For over a decade, Jonellen Heckler has chronicled family life in her poetry, short stories and books, and much of her work has appeared in *The Ladies Home Journal*. *Circumstances Unknown* is her fourth novel and she is hard at work on her fifth. She lives in Florida.

'Jonellen Heckler weaves a suspense tale that draws the reader in from the first line.'

Mary Higgins Clark

'Brilliant, just brilliant. *Circumstances Unknown* is peopled with wonderfully human characters, and the suspense Heckler generates is uncomfortably keen. Bravo!'

Lawrence Block

D1099167

Also by Jonellen Heckler

Safekeeping
A Fragile Peace
White Lies

Circumstances Unknown

Jonellen Heckler

First published in Great Britain in 1993
by HEADLINE BOOK PUBLISHING PLC

First published in paperback in 1993
by HEADLINE BOOK PUBLISHING PLC

A HEADLINE FEATURE paperback

10 9 8 7 6 5 4 3 2

The quotation from *What Cops Know* is © 1990 Connie Fletcher.
Used by kind permission of Villard Books, a division of Random
House, Inc.

All characters in this publication are fictitious
and any resemblance to real persons, living or dead,
is purely coincidental

ISBN 0 7472 4133 3

Printed and bound in Great Britain by
HarperCollins Manufacturing, Glasgow

HEADLINE BOOK PUBLISHING PLC
Headline House, 79 Great Titchfield Street, London W1P 7FN

For Lou again
With love

ACKNOWLEDGMENTS

Sincere thanks to those who so generously gave assistance and guidance during the writing of this novel: Cynthia Cannell; Margaret Goff Clark; Gay Courter; Eduardo Diaz; William Grose; Karen Harmon, Harmon Photographers, Fort Myers, Florida; Lou Heckler; Steven Heckler; Patricia J. Hewitt; Morton L. Janklow; Ralph Keyes; Michael Kneebone, designer/goldsmith, Contemporary Gold Limited, Naples, Florida; Mary DeBall Kwitz; Dr. Lowell Levine, director, Forensic Sciences Unit, New York State Police; Donna and Leo Malaschak; Jerry F. Nichols, CLU; Sally Peters; Anne Sibbald; Eric Simonoff; and Margie Moeller Tingley.

'Most murders are spontaneous. The ones that are pre-meditated, who knows? . . . we might never even find out that they're murders. If the guy is clever enough, he can make it look like a suicide or an accident or even a natural death.'

What Cops Know by Connie Fletcher

Prologue

She walked slowly into his line of sight, straightening the straps of her bathing suit and cinching a towel tighter around her waist. He shifted quietly in the water and moved along the edges of the raft, careful to keep back, hidden, as she left the dirt road and picked her way down the grassy trail to the edge of the lake. At this distance, her features were indistinct, but her silhouette brought a familiar, decisive closing at the center of his heart: legs too thin for the hips, hips too thin for the breasts, breasts too small for the electric torrent of black hair that encircled her head and swept her shoulders.

Warmth flooded his belly, surprising him. He had grown numb waiting for her in the chilly depths while mist rose around him and the sun inched over the horizon.

She draped the towel on a branch, turned in his direction, and sprinted gracefully into the water, diving beneath the surface and coming up gasping. Ragged sounds skipped toward him: the whisper of ripples, a shallow cough. She would swim to the raft, as she did every day. The moment was here. He had dreamed it, planned it, feared it, desired it for so long.

She began to tread water. Gradually, her movements subsided until she floated, almost perfectly still, scanning the muddy banks, the treetops. Did she sense a presence

3

other than her own? He slid completely behind the raft and submerged himself to his chin, forehead resting against the weathered wood. It had the scent of camps and forest lodges, of unused fireplaces and summer loneliness. Now he could hear her cutting sharply through the water, sucking in breath, rolling under, into the silent world, leaping upward with a splash, sighing, rolling under.

It was important to keep it simple. Simplicity bred success in all things. He made a visual check of the woods, the hills. If someone else were out there, he would know. In such cases, the leaves were translucent, and people telegraphed themselves.

She seemed to spread heat as she came toward him. For a few seconds, a question flickered at his eyelids. The answer, which split and fused him like lightning, was an emotion more primitive than passion, more subtle than sensuality, bright, elusive as a star.

The raft undulated before her. And the ladder. Yes. She propelled herself toward it, touched it, drifted upward. A deliberate pressure grazed the top of her head. She stiffened in response.

What felt like a fist seized her hair, pushing her down, holding her down with uncanny force. Hot urine shot between her legs. She struggled, pulling away, wriggling painfully, as fingers, in a circular motion, anchored themselves more securely in her hair. Disbelieving, she reached up. *It was. A man's hand.* He had to be above her, on the raft, lying on his stomach.

Her feet found the 55-gallon drums lashed to the bottom of the raft; she grabbed the pontoon cables with her toes. If she could drag herself under the platform, he would have

4

to slide closer to the edge to keep hold of her. She might have a chance to yank him into the water.

She clasped the ladder, wrenching herself away from him, into shadow, as her scalp tore in a thousand places. He flexed his hand slightly, closed it again. He must have moved just then. Through a golden haze she could see his bare arm, submerged to the shoulder. She caught his elbow, but she had no strength. The weight of the water was crushing her chest. She went limp, coaching herself not to breathe. Her attacker was a person – a human. She could outwit him. He would let go. When he thought she was dead. If she continued to fight, she would use up her air in a matter of seconds.

She waited. His grip remained firm. She would have to breathe the water. Just a little of it. That's all she needed. Water possessed oxygen. She would mix a small amount with the depleted air in her lungs, wait him out. She opened her mouth cautiously. Water jammed her throat, choking her, burning her windpipe, exploding her lungs. A buzzing stung her ears. And then, a profound calm settled over her. She felt the cool water filter beneath her ribs, filling hungry spaces, falling down, a long way down, cool, cold. She could wait like this indefinitely. Wait. Wait him out.

Seven
Years
Later

Sunday

1

He crossed the street slowly and entered Central Park near the boat pond. As always on Sunday morning, children and their parents ringed it, operating remote controls on a fleet of toy sailing ships. He could sense the guardian watchfulness of the mothers and fathers and the nannies as he passed: a radar field, not aimed at him, but general. Their pride was palpable, these sets of people, the boys with the same square chins as their fathers, the girls with the same blond top knots as their mothers. Strolling among them stirred him up.

He was walking in the wake of pride, the sin of pride, flowing off these people like water. He could tolerate it in individuals if it were based on handwrought accomplishments of stature. But *this* pride, pride in contrived relationships, begged judgment. It was based not on skills or talent but on happenstance and will. Woman meets man. Man chooses woman to bear his child. Child is born. Incidents of their own making, elevated into august events.

Look how they close the circle, these people, making fences of their devotion, keeping him back, shutting him out. *My wife. My husband. My family*. A tutored arrogance. A legacy.

Soon, another couple would learn from a great teacher,

11

would learn that it all can end in a flash, would learn that the manufacture of pride is not an enduring accomplishment. He reached into his suitcoat pocket, found and fingered the photograph, the one with man and wife and child. He did not have to look at it to remember their poses and expressions. It had texture, imagined flesh under his thumb. He could feel the sharpness of the man's shoulders as he stood with one arm protectively around the woman's upper back, the other arm extended to press the little boy against a thigh. They were smiling. He could feel the softness of the woman, the moist set of her mouth, the rubbery young bones of the boy. The ink on the back of the photograph seemed raised to the touch: *Tim. Deena. Jon, age 5.*

He had waited years for her to come onto his turf. He had been right to wait, to use caution. But now he would have to be swift. Swift and careful. He fixed Deena in his mind's eye. He could tell from the tilt of her chin, not meek but certainly accommodating, that she would not put up much of a fight.

2

Deena rolled over, pressing her back to Tim's warm chest and abdomen. Gradually, she brought the room into focus, checking for Jon. He was asleep in a warm circle of morning light on the other bed. A little boy now, not a baby, but looking baby sweet against the pale peach blanket. Would she ever get over the feeling of wonder for him? Tim put a hand on her hip and she could tell from the way he lapsed into regular, shallow breaths that he was still dozing. She checked the digital alarm clock: *10:05*.

Her gaze swept the elegantly pleated cornice boards and flowing draperies, the mirrored walls, the burnished Colonial furniture, the expansive plush peach carpet. She pictured the dizzying canyons of skyscrapers beyond the curtained hotel windows and joy touched her. It had been a perfect vacation so far, with more to come. Tonight, they would leave Tim's native New York City for the leisure of the mountains and his boyhood summer home, which she had never seen. He seemed delighted to be here at last, after living with her in California all of their married life.

She went over the morning's plans: 11:30 brunch at Tavern on the Green, two of Tim's old friends joining them as a surprise for him. She hoped he would be pleased, not knocked off balance, by it. She had alternately been worried and thrilled about her decision to secretly invite the men. Surely Tim would be glad to see them. He would never have initiated such a meeting, she understood that, but she could also sense that they all longed to be reunited. When the letters and photos from Martin and Paul arrived once a year, at Christmas, Tim pored over them, putting them carefully away in the album to read again and again. There was obviously genuine respect among the three, a deep bond formed in childhood but tinged permanently by a personal tragedy. It needed to be mended. Although she had never met Paul and Martin, she felt she could mend it. She was good at such things.

Paul had sounded pleased, Martin amazed, by her phone calls. Each of them had said yes at once. The photos of Paul always showed him in his shop, standing stiffly by glass cases of his hand-crafted jewelry. Martin,

13

a courtroom artist, always drew his own cards, the scenes exquisite but unpeopled: a snowy field of pines, a blazing hearth, a frozen lake dotted with the reflection of stars. The only photo he had sent – five years ago – was in three-quarter profile, as if he were afraid of the camera. Neither man had married.

Tim gently bit her neck. She turned over to face him and kissed his chin. God, she was happy. She had been born happy. That was her gift. Her talents were ordinary. Tim would protest, but it was true. She was quite ordinary except for this, a springing buoyancy, an ability to believe the best would happen, a fine appreciation for whatever was in her sphere. She was uncomplicated, she knew. She simply wanted to experience the fun of another day and – most of all – be with Tim and Jon.

3

Sometimes he seemed to cross cosmic paths with one of the nannies at the boat pond or on the street. He had seen them stop pushing their prams and stand motionless with their backs to him, hesitating as if in dread, turning then, slowly, slowly, to stare at him for the first time, a stare laced with recognition. If they were young women, they quickly shoved the prams into motion away from him. The older ones usually narrowed their eyes and assumed a confrontational position, their prams or charges behind them, until he left. Once in a while, a long while, there was one who persecuted him with her gaze from the outset, finding him, singling him out. There was one today, with twins in a double stroller. When he had first traveled through the rings of families by the pond, he had felt himself being snared in the net of her suspicion. She had not taken her eyes from him in an hour, although he had slouched and stretched on a park bench, crossing his ankles and tilting his face mildly to the sun. His was a benign countenance; he had practiced it to an art. His clothes were the clothes of a gentleman. Such women astonished him. He could only surmise that they were instinctively angry when he passed in front of them.

They had reason.

4

Tim reached for Deena in the nest of covers, his hands seeking her waist, grasping it, pulling her up and onto him until they were stomach to stomach, smile to smile. Through her nightgown she could feel the warmth of his solid body, a physique the exact shape and thickness he wished it to be. She supposed he had mentally drawn a plan for it the way he had envisioned and penciled out all his work: residences, office buildings, even an occasional monument. He understood the qualities of permanence and used them to enhance his entire world – career, marriage, self. She had never known a person so surefooted. But not boring. Definitely. And not judg- mental either.

She studied his face, a great face, strongly oval and set with inquisitive gray-green eyes. In the landscape of this face were the trophies of games years past: a bump on the bridge of the nose from racquetball, a slash in the cheek from football, a slight protrusion to the jawbone from a skiing mishap. If there was a sport he hadn't tried, it was one he hadn't heard of.

He kissed her, a kiss of lazy contentment and whispered, 'Let's just order room service.'

'What do you mean?'

'Brunch. I don't want to jump up and rush around, do you? Let's cancel our reservation at the Tavern. Or move it to later on.'

The photographs of Paul and Martin leapt to her mind – the sideways, almost wary glance from Martin, Paul's full-front straight-armed poses that implied a puzzling air of obedience. 'We can't do that.'

'Why not?'

'Well . . . it's Easter Sunday. The Tavern's booked solid, all day. If we give up our spot, we won't get in. And I really want to go.'

He closed one eye, squinting at her.

She hated lying to him. She never did that. And, as far as she knew, he never lied to her either. It would be a relief to tell him, to let him be prepared for the meeting. Should she?

'Okay,' he murmured, pushing her playfully to one side and sitting up. 'I'll get a shower. You wake up the Kid. We'll just make it.'

She watched him stand and walk around the bed in his briefs. He had the football player's gait: slightly stoop-shouldered, body weight balanced on the outsides of his feet. His knees and arches had taken a lot of punishment from high school and college ball. She remembered the first time she'd seen Tim. She'd been sent by *Architect Quarterly* to take photographs of him in business suit and hard hat. He had just come out of college into his first job with an architectural firm. She'd become so infatuated with him she'd taken two rolls more than she needed, just to keep him talking.

When he had gone into the bathroom, she pulled on her robe and slippers and crawled onto Jon's bed. His skin had a distinctive fragrance beneath the smell of clean sheets: a delightfully indescribable one-of-a-kind aroma. She would easily be able to find her son in a pitch-dark room full of children. He opened his eyes, peering at her from the bottom of his dreams. The eyelids sank again. 'Time to get up, Jon. We're going to have fun today.'

'In a minute.' The words were slow. He turned over heavily, hiding half his face.

She moved closer and hugged his shoulders. 'How long is a minute?' His favourite question for her.

This produced an eyes-closed smile. He buried the rest of his face in the pillow.

5

In his dream, Martin was able to tell himself that he needed to wake up. His breathing had shut off again, like the sudden stoppage of a defective machine. The only way to restart it was to try to climb out of the well of sleep. The dream fell away and he was aware of the mattress hard beneath his stomach, but he was paralyzed, a man in a coma, striving to move his muscles, his body dead weight, severed from his mind by some inexplicable short circuit.

This always panicked him, this stage of the struggle, understanding what was happening but not being able to do anything about it. His pulse began to knock violently against his Adam's apple. He tried to remember how to breathe. On previous occasions he had found that if he could make a noise, a grunt or a whimper, he could push himself over the edge into the real world. So he began a mighty effort to produce a sound. He shuddered repeatedly, feeling his face grow slick, fought, forcing his throat open slightly, finally squeezing a thin cry through the long tunnel. He was able, then, to slide a stiff knee over an inch or so, open his eyes, and hungrily gulp air.

The room was a cool cocoon, white sheets and blue walls washed with yellow-gray light fanning from the edges of the mini-blinds. He sat up, his heart slamming against his breastbone, and lurched out of bed, his feet blocks of wood. In the bathroom, he stared into the mirror for reassurance, but his eyes still held the round, blank gaze of shock.

He threw water on his face and brushed his teeth. It came to him what he had been dreaming. *Jenny, his love. Underwater. Losing her life alone, silently.* He had dreamed of her often in the seven years since the accident. She was always propelling herself gracefully upward, up, up, back arched, arms outstretched, bubbles streaming from her mouth as she tried to find the surface of the lake. Her expression reflected hope, not just hope, but expectation: Any moment now, she would be free. Always, he watched helplessly as the light in her eyes faded.

He turned on the shower and sat on the tile floor of the stall, hands to his head, skin stinging in the hot spray. Ever since she died, he had not been in control. The idea of life as a series of accidents had possessed him. The accident of birth, the accident of meeting, the accident of death. All events random, unplanned. No hand turning the moon, no benevolent mind steering the planets, no safety nets, no permanent tethers. Only aimless motion, endless space.

At first, he had believed her spirit would visit him, answer his questions. *What happened? Why did you drown? How?* He had willed it, waiting for her in the darkness, leaving the windows open, the lights off, watching the corners and the ceiling for a twist of air, a dusty glimmer. Always, familiar sounds from the street four stories below gradually magnified themselves into an undeniable message of reality: She was not here, would never again be here. There are questions that cannot be answered.

6

Deena zipped her suit trousers and swept back the drapery to look outside. Their room was on the fourteenth floor, facing west into Midtown where morning sun glittered against a thousand windows. In the few days they had been here, she had noticed a myriad of things that Tim took for granted because he had grown up in the city. This was her first experience with New York, and New York was fabulous, a cornucopia of ripe abundance: narrow stalls overflowing with fragrant newspapers and magazines in a dozen languages, sidewalk displays brimming with brilliant flowers and fruits, shops crammed with shiny golden loaves of bread, exotic salads, filet mignon and fresh fish arranged on ice, jars of fat floating pickles. Whatever the world at large possessed, New York seemed to have more of it. And New York had culled the world's possessions to claim the best.

The adjacent window had a southern exposure. From it,

she could see for blocks down Second Avenue. Traffic was light, a sprinkling of yellow cabs moving slowly south. She raised the sash and leaned over the sill, sizing up the tiny balcony beneath it, more of a decoration than a porch. Since the first day, she had thought about crawling out there. Was it sturdy enough? *Last day, last chance*.

Tim wouldn't like that. She listened to his chatter with Jon in the bathroom, realizing he was getting ready to blow Jon's hair dry. That and the brushing of teeth would take a few minutes. She'd be quick. Lifting her camera from the dresser, she hung it around her neck and climbed gingerly into the biting breeze, the cement floor of the balcony cold on her stocking feet. She was high enough to look down on rooftop gardens: idyllic patches of green grass, small square pools, ceramic basins of red geraniums, plastic tables and chairs, bare-branched trees fuzzy with buds. Frame by frame, she brought the gardens and pieces of gardens into focus with the zoom lens, pressing the button.

To the left, yellow fire undulated on the East River, but the sun itself was hidden by the brick corner of the hotel. Stretching over the waist-high railing, she could see only half of it. She navigated the railing easily and, gripping it, leaned out over the street. The view was perfect, the sun in exactly the right position, an exquisite tapestry. But she needed both hands for the camera. Tucking a knee between bars of the railing to steady herself, she began to shoot the rest of the roll slowly.

'Deena!' She glanced at the window to find Tim in a towel, staring at her in amazement.

'I'm all right.'

'Please come in!'

'I'm almost finished.'

He shook his head angrily and walked away. They had argued many times about what he termed her 'carelessness.' In fact, it was about the only thing they argued over. She could never make him understand that she wasn't being careless. She wouldn't do anything crazy, anything unsafe. She assessed risks accurately. He continually accused her of being fearless, but that wasn't true. She was afraid when it was warranted. But she wasn't unduly afraid. In all fairness to him, what she did seem to have was an unusual tolerance for risk because – and she had thought a lot about this – she had been born without phobias. Heights didn't bother her. Neither did tightly enclosed spaces or snakes or any of the other terrors that plagued humans generally. It seemed upside down and backward to her that she was considered strange for this.

'Mom!' Jon was in the window now, looking at her with sleepy eyes. 'Dad says you should get in here.'

'In a minute.' She squeezed off a few more shots and hoisted herself over the rail.

Tim, adjusting his tie in front of the mirror, watched Deena crawl inside through the window in back of him. 'You're nuts.'

She grinned. 'Nah.'

'You are.'

'Am not.' She laid the camera on the bed and retrieved a fresh box of film from her bag.

'You think nothing can happen. Nothing bad can happen. That's what you think.'

'Nothing ever has.'

Jon sank into the lower part of Tim's mirror view and sat

21

on the carpet to put his socks and shoes on. The way he ducked his head made Tim realize that Jon was expecting the exchange to escalate. He'd keep it light. But, doggone, she had one amazingly simplistic view of the world based on a storybook-perfect childhood. Most people by the age of twenty-seven had been smashed in the teeth a few times. Not Deena. She anticipated only the best. Because it had always been that way. 'If you fell off that balcony, you'd be saying to yourself on the way down, "Well, this is okay. Nothing's happened yet." You'd get that camera up to your eye and take a few more pictures, wouldn't you?'

'Sure. They'd be my best shots.' Deena smiled at Jon. Tim turned away from the mirror and winked at him.

7

Martin stood and soaped himself slowly, leaning against the wall. He had become peculiar, he knew. Distracted and lethargic. The cheery coaxing of friends seemed distant, like conversations overheard, and it was waning as one by one they gave up on him. He was supposed to have passed through the magical process of mourning by now, shedding its stages, regaining his balance, emerging whole. Instead, he still wore the original grief. He had merely broken it in somewhat. It was softer now, hanging loosely over his bones.

Was this Sunday? Saturday? Sunday? Sunday, yes. Oh, Lord. What time was it? He stopped the water and stepped out, dripping his way into the bedroom, flinching when he saw the clock. He was late. He found a towel, hastily tied his hair back, and dug in the closet for shoes, shirt, pants, tie, sport coat. Scuffs. Wrinkles. Spots. Some day he'd get a handle on all this, but most of the time it didn't matter. It only mattered when someone was going to scrutinize him. Like today. He didn't want to take care of a goddamn thing. He didn't even own a houseplant.

When he had dressed, he checked the mirror. The news was not good. He went to the refrigerator, opened it, and plucked his keys out of the bowl, dropping them into his pocket with his change.

In the street, he realized he'd made a bigger mistake than he thought. It was going to rain. He'd never get a cab. And he was sixteen blocks from the Tavern. He began to run.

8

As she pushed her way through the throng in the foyer of the restaurant, Deena looked back at Tim. He had her coat over one arm and, with the other arm, was steering Jon into line at the checkroom. It would take him several minutes, enough time for her to arrange everything. She was grateful for the noisy conversations around her. Tim wouldn't be able to hear what she said to the hostess.

She waited for her turn, eyeing the people who were spilling through the front doors. What if Paul or Martin arrived early, in the middle of this milling crowd? She had deliberately timed their entrance for fifteen minutes after her own.

The man in front of her stepped aside and she was greeted cordially by a tall dark-haired young woman.

'I'm Deena Reuschel.'

The woman consulted her list. 'Party of five?'

'Yes. But I don't want my husband to know that there will be two extra guests until we get to our table. It's a surprise.' She glanced at the checkroom door, seeing Tim handing their coats over the counter.

'Certainly.'

'The others will be here in a few minutes.'

'I'll make sure they find you. May I have their names, please?' Tim and Jon were heading for her now, weaving through the jam of people.

'Let me write it down for you.'

The woman handed her a pen and a small white card. On it, Deena printed,

MARTIN TRAYNE
PAUL KINCAID

9

The sun had left the boat pond. He could smell rain coming. It was time, anyway. He got to his feet. The woman jerked the stroller back a few paces, glaring, waiting. He moved in the opposite direction, west, onto the concrete paths of the park, out of her range, and walked briskly for minutes, working to throw off the spell of her hatred. Joggers streamed by. Old men with poodles on leashes. Little girls in ruffled bonnets. Panhandlers calling to him, gesturing.

He must concentrate now. Think. He must be alert, ready to observe carefully. To this point, Deena had consisted merely of images on a half-dozen pieces of shiny paper. In a few minutes, she would take shape in front of him, bearing flesh and will. He would be able to gauge her strength, her intellect, and guess how she could be brought to her death. He had never been wrong. Except about Jenny. She had been disappointingly acquiescent. His memory conjured Jenny in her coffin, her black wiry hair wild against the satin pillow, her color sallow. It was dangerous to dwell on her.

As the Tavern edged into view, perched on a stretch of lawn, anxiety possessed him. *They would know. They would look at him and know.* Perspiring, he paused at the restaurant's front walk. How could they possibly know? No one on earth could read his mind or view his motives. He was as opaque as others were transparent. He took out his handkerchief and wiped his eyelids. It would be over soon. He reached for the door handle. As he did, he could feel Jenny's hair in his hand. He looked down at his fingers, his palm. He expected to see clumps, strands, curls, etched there like a tattoo. But, of course, he saw nothing.

Inside, the din was disorienting. A hard wall of human backs and shoulders kept him from moving forward. Bodies quickly filled the spaces behind him. Imprisoned, he felt the heat of a hundred brains searing his. He could not wait here. Would not. He began to pinch and elbow people out of his path. He had learned that he could get away with such aggression if he inflicted sharp, sudden pain and charged forward without making eye contact. Even the most hardened New Yorker was momentarily intimidated by it.

The woman at the desk watched him come toward her. He was there in seconds, muted outrage rumbling in his wake. 'Reuschel party.' He phrased it as a quiet command.

25

She blinked at him.

'R-e-u-s-c-h-e-l.'

'You are . . .' She looked down, reading, then glanced up at him. 'Mr. Trayne?'

'Kincaid.'

10

Tim reached down and helped Jon into his lap.

'Who're we waiting for, Daddy?' Jon put a cheek next to his.

'I don't know, pumpkin.' He looked at Deena. 'Who are we waiting for?'

'It's a surprise.' They smiled at each other. One of the principles of their marriage was a wedding day promise: *no surprises*. 'Just this once.'

'Is it two people?' Jon asked, pointing to the empty chairs at their table.

'Yes, honey,' Deena said.

'I thought so.'

Tim shifted to scan the impeccably dressed people flooding into the restaurant from church services but saw no one he knew.

Deena winked. 'Don't try to guess.'

Tim's gaze settled over the Crystal Room's bright splashes of color: tulips, daffodils, irises, and lilies, red, yellow, pink, purple, white. Beyond the giant windows of the restaurant loomed the misting April beauty of Central Park.

He sensed Deena straighten slightly. The waitress was leading a man toward them. *Paul*. No mistake. Shock rippled through him. He rose, lifting his startled son to his feet. The man was thicker than he'd remembered, as though all his bones had doubled in weight and width. The white-blond hair had faded to sand, but the eyes were still an intense blue. Without words, they reached for each other. In Paul's cordial embrace, Tim could feel the hard muscles of his biceps.

'You rascal,' he whispered, shaken.

Paul released him breathlessly. It seemed he could not speak.

'This is . . . Deena.'

She was standing now, holding out her hand to Paul who took it and pressed it between his. 'How nice to meet you at last!' she said. As he let go of her, she impulsively put her arms around his neck and kissed him on the cheek.

'And our son, Jon.'

'Are you Daddy's friend?' Jon asked.

Paul stooped to meet him eye to eye. 'Yes. We grew up together.'

'A long time ago?'

'Yes.'

Jon considered this for a moment and then allowed himself to be hugged.

A long time ago. Forever. He and Paul and Martin had avoided personal contact. An unspoken pact. Deena didn't know. Deena hadn't been there when Jenny was dragged from the lake, bloated and still. Tim hadn't met Deena until ten months later, in Los Angeles. She hadn't been at Jenny's funeral shoulder to shoulder with Paul, weeping, watching Martin weep in desolation. He felt gratitude that Deena hadn't ever undergone events so profound that she would understand the basic principle: Some situations are

27

so affecting that the people involved in them never want to see each other again.

Suddenly, he realized who would be sitting in the other chair.

Deena was more commanding physically than Paul had guessed from the photographs. It had nothing to do with her height or weight, which were average. She carried herself like a dancer, in total control of her body, her movements and gestures mildly dramatic, the voice musical, the diction perfect. Her brown eyes and red shoulder-length hair shimmered. He placed her immediately: the polished product of an upper-class home. Years of piano lessons and orthodontia and museum field trips. The kind of home in which children are not taught manners so much as they are imbued with them. Such women had no problems of identity. They had been told how smart they were from the time they were old enough to listen. And they were generally astute. He turned his smile on her and got an answering smile.

'I can't believe you did this,' Tim said to Deena. There was no edge of accusation in it, just amazement. 'Is Martin coming, too?'

'Yes.'

Tim hesitated, then nodded, looking straight at Paul. 'It was time,' he said. 'I've really missed you.'

Already, Tim felt the searing energy that burned through Paul. It seemed Paul must have been born with it, this terrible hunger that constantly consumed him. Its source was beyond Tim's comprehension, but not beyond his compassion. Joy had eluded the man. Tim could not

28

see why, only that gifts that fell so freely on Tim had been denied to Paul: a close relationship with parents, the existence of siblings, the love of a woman, the birth of a child. Paul had always been a portrait of pursuit and jealousy, and yet his obvious vulnerability was somehow endearing. He evoked a raw tenderness in Tim that would not be healed.

Paul was looking covetously at Deena, a reaction so typical that it evoked instant irritation in Tim. But that emotion was quickly supplanted by another: sorrow mingled with forgiveness. Tim had never been able to mentally disown Paul. It was as though Paul were hanging, terrified, from Tim's hands over a fierce sucking hole that threatened to swallow him for eternity. Tim could not turn him loose.

Deena's nervousness began to dissipate. Paul seemed kind. She should have known from his letters that he had heart. He always wrote long ones, laced with anecdotes and signed with good wishes. They seated themselves, Tim on one side of her, Paul choosing the other chair next to hers. Jon sat next to Tim, buttering crackers.

When they had given their beverage orders to the waiter, Paul asked sincerely, 'Have you had a good visit?'

Tim took Deena's hand, and she realized he was trembling. 'Yes. Lots of sightseeing. And we sold a few things. Deena's photography is in demand these days.'

'With magazines?'

She nodded. 'And syndicates. I'm grateful.'

'She's being modest. She's doing very, very well.' Tim pulled a clean, folded handkerchief from his pocket and wiped his face with it. She realized he was genuinely struggling, working to keep the conversation going. She

had probably made an error in bringing Tim and Paul together again.

'Mostly architectural?'

'I'm . . .' It was too late. She couldn't go back, erase it all. She had to do the best she could from here. '. . . branching out quite a bit. Travel shots. Landscapes and character portraits. Candids. Kids and dogs, outdoors. A little bit of this and a lot of that. Fairly unstructured. I don't work on assignment much anymore. I take the shots that interest me and put them on file with services. Tim's the one who's got a plan and working in the right direction. He signed a contract this week to design a convention center in Arizona.'

Paul leaned around her to look fondly at Tim. 'That's terrific. You deserve the best.'

'I've been lucky,' Tim said.

It was exactly as Paul had thought it would be: the praising and the open touching between husband and wife, an emotional distance from others so complete and rudely unaware that it incensed him. He had known from their correspondence that they were exclusively focused on one another, a pattern he had seen many times before but which always amazed him. Such couples had no concept of the loneliness and yearning of those around them, even their own children. Worse, he suspected it wouldn't matter to them if they did know.

A growing restlessness moved his legs. He found he was no longer listening to Tim and Deena but to a furious, steadily rising inner tide. In his bleakest moments, he believed the insistent force that pushed at him to be self-righteousness but in his best moments realized that it was simply a function of his ordained purpose: to maintain a sort of emotional balance in the world. If he needed to be executioner to this end, he would be. The lost, awed expression of a man whose mate had suddenly been snatched away by death satisfied Paul as nothing else ever satisfied him. An executioner was, ultimately, an instrument of justice.

He studied Deena, mentally moving her over a notch. She was not old money, she was new money – only one, maybe two generations down from shirtsleeves. Old money was sedate and suspicious. New money was casual. Deena Reuschel's parents had, no doubt, insulated their children from the kind of hardships they themselves had endured, thus creating an impression of the world as a generous and benign place.

She would be easy.

'How would you like to excuse yourself from your friends and come talk to me?' A snarled threat.

Paul looked up. A bulky man whose nose and cheeks were tinged red with anger stared down at him. Who? *Someone from the foyer.* Paul rose, following the man toward the corridor. Out of the corner of his eye, he saw Tim leave the table. Paul motioned that he didn't need help.

In the hallway, the man faced him. 'You son of a bitch,' he growled, leaning close to Paul's ear. 'You get away with that stuff all the time, don't you? No one ever calls you on it. No one wants to make a scene. I ought to beat the crap out of you. But I'm willing to entertain your apology.'

Paul shrugged. 'Sorry.'

* * *

The man rammed stiff fingers into Paul's chest, sending him backward against the arch of the doorway. Deena, watching, jumped to her feet as Tim caught her arm. 'Paul can handle it,' he said.

But he *wasn't* handling it. The whole thing was falling apart, the brunch, her plans. What was going on? She walked quickly away from Tim and approached Paul just as he gave the man a return shove. 'Who is this?' she said to Paul.

'I don't know.'

She confronted the man. 'What do you want?'

'Mind your own business.'

She glanced around for the maitre d' she knew would be hovering anxiously nearby and found him. At the wave of her hand, he joined them.

'What seems to be the problem?'

They had the attention of half the room now. She needed to cut this off quickly. 'The gentleman wishes to harass my guest. He is disturbing our party. None of us know him.'

'Will you come with me, please, sir?' the maitre d' said pointedly to the stranger.

She stared defiantly into the man's eyes as he decided what to do and finally turned his back.

'I will take care of it, madam,' the maitre d' cautioned.

As she and Paul made their way to the table, Tim grinned at her and shook his head.

He had misjudged Deena Reuschel. She would be a force. He would need to shut off her breathing instantly, the crook of his elbow snapping around her throat like a well-set trap. He would seize her from behind, lifting her against him, carrying her. He would need to move like lightning.

'What was *that* all about?' Tim said as Paul sat down again.

'Beats me.'

'I can't imagine why anyone would want to pick a fight with you.'

'It happens.' He laughed. 'Welcome to New York.'

Martin appeared as they were beginning to eat their meal. Without words, he slipped into the fifth chair. Tim did a double take, realizing that this was not a street person who had decided to join them, it was *Martin*. What had he done to himself? The wild salt-and-pepper hair: mustache, beard, foot-long ponytail. The starvation build. The wrinkled clothing. Nothing like the old buttoned-down Martin Trayne. Nothing whatsoever. He'd aged fifteen years in the last seven. He had obviously been caught in the rain and toweled off in the rest room. His hair and the shoulders of his sport coat were soaked. His familiar gray eyes peered out from brambles of damp facial hair as though peering from behind a bush.

'Mart?'

'Hey.' He stuck out his hand and Tim shook it. 'Sorry to be late.'

The memory of Jenny hung between them. *The vision of a dusty lane in summer, Tim racing along it toward the lake, Martin staggering away from the steep bank, dazed, meeting him with a hoarse cry*. 'That's all right. Listen, this is Deena.' She nodded warily. 'And Jon.' Jon simply stared.

Paul reached across the table with both hands to welcome Martin. 'My God, it's good to see you!'

Tim was awkwardly aware of the table full of food.

33

'We went ahead and ordered. Weren't sure when you'd get here.'

'That's all right. I'm not hungry.'

'Not *hungry?*'

'No.'

He shouldn't be surprised. That was vintage Martin. He ran on his own schedule. No compulsion to eat when others were eating just because it was the accepted thing to do. Deena wouldn't feel right about it though. She'd think they had offended him. He noticed that she had laid her fork on her plate.

'Okay. How about a drink?'

'Just the water. That'll be fine.' He picked up his glass and drained it.

'We're taking a raft trip tomorrow,' Jon announced.

Deena flinched. She and Tim had deliberately avoided telling Martin they were going to the mountains.

A few seconds of leaden silence passed. It seemed to register with Martin that he was the only person at the table unaware of their plans. 'Where's that?' he said to Jon.

'At my grandpa's cottage.'

She searched wildly for another topic. Jenny had drowned there.

'Sounds like fun.'

'People think it's too cold, but my dad says this is the best time of year.'

'You're staying at the lake house?' Martin asked Tim.

'Yes.' An apology.

More silence. 'Well, give your folks my best.'

'They're in Florida. Only venture north in deep summer. But I'll be sure to tell them.'

Stricken, Deena could not think of a new subject. She sat helplessly as Martin regarded each of their faces without comment. She must have changed color because Martin's gaze came back to rest on her. 'It's all right,' he said.

By the time dessert came, they had rearranged their places at the table. Jon, who regarded Martin with the reserve he used in the presence of people like the school principal, had left his chair to sit on Paul's lap and feed him the cherry from his own hot fudge sundae. Deena had run out of starter conversation for Martin who hadn't picked up on any of it. She was quietly talking jewelry with Paul, while Tim, in Jon's original chair, kept Martin company. *There are two distinct camps at the table now*, Tim thought. Martin did that to a gathering.

In search of a pat cause for Martin's social ineptness, Tim had decided long ago that it was because Martin's parents had given birth for the first and only time in their late forties – to Martin and his twin, Marie. He was out of sync with the culture.

But Martin's loyalty transcended differences. Tim could not remember a single time that he'd butted heads with Mart. The same old-fashioned twist that set him apart kept him from a trace of meanness. As a kid, he'd simply walked away from punches and name-calling. He was the friend you wanted with you on an all-day outing. He wore well.

Paul was flashier. He tended to flattery, and he liked being flattered. Deena was stroking the right spot now with her profuse praise of the wedding rings he had made for them. *Handcrafted and handcarved, precisely matched, no two sets alike*, he was telling her.

'Let me see,' Jon said. She took off the circle of gold and slipped it onto his thumb. 'Pretty.'

Martin tapped the table gently, indicating that he wanted to see Tim's ring. Tim laid his left hand flat against the cloth, palm down. Martin observed it without comment.

The smooth sheen of Deena's neck entranced Paul. He imagined the curve of her bare shoulders under her blouse. An excitement had been pushing through him for an hour, springing unbidden behind his eyes, collecting beneath his skull.

Jon handed Deena her ring and she put it back on her finger. Warmth had crept widely through her as Paul spoke in soft words, never lifting his gaze from her face. She could see why Tim liked Paul. He had a direct charm, a spellbinding friendliness. The contrast to Martin was shocking, as though Paul had received more than his share of personality from the store meant for Martin.

She looked up at Paul again. He was watching her intently, half smiling, admiration in his expression. She smiled back. He continued to stare at her in silence. She glanced away, startled. She had seen this interest in the eyes of men at parties, when she was single. She had seldom seen it since then. Had he thought she was flirting with him? Confused, she touched the tablecloth, then laid her hands in her lap, embarrassed. When she dared look up again, she realized she had been vain to think such a thing. There was nothing other than kindness in his face. Nothing at all.

Deena sighted the three men through the viewfinder. They

were all laughing. Even Martin. She centered them in front of the tulip garden, with the restaurant's glass exterior in the background.

'Ready?' she said.

They put their arms around each other's shoulders and gave her their best boyish grins. 'Go!' Tim hollered from the middle. They laughed again. Martin stuck two fingers up behind Tim's head like rabbit ears.

'I'm waiting,' she called. The fingers disappeared. *Click.* 'One more.'

Paul held out his arms to Jon who walked into the frame. 'Up you go.' He hefted Jon onto his arm. Jon made fists and cocked his head, baring his teeth in a comically fierce expression. She centered the bodies. *Click.* Paul set Jon down and he ran to her.

When she lowered the camera from her eye, the men were already saying good-bye to each other. She stayed where she was to give Tim a chance alone with his friends. He hugged them both, Martin first. As he released Paul, Paul said something funny to him in a low voice. Tim laughed again and kissed him loudly on the cheek.

All things considered, she had done a good thing today.

11

Paul waited until Tim and his family had departed in a cab and Martin had strolled out of sight to the north before he chose his direction. It would be a long walk to the garage, but that would give him a chance to calm down, work off some energy. Deena's perfume still lay on his tongue. He started away quickly, south, and during the next twenty minutes passed through varied sections of Broadway in measured strides, aware of every shape and motion. Loitering men poked their faces toward him as he went by. He did not meet their eyes.

At last, he turned west and, keeping the same pace, began the journey along office buildings into distinctly ethnic neighborhoods: black, then Hispanic, then mixed. Some sidewalks were occupied by playing children. None spoke to him. After nearly twelve blocks, he entered the garage. It was Sunday quiet. Even during the week, there was no attendant – perfect for his purposes. Cars accessed the gate with a plastic card.

His parking space was on the second floor; he took the steps two at a time. Opening the tailgate of the Bronco with his key, he removed his gym bag and carried it down the stairs to the fire exit at the back of the garage. The stick was where he had last put it, above the door, on the frame. He took it down and laid it against the jamb as he left.

Across the street and two blocks away was an eight-story building he had first visited when he was an art student. It housed low-rent art studios and actors' workshops. The graffiti-smeared entrance was never locked; the elevator reeked of mold. He took it to the sixth floor and stepped into an empty hallway. All the doors were shut but one, the rest-room door. He stepped inside and bolted it.

How many times he had dressed and undressed here, he could not remember. He only knew that it was made for him, this actors' bathroom: sink, dressing table, toilet and – most important – a shower. Even during the week, the building had a dilapidated empty air. He seldom saw anyone, and when he did, they looked past him.

He slid into jeans and boots and sweatshirt, folding the suit away, zipping the bag, sliding it behind the dressing table skirt into the dust. The changing of clothes in this room always excited him, filled him with ideas. In the dim mirror, he assessed the resolve in his face: the hunter, undefeated. He had been wise. His unhurried observation of each woman's nature had instructed him on how to capture her. It was nearly mystical, the track in his mind where perfectly formed solutions came forward to fit with his challenges. He trusted it implicitly. Now, he turned Deena over to it. Her case was different. Within days, she would be out of range. And she had an immediate protector who was not likely to leave her alone in the mountains. When would she be vulnerable?

Carmela Azaña undulated into his vision, her breasts ripe under white eyelet, her hair braided with pastel ribbons. He had followed her seven times before she died. She trailed musk and favoured seamed stockings, but her demeanor spoke only of innocence. She was a window shopper, a romantic, something from the top of a wedding cake, perpetually in party clothes that harked back to adolescence. A vision of pink roses bunched against ivory lace in a tight bouquet had come to his mind and stayed there during the time he was contemplating her. In the end, it was simple. He attached the bouquet to a rail on the lower tier of the ramparts where she liked to walk along the East River. She was drawn to it, down the steep steps, approached it cautiously, touched it with wonder, and began to untie it to take home. He had come at her casually, down the same steps, suddenly tangling his fingers in her hair and striking her forehead on the rail with all his strength. His foot found her feet and swept them toward the water. She lay back, in his arms, stunned and mute as he fed her to the fast current.

He needed to relax about Deena. An answer would come.

He let himself out of the bathroom into the echoing hallway, floating, descending in the elevator to the strangely daylit street alone, retracing his path to the garage, shouldering the door, replacing the stick horizontally on the frame overhead, finding the Bronco and backing it into position, jamming it into forward gear, riding it down.

12

Martin paused in the outer foyer of his apartment house and turned his key in the lock of his mail compartment. Empty. Not even a bill.

What was he thinking of? It was Sunday. He closed the box quickly, glancing around, relieved that no one was watching. The sticky inner door took all his weight to open. It had been painted brown so many times that the layers seemed never to have dried completely. The glossy surface was soft and thick. Once on the other side, he had to force the door closed.

His landlady's shuffling footsteps sounded above him in the stairwell. The banister squeaked under her aged fingers as she descended. She came into view, slouching, hips forward to keep her balance. 'There you are,' she said, pausing, pushing her glasses up on her nose to get a look at him. She always pushed them with one hand, by the corners, never by the bridge. And they always slid down again as soon as she let go.

'Happy Easter, Mrs. Swenk.' He started up the steps.

'Not such a Happy Easter for me, don't you know. I was up with Daniel all night.'

Her third husband. The second one had died on a golf course. 'I'm sorry to hear that.' He edged past her.

She followed him with her voice. 'I think this new doctor's giving him the wrong medication, but I can't get a callback and now it's a holiday and it's too expensive to take him to the emergency room, he has six children, *six*, but they've all moved away, don't you see, there's no one to help me and he doesn't have any visitors, he's looking forward to your visit when you have time, of course, that would be nice because—'

There was no way to extricate himself from her tangle of sentences. She barely took a breath between them. Anytime he encountered her, he could plan on spending a polite twenty minutes or a rude twenty seconds. In truth, it didn't seem to matter to her. He had learned to nod sympathetically and keep walking. She would talk as long as he was in her sight.

'— he's getting weaker, I hardly know what to do, don't you know, I only get out to the store, I don't know what to do, he can't be left by himself, don't you see, he can't do —' He nodded sympathetically until he couldn't see her anymore. She stopped speaking, as though someone had lifted the needle from a record.

In the kitchen, he threw his keys into the bowl and slammed the refrigerator. *Doesn't matter. Visit or no visit. Can't change anything.*

What a hard ass he had become. What would it hurt him to give Daniel Swenk half an hour? She'd been asking him for months.

41

Not in his vocabulary. Didn't matter.

The living room was a shady mushroom field. He opened the drapes, releasing dusty light onto a floor piled with short stacks of paperback westerns. He chose one and, lying on the couch, held it over his face, focusing on the words. *The crevice, cleft out of sandstone, was precisely the width to snare a horse's hoof.*

Today's reunion, nice as it was, didn't matter either. It wouldn't affect his paycheck. Wouldn't affect anything.

13

The cottage had somehow escaped acquiring the musty smell of closed-up places. As they turned on the kitchen overhead light and then the living room lamps, Deena saw why. The interior had been kept up-to-date: a modern sectional sofa and easy chairs, bright artwork, plump throw pillows, a fireplace scraped clean of ashes and stacked with logs. Jon ran from room to room, finding the light switches and shouting, 'Look at this!' She and Tim followed him, grinning.

The master bedroom on the first floor was done in antiques and cream colors. The two upstairs bedrooms were quintessential boy's and girl's rooms, obviously Tim's and his sister's. Gail's was pale yellow and pale pink, with a dressing table and a four-poster double bed covered with dolls. Tim's was in earth tones and filled with shelves of model cars and metal trucks. The bedrooms escaped having the atmosphere of shrines, though, because sentimental quaintness had been tempered by new paint, new carpet, new bedding, and new curtains. There was, instead, a settled air of family history and contemporary humor. It figured, knowing the Reuschels, that the summer home of Tim's childhood would be so obviously well tended and cordial.

'Is this my room?' Jon said when he saw the toys.

'You bet,' Tim answered in delight. 'Look here.' He opened a plastic case on one of the shelves. Deena moved closer. 'My Matchbox cars.' There were dozens in a heap.

Jon appraised the room eagerly. 'Can I play with everything?'

'Sure. Why don't you do that while Mom and I get the luggage out of the car?'

'Can I look inside everything?'

'Yes.'

Jon gingerly opened a dresser drawer, finding baseball cards. He checked out the closet. 'I can't believe all this. What's out there?' He pointed to an exterior door with a dead-bolt lock.

'Steps down to the backyard. They're steep. Don't mess with that. I'll show you in the morning,' Tim said.

'Okay.' Jon moved on to the cabinets and sat in front of them, pulling the handles.

Even at five, you could take him at his word, Deena thought. He was always straightforward. If he didn't want to do what you asked, he'd tell you so.

When the suitcases and groceries had been brought inside, Tim and Deena stepped onto the screened porch. Night air spread through her jacket; Tim turned sideways, putting Deena in front of him to shield her from the wind. Black outlines of trees stood between them and the water, a slick charcoal-gray surface glowing dimly under starlight. She couldn't assess the size of it, but she knew from the map that it was a meandering lake, with many parts, wide and narrow, shallow and deep. It ran for miles.

'This is a magical place,' she said.

He didn't answer.

'We should visit your folks here in the summer. They ask us and ask us, but we only see them in the winter, when they're in Florida.'

His arms tightened around her shoulders, but he said nothing.

When she was getting ready for bed, she found Jenny in a wall of photographs between the bathroom and the kitchen. At least, she thought it was Jenny. Martin had his arm around her. Martin as a teenager. Braces on his teeth. Must have been a party. They were sitting on a flowered couch, drinking what? Must have been pop. They were kids, just kids. Both of them were wearing shorts, singing something at the camera, waving their glasses in a toast. Jenny with the dark cotton-candy hair, dark luminescent eyes. She was slightly on the plump side, not much, a little. No, her legs were fairly thin, hips trim. But she was full-busted for a teen. That was it.

The photo was surrounded by many others in silver frames: Tim waterskiing in his bare feet. Gail and her husband Kemp in a two-person hammock. She was eight years older than Tim. She couldn't have shared much of Tim's life on the lake. She was married by the time he was ten. And this one . . . A kid in jeans, bent over with his backside to the camera and looking through his legs. Paul? Yes, Paul. Here was another one of him in a bathing suit, pretending to put a fish down the back of Jenny's blouse. Had to be Jenny. Gene and Barbara nuzzling in the boat. There were other people, all ages. Baby pictures of Tim and Gail, anniversary pictures of Tim's grandparents. And her wedding picture . . . she and Tim, each twenty-one years old. Tim, suddenly beside her in the hallway, pushed his rumpled hair back with his fingers and scanned the array of faces and poses she had been studying. His gaze rested on the girl with the black hair.

'Is that Jenny?' she asked softly.

'Yes.'

'She looks nice.'

'She was.'

'Looks like you all had a lot of fun.'

He nodded.

'Is that why you stopped coming back here? Because she died?' She looked into his eyes, seeing anguish.

'Yes.'

She could envision Jenny in the hazy dawn, swimming alone toward the wooden raft, could envision Martin, discovering her under the raft and dragging her to shore, screaming. The incident had the air of legend, it was so tragic and so vague at the edges. Deena had heard the story only once from Tim, who gave sparse details and was depressed for days after the telling.

'Does Martin come back?'

'No. When he wouldn't, his parents sold their lake house. So did Jenny's. They divorced.'

'And Paul?'

'His dad's still here. Paul visits him. His mother's dead.' Tim put his hands on his hips, frowning at the photos.

'Did I do wrong by inviting them today? I didn't want to hurt you. I wanted the opposite.'

'Lord, no.' He swallowed hard. 'It was okay.'

Tears caught her. 'You still love them.'

He shifted his weight uneasily and shrugged. 'Sure.'

'I'm sorry about Jenny,' she whispered. 'I'm sorry for all of you.'

Until she drowned, Tim could not remember a time when Jenny did not exist. He and she, Martin and Paul, had been babies on a single blanket at lake picnics. In the drifting, rainbow-streaked bubble of summer, the four of them rode the sky together, year after year. In the city winters, they hardly saw each other, but they were inseparable from the Fourth of July to Labor Day. Jenny was their soul, their conscience, the prow of their curiosity. When she was grown, she chose Martin.

It didn't seem that Jenny could belong to simply one of them for eternity, that she could marry Martin. But he bought her an engagement ring, which she accepted. Tim struggled with it in private, suffered, could not eat. He had been raised to marry Jenny Cunningham. Hadn't he?

One rainy morning, he came to a resolve. He would tell her. When she met him by the duck pond, she was crying. Paul, she said, had been at her house and confessed his love, asked her to leave Martin and go away with him. When she refused, Paul put his fist through a pane of glass. Paul's pain hurt her, she said. She was sick with it.

He kept his words that day. And kept his promise to Jenny that he would never tell Martin what Paul had done.

14

Martin lifted the humidor down from the top of the refrigerator and set it on the kitchen table. A heavy black lacquer box with chrome handles, it was big enough to accommodate six dozen cigars – fat, expensive ones. Martin's grandfather had kept it at the center of the fireplace mantel in his home and willed it to his only grandson. Although it still cast a faint aroma of tobacco, it had a different purpose now. In it, Martin saved things he could not bear to part with but which he could not bear to see again. Things relegated to the box did not come out. Martin opened it only to toss items in.

He clicked the swag lamp on and thumbed back the humidor's lid, glancing briefly at the contents of the box. Snapshots, yellowed newspaper articles, a crystal salt and pepper shaker set with sterling silver tops, a woman's handkerchief edged in lace. He averted his eyes and stuck his hand under the layers of paper and cloth, feeling for velvet. His fingers struck the curved surface he was seeking. He brought the ring box up, into the light.

Jenny's wedding ring, and his, against ivory satin. Neither had been worn. Jenny had not even seen hers. He had wanted to surprise her. Their shine had dulled, but the garland of irises that twined around each was clearly visible. They were exactly like Tim and Deena's. Strange that Paul had made the sets of rings identical to one another. He could not have done it accidentally. Martin knew Paul kept a precise record of his designs. Paul had lied to Deena for some reason. But that was Paul. Martin had always noticed that Paul occasionally rearranged the truth to fit his needs.

15

Paul prowled the darkness of the frozen hillside, pausing now and then with his shoulder to a tree. The windows of the cottage were like lighted stages upon which players came and went. Because their house was out of sight of other homes on the lake, the Reuschels usually did not cover their windows except the ones in the bathrooms.

He had walked over here from his home many nights in his youth to hunker in the rotting leaves, fascinated by the parade of people swirling through the glow. They had seemed perpetually happy, the Reuschels. It had both piqued him and inspired him, as a child, to witness the steadiness of their interior life, the effortless weaving of their relationships: Gene in Gail's room building shelves with her; Barbara in the living room rocker, a book on her lap, obviously reading aloud to Tim; the entire family at the kitchen table munching late snacks – pizza and popcorn, the steam of which he could smell. When they did dishes together, there was playful flicking of water at each other and gentle laughter. Sounds from the windows carried perfectly, through the screens and up the hillside, helped along by the acoustically perfect surface of the lake. He had heard singing and secrets through the years, heard the toilets flush and doors slam. Once in a while he had heard crying, but with the crying was almost always another voice, a tender voice offering solace.

Tim's family, his wife and child, were no less than that.

There had been touching tonight and talking, the making of the beds, and the building of a fire. Because the windows were shut tight against the early spring air, the stage shows had been silent movies, their dramas still profoundly affecting. His gaze had followed Deena closely, memorizing her grace. Behind his eyelids he danced with her, moving against her as a husband would move against a wife: with ease, with affection, and with acknowledged need.

She and Tim were turning off lights now. In the kitchen. The living room. The upstairs bathroom. They huddled with Jon on the bed in Tim's old room for minutes, then clicked his lamp off. The staircase light went out and he could see Tim and Deena enter their room, shutting the door, reaching for each other. Their embrace was brief. Deena pulled away and touched the wall switch. The window square went black. Had she sensed his watching heart? She belonged to him as Jenny had. She was his. And she knew it.

The stars grew brighter. A slender piece of moon had risen while he waited. The magic of the cottage called to him. He stood up stiffly, took off his gloves, shoved them into his jacket pockets, and rubbed his hands together. Creeping down the hill, he approached the outdoor stairs that led to the room where Jon was sleeping. He had long ago numbered the steps. There were thirteen, and if he walked to the outside of each step, it would not creak. He took his time climbing, a long, labored journey, and at last knelt with his hands and cheek to the door. The wood was warm, a comfort to him. He owned this house and the aura within it. He came and went when no one was home, wandering the halls like a ghost. The Reuschels had summoned the locksmith to change the combinations on the lock tumblers from time to time but could not keep him out. He had a secret. When he was nine years old, he had discovered a way to get in without a key by sticking a pen knife between Tim's exterior door and its frame and simply pushing the dead bolt back. It was an accidental discovery, based on childish tinkering. When Paul was older, he realized why it worked: A dead bolt has to be fully extended in order to snap into place and stay there. Whoever had installed the original lock had left the bolt hole in the door frame slightly too shallow. In time, he had tested all of the exterior doors in the Reuschel cottage and found he could enter any of them the same way. Once in, he would throw the dead bolt's thumb turn and exit via another door.

The Reuschels had been aware for years that they occasionally had a trespasser but could not figure out how or who.

He didn't need to open this door right now. It was enough for him to know that he could.

16

The pungent odor of old toys woke Tim in the dark. Large oily squares floated by. *Where was he?* At the cottage. In his room. The squares were window shapes pasted on walls. But in the wrong positions.

This was his parents' room.

He was a parent now.

His dreams gradually released him from their rocking motion. What had they been about? He couldn't remember. Great numbers of people, dizzying activity. He had tumbled and spun through them. Birthday parties? Foreign countries? Something like that. They weren't happy dreams. He had awakened with the emptiness of loss. Deena was warm beside him. He touched her to reassure himself. She did not stir.

Finding his flashlight, he followed its beam up the stairs. Jon lay sleeping on his stomach in the double bed, his breaths even and deep, his arms and legs flung out as though he were flying.

Monday

1

Paul approached the chosen area just after daybreak, moving through it cautiously, seeking the exact spot on which he should stand. His visible breath mingled with ground fog as he searched. He knew from experience that there was nothing objective about this phase. He had been summoned to a single location, a stretch of forest where the river widened and straightened. He had left some of his youth here, and the territory bore his unseen mark. The birds did not jump into flight as he walked. The burrowing animals were still.

Head down, he moved purposefully, roving, toward the place where the sticky sweet scent would be most dense and he would stop, awed. He found it in minutes, taking a step or two backward and forward to be certain. The process was mystical. He turned his face toward the river. Tim and his family would pause here. There was no need to track them through the fluttering morning. He would wait and they would be drawn to him.

He saw it clearly, the arrival of the raft and the slow parting of the males from the female, at her wish. Her essence had crystallized for Paul during the night: regal, deliberate, with an innate sense of correctness she will not violate. *He sees her reticence, the males peeing hidden in the underbrush, she selecting another place, separate, well out of the sight of the boy. This place. As she bends, the hunter seizes her. She makes no sound.*

He can never understand why this works, his finding of a single site. Does some fate conspire to help him, or does he will others into his path?

2

Deena lifted Jon into Tim's arms. Smiling, Tim swung Jon high in the air then onto the river bank and turned back to Deena.

'Try to step wide, now.'

Grasping Tim's hands, she put one foot on the rim of the raft and jumped, the camera weighty around her neck. Her boots sank in the soft mud, but she was able to walk easily to higher ground as Tim dragged the raft onto shore. She gazed upriver. For the last two hours they had been floating peacefully through flowering woodland. Her feet were cold, in spite of her boots. The water temperature was below fifty degrees and a chill radiated from the rubber floor of the raft. Nevertheless, Tim had been right. It was a beautiful journey. Each bend in the river brought new glory: mountain vistas, leafing thickets, webs of black branches unfurling gauzy, delicate foliage. And they were entirely alone, suspended in time.

Tim hauled their plastic food cooler and Deena's gadget bag from the raft to a dry spot on the bank. 'Come on, Jon, let's get ready for lunch.' He touched Jon's shoulder and led him into the brush.

Deena watched until she could see them no more. Then she zipped the camera into the bag and walked in the other direction trampling twigs and pulling prickly vines from her slacks with her gloves. Men had it easy. They didn't have to remove any clothes to go to the bathroom. She shivered, thinking of wind on her backside. Nothing to do but get it over with.

3

What the hell was wrong with him? He'd never have a better chance. She was in exactly the right place: totally hidden from the others. And very close to a stream. Her cries, if there were any, would be muffled by the sound of rushing water as it hit stones. The river was silent compared to this tributary. And she would be hunkering down any minute now. Experience had taught him that success was quickest if he caught the subject from above.

Perplexed, he pivoted silently on the ball of his left foot and put his back to a tree. Perspiration was running beneath his sweatshirt. Literally running, dripping. The crashing of his heart seemed audible. He tried not to breathe.

When he pivoted again, slowly, he brought her into view. She was facing the other direction, fumbling with the bulk of her jacket, the zipper of her trousers. Then, the white gleam and grace of her buttocks and thighs startled him, shimmering in his gaze. She squatted as a dancer would squat, with gentle control, perfect balance. He closed his eyes.

4

'Mommy! Lunchtime!' Jon shouted, wiping his river-washed hands on a paper towel.

'Maybe I'll go look for her,' Tim said. 'You start.'

Jon, kneeling at the cooler, fished out a sandwich in a plastic bag.

'Go ahead, pal. I'll be right back.'

Tim stared at the brambles, trying to determine where Deena had entered the woods. Squinting, he searched for her form in the distance. 'Don't go near the water, Jon. Eat your lunch.'

Jon nodded and Tim moved quickly into the forest. Perhaps she had followed the stream. It was alive with fish at this time of year. She may have become fascinated and wandered farther than she thought. Still, it wasn't like her to . . . 'Deena!' The name was carried on the breeze, across the glade and stream and up a steep grade on the other side. 'DEENA!' His voice seemed to stir the underbrush. He heard rustling, but the source was too wide, too general to find with his eyes. He stood motionless, a fine dust stinging his face.

'Tim?'

Deena materialized in beige sunlight ten yards from him. Relief touched his breastbone like a finger. 'You okay?'

'Sure. Just takes me longer.' She scrambled over a pile of fallen pines, flashes of gold shining in her hair, and looked at him with glad eyes.

When she came within reach, he slid an arm around her waist.

'Were you worried?' She shoved a hand into his jacket pocket.

Was he? *Really?* 'No.'

5

Tim couldn't remember every turn of the river. It had been a decade since he last navigated it. He sat on the bank munching an apple and watching the current, tracing in his mind the way they had come. He wasn't sure exactly how far it was to white water, that lone unpredictable stretch of Class II rapids that boiled among rocks for half a mile. It was too cold a day to get wet. They'd carry the raft past that point and re-enter the river where it calmed. But was it just ahead or farther on? He'd better walk downstream to scout, using the far ridge as a vantage post. From there, he was sure he could see at least two miles. It wouldn't take him more than fifteen minutes to check it out.

Jon, who had been playing behind him, suddenly thudded against Tim's back, putting his arms around Tim's neck in a bear hug. Tim teased him by leaning forward until Jon's feet left the ground and then standing up quickly. Jon, still hanging on, squealed with delight and wrapped his legs around his father's waist. 'Take me for a ride,' he commanded.

Tim looked at Deena. 'I think this might be the place for portage, but I'll walk down a ways and see.'

'Okay,' she smiled, shoving their bread crusts and wrappers into a paper bag.

Could he carry Jon? The kid was a brick. 'Do you want to go, pal? You'll have to walk most of the way.'

'Yes!'

Tim started off at a gallop, bouncing the boy up and down on his back. At about forty paces, Jon began to feel heavy and Tim stooped to let him down.

'I want to ride,' Jon said, clinging.

'No, you'll have to walk.'

'I don't want to.'

Tim leaned to one side until Jon dropped to his feet. 'Then stay with Mom.'

'I don't want to.'

Ah, the logic of five-year-olds, those adorable one-trackers. Tim glanced back at Deena. He could barely see her. She was sitting on the cooler, facing them. 'I want you to run back to Mom.'

'I don't want to.'

'Jon, *walk*, or go *back*.' He must have struck the right tone, the one that mingled authority with affection. Jon began to run toward Deena. Tim watched until he saw her catch him in an arms-wide embrace, then waved at her and sprinted decisively out of their vision. If he lingered, Jon would change his mind.

6

The river was bordered by huge numbers of dead trees poised at varied angles of falling. Storms were frequent here and volatile. If wind didn't move the timber, rapidly rising water did, eating quickly at the roots, dredging them up, sending the tall trunks groaning earthward, spilling into the turbulent flow. Some had been split by lightning, cleanly, as if with an ax. Blankets of twigs and branches rotted underfoot, mixed with the crumbling slippery leaves of another season.

Tim started up the incline, beginning to work a little harder to draw breath. Deena and Jon came into his mind. From the ridge, he might be able to see them. As he neared the top, he tried, but the woods behind him were deeper than he thought. He approached the summit and stared out at the vista. The river widened in a grand sweep to the left around the bluff. He remembered it now. After that it hit a downward slope, studded by a few perilous rocks, and commenced the rippling and rushing that heralded rapids. His eyes followed the course, which gradually turned foamy.

He took a few steps toward the edge and gazed straight down. In the years since he had been here, the river had gouged the land at the base of the ridge and taken it over. He was standing directly above the flow.

He heard a sigh, close, over his shoulder.

An explosion shattered his legs, hurling him forward. He was in the air, plummeting chin first towards the river, slamming his knees, an elbow, falling again, this time straighter, in a straight line, but suddenly being snagged by poles from trees, his flesh poked instantly raw through his clothes. The water came at him faster than he imagined possible. He hit it on his side, going under like a stone, freezing. *God. Freezing. Where is up?* The current tore at him, snatched him away from life. He reached out for anything, could grip nothing. And then miraculously his head was above water. He gasped, noon sights glinting through a torrent. The ridge: someone scrambling down the face of it, a man, dressed darkly.

Fear stunned him for the first time. *Hurry. Go.* His

bones were heavy, his chest kept sinking. He was picking up speed, bumping painfully along a line of submerged trees. He put his arms out in defense, the blood draining from his head as he fought to stay conscious. Branches whipped his face. Choppy glimpses of the riverbank showed a blur running beside him, pausing, running, pausing, mirroring his progress, his descent. *Paul!* It was *Paul*, in a black stocking cap and black hunting jacket. Paul was the man who had climbed down the ridge. But where was the other man, the one who hit him?

He needed to help Paul. Paul would not be able to reach him, to rescue him, if he didn't take action *now*. The initial numbness had worn off slightly. Tim could feel his heart pulsing heat. He could feel the current too, its insistent direction, as it pummeled his body, his head. He managed to get his arms up, toward the sky, and maneuver his legs into position at a right angle to shore. He was in the rocks, among them, being smashed, scraped, knocked windless; he was in the trees, hitting with force, stopping sharply, groping. Through the water, he heard the rubbery bass-pitch cadence of wading. And then Paul was leaning over a log above him, urgently reaching for him with both hands, grasping his hair, yanking his head sideways, viciously, painfully, down, down.

Truth slammed, whole, into his brain. In a single second, he understood. He wanted to stand, to be on equal ground with Paul, but it wasn't possible. He struggled to slide away. The fingers held fast. Water pounded at his eyes, seared his nostrils. He couldn't breathe. *The shit. The fucking shit*. Anger gave him strength. He jerked backward, felt Paul follow him effortlessly. *Pull him in. Pull the fucker in*. He grabbed Paul's wrists. They turned to cotton under his fingers. He couldn't get a grip. They gave. Soft. He squeezed, kept squeezing, pinching the cotton with such force he touched his thumbs through it. An electric hum began in the recesses of his brain, behind a distant door. Its piercing pitch broke his concentration. He would have to see about it, stop the noise before he could do anything else. The hum grew louder as he walked slowly back through the long shadowy corridor. Far. Farther than he thought.

When he finally reached the door, he was able to open it easily.

7

Holy Mary, Mother of God, Mimi Trakas prayed silently, ringing the bell on her wrist, shaking her arm, back and forth, back and forth, back and forth until her head vibrated with the noise. Why didn't Arlene *come?* The man who had been pushed under the water was thrashing wildly, grabbing and grabbing at the man who held him down. *Mother of God.* As she watched, the poor soul's frantic, grasping motions began to subside. *Pray for us sinners . . . pray for us . . . pray for us . . .* When they stopped, the attacker stayed perfectly still, lying across the log, with his arms submerged. Finally, he eased himself to his feet, straightening his legs and his back and raising his chin to look around.

Evil incarnate. The devil himself! Who *was* this? Anyone she had seen before? Impossible, at such a distance, to make out his features. Mimi shifted her gaze through the gauzy green and brown web of branches outside her closed window to the spot in the river where the drowned man's body would appear momentarily if, indeed, he had died. She had been born beside this river and knew it well. It was angry this afternoon, roiling, but it had utterly predictable patterns, patterns she had watched for eight decades. She could feel her windpipe tightening as she eyed the Chute. Her brother Fred had named it, the wide sucking passage between Billy Rock and Skytop Rock. At that point the current was inescapable, and halfway through the Chute, there was a shallow place. Fred had broken his leg there once, on the sudden stretch of higher ground, and had been carried downriver three miles beyond it before they could get him out.

As she stared, a gray-white balloon appeared, bobbing through the Chute. The man at the edge of the river saw it, too. He left the water and loped along the bank, shading his eyes with his hand.

This was a human face, bobbing. She couldn't see it clearly from so far away, but she knew. A face. One with no life left in it, part of a body with no resistance left in it, no resistance to the flow of the water.

She stopped ringing the bell. It was too late now for Arlene to see what she had been watching. Mimi had realized from the beginning that this was going to be a murderous fight. She had awakened from a doze to the vision of one man creeping up behind another man, hitting him, sending him sailing from the cliff. She had been ringing the bell from the very beginning. From the start. Where in the world was Arlene? The frustration was suffocating. She could hear her breath groaning in her throat.

Waves closed over the face. The other man still stood

on the riverbank, his hands in his pockets. He turned in her direction and then away, striding in a circle. Could he guess she was there? He seemed to be familiar with the woods, the river. Surely he knew of the house. Her heart moved in her chest.

Maybe not. The house was new. If he hadn't been in the area recently, he might not be aware of it. *He didn't know.* If he had known, he wouldn't have worked his evil within sight of it. *Would he notice it now?* Her son had designed this home to blend with the setting. The color of old leaves and forest straw, it sat high in the woods on a flat ridge, with only the roof and second story visible from river level.

She shouldn't take the chance. She should try to get up, get out of bed, make it to the head of the staircase, and ring the bell again. Perhaps she could even navigate the stairs. She still had a fairly usable arm and leg. But how would she grip the banister? Her fingers had no strength, no dexterity. And the paralyzed side of her was amazingly heavy, like another whole person to be carried.

The man was walking away from the river now, out of her vision, probably toward his truck. The truck, that was what had first caught her attention, well before breakfast. She had been astonished to see it cutting through the mist and tall weeds of Tommy's Field more than two miles from the main road. It had driven across her vision like an apparition, leaving the dry grasses waving when it vanished.

'Yes, Mom?'

She glanced at the doorway. Arlene was leaning against the frame. She was wearing a familiar tolerant smile, the one that meant, 'You ring the bell too much. I just can't drop everything and run up here right away every time you ring.'

Mimi raised her good arm toward her daughter-in-law and then moved it toward the window. The sound of the bell on her wrist caused Arlene to sigh. She crossed the room and stood beside the bed. 'What is it?'

The man had gone.

'Ewaaaaaaa.' Her own voice always took her by surprise now. She could no longer form words and the tone was uncontrolled, a guttural wail. Defeated, she let her arm drop to the blanket.

Arlene looked at the window, studying the frame and sill. 'I'd better not open it, Mom. It's pretty cold outside.'

'Aaaawwwwwwaaa.' *A man died, died before my eyes. Another man killed him.*

'It's frustrating, isn't it? I'm so sorry. If only you could write it down. It must be so hard not to be able to make yourself understood.' Arlene bent over and gently put a cheek to hers. Mimi couldn't feel it. 'Do you want me to take off your glasses so you can rest?' She paused, waiting for an answer. 'No? Then, I'll bring you some pudding. Shall I?'

Tears had been amassing in the center of her brain for months, hardening into a large stone. She had been shocked, following the stroke, to find that she could no longer cry. When she wept, which was often, she wept in the core of her soul, dry-eyed and stiff-lidded, bereft.

8

Paul hesitated with his hand on the ignition key. An intrusive presence had followed him along the river's edge. He was out of its range now, but it still made his blood hum. A person. *A witness?* He had turned slowly in all directions, his radar seeking the source. But he couldn't find it. Didn't have time to find it. He needed to get out.

He yanked the Bronco into gear and nudged it forward, feeling the left rear tire sink slightly then pop onto firm ground. Holding the wheel steady, he plowed cautiously though the brush. *Concentrate.* The most important thing was not to get stuck. There were a blue million snares between here and the road.

The presence, still raking his veins, disturbed, distracted him. A fatal presence, perhaps. His undoing. If he had been aware of it at the outset, he wouldn't have begun with Tim. He would have walked away from opportunity, as he had so many times before.

But he hadn't felt it at first. Perhaps the person hadn't been there at first.

There was no recourse. He couldn't stay, couldn't back-track later without the risk of being caught. It was over. He just had to hope he was wrong.

9

Something must have happened. Tim would never leave them for this long. In the half hour he'd been gone, the sky had filled with clouds and a mistlike rain had enveloped them. The temperature was dropping. Deena pulled Jon's jacket hood over his shiny blond hair and tied it tight. 'Put your gloves on, honey.'

'Where's Dad?'

'I don't know.' She stared at the place she had seen him last, the entrance to a tunnel of trees. Surely he would appear there any second now. But she had been thinking that for the past fifteen minutes. She stooped to help Jon with his gloves, startled to see that his eyes were rounded in fear. She realized that he was imitating her expression. She consciously relaxed her face. 'We'll just go see what Dad's up to.'

Jon grasped her hand and walked beside her in silence. She took small steps, allowing him to set the pace, not wanting to alarm him by rushing. She watched the trail closely, looking for signs of Tim, but there were none. She could hear nothing but the whoosh and gurgle of the river, the occasional whine of wind through branches, and a few lone bird calls. Where had he gone? To the ridge. That's what he'd said. She contemplated the ordeal of helping Jon climb it and – for a second – the possibility of leaving him at the bottom to wait. Anger flashed through her. She felt her cheeks redden. Where was Tim? He had to know they were looking for him. Dismay quickly replaced the anger, and another mood began to possess her, a flat despondence that deepened into dread.

By the time they reached the foot of the hill, panic had energized her. She took the grade as rapidly as possible, tugging Jon by the hand, hefting him over logs, carrying him in spurts. She was sweating heavily and could hear herself wheezing. Halfway to the top, she had to sit down. She pulled Jon into her lap and held him tightly. They stayed there for minutes, not speaking. She could feel, through their many layers of clothes, Jon's tremulous heartbeat. At last, they got up and climbed the rest of the way in an even rhythm, the breeze of the crest flying at them well before they reached it. They approached the peak slowly, watching a panorama rise into view: mountaintops, forests, the wide hooking angle of the river, the rapids beyond it. She could tell there was a sheer drop ahead. 'Jon, stay back.'

Jon stopped and she inched forward. Yes, it was nearly straight down from here. The river was right under them.

Could Tim have fallen? Not likely. He was careful, always. Unless he had become dizzy or ill. To fall would mean hitting stones once, maybe twice on the way down. And hitting debris, too, in the water. She winced. She had to stand for a minute and simply stare, looking for him, searching the swirls and foam of the river, the rocks. The driftwood stuck in silt. The other bank.

She turned swiftly to check for Jon. He was still there, right where she had told him to stay, hunkering, peering at something under a swatch of dead leaves. All remaining courage left her.

'What did you find, sweetheart?' she asked, careful to keep her voice gentle.

He looked up at her with wonder and lifted the rotting mass so she could see. A black beetle, the size of a silver dollar, lay on its back in the soil, legs clawing the air in protest against the invasion of light and air.

10

Should she go back to the raft? Would Tim be there?

Why would he be there now if he hadn't been there before?

No, she probably should get help. Downriver. That would be quickest. Their trip had been more than half over when they stopped for lunch. She had no idea how far it was to the ranger station where they were to have taken the bus back to their car. And was it on this side of the river or the other?

She slipped and slid down the incline the remaining few yards to level ground and reached behind her for Jon. 'We're going to walk to the ranger station.'

'Where is it?'

'Not very far.' Why did she say that? She had never lied to him, not even about Santa Claus. 'Listen . . . I'm not sure. Do you think you can make it or are you too tired?'

'Too tired.'

'Do you want to rest a while?'

There was something so poignantly manly in the way he shook his head that she nearly wept.

'Let's go, then,' she said, and they started off slowly, pushing the limbs of saplings out of their path. If they kept going to the right, around the ridge, they would find the river and walk beside it until dark. That was as far ahead as she could plan.

11

Paul leaned out the window of the Bronco and stuck his plastic parking pass into the metal clock. The gate rose. He accelerated slowly up the steep ramp, positioning the truck perfectly in the slot. Climbing down, he walked around the vehicle once, checking for mud. He had done an exceptional job in the self-wash. If he kept following procedures, he would be fine. The Fire had finally stopped rolling at him, yellow clouds with ragged white holes at their centers, waves that struck powerfully and receded quickly leaving him stunned and weak. They scared the crap out of him.

He had control now, had regained it by erasing memory and locking onto procedures. The next hour was crucial. He would do what he had always done. And he would be fine. He saw himself in the actors' bathroom cleaning his boots, showering, shaving, rinsing the sink, dressing in his suit, carrying the bag of dirty clothes and towels and rags to the laundromat, washing and drying its contents beside the disinterest of sloppy-fat women, returning the bag to the truck, walking down into spring air.

He would be fine.

In the cement stairwell of the parking garage, the Fire came for him again. He kept just ahead of it, taking each new step with his strong right foot. He had been willful, the Fire said, ungrateful. He had not obeyed.

12

Jon was behind her now, stepping exactly where she stepped, as though he could see her footsteps in imagined snow. She guessed it had been three hours since they left the raft to look for Tim. It wouldn't be dark for another two. Surely they could make it to the station. She didn't want to think of the alternative. The day had continued to grow colder, perhaps close to freezing. Following the river had been a little easier than plowing through the woods, but not much. There were intermittent stretches of muck that couldn't be avoided. Luckily, they had not been forced to wade. They'd managed to stay fairly dry. And the mist had cleared up.

Her eyes were tired from watching, hunting, along the bank for a sign of Tim. She had grown past her earlier emotions into a state of weary resignation. Whatever the truth was, she would handle it, if not for her own sake, then for Jon's. The immediate task was to survive.

'I'm cold, Mommy.'

His voice startled her into a recognition that she was losing her mental alertness. She shook off the cobwebs of ice in her brain and touched his shoulder. 'I'm sorry.' Why hadn't she brought the remaining sandwiches with her? Or any of their other supplies? 'I'm cold, too.' She scanned the horizon, seeing no movement. Even the birds had disappeared.

The clamor of the water leapt into her consciousness. Maybe they would be warmer if they left the river and walked through the woods. As she considered this, she contemplated the marshy brush and the brambles beyond. Her eye tracked trees and river to a convergent point where a tiny, upright brown rectangle shimmered faintly behind a storm of branches.

'Honey, come here. Let me hold you up.' She reached under his arms and, with difficulty, lifted him. 'Look down there. See that little house?' She pointed.

'Where?'

She pulled off her glove. 'Follow my finger. Right there.'

His eyes widened.

'You see it?' Excitement pulsed through her. 'It's . . . maybe . . .' She set him down again. '. . . where we're going. We'll keep on, okay?'

'Okay.'

They trudged in silence for a long time, the weathered structure gradually resolving in her vision, slowly growing larger. Too big for a cabin. Had to be a public building.

It puzzled her that she saw no one moving about the grounds. Was it abandoned? She watched intently as they approached. When they drew closer, she began to have an eerie sense of Tim's presence there. He must be waiting for her. It was logical – the natural spot to find each other again. She cautioned herself not to run. She needed to save the last bits of her strength. Besides, Jon would not be able to keep up.

Like stepping into a dream, she and Jon finally stepped into the deep clearing surrounding the station. She was sure now that she was in the right place, simply coming at it from the back. The station probably faced a road she couldn't see yet. The massive windowless structure blocked her view. The river was especially loud at this stretch, almost howling in the wind and flowing as swiftly as a waterfall.

She grabbed Jon's hand and crossed the yard, rounding a corner and opening the view wide before her. *An ambulance. Three police cars. Uniformed people in conversation.* The event that had brought them here was over. There was no doubt. They had the sad, slow movements of people in the wake of tragedy. She knew at once what the tragedy had been.

13

They saw her. One by one, they turned to stare. She slowed her pace in horror at their expressions: surprise and recognition, sympathy and apprehension. None of them moved. She wandered, dazed, across the vast insurmountable distance, dragging Jon with her. He hung back, heavy on her arm. Whatever was to come, it would be vivid in his memory for the rest of his life. She must put her own feelings aside and guard his. She pulled him to her. He grabbed the pocket of her jacket and clung to her side.

As they picked their way through the mud, one of the policemen came toward them. He approached cautiously. When she was close to him, he asked softly, 'Mrs. Reuschel?'

He had found Tim. How else would he know her name? She nodded.

'I'm afraid I have some bad news for you.'

His tone was confirmation enough. Tim had died. She didn't want Jon to hear this, not from a stranger. 'Could we . . .,' she began.

His gaze flickered to Jon. 'You cold, son?'

'Yes.'

'Let's go sit in the car, how about it? I'll put the heater on.'

'Okay,' Jon said.

'I'm sorry you two had to walk down. We were just getting ready to hunt for you.'

'Is my dad here?' Jon asked.

The policeman shot her a glance.

'Is my daddy here?' Jon repeated.

The policeman hesitated, choosing a word. 'No.'

14

Paul left the bus at 32nd Street and eased his way toward his studio. There was no hurry now. He had completed all of the tasks and no longer had the sense of being followed.

Home was not a good place to be after a day like this. Nothing gave him comfort but his work. The thought of his living room, the sterile cushion fabrics and the barren stretches between glossy tables, created a great emptiness in him. He preferred the studio with its orderly clutter, its collection of unique pieces crafted by his own hand. They affirmed that, as flawed as his thoughts might be at times, he had a worthy soul. He could consistently bring forth beauty from it. He liked to be surrounded by his art.

Even the building itself gave him a sense of peace. As he approached it, he began to relax. Inside, a honeycomb of glass-front studios spread before him, each filtering dusk into the corridor from its massive windows. There were not many artists working at this hour and hardly any customers drifting about. That was fortunate. He did not want to talk.

One by one, he lit the glass cases in his shop, admiring their contents. The gathering glow reassured him. It climbed the brick and fanned out overhead like an umbrella. He was safe under it.

15

The first policeman kept on talking and talking to his mother, but Jon couldn't hear him with the window up and the car turned on. She wasn't saying anything back, just looking sad. If his father were here, he would never let his mother look this sad. Sometimes, her chin went up and her mouth opened and her eyes closed tight. When she did that, the man would stop talking and wait for her to open her eyes again.

The second policeman sat next to Jon on the back seat of the car in the heat. He hadn't said anything to Jon. The metal stuff all over his uniform smelled cold, and he took up a lot of space.

Now his mother and the first policeman were going away from him, toward the ambulance. He wanted to run after her, but she wouldn't like that. She had told him not to get out of the car. Was the man going to put her in the ambulance? What if they took his mother away? He looked for the door handle but couldn't find it.

'Why don't you stay here with me?' the second policeman said, patting Jon's leg.

Jon watched his mother walk from the side of the ambulance to the back of it. The first policeman opened the two doors for her and she went behind one of them. 'Are they taking my mother somewhere?'

'No, she'll be here in a few minutes.'

It didn't seem to be a lie, not the way he said it. It seemed true. But Jon kept looking for the door handle so he would be ready to run after the ambulance if it started up.

16

The interior of the ambulance had a distinctive odor that met Deena as soon as the doors were opened. She had never smelled it before but knew it was that of a lifeless body. Harsh overhead lights were on inside, illuminating every corner of the rectangular compartment. On the left was a stretcher and the form of a man totally covered by a bright blue blanket. On the right a thin, uniformed woman about Deena's age sat on a bench. The woman beckoned

Deena to sit next to her and she did. The policeman closed the doors.

'I've been staying with him so he wouldn't be lonely,' the woman said. 'I always think they must be lonely at first.'

The comment piqued Deena. 'I want to see him.'

The woman knelt beside the stretcher, lifting the blanket up and folding it back. *Tim.* Battered and dirty, his eyes and mouth closed, his hair stiff. Involuntarily, she cried out. He must have died in agony, beaten cruelly, fighting. Her vision narrowed and nausea wrenched her. *He couldn't be dead.* If she screamed . . . screamed loud enough, long enough, she could change this moment, make it disappear, swallowed by time as though it had never occurred.

Even as she thought it, she knew it was not so. Nothing would change this. The scream came out as a sob.

'He knows you're with him now,' the woman said, smoothing Tim's hair. 'And that's a comfort to him.' She put her other hand gently on Tim's elbow. 'He had a hard ride down that river.' She was speaking about him and touching him as though he were an ill child. 'This is a good man. I can tell that.'

'Are you the medic?' Deena whispered.

'One of them. There wasn't anything we could do. He was already gone when they brought him up from the river.'

'What happened to him?'

The woman shook her head. 'The pathologist will have to tell you.'

'Is that where he goes next?'

'Yes. To the hospital.' She turned to Deena. 'Don't you

77

want to touch him? I've found out it helps in the long run. To let him go.'

Deena hesitated, then got to her knees. The odor of him seemed overwhelming now. The woman looked at her with compassionate eyes. Deena laid her cheek against Tim's chest and wept.

17

The most difficult thing about the situations he created was waiting for news. It was imperative that he ask no questions of anyone, that he let the facts drift back to him at their own speed. Sometimes it took weeks or months. Sometimes he never learned what he wanted to know, although he listened intently to gossip and to broadcast accounts and read every paper he could find. He had discovered that the periodical sections of small libraries near the murder sites were excellent for providing fairly detailed information. Local newspapers had the space to run more than a cursory account of circumstances, survivors, arrangements, speculation. Without exception, the deaths of his victims had eventually been ruled as accidental. But comments from investigators were always deliberately sparse and vague in the meantime. He had no way of determining whether foul play was suspected. He always felt uneasy, darkly moody after a search for details. Still, the discipline he had been forced to use, time after time, had matured him. He was getting more philosophical and much better at waiting.

This time would be especially difficult. He had broken

his pattern and perhaps his luck. The nourishing relief he usually felt after an episode had been displaced by confusion and awe.

He had killed Tim.

He did not kill men. Ever.

He went to his workbench and straddled the Balans chair. Selecting a narrow strip of sheet gold from a drawer, he laid it in front of him, contemplating its smooth brilliance.

What had possessed him? Deena's bare skin, her silken buttocks? She had sent up a gravity that pressed him flat against a tree. He had to peel himself off the landscape when she walked away. She had a distinct air of resistance. He couldn't possibly have taken her.

Sliding his glasses onto his nose, he lit the soldering torch, picked up the gold with tweezers, and moved the flame across its surface. In seconds, the gold began to glow a dull cherry red. He shut off the torch and, selecting a rawhide mallet, delicately hammered the softened strip around the size 5 mark of a mandrel.

Lighting the torch, he soldered the ring into a smooth circle and lowered the ring into pickling solution. It came out cool, free of fire scale. He studied the unfinished wedding band, contemplating the bride who would wear it: Ms. Stephanie Johnston, a slight woman, perhaps twenty-two years old, with long black hair and an unexpected solemnity. She reminded him of the pioneers who stare gravely out from black-and-white photographs in museums. He had seen her twice. On each occasion, she spoke to him in tones he had to strain to hear. But when she spoke to her beloved, her voice was stronger, and she smiled a faint smile of delicious secrets. He could see the man respond with pleasure. Mr. Jason Weingarten.

He sat perfectly still, listening to the counterpoint of his feelings, a wordless, soundless tapping against a wordless, soundless pulse.

For hours he had been telling himself that Tim had been the recipient of shunted energy. But that was not the truth.

Deena Reuschel was alive because he wanted her.

And Stephanie Johnston? He meditated for a moment on Jason Weingarten's fingers caressing her elbow, rubbing the nape of her neck beneath the waterfall of her hair. Somehow their relationship did not evoke in him the lash of despair he had experienced watching other couples touch and whisper in the sanctum of his shop.

He would let her go.

He selected an engraving tool from among the instruments in the well of his bench and began to carve a design into the ring: the vine of life.

18

After a while, his mother walked back from the ambulance by herself. It was getting dark, but he could see that she was mad and her hair was all messed up. He felt scared. The second policeman got out and she got in. She shut the door.

'Where's Daddy?'

'He . . .'

The first policeman opened the front door by the steering wheel and leaned in. A light went on. His mother yelled, 'Stay *out* of here! I want to talk to my *son*! For *God's* sake, give us some *privacy!*' The man shut the door. The light went off.

He had only heard her shout like that one other time, when he almost rode his tricycle down the basement steps. 'Jon . . .' She sounded like she was choking. She grabbed him in a hug that hurt. 'Daddy died,' she said. 'Somehow he fell in the river. Do you know what that is, to *die?*'

Jon stiffened. Allison Lucas's father was dead, killed in the war. He didn't live at their house anymore.

'Yes. Is he coming back?'

She started to cry. 'No.'

He knew that. You never saw dead people again. But, maybe sometime, someone might come back. Maybe his dad. 'Are you sure?'

'I'm sure. He might want to, but he can't.' She kept crying.

His dad had told him once that nobody could know everything about the world. Maybe she didn't know everything about dead people. His dad wouldn't leave him. Not for very long anyway.

'Jon, do you understand what I'm saying?'

'Yes.'

She put him on her lap and held him there. He felt sleepy and hungry and sick all at the same time. His mother rolled the window down a little bit and one of the men stuck his eyes in the slot. 'We can go now,' she said.

Two policemen sat down in the front seat, making the car drop and come back up. The air outside started flashing red.

The ambulance was flashing, too. It moved over in front of them. They followed it up a high hill.

19

Barbara Reuschel loosened the last switch plate, plucking it from the wall and laying it, with its screw, on the windowsill. She should have quit painting before dinner, but she was almost done, would be done with the entire project by bedtime. She made a summary check of her handiwork in the spotty circles of light cast by lamps she had set on the sheet-covered carpet. Excellent, what she could see of it. Three days of work had brightened the guest room considerably.

The aroma of the apple pie Gene was baking drifted to her. The phone rang three times, stopping in mid-ring. He must have answered it. She touched the roller to the pale yellow paint in the metal pan and evened it out gingerly before applying it to the area around the outlet. Some of her muscles were complaining about the ladder climbing she had done, but satisfaction overrode any discomfort. She had never hired a painter, never would as long as she could still move her bones. Painting was a happy job.

The warm Florida breeze wafting in from the Gulf dried the paint quickly. The wetness on the wall faded as soon as she left each section. She sensed Gene's presence in the doorway and waited for him to speak as she wiped splatters from the baseboard with a damp rag. He did not. She dipped the roller into the paint again. What had he come to tell her? She looked up, jolted into terror by his expression.

20

'What should I do, Gene?' Over the hospital pay phone Deena could hear Barbara's muffled sobbing, but her father-in-law spoke clearly from the extension. 'What do you want, Deena? Do you want to take him home to California?'

She had been talking to her in-laws for so long now, nearly half an hour, without anything having been decided. She was aware that she had passed into a state of numbness in which her thoughts were wound around each other, immobile. Everything she had done to this point seemed wrong. She shouldn't have let Tim go off by himself. She shouldn't have wasted time following the track of the river. She should have traveled perpendicular to the river until she found the road and was able to flag down a car. She had not been incisive, and that might have cost Tim his life. She glanced at Jon who was sitting halfway down the hall in a plastic chair, with his feet straight out in front of him. His shoulders were rounded, his head bowed. He was almost asleep. 'I don't know. I don't want to prolong this, the funeral and all. I don't want to put Jon through any more than necessary.'

Barbara now: 'He loved the lake. How would you feel about having him buried near there?'

The lake. 'I don't know.' It was barely audible.

'You want to bury him there?' Gene's voice.

'All right.'

'I'll take care of everything,' Gene said. 'I know who to call. I'll let your parents know about the arrangements.

You won't need to talk to them again tonight unless you want to. And I'll get the phone company to turn on that line at the cottage. It might take a day or two, though. They're not too efficient up there.'

'Will we need it, Gene?' Barbara said. 'We'll probably all leave the cottage by Friday to go home. By the time they turn it on, they'll just have to shut it off again.'

'What would you like, Deena?' Gene was beginning to crack again. She could hear it in the husky tones.

'It won't matter.' It would be a relief to leave it off. She didn't feel like talking to the people who were bound to call when they heard about Tim.

'We won't bother, then,' Gene said. 'We can use a neighbor's phone.'

'You should have someone with you, right now, a friend. Is anyone there?'

'No.' Who would she call?

Barbara coughed, blew her nose. 'Well . . . we have friends at the lake. I'll get someone to come over to the cottage. Right away.'

The thought of strangers at the house was intolerable, even one stranger. Their evening had been filled with strangers, taking their temperatures, blood pressure, asking questions, filling out forms. She had told her story a dozen times, how Tim had left and how they had gone to find him. She was tired of curious stares, tired of mechanical sympathy, tired of defending herself and Tim against insinuation. *He left you and your son in the woods? Had you been arguing? Are you sure he hadn't been drinking? Was he on any drugs? Was he depressed about anything? Would he have had a reason to take his own life?*

'Don't do that, Barbara.'

'Surely you don't want to be alone,' she said. 'These are long-time friends. They'll help you.'

'Please don't.'

'We won't,' Gene stated flatly. 'We'll be there by tomorrow afternoon. We love you.'

She placed the receiver in its cradle and picked up from the floor the small cardboard box the nurse had given her. She had signed a receipt for it. In it was Tim's jewelry and the contents of the zippered pockets of his jacket. She would need the car keys.

She tugged the lid off the box, retrieving the keys and staring for the first time at the collection of items that rested in a bed of cotton. *His wallet*, limp from being soaked – although someone had obviously made an attempt at drying it off. She picked through it. Tim stared at her from the photo on his driver's license. There was plenty of cash in the bill compartment. His credit cards were in place in their slots. *His watch*, waterproof and still running. A wet packet of matches. An assortment of change. A penknife. His wedding ring. She touched the ring. It matched hers, a golden circle of irises in full bloom. Would Tim want to be buried wearing it? He probably would. She thought of Paul and his careful shaping of this ring, an act of devotion. The rings had been his wedding gifts to them. He would be devastated by the news. The thought of Paul embracing Tim at the brunch, obviously overwhelmed to see him again, made Deena wince. They had played together as little children. They had a common history. Of all the people she had seen respond to Tim, few had responded so warmly.

She looked at her precious son who was asleep in the chair, with his chin to his chest. Agonizing empty hours lay ahead of them in a house overflowing with reminders of Tim. She was lost. There was no comfort here, not a single person she knew and trusted and who had cherished her husband. No one to mourn with. No one to hold her up, as she would have to hold up Jon.

The image of Tim kissing Paul exuberantly as they parted on Sunday swept into her mind. If *she* had drowned in this place, Tim would have asked Paul to come. She was sure of it.

She would call him.

21

Barbara stood paralyzed as Gene came to her, enfolding her in his arms. As they pressed together in wordless grief, it seemed there was no longer a roof on the house. It had disappeared into the vast universe. Their heads and shoulders were bare, exposed to wind and the whim of God. She had spent her life layering their shelter, paint on paint, fabric on fabric, item on item, prayer on prayer, until there was not the tiniest cleft where sorrow could enter. When they were in financial jeopardy, she had found new ways to save. When their babies were ill, she had summoned the doctor immediately. She had laid up the garden's bounty in cans and jars against the encroaching winters. She had cautioned the little ones about strangers. She had orchestrated weddings for the children and sewn christening gowns for the grandchildren. Her home-grown wisdom had anticipated and circumvented every lack, every danger. Everything but this.

Tuesday

1

Deena lay in Tim's old bed next to Jon, listening to his ragged breathing in the dark. He had cried so hard on and off throughout the evening that she became afraid for his health. She had made up her mind to sleep with Jon the rest of the time they remained at the cottage. Because they would wake up over and over again to the stark fact of Tim's death, she would make sure Jon was constantly comforted by her physical presence. She would not leave him.

The new moon cast a sinking silver light against the shelves containing Tim's books and model cars. Jon had been asleep for hours while she, trapped in an endless cycle of the day's events, ceaselessly reviewed them. Tim must have had a sudden health problem, like a heart attack or an aneurysm. She knew with certainty that he had not killed himself. She resented the implication of suicide, resented the total loss of privacy she had endured thus far. With Tim's death, she had been catapulted into a strange realm, one in which their past, their comings and goings, their health, financial matters, and marital condition were subjects for official scrutiny. She was no longer in charge of what happened next. She could only be patient and wait for the coroner's report to exonerate them. How many days would it take to get it? What kind of intrusion would she have to bear in the meantime? A policeman had stayed with her and Jon at the hospital, one who had definite ideas on the procedures she should follow. When she had insisted that they be taken back to the rental car they left up the river that morning, he had insisted she was in no shape to drive. She had won but ended up agreeing to follow the patrol car to the cottage. How eerie it had been to adjust the driver's seat and the mirrors from Tim's positions to her own. She supposed that for months she would be finding things as Tim had left them.

Illumination swept the wall. She sat up in bed to look out the window. Headlights were growing larger on the gravel driveway that wound through the trees. A car materialized, slowing when it approached the house. She buttoned the waist of her jeans, pulled a sweater on over her blouse and slid her feet into her sneakers. The vehicle had stopped, out of her sight. She could hear the motor die. It was probably Paul. She hoped it was Paul.

Tying her shoes, she raced downstairs and through the kitchen to turn on the outside light. In the flooding glow, she saw Paul running toward her. She struggled with the door, opening it to his anxious gaze.

'Oh, Deena!' he said as she let him in. 'How could this happen? I'm *sorry*!' He pulled her to him, and she rested her feverish head against his shoulder.

2

It was so easy. She wasn't shy with him at all. She let him put his arms around her waist. Her body was hot, as though she had come to him from her bed. She filled his senses, the tangled silk of her hair soft beneath his cheek, the sensual mingling of perspiration and perfume, the slim, surprisingly powerful shape of her back and hips. She was taller than he had remembered and substantively stronger, as though Tim's death had caused a flowering in her. He was careful to hold her lightly, very lightly, conscious of the times when he had been too eager with women and provoked their apathy.

She released him and stepped away, her face turned up to his. He noticed that she still had on the clothes she had worn in the woods. It struck him as odd, pitiful, that she had not changed, had not bathed. Her appearance was a link to Tim and the events on the river. He had wanted to start fresh with her. 'Thank you for coming,' she said.

'I loved Tim,' he answered simply.

This seemed to be what she wanted to hear. She took his hand and led him into the living room, where there was a single lamp burning on a corner table. From now on, he would be whatever she wished him to be. He would live inside her reality. His memories of yesterday would disappear altogether. He could do that, could effectively block the past. He had done it before. And he would be patient with her grief, waiting for her to gradually accept him.

She sat on the couch, watching somberly as he kindled a fire in the fireplace and set the screen in front of it. She blinked at the flames, tears flowing down her face and dripping from her chin, which she rubbed with the sleeve of her sweater. 'I don't understand how it happened,' she said. 'He was a good swimmer. Maybe he was unconscious when he fell in.'

'Maybe.'

She reached out to him, and he went to sit beside her, taking her hand.

Subtle noise on the stairs made him turn his head. Jon stood near the bottom of them, in his pajamas. A beautiful child, gentle and appealing. He would be good to him, better than a father. He had dreamed it would be like this.

Groggy, Jon squinted at the couple on the sofa. His mother. And? *His dad?* He *had* come back! *He had.* He opened his mouth. His dad started toward him but it wasn't his dad it was someone else the man from the restaurant where was *Daddy? Still dead?*

Paul crossed the room to Jon and picked him up.

'Nooo!' Jon cried, bucking wildly in his arms. 'No! No! Mommy! Mommy!'

He couldn't keep hold of Jon, but he couldn't put him down either. The arching and kicking knocked Paul off balance. Jon's heels bruised Paul's legs. He nearly fell against the banister trying to put the boy safely onto his feet. Anger ripped through him. Deena was there now, lifting Jon, carrying him toward the rocker. As Deena walked away, Jon glared at Paul over her shoulder. She held Jon in her lap, rocking gently as Paul fought to calm himself. He felt like snatching the child from Deena, shaking him, slamming him against the wall. He retreated to the easy chair by the French doors. Mother and son had formed a unit, chest to chest, in the creaking chair. They moved as one being in a slow ride of which he had no part. Absorbed in each other, they forgot he was there.

Minutes passed, marked with the rhythmic rocking. The

rapid rate of his heartbeat did not subside but grew more insistent. He understood human devotion in all its forms, and this form was the most narcissistic because it was exclusive. It took place inside an invisible circle barely big enough for two. His parents had existed in a single shell like this one, a soundproof shell through which his voice did not seem to penetrate. They had seemed always to have their backs to him, to be in a perpetual state of going away from him. His father had eyes only for her, his mother. Gifts only for her. Laughter and journeys for her, for her. From them he had acquired wisdom regarding such a relationship. It fed itself in a symbiotic way, round and round, gathering force, unstoppable. The only thing that could halt it was the permanent absence of one of the partners.

He saw the future. Jon: all that was left of Tim. Deena: obsessively treasuring that remnant. No emotional space between the two of them, no space for anyone else. He couldn't allow it.

Deena did not look up. Her head was bowed against her son's. With their eyes closed, they continued to rock, breathing only the breath of each other. It infuriated him. She would never be free for his own love as long as she had this one.

3

Martin had learned not to slink to his desk, although he was inevitably late for work. He stood tall on the long escalator that rose from the cavernous first floor of the newspaper building to the jumbled offices of the second

93

and, upon reaching the top, plodded silently toward his alcove. No one spoke to him: a friendly conspiracy to keep the editor from noticing what time he arrived. Chalmers usually noticed anyway and relished calling him on it.

As he approached his desk, he pondered the usual collection of garbage that had piled up overnight: clippings, returned sketches, pink telephone notes, computer printouts. One of the printouts was rolled up in his mug, a signal. There had been a drowning within a one-hundred-mile radius of Manhattan in the last twenty-four hours. This would be an account of it, taken from the wire service and delivered to him courtesy of Harvey Delittuso. Harvey, the garden editor who occupied the desk next to his, had observed Martin pulling drowning stories from the wire over a period of months and had finally asked about it. By tradition, nobody at work asked Martin anything personal. He cultivated a deliberate aloofness. Harvey's inquiry had been an overstepping of boundaries and Harvey knew it. But the man was irresistibly earnest. And he had asked privately. So Martin had told him. Thereafter, Harvey began to pull the stories himself during his early-morning scans of the wire and place them, without comment, in Martin's coffee cup.

Martin slipped the paper from the mug and unrolled it. In the past few years, he had distilled a giant mass of drowning stories to a group of eight that fit a subtle but perceptible pattern. The rest were throwaways, people who obviously did themselves in or made fatal mistakes or people who definitely were murdered. The more concretely he formulated his theory, the more curious he became, and the more anxious he was to analyze each new account. He smoothed the paper out on top of a stack of drawings and started to read.

Harvey Delittuso, carrying a pile of boxed garden books mailed from publishers, navigated several turns and dropped them next to his chair. Mart must have just come in. He was still wearing his coat while perusing the rubble on his desktop. It wasn't like Martin to take such a high profile. He'd usually roll the coat up right away and toss it under the desk, slip into his chair fast, with his head down. They never spoke first thing. Mart turned in his direction, the whole body at once, his face contorted.

'Hey . . . you all right?'

Martin shook his head.

'What's the matter?' Harvey took the piece of paper Martin held out to him. It was the wire service article from the morning feed. The drowning of a vacationer in the mountains.

'I know this one.'

4

Six hours since he'd been alone with Deena. The child had roamed between them minute by minute, separating Paul from her. Jon was eating Cheerios from a bowl at the kitchen table. Deena sat at the other side of it, resting her forehead on her hands.

Paul stirred the eggs in a skillet and dropped bread into the toaster. During the darkness and the seeping sunrise, he had thought carefully about Tim's son. It wasn't just that Deena had rapport with Jon. They were bound together spiritually. He was powerless to alter that. Paul would always be second to him, would always be suppressing his own fury, the kind of fury that pounded through his brain right now, demanding an outlet.

The toast popped up. He buttered it and spooned the eggs onto their plates. Another slice of bread went into the toaster. He pushed the handle down.

And he had a greater problem: Deena would probably leave at the end of the week, taking Jon with her to California. He had not thought that out in advance. He had not thought anything out in advance. He had let it all get away from him.

His actions from now on would have to be precise.

What actions? He could do nothing. He had broken his own rules by killing Tim. He'd be lucky to get away with that. Killing Jon, even if he made the death appear to be an accident, was out of the question. No one would believe it could happen twice in the same family. He'd trigger a manhunt.

Even if Jon died, Deena would go home. And it would crush her. It would be pointless.

As he set one of the plates in front of her, Deena's air of gratitude engulfed him. She folded her hands together and gave him a tingling half smile. *In his fantasy, she rose purposefully and caught him around the neck, covering his mouth with her own, pressing the lean line of her body against his chest, his abdomen, his groin. He put the palm of his hand flat against the small of her back, feeling her instant response, the arching of her spine, a quickening of breath*. She was worth whatever risk he had to take, worth the risk he had already taken. How could he keep her with him?

He gave the other plate to Jon, who sniffed at it.

'Say thank you, honey,' Deena whispered.

'Thank you.'

The toaster flipped the bread up and onto the counter. Paul retrieved and buttered it. As they ate silently, the sweet aroma of Deena's skin teased him. She still had not bathed or changed. Excitement rippled through him. She set down her fork and looked into his eyes with a degree of surprise. Was she reading his mind? It startled him when she said with resignation, 'I guess I'll go shower. Thank you for making breakfast, Paul.'

She was gone. He studied Jon who was picking flakes of pepper out of his egg. Somehow he could see Jon more clearly with Deena absent. The boy seemed solitary now, vulnerable. When she was present, she set up a protective atmosphere around him, a fog of slowly circulating atoms.

If Jon were missing. Not dead, merely missing. She would stay. Indefinitely.

It would solve both problems.

A child terribly upset by his father's death might run away, might disappear and not be found. It was plausible.

Do that? How to do that? Jon was never out of her sight.

He would find a way.

5

Martin listened to the sound of his own voice growling at him over the pay phone. 'Hi. Leave a note. I'll get back.' He punched the number 4 and waited. No beeps. No messages. He pressed 6, hearing the mechanical gurgle that meant the machine was resetting itself. No one had called him about Tim. As soon as he'd seen the article from the wire, Martin had phoned Paul's home and his workroom but got answering machines both places and hung up without saying anything. Maybe Paul had tried to reach him and done the same thing. More likely, Paul didn't know about Tim yet. It was exasperating not being able to get hold of people. He'd tried to contact Deena at the cottage, but that phone had been disconnected. He had even tried Tim's parents in Florida without success. The phone had rung thirty times. What, in God's name, had happened out on that river?

He didn't have another second to fool with it. Snatching up his portfolio, he sprinted down the courthouse corridor. The bailiff saw him coming and opened the door. The trial was already in session. He slowed to a walk as he entered and went straight to his seat in the usual row of reporters, avoiding eye contact. As he took his place next to Rachel Culver, she acknowledged him with a hiss. '*Tardy.*' Greeting, not condemnation. His nickname: Tardy Marty. He dug in his portfolio for charcoal pencils, pastels, and sketch pad. Had he missed anybody crucial in the first twenty minutes of this fiasco? Doubtful. It was the same cast of characters day after day. An exhaustive million-dollar trial for a two-bit gangster. A waste.

He began to size up the witness, drawing the oval shape of her skull and jaw, the outline of her shoulder-length straight hair. He split her head in half with a faint horizontal line and placed another delicate line down the center of her face. Then, he marked the vertical line in the spots where he would place the end of the nose and the meeting of the lips. He assessed the woman's eyes.

Sorrow and guile. He hadn't been here long enough to get the gist of her verbal testimony, but he didn't have to. Her appearance was testimony. He needed to capture that. Rachel would get the rest. Rachel's words and Martin's drawings: a matched set.

Who was this female? He glanced at Rachel. She pointed to the name on her tablet. *Georgette Henninger.* Georgette clearly had something to hide. He gauged the proximity of the eyes and shaped them on the horizontal line. The mouth was not small but appeared small because she was pursing her lips in a subconscious statement of stonewalling. He judged the size of the mouth and put it in lightly. He had spent his entire adult life this way, in anonymity behind a wooden rail, his fingers coated with charcoal and chalk, seizing the essence of defendants and witnesses, translating it onto the page. In time, he had come to know which were innocent and which were not, who was lying, who telling the truth, by subtle signs of guilt: a greenish cast beneath the lower lip, unwarranted indentations at the outer corners of the eyes, a disposition to lean to one side of the buttocks on the stand. Georgette was lying. He guessed it was a lie born of fear.

There was plenty to be afraid of in anybody's world.

His vision went soft, and he realized he was blinking back tears.

6

With a grunt, Dr. Frank Halligan straightened up from the body of Tim Reuschel and continued to stand in the halo of the lamp, meditating on his discoveries. All of the wounds were consistent with the theory of a fall into the river and a subsequent swift journey downstream, perhaps for several miles. He probably had tumbled – or leaped – from a height of approximately forty feet and had been alive when he hit the water, drowning shortly thereafter in an area close to the point of entry. Injuries before drowning were mainly from green wood – broken tree limbs, most likely; subsequent injuries were from impact with submerged decaying timber and smooth rocks. The torso and arms had been protected somewhat by a long-sleeved down jacket, but the face, hands, and legs – in spite of blue jeans – had suffered considerable trauma including a number of punctures.

Reuschel's brain and heart were sound, so – unless toxicology turned up something unusual – they were probably looking at suicide or foul play. He considered the latter because a faint pattern injury ran across the backs of the knees, seemingly the mark of a large branch or something similar. The subject might have been struck from behind with just enough force to topple him from wherever he was standing. On the other hand, he could have received this blow during his fall or in the river. Possible. But unlikely. The pattern formed a line across both legs, indicating that the legs had been roughly parallel to each other at the time of the injury.

He grunted again. At sixty-three, he tired more and more easily. He also noticed he had less and less patience. He would receive his gold watch or whatever the hell they'd hand him in precisely eight months. And then he was going to sunny Phoenix, Arizona, to live with his daughter and forget all about Cameron County. He felt sorry for every poor bastard who died of unnatural causes here these days. Incestuous politics had produced a law enforcement monster, a sluggish system that had a dismal apprehension and conviction rate. Cameron County law enforcement had become a joke, the shame of the state of New York. And he had been under increasing pressure, for nearly a decade, to term as accidental or suicide any death that wasn't clearly murder. To catch a suspect, the sheriff's department needed enough clues for a board game.

This one wouldn't be a simple case. The deceased was a tourist, home state California. A lot of police paperwork and useless expense and wild goose chases, that's what it would be. They'd try to fire his ass for it, too. No, he'd better not raise the question of foul play on this one.

The alternatives weren't any better. He didn't have enough evidence to call it a suicide. That designation required proof. But if he called it an accidental death, he might trigger an insurance investigation on a double indemnity clause. Depended on how much insurance Reuschel was carrying.

This insurance thing had become his biggest problem. He had passed over too many mildly suspicious deaths, handing them off to the insurance companies as accidental. Their investigations could – and sometimes did – lead right back into his office. He'd been in court more than once and had prevailed, but he didn't want to trigger so many inquiries that he set up a pattern centered on him. Insurance companies were sharpening their teeth. Just last summer, the Dunbar Country pathologist lost his job and his pension that way. Rumor had it that he'd answered his home doorbell one June evening to find a gorgeous young woman standing on the porch. She turned out to be the insurance investigator who instigated his removal by filing a major lawsuit against him in a suicide he'd termed accidental.

So. What to do?

He was a gambler. He could run between the raindrops for eight months.

7

'Someone's here,' Gene said as they approached the cottage. 'I'm glad she called somebody. Who is it?'

'I don't know.' Barbara squinted at the two cars that were side by side in the garage, one red, one beige, both fairly new.

They parked on the grass. Jon burst from the kitchen and came running, with Deena behind him. Barbara opened the car door and Jon jumped inside, into her arms. They hugged each other tightly.

'Grandpa . . .' Jon held out his hands toward Gene who pulled Jon into his lap.

Barbara stood up, embracing her daughter-in-law, kissing her. They had been friends from the start, and she could sense that there was no emotional separation between them now. She reminded herself that she needed to be strong for Deena and the rest of the family. She mustn't be self-pitying.

As she and Deena parted, a man started toward them from the house. She realized with a rush of affection that it was Paul Kincaid. She hadn't seen him in years. He approached shyly. When he reached her, Barbara hooked an arm around his waist. 'Paul – I'm so glad to see you. Thanks for being here.'

'He's been cooking for us,' Deena said, touching his shoulder.

Gene, carrying Jon, shook hands with Paul. 'Good of you to come.'

'I'm sorry about Tim,' Paul answered.

Barbara released him. 'Oh, God. It's unbelievable. I'm so sorry for you kids.' *Paul, Tim, Jenny, Martin.* A strangely ill-fated group, this beloved and pampered group of children. Who could have imagined what would befall them? Their lives on the lake had been ordinary – she had striven to make their upbringing and surroundings ordinary, low-key. She used to regard that cloistered pattern as a protection from extraordinary events.

'My daddy died,' Jon told Gene.

Gene patted Jon's back. 'I know, buddy.'

'I've got to get going.' Paul seemed embarrassed, uneasy, 'To work.'

'We understand,' Barbara said. 'It was generous of you to give up so much time. It means a lot to all of us.'

'Thank you, Paul.' Deena shook hands with him and he started away, with his head down.

'I guess we'll see you some more over the next few days,' Gene called after him.

Paul turned back briefly. 'Sure.' His gaze focused on Jon. 'Good-bye.' Jon hid his face against Gene's neck.

They got out of the way as Paul backed the red car into the driveway and turned it around. He didn't wave at them as he left. Barbara felt heartsick watching him go. It couldn't have been easy for him to come here in the middle of their grief. She had to give him a lot of credit for the effort. He had lost so much himself. Drowning had haunted his life thus far. Tim. And Jenny. And, of course, his own mother.

8

Tim's parents gathered her and Jon to them in the living room. They stood in a huddle, embracing, weeping. Jon began to screech, sitting and then lying on the floor, beating his fists on the carpet, kicking his feet. No one tried to stop him. Finally, weak and choking on bitterness, she and Gene and Barbara separated, collapsing into the chairs, silent, spent. Jon grew silent too, face down, his head on his arms.

Barbara and Gene asked her questions. She told the story and pieces of the story over and over, and still they had questions. She realized they were trying, through repetition, to make the tragedy real in their minds, to accept it. Instead, the telling seemed to become increasingly bizarre, until she wasn't sure that what she was saying was the truth. The events as she remembered them couldn't be so. He couldn't have died.

She wore herself out with it, the unrelenting grief and total despair. She lay on the couch listening to her in-laws moving about, bringing their things into the house, getting lunch started in the kitchen. How could Gene and Barbara go on? She did not want to go on.

Now and then, Jon would come and sit on the floor

beside her, putting his head on her stomach, rubbing her arms. When he did that she felt a small quiver of energy. When he went away, it went with him.

9

After lunch, Deena, trying to work a jigsaw puzzle with Jon at the coffee table, heard Gene open the back door and speak to someone. The visitor's tones were clipped and slightly too loud for the setting, but his sentences were indistinct. She rounded the corner to the kitchen, as Gene came inside. 'They've brought back your things from the river,' he said.

She approached the screen door. Two policemen were in the carport, one of them struggling to stand the raft sideways against a wall, the other carrying the cooler with her camera bag on top of it. He set the cooler and bag side by side next to the sink.

'Mrs. Reuschel?'

'Yes.'

'Would you come with me, please? We'd like to talk to you for a minute.' He looked meaningfully at Gene. 'By yourself.'

Jon came up behind her. 'Is this about my dad?'

The man gave him a sympathetic glance. 'Yes.'

'I want to come, too.'

The officer waited for her to say no to Jon. She couldn't do it. 'Get your jacket.' Jon grabbed it from the low set of pegs and put it on. She buttoned her cardigan as she followed the policeman down the steps with Jon at her heels. The other man was leaning against the patrol car, his backside against a fender. Before either of them spoke, she knew she would resent the conversation. Their postures smacked of arrogance, as if they knew something she didn't, something she wouldn't be smart enough to understand. She set her face in a mask of challenge. This had the desired effect on one of them. He looked at the ground. She read his name tag: *TABOR*.

'We need to ask you a few questions,' the other one said. *BAEZ*.

'Officer Baez, I've already gone over everything I know. Many times.'

'Yes, ma'am.' A dismissal of her protest.

'What is this about? Get to the point.'

'Are you aware that your husband had quite a bit of debt and quite a bit of life insurance?'

They think he was a suicide. Anger stung her. They had done some rapid and deep investigation to come up with this. 'He started an architecture firm of his own. Three years ago. It takes capital to get a business up and running. He took out a bank loan. Naturally, he raised the amount of his life insurance to cover it.'

'He had significantly more life insurance than he had debt.'

The comment hung in the air. An indictment. 'He wanted me to be able to stay at home with our son and raise him without worries about money. We talked it over. It makes perfect sense to *me*.'

Baez watched her face carefully. 'Was he seriously depressed about the amount of debt or about anything else that you know of?'

'He didn't kill himself. And I suggest you save the rest until we get the results of the autopsy.'

The eyebrows raised slightly.

'Or do you have them now?'

Baez considered this. The hesitation told her he was cautiously formulating a reply. 'No. And if I did, I wouldn't be allowed to give them to you verbally. You have to request that, in writing, from the coroner's office.'

She waited, staring pointedly at him.

'We're sorry about your husband, ma'am. There's no disrespect intended. We're just trying to determine what happened.'

She turned away, placing a hand on Jon's head and propelling him toward the house.

10

Deena leaned over the side of the tub, bathing Jon in preparation for his nap. They had both been silent through the whole procedure. An almost irrational rage had possessed her in the encounter with Baez and it would not subside. So many foreign emotions had surfaced in her during the last twenty-four hours. She felt hopelessly incapable of controlling them. Her flesh literally throbbed from her anguish. She could no longer sort out what was and wasn't true. Was what he had said logical and not meant to provoke her?

She soaped the washcloth and rubbed it on Jon's back.

'Do you think Daddy did that to himself?' he asked.

She stopped scrubbing. He was looking at his toes, expressionless. She let the cloth sink into the water and shifted from her knees to a sitting position where she could see Jon's eyes. 'No.'

'The policeman does.'

'He's wrong. Daddy loved us. He still loves us. He wouldn't leave us unless he had to.'

'Do you think someone hurt him?'

'I think he got sick and fell into the water. There's a doctor who's going to tell us why that happened.'

'How does he know?'

Should she be getting into all this? She studied Jon: the searching blue eyes, sandy hair, the brave straight shoulders, the mouth she had seldom seen droop in a frown as it was drooping now. It had been her policy, from the time he could talk, to answer all of his questions on a certain topic, for as long as he wanted to ask them. But not to volunteer information past that point. 'He will check Daddy over, the way your doctor checks you.'

She could see him accepting this concept. He was quiet while she found the washcloth and rinsed him. She released the drain stopper and helped him out of the tub onto the bath mat, wrapping him from head to toe in a huge towel.

'I think the man in the woods hurt him,' he said.

Her breath froze in her throat. '*What* man?' She knelt in front of Jon.

'Didn't you see him?'

'No.'

'He had on black all over, but his skin wasn't black.'

'Where was he?'

'In the trees, when I ran back.'

'Ran back to me from Dad?'

'Yes.'

The suspicion she had been suppressing from the beginning leaped at her. *He could have been murdered.* A twenty-seven-year-old man who has recently had a perfect physical exam does not die of natural causes. He may have stumbled upon a crime being committed in the woods, a witness who could not be allowed to go free. 'Did you see his face?'

'No, his back.'

'How do you know he had white skin?'

'His hands were white.'

She got to her feet, leaning against the sink counter for support. 'Why didn't you tell me *then*?' she whispered.

'I thought other people were allowed to be there. Aren't they?'

She wrenched the door open, stumbling into the hall. 'Gene!'

'Yes?' His voice came from below, possibly from the kitchen.

'Will you come up here?' As she went back to the bathroom, she could hear him on the stairs, Barbara's footsteps joining his. He appeared in the doorway wide-eyed at the urgency of her shout. Barbara peered at her from behind Gene.

'What is it?' he said with a worried glance at Jon.

She motioned him closer.

'Jon saw somebody in the woods, right before Tim died.' She nodded at Jon. 'Tell Grandpa.'

'A man,' Jon said.

Gene squinted at this vision. 'A man . . . Did he go near your dad?'

'No.'

'What was he doing?'

'Walking away.'

'Did he say anything?'

'No.'

'Did you see him after that?'

'No.'

A peculiar silence followed in which both Gene and Barbara seemed puzzled. Then, Barbara moved forward, picking up Jon, towel and all, and carrying him from the room.

'Deena,' Gene said softly, 'let's try to keep him as calm as possible.'

She understood at once. Gene was responding to what he perceived as hysteria on her part. Jon's revelation had meant nothing to him, had proved nothing. He believed her alarm was at best premature and at worst completely unwarranted.

Embarrassment crept over her. He was right. She was acting foolish.

11

Leaf shadows trembled on the walls of Tim's room. Jon lay napping in the bed while Deena folded Tim's suit and shirt and tie into a plastic bag. He would need dress shoes and socks. Wouldn't he? She located them in his suitcase and placed the socks down inside one of the shoes. Was he supposed to have underwear? She knew nothing about funerals and burial. Even her grandparents were still living. She wished her mother were here, but she would not arrive until tomorrow. She couldn't ask

Gene. She wiped her eyes with a tissue. She would put the underwear in the bag.

Did she need to decide about the ring now? It glittered in the sunlight on the nightstand. She picked it up, running her thumb over the carved iris garland. He had worn it constantly, never taking it off. Would he feel abandoned without it, separated from her love? Did the dead have feelings about what happened to their bodies? Was a body still a person? Did a person have a spirit that outlived the body? The old questions.

She was no closer to the answers than she had ever been. She had no sense of Tim's soul beside her, trying to comfort her. She had not been aware of Tim's distress or of his ghostly presence at the instant he died, and she did not know where he was now. She walked through this endless dream surrounded by emptiness.

She wanted his ring as a reminder of him. She did not want it to be underground, gone forever. But if she kept it, he, shut away from life and joy, would have no tie to her, to her enduring love. He would want to wear it. He must wear it.

In the end, she couldn't decide. She put the ring back on the table. She would keep it a day longer. She closed the bag and carried it and the shoes into the hallway where Gene was waiting.

'You stay here with Barb,' he said to her quietly. 'I'll deliver these. And I'll take your letter to the coroner's office. Maybe I can hurry the report along. Then you can put your mind at rest.'

She found her mother-in-law on the screened porch, gazing blankly at the lake. 'Mom, are you okay?'

Barbara looked through her. 'It can't be over. It can't be. It was so short. How could he be gone?'

Deena shook her head.

'He was like Jon. So bright. He was so much fun. I try not to dwell on the past. You know that. I don't talk about his childhood, I talk about today and what there is to look forward to.'

'Yes.'

'He was a great kid. Always a joy. He wanted to help with everything. He used to climb up on a stool and cook with me. Three years old, four. I would measure the ingredients and he would pour them into the bowl. It seemed like we had forever then. And now it's over. He isn't here anymore. That's the end of it.'

Deena drew Barbara to her and they held each other for minutes. 'I'm glad you and Jon are all right,' Barbara whispered. Gently separating from Deena, she went into the house, to the master bedroom, and closed the door.

Barbara's reminiscence had made Deena almost dizzy with empathy. To be a mother . . . and to lose your child . . . The perspective deepened her wound. Her chest ached with emotion.

She had to let it out.

She left the porch and fell into the sunlight, running. Where could she go that Barbara and Jon would not hear? Sound carried a long way because of the water. Hands on her hips, breathing in fits, she walked around the side of the house.

The car.

She crawled into the backseat and shut herself in. With the windows up, it was nearly soundproof. She had wanted to scream from the instant she had seen

Tim's body in the ambulance, scream until she had no voice.

The sound came out of her in hard, low bursts and gradually became louder, more shrill. She was on the river again, waiting for Tim in the freezing wind, anxious, hopeful, zipping up Jon's jacket and tying his hood under his chin. She was staring at the tunnel of trees through which Tim had departed smiling at her, waving. She could change it all, make him come back.

Couldn't she?

12

Deena sat watching Jon sleep as the afternoon shadows grew larger and inched across the room. Tim seemed far away, but Jon nearer than ever before. He looked so much like Tim and yet he had her eyes, exactly. She had always felt this meant she and Jon had a shared view. They did not disagree about much of anything, as though he had been born with a genetic copy of her philosophies. He was still acquiring her values, but it had been obvious from the outset that they thought alike. Now, his fears about Tim mirrored her own.

She had relived again and again, in detail, the minutes and miles from the time she had last seen Tim alive until she had found him in the ambulance. There were no clues. None. Except for the man Jon had seen when he ran back to her from Tim.

What happened right before that?

They ate. And before that?

They brought the food out of the cooler.

And before that? *They washed their hands*. And before that? *They went to the bathroom, Tim and Jon yards away from her in the brush*. Was the man there then? Watching Tim? Watching her?

Back up. They got out of the raft. Tim first, lifting Jon, helping her. *Go back*. They are in the raft. Tim has the lunch spot picked out. He has been there before. Over and over. But as a child. Not recently. *What do you see?* She is relaxed, unaware of danger. The vista is in sections through the tunnel of her camera lens.

The camera.

She got up and went downstairs. The master bedroom door was closed. Through it drifted the hushed shudder of Barbara's weeping. In the corner of the kitchen, the cooler and the gadget bag were just as the policeman had left them, the top still on the cooler, the gadget bag zipped shut. The bag was grimy to the touch, tacky and damp. The snaps and the zipper were stiff from a day and a night in freezing temperatures and rain. When she put her hand inside, the moisture told her the camera was probably ruined. She hefted it and dried it on a dish towel. The automatic rewind was stiff but hesitated only slightly before lurching into action. When the whirring stopped, she opened the camera and released the roll of film. It did not seem to be wet. And freezing temperatures wouldn't have hurt it.

She would have to be careful about where she got it developed. If Tim had met with violence, she had no idea who was involved. Or why. She did not like the authorities in this place. It would be best to drive out of Cameron County toward New York City as far as she needed to, until she felt safe.

13

'I'm disappointed that you wouldn't eat your breakfast or your lunch today,' Arlene said, placing a vase of spring flowers on the dresser where Mimi could see them. Her mother-in-law seemed shrunken and distant, despondent. 'You don't seem to feel well. Would you like me to call the doctor?'

Mimi did not ring the bell. That meant no. Who could blame her for giving up? What did she have any more? She needed help with even the simplest tasks like eating and bathing. She had no entertainment except the television. She could not speak. Her only fresh air came to her through the window when it was warm enough to open it. The only people she saw were those who came into her room. Yet, she seemed to have dipped significantly since yesterday. Some memory or pain had upset her in the early afternoon. She had rung the bell incessantly and, when she stopped, had begun a noticeable decline.

'We care about you, Mom,' she said. This drew the notice of Mimi's eyes, but her attention wandered back to the window. *What she sees out there is all she's got left of freedom*, Arlene thought. She kept Mimi's view as pure as possible, cleaning the glass every few days, making sure the television was off during the news hour when terrible things were said. She had instructed her children not to bear tales of sorrow into this sanctuary. Health, or lack of it, had much to do with the state of one's emotions. She would not, for instance, allow Mimi to be told of yesterday's river drowning. At

Mimi's age the news should consist only of pretty and pleasant things.

14

The color photographs from the envelope slid out into Deena's palm. She could tell immediately that the film had not been damaged by the weather. The scenes were crisp and in the correct hues. She pushed the envelope aside and started through them quickly. The ones on top were the shots she had taken from the hotel balcony. The developer must have kept the roll in chronological order. She slipped a print from the bottom of the pile but could not look at it. She would see Tim in his last hours, happy, unknowing. *Oh, God.*

She forced herself to stare at the picture. *Tim, dragging the raft up onto the bank, grinning:* a close-up, taken from the raft. Tim, alive and healthy. She rubbed at her eyes, her throat dry. If she could stay on task . . . What about this photograph? She dissected it mentally. Not useful. Hardly any background.

She laid the next-to-the-last one on top of it. *Here.* The river bank and the thick woods, as they paddled in. She remembered this moment because they were suddenly blessed with sun. The morning had been cloudy, her photography handicapped by drizzle and haze. At this second, sunshine had filtered among the trees.

There were numerous dark patches in the photograph, though, because of the density of the forest. She shoved the print under the counter lamp and held the magnifier over the scene. There was no mistaking one of the dark

116

half-forms among the trees. A human. *He had been watching from the very beginning*. His partial silhouette was attached to a tree trunk, as though he were leaning against it or getting ready to hide behind it. No visible facial features. Head and neck flaring to a shoulder. The bulk of a long jacket. The tapering of a thigh to a foot.

She studied the other blotches. None of them seemed to suggest a human shape. They must have been bushes or logs propped at angles. She moved the magnifier back to left center, to the man. But the outline no longer looked human. The landscape was cluttered with charcoal and black etching. This was merely more of the same. What she had thought was a man might be split timber or a cluster of saplings or the projection of rocks from the far hillside. Who could say? She touched the bell on the counter and the proprietor stood up from his desk in the back of the shop, smiling.

'I'd like you to enlarge a couple of these for me, please.'

At that, Jon got out of his chair and came over to her, tapping her arm. She lifted him up, centering the magnifier over the picture. He looked through it carefully, sucking on his lower lip, but said nothing, as he had been told.

15

'*Hi, leave a note. I'll get back.*'

'Shut up,' Martin muttered, hitting the number 4 on his office phone and waiting for the answering machine to go through its paces. No beeps. No one had called him about Tim. It was puzzling, almost as though Tim's death were fiction, something Martin had made up. He touched the 6 and the machine reset itself.

Paul surely didn't know. He'd have to go around there, to Paul's workroom, and tell him, either tonight or in the morning – whenever he could catch him. He tapped out the number and waited. A human voice startled him.

'Paul Kincaid.'

He was there now. Martin hung up.

16

'Is this what you saw?' Deena whispered, laying the final enlargement in Jon's lap and huddling with him on the plastic chairs in the waiting area of the photo shop. They were essentially alone. The proprietor had gone back to his desk. Jon gaped at the grainy image. It was as large as it could be made without losing clarity altogether. This was the third successive blowup of the original photograph. On each eight-by-ten she had marked a section to be enlarged. Gradually, the questionable object had grown more distinct and more manlike. It filled the frame now, to the very edges, but was still basically unrecognizable. To her, it suggested a three-quarter back profile of a white man wearing a stocking cap.

Jon rubbed his fingers on the slick surface as if trying to get a sense of texture: wool and leather, human skin. 'Sort of.'

'Let me . . .' She picked up the photograph, held it vertically in front of his face and moved it slowly away from him. His eyes followed it, narrowing with recognition, as she stood and took small steps toward the counter.

He nodded.

17

He knew where Paul's shop was. He had passed the building a dozen times or more in the past six years. Each time he had approached it, he intended to go inside to visit Paul, but he could not make himself do it.

The building was an ancient red brick school, abandoned by the city and resurrected by a league of artists. He had read about the renovation, but seeing it was a different thing entirely. The immense interior had been totally gutted to make way for an impressive series of glass-front studios, each designed to showcase a single artist, who created and displayed his or her work in the space.

The directory told him that Paul's studio was on the first floor, at the east end. He noticed, as he drew close to it, that the door was open. Paul was alone, polishing a silver necklace at the counter. He seemed astonished to see Martin.

'Hi, Mart.'

'Paul.' He was already choking up. *Say it and get out.* 'Hey . . . I'm sorry to be the one, but I'm here to tell you some bad news. Tim . . . Tim . . . died. He drowned yesterday on the raft trip.'

Paul's eyebrows raised slightly. 'Deena called me.'

'Where is she?'

'At the cottage. I was with her all night.' There was a baffling tinge of pride to the sentence.

'What happened to him?'

Paul shook his head.

'Are there funeral plans?'

'Not yet.'

'Where are they going to bury him?'

'At the lake.'

Piqued, he studied Paul who rearranged his expression to look earnest in spite of the minimal information he was providing. Paul was the perpetual king of defense. What difference did it make what he told Martin? What did this posturing mean? With Paul, it meant something. Guaranteed.

Shit. Martin had always been odd man out with Tim and Paul. The implication here was that Paul would handle things with Tim's family. Martin needn't be personally involved. He should merely show up for the memorial service. If he could find it. 'Why didn't you call me?'

'I did. You weren't there.'

'Where? Work or home?'

Paul assessed him cautiously. 'Home.'

'I've got an answering machine.'

'Have you been home today?'

'No.'

'I left word.'

'I phoned my machine, Paul. A couple of times. You didn't leave anything.'

The verbal sparring had brought Paul to attention. 'Mart, what's this about?'

'When were you going to tell me? I walked all the way down here to tell you in person.'

'When's the last time you tried your machine?'

'Before I left the office to come over here.'

'I just got back from the lake. The phone's not hooked up in the cottage. As soon as I got in this room, I called you. A few minutes ago. You must have been

120

on your way. Use my phone. Try the damned thing. I'm on it.'

This was insane. They were arguing over nothing. It didn't matter. Tim was *dead*. 'I don't need to do that. Look, Paul, I'm sorry. I'm upset. I found out about it by reading it off the wire.'

'Jesus.'

'Just . . . let me know about the funeral, okay?'

'Sure.'

Mute with agitation, Martin strode out of Paul's shop and headed for the outer doors. When he had almost reached them, he heard his name and looked toward the sound. A stocky, familiar-looking man in shirtsleeves was barreling toward him. *Derek Vealey.*

'Mart! I thought it was you!' Derek grabbed him in a friendly bear hug that brought Martin's feet off the floor.

Martin hugged him back. 'Hey, D.V.' He hadn't seen Derek since they were senior-class roommates at RIT. That great whimsical face was the same, but Derek had put on a few pounds. 'What're you doing here?'

'I'm the manager.'

'Of?'

'This building.'

'No kidding! Congratulations.'

'You shopping?'

'Visiting.' Martin shrugged. 'Paul Kincaid.'

'You grew up with him, right?'

'Right.'

'I had kind of forgotten that. He came to see you at school a couple of times.'

Martin nodded.

'Small world.' Derek playfully scrutinized Martin's beard and tugged his ponytail. 'You in disguise or what?'

'Yah, I'm famous now.'

'You *are*. I see your sketches in the paper all the time. I tell people I know you. A slight exaggeration. Haven't seen you since we used to be handsome.'

He had loved rooming with Derek. The guy had an incurable sense of humor and an uncommon loyalty. They had been close since freshman camp. It was Martin's fault that they lost touch after graduation. Martin had let everything go.

'You look dragged out, Marty. What's the matter?'

'Having a bad week.'

Derek digested this. 'You married yet?'

Martin knew Derek was thinking of Jenny. 'No.' Derek had carried Martin through the worst year of his life: the first year after her death. 'How 'bout you?'

'No.' He grinned. 'Are we a couple of losers or what?'

'What.'

'I agree. Listen, I gotta go. Late for a meeting.' Derek started up the stairs that led to the second-floor balcony. 'You want to meet me at Gino's Friday night? It's a ritual. T.G.I.F. We start about ten and party 'til we fall down.'

Martin's throat started closing again. He couldn't do it. And he didn't want to explain why. 'Sorry.'

'You're not going to disappear again, are you, Mart?' There was affection and understanding in the sentence.

'I'll be in touch. Promise.'

Derek was on the balcony now, peering at him from above a huge, round full-length portrait of Marilyn Monroe. Martin recognized Derek's style in the painting. Marilyn was wearing the famous halter dress and standing in the classic windy-day pose. 'You like my invention?'

Martin did a double take at the portrait. It was a clock. The 'hands' were Marilyn's legs. She was balancing lightly on her right foot.

Derek gave him a dramatic smirk and wiggled his eyebrows. 'Come back at ten past ten.'

Paul watched Martin through the glass until he finished talking with Derek and left through the main entrance. Then, he picked up the phone and dialed Martin's number. The machine spat a couple of sentences and gave him a squawking tone. 'Mart, this is Paul,' he said quietly, giving his voice an ominous tinge. 'Call me as soon as you can. I'm at the studio.'

18

Driving back into Cameron with Jon, Deena tried to memorize the terrain. Every turn of the road seemed to hold vital knowledge, possibilities. She had studied the map of Cameron County while she waited in the photo shop. She wanted to know who lived here and why.

The town of Cameron was located two hours northwest of New York City, eleven miles above State Road 17. Once through that intersection, there was not another town until Somerset, nineteen miles north. The desolate stretch snaked through farmland and mountains. In the farmland there was a large meandering lake and in the mountains there was a beautiful, treacherous river.

She had seen nothing of the village or the farmland

Sunday night when Tim had taken them to the cottage in the dark. Nor had she truly seen the mountain area Monday night as she followed the police car to the cottage from the hospital. Until today, her only glimpses of the surroundings had been during Monday morning's trip to the river. She hadn't paid much attention as Tim pointed out the sights. She had been feeding Jon and Tim muffins and milk.

Now, she turned down almost every block in town, taking her time, cruising the sparsely populated streets, intent on details. The windshield flashed the orange cast of sunset steadily into her eyes. There were no surprises. A fire station, a couple of restaurants, a grocery store, churches, clothing shops, an aging inn, well-kept white houses interspersed with commercial establishments. Most of the houses had American flags flying next to the front door.

'Where are we going?' Jon asked.

'Just taking a ride.'

'I want to go home.'

'We will. We're almost there.'

'*Really* home. To my house. My *real* house.'

The pain he reflected stung her. 'We will, honey. In a few days.' She swung the car onto the river road and they left Cameron. She knew it was three miles to the lake and twelve miles to the river from this point. Seven miles beyond that was Somerset where they had been examined at the hospital and where the funeral home was located.

They passed chicken farms and another inn on the right; on the left, meadows and cows and wire fences sprawled to the horizon. The lake road cutoff was marked only by a gray barn. She turned right onto the six-mile loop that varied from dirt to gravel to macadam. Cottage after cottage hunkered almost in the water of the lake. On the opposite side of the road, farmhouses in varying conditions perched in deep fields.

'I'm afraid of the man, Mommy.'

'Who? The man in the picture?'

'Yes.'

What had she done, scaring him like that? She covered his hand with hers, squeezing the little fingers. He squeezed back. She regretted taking him with her. 'We aren't sure that man did anything to Daddy. He probably didn't. Don't worry. I'll be with you all the time. To take care of you. Or Grandma and Grandpa will.'

They bounced down the driveway and into the carport. 'Listen, Jon. Don't tell Grandma and Grandpa about the pictures. It might upset them. I don't like to ask you to keep secrets. You should be able to say whatever you want to say. But right now it wouldn't be good to share this with them, okay?'

'Okay.'

She leaned over and hid the photograph package under the front seat.

19

The apartment was dark when Martin let himself into it. The only light was a red dot blinking on the answering machine in the corner. Martin could count the cadence of the blinks from across the room. There had been one call.

He flicked a switch and a dim lamp sent a yellow circle

against the ceiling. Throwing his overcoat on a chair, he thumbed the playback button.

Paul, hushed and sorrowful. It was the message about Tim. He'd made an ass of himself, getting on Paul about not calling. The guy had made the effort. He'd simply missed him.

Martin checked the digital readout. 17:33. Just after five-thirty. He'd left Paul's studio about that time.

Hadn't he?

The crazy Marilyn clock jumped into his vision. She'd been standing with all of her weight on her right foot, her left foot slightly raised. That was . . . five-thirty. The bastard had called after Mart chewed him out.

20

Barbara put her arm around Deena and walked her away from the cottage, toward the lake. It was a flat blade under the wisp of moon. 'I wanted you to come outside with me because I have a piece of news,' she said. 'About the autopsy.'

Why had Barbara waited until now, out of Jon's hearing, to tell her? Deena must have been right in her suspicions.

'Gene talked with the coroner. The coroner's pathologist couldn't find anything wrong with Tim. No natural cause for his death. No unnatural cause either.'

'What do you mean?'

'They're still running tests on Tim's blood and tissue samples, but he was healthy as far as the pathologist could see. Nothing unusual. Nothing at all. They're rushing it through for us. We may have something in writing by tomorrow.'

'I don't understand. What killed him?'

'They don't know. We may never know. The coroner told Gene the autopsy was inconclusive.'

She faced her mother-in-law. 'Does that make sense to you?'

Barbara didn't answer for a minute. Then she said. 'No. But much of life does not make sense to me now.'

21

From the foyer, Paul assessed his condominium the way a visitor might – a game he played almost every time he entered it. It was a model home, in his opinion – professionally decorated, but not overdone, and strikingly clean. It had the hallmarks of status: oriental carpets and hardwood floors, traditional but rather massive furniture in subdued solid fabrics, track lighting, a large curving wet bar, an elevated view of Central Park. And yet it was not pretentious in the least. Not in the least.

He could not remember the last time a visitor had been inside this place or even if there had been a visitor. He supposed not. Except the decorator, of course. But that was the week he moved in.

Hard to believe he'd been here more than six years. Everything looked as bright now as it had in the beginning. He'd made sure of that, polishing and vacuuming on a regular schedule, washing windows, scrubbing the bathrooms. It satisfied him enormously to know that he was steadily outsmarting the smug psychiatrists and the savvy detectives, whoever they might be. He did not fit any of their profiles. He didn't keep delicious diaries of his deeds or yellowed newspaper clippings about victims or leave his 'signature' at crime scenes. In fact, he could not imagine anything more stupid than leaving, say, a bite mark like Ted Bundy did. No, the best and most clever perpetrators were those who remained totally invisible because their work simulated suicide or accidental death. There were many, he felt certain. Masters all.

He kept his home in order on the remote possibility he should ever become suspect. He lived in the finest building he could afford, on the highest floor he could afford. Below him, a well-groomed doorman in a uniform stood guard and, below that, Paul always kept a whistle-clean late-model – but not showy – car in the condominium's secure parking deck. The central credit bureau computer had nothing but kind things to say about him: He paid his bills on time and owed only enough money on his mortgage and auto loan to make him human. He subscribed to upscale magazines and kept the most recent copies in a wicker basket by his reading chair. His kitchen cupboards were well stocked and pleasantly jumbled. He gave the mailman a nice tip each Christmas. Criminologists underestimated their prey when they assessed them as insane. An insane person couldn't possibly do what he did and do it this well.

He went to his bedroom and began to remove his clothing, carefully considering the pieces and sorting them into hampers at the back of his closet. Laundry, light. Laundry, dark. Dry cleaner. Nothing for the hanger. His clothes were wilted today from his long hours. Naked, he confronted the floor-to-ceiling mirror that filled one wall of the bedroom, admiring his lean torso, the powerful upper arms and chest. He did not rush. The ability to honestly appraise one's body was the mark of a straight thinker.

He stared for a good five or six minutes, then donned support briefs and a T-shirt, cushioned socks and re-inforced shoes, lacing them securely over his ankles. There was only one right way to lift weights: properly supported and properly warmed. He began to stretch in preparation, moving through a memorized series of toe-touches, deep knee bends and sit-ups, feeling an intense heat build at his core.

At last, he allowed himself to chalk his palms and approach the bar. One hundred and ten pounds. No reason in the world why he would need to lift more than that. No reason in the world. There was only one true way to avoid injury and that was to lift appropriate weight in an appropriate manner.

He began palms down, methodically; floor, knee, waist, shoulder, waist, knee, floor, knee, waist, shoulder. Many of his finest ideas had come to him while lifting. He was in tune now, waiting, *waist, knee, floor*, visualizing Jon, watching the boy's vulnerable little legs and arms, the innocent shape of his head. He watched Jon, watched, watched. Power burst through him; he pushed the bar up, over his head, arms fully extended, and brought it to his shoulders again. Up. Down. Up. Down.

A yellow tinge invaded the edges of the room. It caused him to falter on his eighth full press. A small knot arose in the left side of his neck. He continued his program, *shoul-der, extend, shoulder, extend, shoulder, extend*, ignoring, defying the intruder. He knew why it had come. Paul had always done exactly as he had been directed. Now he wanted to be free, had already taken the first step. He lowered the bar to the floor, rechalked his hands and slid them, palms up, under the bar. He was stronger than any other being. Hadn't he proven that from the age of twelve? He alone would decide his future.

The smoke faded from his peripheral vision, exhilarating Paul. His perspiration-soaked shirt spread a sudden chill across his back. He thought again about Jon and where to hide him, saw him in a river cave, the deepest part, where lack of moisture had turned the ground to dry powdered sand, saw him in a sack, like a sleeping bag sewn shut.

He hefted the weights to midthigh and began his curl, pulling them toward his shoulders, elbows and breastbone straining, something akin to joy rolling in his chest. *Shoulder, thigh, shoulder, thigh.* How would he feed Jon? How often would he have to risk going to him in order to keep him alive? The answer sprang to the center of his mind, steady as a compass reading: He could not go back. It was too dangerous. If he hid Jon, he would have to abandon him. The thought broke the rhythm of his lifting. He set the weights at his feet and sat on his heels, gasping.

Energy coursed upward through him, the same demanding energy that had owned him many times before. He would have to hold it back for days. He moaned and put his fingers to his eyes, crouching for minutes as thunder took him: massive, wild, overwhelming.

Wednesday

1

Deena stared at Tim with wonder as she approached his coffin. He was a wax carving, the ivory skin of his face glossy and firm, touched here and there with rose highlights and taupe shading. Shocked, she glanced at her father-in-law who stood arm in arm with her – the only person she had wanted to be present for this first viewing.

'My God,' he said softly.

She wished she had the physical strength to pick Tim up, out of the casket, carry him away from the suffocating scent of carnations into the early morning sunshine and fresh air of the funeral home's front porch and beyond. She would run, with him in her arms, run until no one could find them. He did not belong here in this room in this town. It was wrong for her to passively accept the standard trappings of death. Tim's death was not standard, it was suspect. But what could she do? If she could bring it all down to a sentence, if she could effect anything, what step would she take next?

She could push for a second autopsy. Surely it was a simple matter of transferring Tim's body and samples to a neighboring town, to the state capital, or to a medical school. 'Gene,' she whispered, 'I want someone else to look at Tim.'

He glanced at her warily. 'What?'

'Get a second opinion – away from here.'

'Why?'

'I'm not satisfied with what the coroner is saying.' She was astonished at her father-in-law's slowness in understanding her.

He pondered this, finally shaking his head.

She regarded Gene's weathered tanned face, the wise blue eyes, the gray hair, which would not lie down when he combed it. Her husband's father: a man who by Tim's account had been a good-natured playmate and friend to his boy. A man who built tree houses and helped with school science projects. A man who had treated Tim – and her – with great respect, always.

He looked at her with empathy. 'Deena, I've seen a lot of death. I lost a sister when she was four. All my grandparents died. My parents are dead. The thing I've learned is not to struggle – to open my hand and let them go.'

'This is different.'

'It *isn't*. We have to have something to blame, so we'll feel better. We blame the doctor who did the best he could. We blame the patient for not taking better care of himself. We blame ourselves for not being able to prevent death, which is as natural as life. Deena, the pathologist did the best *he* could. We have to believe that. There's no reason not to. If the man can't find a specific cause, then he can't find a specific cause. Part of maturity is accepting that life has mysteries.' He spoke with passion.

'I'm not asking this out of guilt, Gene.'

He gazed at her, kindly, for a long minute. 'Tim's my son. My feelings for him are similar to your own. But it's over. I'm just here to do what needs to be done.'

His tense shoulders drooped in weariness. She suddenly became conscious of the fact that he was in an emotionally precarious condition. She mustn't vex him. He needed to cope in his own way. In response to her silence, he asked gently, 'Will you let us bury him tomorrow?'

She thought of the dear people who were gathering to sorrow with her, people who would be further anguished by delay and doubt. She thought about Jon begging her to take him home. She had probably been possessed in the past two days by a madness born of grief. She needed to give it up. There was no concrete reason to prolong the inevitable process of saying good-bye.

Gene put his cheek lovingly to Tim's forehead, then straightened again, turning to her for an answer.

'Yes,' she sighed. 'All right.'

2

Barbara Reuschel, rinsing breakfast dishes, assessed the sky through the partially opened window above the kitchen sink. A gray fog was amassing in the treetops. The new leaves flashed their undersides, blown by a gusting breeze that seemed to rise straight up from the ground. It would rain within the half hour, large heavy drops.

Untying her apron and folding it, she checked on Jon who was in his pajamas watching television cartoons. As she passed through the living room, he held out his arms to her. She knelt with her cheek to his chest and he wrapped his arms around her neck. She hadn't seen Jon much since his birth because he had lived so far

135

from her, but he was always easy – comfortable with himself and with her. She gave her son and Deena a lot of credit for Jon's warmth. He was obviously a beloved child, treated gently.

'When is my other grandma coming?' he asked.

'Sometime before lunch. Do you want to get dressed? I brought your clothes down. They're on the rocking chair.'

'Okay.'

'Do you need help?'

'No.'

She patted his cheek and squeezed his hands. Moving slowly through the house, she began to shut windows against the impending rain. Vivid memories of Tim rose in front of her at every turn. She felt his presence so keenly that she stood still a time or two, listening for his voice, squinting at shadows. She could understand now, more than ever, why Jenny's parents had sold their cottage and not returned to the lake. But it could not be like that for her. She would stay.

Back in the kitchen where drops had already begun to splash the sill above the sink, she lowered the sash while staring at the driveway. Deena's parents could get soaked just walking to the house from their car. Or they might pull into the empty space in the carport where Gene would want to park when he brought Deena back from the funeral home. The thing to do was to back Deena's rental car out of the second space and park it in the driveway to make room. Had Deena left the keys?

They were on the kitchen sideboard. Barbara grabbed them and went quickly out into the gathering mist that

136

had begun to flicker with distant lightning. In the dimness, Barbara could see as she opened the car door that the seat was too close to the steering wheel for her long legs. Finding the lever, she repositioned the seat and slid in, aware that something slippery was on the floor under her feet. She reached down and shifted the item over onto the floor of the passenger side: a big envelope with a small and fairly weighty wad in it.

She edged the car into position halfway up the driveway, stopping as rain began to fill the windshield. The crash and clatter of the downpour intensified suddenly, obscuring her view. Lightning overtook the car in brilliant sizzling flashes. Thunder vibrated in the dashboard. She thought apprehensively of Jon. He must surely be looking for her. She hadn't told him she was leaving the house. And now she was stranded in the storm.

Perhaps she could drift the car carefully down into the carport. No. She couldn't see to do anything just now. She would have to wait. The worst of it couldn't last more than a few minutes. Jon was a trustworthy child. He'd be all right.

She idly read the return address on the envelope, realizing that it was that of a camera shop in Bridgeville. There were no other markings. Instantly curious, she put the envelope in her lap. The shifting weight inside must surely be photographs. But Tim and his family had been at the cottage less than twenty-four hours when he drowned. And they had come here on a Sunday. When would they have had these pictures developed?

Deena. And Jon. Deena must have taken Jon to Bridgeville yesterday.

Barbara lifted the flap and shoved her hand inside,

137

touching the contents. Photographs, beyond a doubt. But they were not hers and this was not her car. She was trespassing. An unforgivable act. She would not spy on Deena. Whatever Deena had done, it was in good faith and not Barbara's to know.

She laid the envelope aside, then picked it up again and brought the pile of photos out into the light to look at the top one: New York City as seen from a height. Nervously, she began to flip through the rest: New York, more New York, a sunrise, shots of Tim and Jon with Martin and Paul, tulips, daffodils, Jon and Tim, Jon in a life jacket, trees and water, water and trees, Tim and the raft ashore. It was a chronicle of the hours leading up to Tim's death. The power of the silent story riveted her.

There was more in the envelope. Negatives in plastic sleeves. Enlargements, some marked with grease pencils. These were copies of some of the last few shots. The river's edge. The forest. The enlargements were out of order but there was a discernible sequence to them. They centered on a section of woodland.

Deena must have been looking for the man Jon said he saw. She evidently believed the unthinkable. Why else would she have hidden the envelope? Barbara studied the enlargement that had no marks, the final one. Did it bear the silhouette of a person in among the trees?

She became aware that the rain had lessened and that the car windows had steamed over. She mustn't leave the car here. Deena would suspect immediately that she had found the photos. Wiping the windshield with her fingers, she cleared her vision enough to release the emergency brake and roll the car into its previous position. Then she drew the driver's seat forward and replaced the envelope under it.

Inside the house, she found Jon engrossed in cartoons, still wearing his pajamas. He hadn't missed her. She got a glass of water from the kitchen tap and drank it rapidly, leaning over the sink. Her daughter-in-law was one of the most logical people she had ever known and one of the smartest. She had to have felt pretty strongly about this matter to pursue it to such an extent. Was it possible she was right?

The photographs could not be mentioned. If Deena discovered that Barbara had violated her privacy, their relationship might be destroyed. She couldn't tell her husband either. She knew what his stance would be. He was a dear and good man, who operated exclusively in the literal and linear world, without imagination. Things unproved simply did not exist.

3

Squinting through the chain-link fence that sealed his basement storage bin, Paul thumbed the padlock in the glare of an overhead bulb. The smell of hot water and liquid starch wafted to him from the laundry room down the hall. He had noticed when he came past it that a white-haired woman was hunched over the utility sink rinsing clothes. She would not interrupt him. Women were cautious about entering this stale maze of passageways.

The padlock snapped open. He put his fingers through the mesh, tugging at the door. As it swung toward him, its metal frame scraped the cement floor. He had to pull up on it to get it open all the way. The bin held the sum of his ingenuity. Eight by eight by eight, it housed the overflow from his condominium, plus a vast accumulation of flea market treasures. He was a compulsive saver and an impulsive buyer. Boxes crowded the cubicle, piled to the ceiling.

He prided himself on this stash, a prop room for the drama of his life. No item in it had been acquired illegally and none could be traced. Each was innocent enough. It was his mix and use of the items that gave them character. His special vision.

From this storehouse, he had concocted the lacy, ribboned nosegay that lured Carmela Azaña down the promenade stairs. A few blossoms from a street vendor was all he had been forced to buy that day. He was cautious. He kept no remnants from a special project but discarded them into sidewalk trash cans.

The box he was seeking now was within easy reach. It almost seemed that the bin's contents continually rearranged themselves in his absence, in concert with his needs. He never had to look far. As he put his hands on the box, he paused, waiting for sanction, a sign that he was correct. It flowed to him as a wispy current of satisfaction. He put the box behind him, in the hallway, closed the padlock and turned out the light.

The elevator was empty. Its cables sang softly in the shaft as he rode it to the ninth floor. He stepped into an empty hallway. How fortunate he was to be able to afford residence in this building where the inhabitants were wealthy enough to desire intense privacy but not so well off that they could stop working. Most days, he saw no one but the doorman.

His hands coated with flaking cardboard and dust, he knelt on the living room rug before the box and peeled tape from its seams. An odor wafted to him in strands, a mixture of the comforting and the terrifying. Pine needles, dog dander, charred marshmallows, chocolate, human hair, stones and clay, dew. The attic beast: summer heat entrenched in cedar, the dry fading fabric and trim of dresses hung from rafters. Yellowed newsprint around glass.

He lifted the sleeping bag from its nest and laid it out flat. He had forgotten how small it was, how much joy it had brought him nights under flying clouds, how stricken he had been when his father as a punishment stowed it high under the eaves.

The right size. He ran his fingers over both sides of it, then turned it again. Still supple, waterproof. He would bet on it. He unzipped it all the way around, leaving a hinge of barely four inches, then laid the halves together.

This morning, he had dreamed of the bag in the last flickering minutes before he awoke. It was a black rectangle on an X-ray. Within the dark shape were the white bones of a skeleton. Jon's skeleton. Paul had come awake knowing that he'd somehow got everything wrong, reversed. His plan for Jon was not the right one. He had lain motionless trying to understand while the sleeping bag, three dimensional and tightly closed, hovered above him, the child's form filling it. He had reached up and touched the zipper, sliding it, watching the track of metal teeth yawn open. Water trickled out.

141

4

When Martin reached the top of the escalator, Harvey Delittuso was waving at him with one hand and holding the receiver of Martin's desk phone in the other.

'A woman,' Harvey said as Martin drew closer.

Martin fired a glance in the direction of Ella Chalmers. She was on the phone in her glass cubicle with her back to him. It would be just like her to call his line when she saw him coming in and give him hell for being late.

'Who?'

Harvey shrugged.

He spoke into the mouthpiece with authority. 'Trayne.'

'Hey, Martin.' Feminine tones.

Martin pursed his lips at Harvey. 'Hey yourself.'

'Am I catching you at a bad time?'

It wasn't Chalmers. Too subdued. 'I leave for court in twelve minutes.'

'This is Deena.'

Deena.

'Reuschel.'

'I know.' He tried to think of a sentence.

'Did anyone . . . did Paul . . . tell you . . . about Tim?'

'I heard. I'm sorry.'

'Well, I wanted to make sure. I've been . . . kind of messed up. Not thinking right. I just remembered you. The funeral's tomorrow morning at ten. Church of the Redeemer, in Cameron.'

'I'll come.'

'Well, I'd better let you go.' An apology.

142

'Wait . . . what happened?'

'To Tim?'

'Yes.'

'I don't know.'

Martin slipped his coat off and sat down. 'You didn't see it?'

'No.'

'What about the autopsy?' *Don't push. It's none of your business.*

'So far it's been inconclusive.'

He'd rarely heard that term. In his six-year career with the newspaper, hanging around courts and jails and morgues and hospitals, he'd heard it used maybe three times. 'I don't understand that.'

'Neither do I. But if it turns out that way, I guess I'll have to accept it.'

Inconclusive? Inconclusive was for veiled suicides. For old people who had so many things wrong with them that it was a matter of speculation which time bomb went off first.

'Martin . . . you still there?'

'See you tomorrow.'

5

'What did Martin say?' Her father-in-law took her arm as she emerged from the funeral home's private lounge into the main lobby.

'He knew.'

'Is there anyone else you need to call before we leave here? I should have had the cottage phone hooked up so you could use it.'

'It's okay. I can't think of anyone.' She peered toward the room where Tim's body lay. This brought a hug from Gene. 'Let's go home.'

The conversation with Martin had stirred her. She had perceived his unspoken criticism that she should do more for Tim. 'Inconclusive' wasn't good enough.

She was surprised to find the front walk damp. It must have rained while they were inside. A suited man with slicked-back hair reminiscent of the fifties was walking toward them from the street. He shook Gene's hand, then hers.

'Deena, this is Bob Norville.'

The funeral director, who was also the coroner. 'Hello.'

'I'm pleased to meet you,' he said. 'I regret that it has to be on this occasion. Gene and I have been friends for many years. I knew your husband.' He did not add 'and liked him very much' but she could glean it from the way he spoke. This was someone who had feeling for the Reuschels. 'Are the arrangements as you wish them to be?' He was asking *her*. She appreciated his recognition that she was the widow and she was in charge. She realized suddenly that she had been overshadowed by Gene in the past twenty-four hours because of her reticence.

'Yes. Except . . .' Why had she been so acquiescent? Why had she sent Gene to speak for her? It was time to take over, to be direct. 'I'm not satisfied with the results of the autopsy.'

Norville straightened in attention. 'There are no results yet.'

'I understand your pathologist couldn't find anything wrong with Tim. Is that true?'

'Dr. Halligan has rendered a preliminary opinion to me. And that is of accidental death.'

'I want to talk to him.'

To his credit, Norville did not look at Gene. He blinked at her, the pose of a man sincerely considering her request. 'That can be arranged.'

'When?'

Gene shifted his weight uneasily but said nothing.

'It might be well to wait for his written report. Then you'll have something concrete to discuss.'

'I don't want to wait.'

Norville seemed to be measuring her mood, carefully formulating his next remark. 'If you approach Dr. Halligan before that, he may consider your inquiry as pressure. I'm sure you don't want to interfere with his objectivity.'

She was aware of the growing warmth of Gene's hand on her elbow. She glanced at him and saw that he was pale.

Norville was also noticing Gene's color. 'I promise you, Mrs. Reuschel, that I'll obtain final word in writing from Dr. Halligan as quickly as possible. Will you count on me?'

There was no deception here. The man was doing his best. She looked him full in the face one last time, then answered, 'Yes.'

6

Paul leaned against the jamb and listened. In the canyon of concrete and steel, twenty-four studios were being unlocked and opened nearly simultaneously as twenty-four artists began their workday. He loved these few minutes surrounding 10 a.m., the blend of voices, the click and ping of keys and locks, the whine of hinges, the shifting wind that rolled through the hallways with the swinging of the doors. By ten past the hour it would all be over, the strange symphony fading, being replaced by muted taps and clunks from shop interiors, the sound of water rushing into the scrub sinks at the far ends of the building. Ideas were electric in this atmosphere. He had merely to receive them.

He thought again of the sleeping bag, curled beside his suitcase. He had lifted the trunk lid of the Maxima twice to look at it in the studio parking lot before he came inside. The bag would be a prison, waterproof and warm, destined for the vacuum of a cave. And yet, the morning's dream nipped at him, the image of water leaking from the lining.

The boy could not be contained. The boy could not be hidden. The boy could not be stolen. These plans were useless.

Stricken, he forced himself to continue standing in the scrambled noise of the hallway until he understood. *The purpose of the bag was not to keep water out, but to keep water in.* He could be successful with Jon, as he had been with the others. But he would have to handle Jon the way he had handled the others: by drowning him. Swiftly, very swiftly. Thrusting him fully beneath the surface before Jon could even guess Paul's intent. Then he would place him in the bag and seal it.

7

Mailboxes and dirt lanes flashed by, acres and miles of unfamiliar country: so many possibilities that Deena could not imagine a logical starting point for inquiries about

Tim. The seat belt strained against her hip bones as the car traveled rapidly along the mountain roads. Gene was driving too fast. He always drove too fast.

'I know what you're thinking,' he said. 'I didn't see it before. This is your first time in Cameron County. It's all foreign to you. I don't blame you for being uneasy. I wish you could see it as I do. It's my home, and the people here are my friends.'

'Do you know Dr. Halligan?'

A pause. 'Never met him but he's been in this area forever. Well respected. He lives along this road, in fact, on a big chunk of land his grandfather owned. He's okay. Believe me.'

It was no use. She had set off Gene's defenses again. She crossed her arms and stared at the curving yellow lines that led up sheer hillsides and through glens so sheltered by overhanging boughs that the markings on the cement seemed to disappear.

He noted her posture and shook his head. 'Be careful.'

'Meaning?'

'I've seen families break apart after a death. Siblings fighting over furniture and money. Couples divorcing. Cousins not speaking. It's an emotional time. Let's stay together.'

The words held no edge. She touched him on the shoulder. 'We'll be together. I've always liked you, Gene, but even if I didn't, I'd owe you one for the way you and Barbara raised Tim. You made him into a fine person who was a wonderful husband and father. I won't forget that.'

Neither of them spoke for minutes. She took a tissue from her purse and blew her nose. Gene slowed the car a little, pointing through the windshield as they started down a slope. 'Frank Halligan lives right over there. That's his mailbox, the blue one. Folks who know him tell me he's got heart. He's not going to screw anything up. Don't worry.'

A quilt of fields and meadows stretched before them in hues of brown and green. If anyone knew the land and its inhabitants, Gene Reuschel did. He was a potential source of in-depth information. When they had reached the far horizon, she said. 'You're right. I can't see it as you do. Help me.'

Probing questions from her might pique him. She determined to keep quiet and wait for whatever he might offer. His comments were sparse and vague until they arrived at the lake circle. Then, forced by uneven pavement and mud to drive more slowly, he began to relate the history of some of the homes. Her eyes became her camera, recording each one in turn as she memorized what he told her. The houses were modest in size but surrounded by huge buffers of woodland. Deena was surprised to see that Martin's and Paul's summer residences were in fair proximity to the Reuschels'. The Traynes had sold their cottage, Gene said, but Mr. Kincaid, a widower, now lived in his full-time. Gene passed his own cottage and made the entire six-mile loop around the lake, coming to a complete stop briefly, at the spot where Jenny had drowned. It was a swimming area from a children's book: picturesque, adorned by a rope swing and a wooden platform and surrounded by a spectacular bowl of trees. As they passed along the opposite side of the lake, he showed her Jenny's house. The three-story farmhouse was not lakeside but across the street from newer Cape Cod-style homes on the water.

As they went by Paul's cottage again, Gene said, 'I rarely

see Mike Kincaid. I got the impression he hit tough financial times after his wife's death. I'm not sure why, because she came from old money. He wasn't employed while she was alive. He's an accountant now. Works from his home. They always kept to themselves, he and she. But Paul was at our dinner table more nights than not.'

Gene eased the car down his driveway into the carport and Deena stepped out, into a puddle. She looked down, realizing that the puddle was a ring of water all the way around her rental car. Raindrops shimmered on its top and hood. Barbara must have driven it.

'I'll be there in a minute,' Gene said. 'I'm going to check the tires. This road always knocks them to pieces.'

Deena climbed the steps and entered the kitchen. Barbara stood by the table, spooning cookie dough onto a metal sheet. For a few seconds she did not look up. Then she raised her chin and Deena saw the truth.

'You found the photographs, didn't you?' Deena said to her.

'Yes.'

'What photographs?' Deena turned at the sound of Gene's voice. He came toward her from the screen door.

Barbara waited for her to speak. 'From Monday, on the river,' Deena answered. 'Gene, you won't like this. You won't want to hear it.'

'Show me.'

Jon was suddenly beside her. 'Jon, get the pictures for Grandpa.' He went outside and returned carrying the envelope. Gene took it into the living room and sat heavily at the end of the couch, putting on his reading glasses. He began with the enlargements.

'What's this?'

149

'The man, Grandpa. See?' Jon sat beside him and put his finger on the dark blotch.

'This looks like a man to you?'

'It does to me,' Jon said.

Gene studied the enlargements and then the smaller photographs, finally laying the batch aside on the end table. 'Why are you doing this?' he asked Deena. 'Don't do this.'

'It's him,' Jon said.

Gene got up, facing Deena, frowning. 'Don't do this.' He turned to Jon. 'If it is a man, he has the right to be there. I want you to listen to me.' He gripped Jon's shoulders. 'You are *safe*. You live and walk in safety. You lie down at night in safety. Nothing is after you. No *one* is after you. No one was after your father! He *died*. People *die* – usually when they get old, but sometimes it happens sooner. I don't want you growing up thinking that you are being watched, that you are in danger. I don't want you growing up frightened. There's no reason for it!'

The crunch of gravel. More than one car was coming down the driveway. Her mother and father. Possibly her sister or Tim's sister.

Gene released Jon and thrust the photos into Deena's hands. 'Put these away.'

8

'You again?' Sergeant Ed Flanders said, staring at Martin through the bullet-proof glass above the counter.

'Me again,' he answered tersely, signing the Property Room book with his name, the name of the requested item, and the name of the court case. He shoved the book into the well under the window.

'What is it this time?' Ed squinted at the page. 'What tape recorder?'

'People versus James Dario. Can't you read?'

'I don't have it.'

It was a game they played often, but today it was without charm. Martin took two steps to the left and waited for Ed to unlock the door. A stranger watching them would think he and Ed were barely acquainted, Martin thought. They always exchanged as few words as possible. They had discovered early in their six-year friendship that they were so much alike they needed only verbal shorthand to communicate.

'People versus James Dario, huh?' Ed put his key in the lock and admitted Martin to the evidence bin. 'What did *he* do?'

There was no need to answer. Flanders had memorized the blotter of every hoodlum and defendant in the city of New York. And his sixth sense was better than Martin's. He had an antenna for guilt.

Flanders led him halfway back along one of the aisles and pointed at a shelf. 'Shall I get you a chair and a cup of coffee, Mr. Trayne?'

Same old nonsense. Martin always said yes and Ed never brought a thing. 'If you please.'

Flanders lumbered off. Martin moved closer to the shelf and stared at the microcassette recorder that had perfectly captured the words and gunshots of Dario as he killed his real estate rival, Ellen Patteka, in her car. Patteka had placed it in her coat pocket prior to the meeting. This sort of paradox was always a marvel:

151

a woman clever enough to carry a tape recorder but naive enough to go near a man like Dario. Martin was the only courtroom artist he knew who considered inanimate objects from crime scenes nearly as interesting as the people involved. The attendant objects were an intriguing part of any story, and he, against the city editor's wishes, rendered them on paper nearly as often as he did people. Martin took his briefcase from under his arm and, extracting his pad and a charcoal pencil, began to sketch the item – the last one he needed for the montage on the Dario trial.

'Here we are, Mr. Trayne.' Flanders was wheeling a chair on rollers toward him and carrying a cup of steaming coffee.

'Allow me.' Flanders held the chair for him. Martin sat. 'Two cream, one sugar, right?'

'Right.'

'You just take your time, Mr. Trayne.' Ed put the coffee on an empty shelf. 'Yessah, you just take your time.' He had shifted into the patter of mock subservience.

Martin considered the man's beefy black cheeks, the glittering street-smart eyes. 'What are you up to?'

'You don't look good today.'

'I don't?'

'You don't.'

'A buddy of mine died, okay?' He continued to sketch. Minutes went by. Flanders didn't move. 'That will be all, Edward,' he said without glancing up.

'And you think it smells,' Flanders said slowly.

Martin shot him a frown. 'No.'

'Yessah, you do.'

'How did you get that?'

Flanders pointed two fingers at his eyes and then at Martin's.

'I have news for you, Ed. Not everyone in this life ends it by being murdered. You've been on the force too long. Thanks for the sympathy.'

The man continued to watch him. 'Are you going to do anything about it?'

Martin sighed. 'I have a dirty little secret, Edward. For your ears only. I've become paranoid. People who sit in court for years drawing perpetrators and victims of violence become paranoid. They think everything's a plot.'

'You going to do anything?' More softly now.

He put his pencil down and held it to the pad with his thumb, examining his handiwork. The tape recorder needed a little more texture. It seemed one-dimensional. He scanned Flanders' shoes. Shiny, not a scuff. The pants to the uniform were showing a little wear, though. He skipped the shirt and focused on the casually curious face.

Martin had drawn this face on countless occasions: the whimsical lift to the brows, the intelligent piercing gaze, the flat nose, wide flawless dental arch, and prominent chin. He couldn't remember precisely the first time he had seen Ed Flanders, but it was, no doubt, at a trial. During Martin's first four years on the job, Flanders had been present in the courtroom a lot, testifying in one arrest or another. Ed had been incredibly clever for the most part, careful. His arrests were airtight. Martin had built up a respect for Flanders long before they'd ever had a conversation, long before Martin learned that in the NYPD Flanders was universally revered.

Ed had been tough and shrewd on his beat. Formidable.

153

A target that someone finally hit. They had broken most
of his bones when they finally got him alone. Martin had
recognized him only by the name on the chart at the end
of his hospital bed. In the past two years, Ed had regained
the use of everything but his courage. He'd asked to be put
on quiet duty. Hence, the Property Room. Martin understood this, the sudden intolerance for risk, the need to
be cloistered, shielded emotionally. The games he used to
play with Flanders had come to an instantaneous halt. He
had been used to prowling coffee shops and street corners
for Flanders, sizing up Ed's current mark, using his artist's
sense to verify or nix one of Ed's theories about a situation.
He had caught things Ed missed, like the time he'd trailed
the honest guy who just couldn't have killed his wife and
noticed that in every restaurant he deftly filched from the
table the tip left by the previous customer. Little things.

Flanders towered above him now, unmoving, waiting
for an answer.

'Maybe.'

9

Paul left his workbench and rounded the corner of it
quickly, wiping his hands. He recognized the customer:
Carlos Leal, who wore the dark clothes of mourning.
Awe and pleasure surged through Paul. He seldom had a
chance to look directly at the results of his efforts. He had
to settle for newspaper accounts detailing the anguish of
the bereaved fiancé. In the case of Carmela Azaña, there
had been no mention of Carlos Leal in the article.

'Mr. Kincaid.' An acknowledgment, not a question.

Paul positioned himself so that the counter was safely between them. Soft rays from the huge northerly window played across it as Leal opened his wallet and thumbed through the contents. His impending request was predictable. He would ask for his deposit to be returned. And Paul would give it to him. Usual, except that a grieving fiancé generally sent a close relative to retrieve the money.

'I have come to pick up my rings.' He found the receipt and held it out.

'Your *rings?*'

'For the wedding.'

Confounded, Paul assessed the young man's brown eyes, the angle of the chin, then cautioned himself against admitting knowledge of Carmela's fate. 'I thought you would bring the lady with you to try them on.'

Pain now, registered in the brow, the mouth. 'Did you not know? She has died.'

He mirrored the man's expression and saw the effort touch him. 'How?'

'She drowned.' Leal dropped his gaze. 'I must have the rings to remember her.'

'Of course.' Paul took the receipt. 'I will get them.' He was in an untenable position. He had to appear to cooperate. He felt a peculiar shortness of breath as he blocked Carlos Leal's view with his body and rotated the dial on the safe. Inside, nine velvet-lined boxes stood open side by side. The first two were empty; the other seven each bore double wedding rings – a man's and a woman's. He selected the last box in the row. His best work, these. Naturally. They were the newest fabrications in his special collection. He had become much more proficient since the creation of the first set. But he had only been in college then. With a clean polishing cloth, he plucked the two rings from their slots and tapped them into the slots of another box, carefully putting the empty box back into line. Closing the safe, he approached Carlos Leal. 'Here they are.'

Leal's eyes widened with appreciation as he contemplated the gold bands. 'Lovely.' He touched them, running a finger over the shallow carving on the smaller one. 'Lovely flower.'

'Iris,' Paul said.

Leal reached into the front pocket of his slacks and produced a roll of wrinkled money. 'A balance of four hundred dollars, correct?'

This was his opportunity, possibly the only one. 'Although these are custom designed, I would – under the circumstances – be most willing to return your deposit.'

A brief pause, as though Leal were considering the option. 'Thank you, but I wish to buy them.'

Once out of his possession, the rings would be impossible to retrieve, as they had been with Martin and Jenny, with Tim and Deena. The thought of losing these agitated him. 'If I may . . . a suggestion. A fine customer of long-standing found himself in the unfortunate situation you are now facing. He chose to take the rings. A month later, he returned them. He had discovered they were a permanent reminder not of his beloved but of his loss.'

This seemed to have impact. Leal's gaze skimmed the circles of shining gold, then rested on Paul. 'That may be true for me also. But my heart tells me to keep them, if only for now.'

Further resistance would heat the exchange, and he avoided conflict whenever possible to escape scrutiny. He would have to comply. 'Very well. Four hundred dollars.' The words had an unintentional edge to them.

Leal did not appear to notice. He counted four bills and placed them in Paul's hand. 'Thank you, Mr. Kincaid. They are beautiful.' Closing the box, Carlos Leal placed it in his breast pocket.

In a moment, it would be over. Paul groped for an idea, another chance. 'You're welcome. My condolences. And . . . should you, at any time, change your mind, please come to see me. I will honor your request.'

10

On the sidewalk, Carlos put his hand against his chest, pressing the ring box to his thudding heart. The memory of Kincaid's face inflamed him, the pretense, the deliberate mocking. Did he think Carlos could not imagine that he had killed Carmela? The vanity of American men astounded him. They underestimated their enemies. He had seen Kincaid's lust on the first day, when Carlos had come with Carmela to that same counter to order the rings. Did Kincaid believe she had not noticed him following her in the streets? *He was there again this afternoon*, she had told Carlos. *He watches me*.

He should have confronted Mr. Paul Kincaid at the outset, when Carmela had first told him her fears. But he, too, had been afraid – afraid of a fight in which he might be arrested and deported, sent away from her. Had he understood when he left Argentina that he would be totally powerless in this country, he would not have come. Entering America illegally had rendered him impotent. In all matters, he had no recourse. Could not complain about wages. Could not freely choose a residence. Could not defend himself. Could not ask for the protection of the law. He had learned to be invisible. And he had learned to hate himself.

Sometimes his homeland rose up before him like a path. He could smell the smoke of a roasting pig, the vapor of orange slices squeezed into pitchers of wine. At home, he would not have hesitated. He would have had help, the help of half a dozen men, to drag Mr. Paul Kincaid from his bed at midnight and cut his confession from his throat with the point of a knife.

Here, he would have to wait, seeking cautiously the hour of justice and revenge. He would slowly crush Kincaid's jaw, his skull, under his boot even as the man's tongue pulsed out the story of Carmela's death. If he chose the right time to execute Kincaid, he might never be caught. Carlos Leal did not exist.

11

The cottage teemed with visitors: relatives and friends. The odor of fried chicken and egg salad hung in the air. People sat on the staircase with paper plates on their laps, others packed the screened porch. There was a collective murmur like the swarming of insects. Deena and Jon occupied the rocking chair in the middle of the living room, clinging to each other. Within her sight were her mother and father, her sister Linda and brother-in-law Christopher, Tim's sister Gail and her husband Kemp, Barbara, Gene, neighbors from the lake, neighbors from town. So many new faces. She had concentrated on each during the introductions. But none of them had touched the well of suspicion in her. They were female homemakers and elderly couples for the most part. Wednesday noon was not a convenient time for men to leave their offices. She would have many more faces to assess tonight at the funeral home.

It seemed as though she was looking from a great distance at all the acquaintances who had come, and at the family members, dear as they were. Only Jon was close and real. The two of them had shared a day so profound that it sealed them forever in a separate compartment. The rest of the world was muffled and veiled. She knew Jon felt it, too. His body was damp and hot as he leaned against her. He had not left her for a moment since the incident with Gene.

Gene's rebuff had demonstrated clearly why she needed to keep her thoughts private, pursue the possibility of murder on her own. In this group there was no one who would leap immediately to her side. As much as they loved her – and she had no doubt they did – they would, at least initially, find her outlook peculiar or be emotionally threatened by it. She studied them one by one, giving up, deciding to be prudent. Even her sister Linda, whom she admired for many reasons, was not capable of the rapid jump that would be required. She was too much like their father, prone to placate, keep the status quo.

Deena's limbs were sore with impatience. She was not used to being confined like this, hemmed in by tradition, stuck helplessly at the center of ritual. In the brilliant April noon beyond the windows, the clues to Tim's fate were cooling and evaporating; the river was gradually changing course; the sky, which must have been fragmented by the shout from his soul as he drowned, was settling peacefully over the woods again. Soon nothing would remain of his struggle. Perhaps there was nothing now.

12

'I don't want to take a nap.'

Deena put her finger to her lips, guiding Jon into Tim's old bedroom and closing the door. 'I'm going out for a while,' she whispered. 'I wanted to bring you up here to tell you why.'

'Can I go?'

'Grandpa Reuschel would be upset if I took you. We don't want him to get angry. He's already sad enough.'

'Where are you going?'

She held out her arms. 'Come here.' He hugged her and they sat together on the bed. 'I don't want to tell you. Then, if someone asks you, you can honestly say you don't know.'

'Is it about Daddy?'

'Yes.'

'You still think the man hurt him?'

She contemplated Jon's blue eyes. He was too young. She shouldn't be confiding in him. But to shut him out would be worse. They were in this together, no matter what. They counted on each other's frankness. 'I'm not sure.' She shifted the digital alarm clock on the table until they could see its red numbers. 'What does this say?'

'One, two, seven.'

'Could you stay in here and pretend to be sleeping until three, two, seven?'

'Why?'

'You'll be keeping my secret. When you get up, I'll be back.'

'Will you tell me where you went?'

'Yes.'

His shoulders sagged in resignation. If he asked her not to go, she would have to stay. She would not discount his needs. 'What if the man hurts *you?* What if *you* die?'

The thought that such a person might exist incensed her. 'I won't. I refuse to die.' She believed it.

He straightened his back and stared at her. 'Because you're mad?'

'I guess I am.'

'Mad as hops?'

She couldn't help smiling at him. He gave her a half grin in return. 'Hopping mad,' she said.

He began to untie his shoes. 'So am I.'

13

When she came out of the bedroom, Gene was leaning against the wall, waiting for her. Had he heard what she said to Jon? She could tell by his expression that he hadn't. He gazed at her with obvious and sincere affection and took her hands in his. 'Deena,' he said quietly, 'I'm sorry I got upset about the photographs. I understand where you are. Believe me, I understand.'

Relief and hope flooded her. 'Thank you, Gene.'

'I was watching you downstairs. You don't want any part

of all this ceremony, do you? I really care for you and I want you to please listen. I know it seems like a wretched formality, the funeral and everything that surrounds it. In your heart, you don't want to participate. You want to ignore all this, pretend it isn't happening. I used to do it myself when I was younger and getting used to the idea of death. This is your first experience with it – a horrendous one. Terrible. No one would blame you for doing what you are doing. But . . . becoming involved in suspicion and staying preoccupied with the man in the photographs and questioning the doctor who did the autopsy is simply a way to keep busy. A defense mechanism, you see? A way of denying the pain and deferring the grief. It's important for you to stop doing that and go ahead with the process of mourning. It shouldn't be postponed. Allow yourself to grieve. And allow yourself to be comforted. It's the path to healing. Even the act of comforting others is healing. Please be part of our circle.'

She felt as though he had struck her. He meant well. Gene always meant well. But he was wrong. Yes, she was deferring her deepest grieving. Yes, yes. Shoving it away on purpose. She could not allow herself to grieve to the fullest extent of her feelings just now because it would paralyze her, keep her from doing the most important task: uncovering the truth and doing it quickly. Her mourning could be deferred, but her inquiry into Tim's death could *not* be deferred. She could lose the trail, allow the murderer to get away – if there was a murderer. Tim himself would understand. He would tell her she was right.

But Gene was not Tim.

'I will be part of the circle, Gene. Am part of it.'

'No, you're holding back, wanting to be absent from us, shut us out. Let's be in this together.'

'We are, Gene.' She squeezed his hands and let them go.

'Mourn while we're here for you. Let Jon mourn. Don't distract him with these other things. Frankly, Barbara and I need your help handling our loss, too.'

Sorrow and loneliness welled up in her. She found she could not answer.

'Stay with us,' he said, kissing her forehead lightly. 'Let's stay together.'

She nodded.

He walked slowly down the stairs. She hesitated, confused. After a moment, she descended the staircase into the crowded living room. Gene was sitting on the couch with his back to her, talking to Gail. Deena passed behind him, into the kitchen, and retrieved her purse and keys from the counter. The three women working at the table, replenishing trays of food, noticed her but did not ask questions.

14

Deena watched the roadside for an opening in the thickets. She would have to get her car completely off the highway and hide it in order not to attract the curiosity of locals or the police. The morning's rain had left huge puddles at the shoulders. The soil in the woods was bound to be muddy. Did she dare risk getting stuck? She pressed the thumb and middle fingers of one hand to her cheekbone to relieve the pressure in her head.

A slight clearing in the brambles caught her attention. As she neared it, she realized it was a rutted lane, overgrown with weeds. She tried to remember the map. Was this close enough to the place on the river where she and Tim and Jon had stopped for lunch? Or would she have to walk a long way?

She'd chance it. She took the turn gingerly and bounced onto the path, tall brush whining and scraping against the front bumper as dense clumps of it were forced under the car. In seconds, she could barely make out the way. The ruts disappeared and, in their place, were low mounds of soggy leaves under towering oaks. She guessed the path by gauging the distance between trees. One of the front wheels struck something hard. She hit the brake and looked behind her. She was far enough off the road not to be seen. No sense in going farther. She cut the engine and spread out the map, tracing the way she had come with a yellow marker. She was in proximity to the right area. She just needed to get her guts up and get going.

She snugged her boots up over her jeans, tucked the map in her jacket pocket and put on her gloves. Getting out of the car, she paused. She always felt naked without her camera, helpless, as though it were a weapon she could use to defend herself. She had deliberately left it behind at the house. It would slow her down.

She started off at a trot, the threat of danger at her heels. Now and then, she would stop suddenly and check the way she had come, seeing nothing but wilderness. But the vision of the watcher stayed with her and she quickened her pace until she was running.

She emerged next to the river, panting, searching for a landmark she would recognize. Nothing was the same.

Two days after Tim's drowning, every trace of their visit was gone – everything she had seen, everything she had photographed. She wandered the riverbank, lost, uncertain she could even get back to the car.

The map, unfolded and flapping in the chill wind, reassured her. She was upriver from the site. She forced herself to walk slowly toward it. Rushing had been a mistake. She didn't want to miss what she had come to find.

When she arrived, the scene of the picnic seemed colorless, undistinguished. Such an important spot, yet it bore no special air. The marks the raft must have made when Tim dragged it ashore were gone, washed away. There was no litter. The indentation of the cooler had disappeared. She spent a long time among the trees, mentally marking the location where the watcher must have stood, if he existed, and digging at mulch with the toe of her boot wherever she thought she saw a foreign object. It was fruitless. She gave up and went downstream, scrutinizing the stretch of land where Jon had seen the stranger retreating. Now she was Tim, following his son with his eyes as he ran back to Deena, being followed as he dashed toward the ridge. What had he seen or done that made him a target? And where had he actually died?

She checked her wristwatch. An hour and twenty-five minutes since she had left home. Much longer than she thought. Jon would worry when he woke up. She might have to come back another day to finish.

If she left now, she would not come back. She would take Jon home to California after the funeral and sleep with nightmares the rest of her life.

She moved cautiously and deliberately toward the ridge, scanning the layered forest, Tim's footsteps invisibly

165

guiding her own. He had been here. And here. She began to climb, the muscles of her calves hardening with the effort. He would have taken this hill easily, quickly. He was in shape.

He had fallen into the river from the crest. There was no other explanation, no other point where he had been in such close proximity to the water that it could snatch him. But why did he fall?

At the peak, she curled each hand into a circle and put them to her eyes like binoculars – a 'kid' trick that shaded glare and focused attention on a small area at a time. Standing like that, she painstakingly swept the horizon, finally pausing at an inverted V nearly hidden behind a shower of new leaves. She took her hands away and stared. It was the roof of a house on another ridge.

15

The laundry on the line was stiff with the cold, but dry. Arlene Trakas pulled the wooden pins from the clothes and folded each piece into the plastic basket, blowing on her fingers to keep them limber. She was the only person she knew who – by choice – did not own a clothes dryer. In winter's worst days she used the basement, crisscrossing it with lines, but most of the time she depended on God-given outdoor air to dispel the germs from her wash. No member of her family, except Mimi, had ever been in a hospital except during the birth process. Nor did they lose time to days sick in bed. Arlene's healthful handling of the laundry was one good reason why. Arlene ironed everything, even underwear and towels, to restore their softness. The heat of the iron released the smell of wind and sun into her kitchen. There was no other smell like it in the whole world. No clothes dryer could do what she did with the help of God.

She straightened from the basket, the pins clattering in the wide pocket of her apron. A woman was approaching her, across the expanse of dormant grass. Arlene seldom saw visitors and this was no one she knew. Boots, jeans, stringy red hair, and dark, empty eyes. There was no help for it now. Arlene was out in the open, too far from the house to go in and bolt the door. Reflexively, she glanced at the garage, seeking Jasper's protection. How many months would it take her to get over the habit? She'd had that precious dog seventeen years before she found him in the rose bed, gone.

The woman kept her distance, as if aware of Arlene's vigilance. 'My name is Deena Reuschel,' she said. 'My husband drowned in the river on Monday. Did you hear about it?'

The widow. Lord have mercy. 'Yes.'

'May I ask you a couple of questions?'

'First of all, I'm so sorry for you, my dear. It's a terrible thing. But the police have already been here about it. Yesterday.'

A new level of intensity in the eyes. 'Did you see anything unusual on Monday? Did you see *him?*'

'No.' The word hung between them, a refusal. Was she so divorced from another's pain that she could not offer this child a single symbol of hospitality? 'Would you like a cup of coffee?'

A nod. As Mrs. Reuschel followed her toward the house, Arlene thought of Mimi. Arlene had deftly kept her from knowing the police had come. She had run outside without her coat when she saw them arriving and had spoken with them in the yard, well away from Mimi's window. Mimi still did not know there had been a fatality on what she considered her property.

She could take Mrs. Reuschel in the side door to the sitting room next to the kitchen. Their conversation would not be overheard by her mother-in-law, who was more than slightly deaf anyway. Mrs. Reuschel followed her in a dispirited manner that tore at Arlene's heart.

'I can't stay,' she said when they bumped their way into the kitchen, Arlene depositing the clothes basket under the ironing board. 'I have to get back to my little boy.'

'Well.' Arlene shut the door to the dining room anyway, just to be sure about Mimi. 'I have a small thermos bottle with a dinosaur on it. I'll put your coffee in that and you can keep it for your son.' The woman's emotional injury was so powerfully apparent that she did not respond. Arlene struggled to decide what else to say. The coffee she poured for Mrs. Reuschel did not change her expression. 'Cream? Sugar?'

'No.'

Arlene twisted the plug into the neck of the thermos and, winding the cap on tightly, put it into Mrs. Reuschel's hands. 'How else may I help?'

'Were you the only person here on Monday? Do you have children or a husband?'

'I have both, but they don't come home until late afternoon. My husband works, and the children are in school.'

'Are there any other houses nearby?'

'Not close. This area was a state preserve until recently.

168

We were the first family to obtain a building permit. After we got it, the state changed its mind and enforced the preserve laws again. But we were allowed to go ahead and build.'

Mimi began to ring her bell, the rhythmic ring that meant she simply wanted company. Mrs. Reuschel looked toward the sound and then at Arlene, her mouth opening in a wordless question.

'My husband's mother. She's an invalid.'

'Could she have seen something?' A whisper.

'She's very old and feeble. She's had a stroke. She lies in bed all day. She doesn't even know about your husband. We keep bad news from her.' Arlene's tone was pleading – she heard that in herself. But she couldn't allow Mimi to be disturbed. It would be pointless. And it might kill her.

Mrs. Reuschel nodded and wordlessly stepped out onto the stoop. 'Thank you,' she said. Her gait was stiff as she walked away, shoulders rounded, the posture of those without hope. Arlene thought of calling to her, some last phrase of kindness, but she couldn't think of what.

Mimi had been good to Arlene, good for Arlene. Mimi, before her stroke, was a laugher, organized, and bright. A confidante. In her waning years, Arlene would protect her. No matter what.

She poured apple juice for Mimi, plucked a spoon from the drawer, and started for the stairs. The bell was still ringing. Mimi would be disturbed to learn that Arlene had called the doctor and that he'd be coming by. A betrayal on Arlene's part. Mimi hated doctors. But she hadn't eaten much of anything since Monday.

Since Monday.

Arlene set the glass and spoon on the foyer table and ran through the dining room and sitting room to the side door. Mrs. Reuschel was barely visible at the bottom of the hill, too far away to catch. Arlene rushed outside and stood on the stoop, crying, 'Come back! Come back! Mrs. Reuschel! Come *back!*'

The face and then the shoulders turned in her direction. Arlene waved.

16

Deena sat on the stairs, listening to Arlene's hushed voice float down to her from Mimi's room.

'Mom, I know you've been depressed. I want you to tell me why. I've asked you before, but now I have a new idea. Is it, maybe, something you saw out the window that upset you? Is that it?'

The bell.

'Was it a man, something about a man?'

The bell.

'Did he . . . drown?'

The bell, loud and continual, the noise ending abruptly. Deena had the impression that Arlene had embraced her mother-in-law. There was no sound from the room.

Finally, Arlene began again, her voice lower. 'A lady came to talk to me. It was her husband, the man you saw, the one who died. She's very nice. She's here, downstairs. Could I bring her in? I want her to hear what you have to say. She's very nice, Mom.'

The bell, followed by creaking overhead. Arlene appeared at the top of the staircase and beckoned Deena. 'She answers by ringing,' Arlene said. 'If she doesn't ring, she means *no*. Her name is Mimi. She likes people to call her that.'

The bleak and airless hallway opened into a bright room. Next to a large bay window was a hospital bed cranked partially into sitting position. Mimi occupied a small portion of it, her head and knees elevated by the angles of the mattress. She was a study in white and gray against vivid pink sheets. A silver cow bell was attached to her wrist with a piece of white yarn. Deena could not see her eyes at first, but skirted the bed until she was fully in Mimi's vision. They were black eyes, startlingly alive in a crumpled body.

'Mimi? I'm Deena.' She glanced at Arlene for permission to continue.

'Go ahead,' Arlene said.

'You think you saw my husband?'

Mimi jerked her wrist upward until the bell clanged.

'Let me . . .' Deena walked around the bed until she stood behind Mimi's head. Mimi's window view was of leafing treetops, a field, the opposite ridge, and a section of river that swirled beneath the bluff and along the gorge. In a week or two, the scene would be almost obscured by the foliage of the oaks. If Deena had come back then, she probably couldn't have seen Arlene's house from the ridge.

Arlene was bringing a chair for her now, placing it at Mimi's bedside. Deena sat in it, and Arlene sat on a cedar chest in the corner where Mimi could watch her.

'I think my husband – his name was Tim – fell from the cliff. Is that right?'

Mimi shook her hand toward the window. The accompanying rapid clang of the bell carried with it such a sense of agitation that it frightened Deena. This was not an unintelligent woman. This was not a woman who had lost her awareness with the stroke. The intensity of Mimi's reaction was a warning. She leaned toward Mimi. 'Was someone up there with him?'

The bell continued, reverberating along the walls, the ceiling.

'A white man in black clothes?'

Still the bell.

'Did he push Tim?'

Mimi's arm came to a rest. She did not stir. Perspiration began to flow from Mimi's scalp, down her forehead. Arlene jumped up from the cedar chest and put her fingers to Mimi's face. 'She's clammy.' Arlene slid her hand on down, feeling the shoulders of Mimi's gown. 'Wet. Maybe this is too much for her. Mom, are you sick?'

Mimi didn't move. Perhaps she was losing consciousness. Arlene took up a towel and began to gently press it to Mimi's neck and temples. Mimi's weakened gaze stayed on Deena.

'Should I go?' Deena asked Arlene.

'No,' Arlene said. 'Finish it.'

Deena hesitated.

'She wants you to.'

Make it more general. 'Mimi, did the man kill Tim?'

The bell.

Horrified, Deena put her hands to her ears. 'Did he sneak up on him, surprise him?'

The bell.

'Did he hit Tim?'

The bell.

'He *hit* him?'

The bell.

'Jesus!' Deena began to sob. 'What did he hit him with, his fists?'

Mimi, gasping, lay still.

Deena lowered her hands. 'Not his fists. He hit him with. . .' She stood up. 'He hit him where?' She pointed to her own head. Her back. Her waist. Her buttocks. Her legs. Mimi rang the bell. 'On the legs. *With* something?'

The bell.

Deena went to the window and stared helplessly at the phantom scene. 'And that knocked Tim into the water?'

The bell, the bell.

'What happened then?' Not right. She had to rephrase it.

'Let me try,' Arlene said. 'Did the man go away after that?'

In a heaving rush, Mimi vomited. Arlene lunged forward and gently rolled Mimi onto her side. 'She'll choke. Help me.' Deena tipped Mimi's head forward and tried to clear her mouth with the corner of the towel. The stench was reminiscent of the odor in the ambulance.

'Awaawwaaaa.' A wail, primitive and guttural.

Deena wept. 'What should we do?'

'She'll be all right. You're all right, aren't you, Mom?' Arlene smoothed Mimi's hair back. 'She's all right. Here, I'll take this.' She folded the towel into a ball. 'I'll bring a washcloth. Just a minute.' She left the room.

Deena sank into the chair. She and Mimi regarded each other in exhaustion. *Ask me*, Mimi said wordlessly.

'Then . . . he climbed down to the river,' Deena whispered, 'and pushed Tim under, held him under, didn't he?'

Mimi's arm flew convulsively upward, against her hip. The bell caught in the bedclothes with a faint chime.

17

Deena and Arlene huddled together in the wind of the side yard. 'I didn't want to talk about it in the house,' Arlene said. 'I didn't want her to hear us.'

Deena nodded.

'They won't believe her, you know. An old woman who can't speak. She's senile.'

'Do you think so?'

'That's what they'll say.'

'*I* believe her.'

'Beyond question.' Arlene shoved her hands into the pockets of her sweater. 'She saw it.'

The vision of Tim being struck sickened Deena again. She folded her arms across her stomach. 'I should have asked her whether she recognized the man.'

'I'll find out.'

'I don't have a phone number here. I'll have to contact you.'

'It's in the book. N. R. Trakas. Call me in the middle of a school day. I can't tell this to my family.'

'Don't.'

Arlene rubbed at her cheeks as though trying to assure herself that she was awake. 'We could all be targets, couldn't we? If anyone found out?'

'When the police came, did you mention Mimi?'

'Most folks know her, know she's here with us. She was born in this county. But to them she's no longer alive. Total invalids are ignored, as though they're already ghosts.'

Laughter. Three children carrying books were chasing each other at the bottom of the hill.

'Mine,' Arlene said with finality.

Deena hurried down the slope past the children who looked at her only fleetingly as she went by.

18

The tires hit the berm of the highway, jerking the car to the right and startling Deena. She yanked at the steering wheel to keep from running completely onto the shoulder. Rubber rumbled and skidded over stones and dirt, bouncing her against her seat belt before the car popped back onto the pavement. The motion gave her a stab of adrenaline. *Pay attention*. She'd been all over the highway, repeatedly crossing the center line and jamming down too hard on the accelerator. She was in Mimi's room, in the chair, listening, watching Tim through Mimi's eyes, watching his attacker. Anger repeatedly ripped at her as though she were being clawed. No, not anger. Not rage. This emotion had no name.

She turned suddenly onto the lake road, sliding sideways, braking, putting her foot down again. The car lunged over cracks and holes, shuddering, sending up a trail of dust in the rearview mirror. Tim had been struck across the legs, hard enough to topple him. It had to have left marks on them. Was Halligan blind? *Calm down*. There must have been countless marks on Tim's body. She had seen the battered flesh of his head. Perhaps Halligan couldn't distinguish one kind of blow from another.

The cottage jumped into view. Only a few cars left. Family, she supposed. She raised her foot from the gas pedal and let the remaining momentum carry her down the driveway. At that, she had to hit the brake hard to stop. A squeal echoed in the carport. She snapped the key a notch to the left and the engine quit. Without the motion of the car, the motion inside her intensified. She wondered if she could get up. Gene appeared at the window beside her and tapped on it lightly. She rolled it down halfway.

'Did I make you feel you had to leave?' he said anxiously. 'I apologize.' He reached in and tugged at the lock, then opened the door for her. 'Forgive me.'

She got out and stood with him for a moment. He was a portrait of intractable sorrow. No future joy could ever fully touch this man. 'I didn't leave because of you. I'm just going to need a lot of space.'

'Done. You tell me when, and I'll help you.'

She put her head against his chest and let him hold her.

'Deena, I want to tell you something before you go inside. Bob Norville dropped off an envelope this afternoon. It's a brief statement from the pathologist. Not the full autopsy report. We'll get that later on.'

She drew away from him. 'Where is it?'

'Here.' He pulled a piece of paper from his back pocket.

It was a form. Her eyes skipped the printed words and went immediately to the handwritten entries: *Drowning.*

176

Accidental death. Circumstances unknown. Jumped or fell.
F. S. Halligan, M. D.

19

After he hit U.S. 6, Paul took the first exit ramp and got into a drive-through lane for fast food. Wedged between two pickup trucks in the endless snaking line of vehicles, he closed his windows against gritty fumes. If he weren't so hungry, he'd skip it: the disembodied voice squawking at him from the menu board, the high curbs blocking his escape, the oily women palming his food. He detested experiences in which he was herded. He was not like other people, not remotely like others. He gave his order and turned the bend. Ahead of him, money was changing hands, soiled and seamed paper bills, filthy coins. He could picture the hamburgers leaking grease spots into the bottoms of cardboard nests, leaving their mark. The sleeping bag came into his mind, nestled safely in the trunk of the car.

Leaving its mark.

What had he been thinking of? He was losing his mind, starting to make some illogical decisions. The bag would leave fibers, had already left fibers, in his living room, on his clothing, and in the car. If he put Jon into it, he would have to get rid of the whole thing forever.

The blast of a horn jolted him. He eased his foot off the brake and moved the car forward, fumbling for the right change in a well of quarters. He would have to throw the sleeping bag – and its human contents – where it could never be found. And there were few such places in the universe.

20

Jon stood up in bed. 'Mommy, it's four, four, seven.'

'I was away longer than I thought I'd be. You helped me a lot. Thanks.'

'Where did you go?'

She beckoned him closer and whispered in his ear. 'I went back to the river, to where we had the picnic.'

He put his mouth against her ear. 'Did you see the man?'

'He wasn't there.'

'What did you see?'

The sharp-angled roof appeared in her memory, Arlene hanging clothes in the yard, the brilliance of the sickroom, Mimi outlined against the window. How much of it could she share with Jon? *None of it. For his own protection.* 'The doctor who examined Daddy sent us a note today. It said that Daddy died by accident.'

'What happened to him?'

'He isn't sure.'

'He's supposed to know.' Jon sat down suddenly, then lay back on the mattress glaring at the ceiling. 'He's stupid. Ask someone else.'

They were always of like mind. She could count on him to voice her thoughts. 'It isn't that easy.'

'Why?'

'Come on and get up now. We're going to have a good dinner.' She patted his leg.

'Didn't you see *anything* when you went there?' His gaze was direct and piercing.

He could tell that she was evading his questions. And he would know if she lied to him. 'Let's go.' Her words seemed to jab him, but he let her pick him up and carry him from the room.

21

Myra Swenk dragged the footstool over to the door so that she could stand on it to look out through the peep-hole. She hated to use it for that purpose. Her sister had made the needlepoint cover for it: lily bells on a lavender background. She needed to buy another stool, that's what she needed to do, one without a cover, a metal or plastic stool, no, not plastic because it might tip. Someday she would. Hands against the door, she hoisted herself into position and put her eye to the circle. Whoever it was, was too close and it was too dim out there to . . .

It was that Mr. Trayne. He always looked like a hobo she thought, with all that facial hair, scruffy. Like the silly TV chef who had the grungy beard. Every time she watched that man cook, she could just see those little hairs dropping into the food. He always looked sleepy, Mr. Trayne. Maybe he was drugged on something all the time. She hadn't thought of that before. He had droopy eyelids. But no, the whites of the eyes were always clear, not bloodshot. She watched for that in people, the condition of the eyes. Eyes are windows to the soul.

Mr. Trayne. That one always walked away from her when she was talking, right past her like he didn't hear her or like what she was saying made no earthly sense. And he only knocked when he needed something. What was it this time? She sighed and got down carefully from the stool. Maybe he had the rent for her. Fat chance about the rent. Mr. Trayne was always out of money or pretended to be. Maybe he had come to see Daniel. She'd drop her teeth if he asked for Daniel. The boy was unfeeling. They all were, that generation. Like Daniel's children. Well, nothing to be done. It's what we taught them.

She dragged the stool back to its spot in the living room and began to work on the locks. She needed three. People say you can't get out in a fire with that many, but burglars were more likely than fires. Undoing the locks always gave her pause, she imagined that while she was undoing them whoever she had looked at through the peephole had gone away and now there was a hoodlum there ready to choke her. She always left the chain lock on for good measure, although she'd heard that a good shoulder to the door could break it right off the frame. She left it on and peered out cautiously. Mr. Trayne was still there, wearing his beggar's face.

'Hello, Mrs. Swenk. I've come to see if I can borrow your car.'

Right into it like that without even a how-are-you. No manners, none at all. 'Last time you borrowed my car, you brought it back empty and I can't have that, don't you see. I need that car, what if I'd have an emergency?' He was harmless but negligent, she'd decided, harmless but negligent. Take for instance his apartment, she couldn't believe it when she went in there, not dirty, thank goodness, that was a blessing, but cluttered, *my land*, books

180

all over the floor, clean dishes, clean I'll grant you, all over the counter like he washed them but never ever put a one of them back in the cupboard, if they had ever been in the cupboard to begin with, which she doubted. And half his clothes on the floor of his closet like he didn't own enough hangers and couldn't afford to buy any. Then he changed the lock on her, they could do that, the tenants, without permission, but she took it as an insult nonetheless when they didn't bring her a new key. When she walked by his apartment now, she expected to see the mess oozing out from under the door. She thought about it a lot sometimes, what it must look like in there these days.

'I have to go to a funeral tomorrow morning, out of town. I'll fill it with gas. I promise.'

He was eyeing the keys on the hooks. She should move that pegboard into the kitchen, by the front door was not a good spot, but she couldn't move it, Daniel always did that kind of thing, she wasn't Daniel. 'I thought maybe you had the rent for me. I can't go on like this month after month, don't you see, I have to make a living and with Daniel sick . . .'

'I pay.'

'You pay *late*.' She got through to him on that one, maybe, she thought she saw guilt cross through the wilderness of that awful facial hair. The man had a conscience, she had discovered that over time, but he didn't act, didn't get off his behind and *do*. Well, maybe he really did have money problems or something else terrible, he always looked stunned, as though somebody had just hit him over the head. She could be lenient, was lenient, she had always thought it was better to have a reputable renter who was late paying than to let him move out and take chances trying to find a new tenant. Russian roulette these days even to interview people.

'Well. Can I borrow it or not?'

'Daniel's looking forward to your visit. When will that be? He's sleeping right now.' Barter was a way of life in some countries and in some parts of this country.

'When I bring the car keys back?'

God only knew when that would be. Last time, she had ended up sitting in a chair in the hallway, right next to his apartment, waiting for him to come home so she could demand he find them. He had mislaid them, he said. He rooted through his belongings for half an hour while she sat in the chair, listening. No wonder. No *wonder*. Maybe a lady could straighten him out, but she never saw him sneaking the ladies in overnight like some. No ladies in the daytime, either. Maybe he wasn't one for ladies. She hadn't thought of that before. They say the ones who don't like the ladies didn't like their mothers. Maybe if he didn't like his mother, his mother didn't like him. That would explain the lack of manners. Mothers were the standard bearers. Well, if he never had a mother . . . That got to her, in the soft parts under her ribs. Mrs. Daniel Swenk could give him a little leeway, she supposed, and a good push now and then, when he needed it.

She never could see which key was which. She touched most of them, squinting at their labels, trying to find the car. Truth was, she hardly ever used it, but he didn't need to know that. She took up the correct set and held them under his nose. 'You bring these right back

182

to me. Understand? Right back. And bring me your rent check.' As he took them from her, she thought she saw a little appreciation in his eyes for her motherly tone, but maybe not.

22

Paul kept the beam from the battery lantern trained on the frost beneath his feet. High above him, the arched ceiling pulsed with a thousand bats. His skin tingled from the perpetual fine mist of droppings. The first day he had been brought into this series of connected caves, when he was ten, their diversity and splendor had dumbfounded him. This cave, the Ballroom, was the most impressive: immense, artfully sculpted, rising like the interior of a grand cathedral over a vast and level sheet of ice. The smallest cave he had found in here was unnamed, a long blind tube barely big enough to accommodate a man crawling on his belly through soil so dry and sandy that it cut flesh. How many caves existed in this maze, he could not guess. He only knew they had not all been mapped.

At this time of year, spelunkers shunned the Angel Caves. They were treacherously cold and notoriously intricate. They had never become a public attraction because they posed so much risk.

How difficult would it be to carry Jon's body across this slippery surface? An immobilizing injury would trap Paul. He would not be found for weeks.

The golden shaft from his lantern located what he was seeking: the Devil's Staircase, in a corner of the Ballroom.

He edged closer. Closer still. Nature had carved stone steps leading down and away, seemingly into the wall. Upon first examination, they appeared to be connecting the Ballroom to a lower cave. Inexperienced explorers might be seduced by the evenness of each tread and the glistening beauty of the formations hanging overhead. But the staircase ended abruptly over a pit. He had thrown stones into it and heard them hit faintly many seconds later. Nothing that went into that abyss ever came out.

Three or four minutes. That's all it would take from start to finish, the car looping into the deserted parking area and backing down the incline almost into the entrance, the package being lifted and carried through the outer cave, into the Ballroom, and then gingerly across the ice, hurled into the blackness. Once he had let go of it, once it had gone out of sight, nothing could be proved.

23

Whose house was this? There were curtains and rugs and chairs and tables. No toys, though. He could tell that just grown-ups lived here. He wished there were kids. Why did they bring his dad to *this* funeral home? Why didn't they bring his dad to his grandpa Reuschel's funeral home on the lake? Nobody seemed to be the mommy or grandma at this funeral home. Nobody had offered him juice or showed him the other rooms. Nobody must live here. He'd thought that as soon as he came in. There weren't any books or a TV or a cat or mail. This was the loneliest he had ever felt. Ever. On the way in the car, he had been excited about seeing his dad. He ran through the parking lot. But then, when he saw him, his dad looked like a big doll in a bed. His dad couldn't speak to him. His dad wasn't even here. Just the big doll was here. And he knew he couldn't call his real dad on the phone or find him anywhere in the whole world. Even at home in California. It made him cry.

There were too many people around him and his mother. They kept pushing in, more and more. The men had hot hands and they put their faces right down in front of his. Nobody seemed very nice, just like they were trying to be nice. He kept looking for the man from the woods, the jacket and hat, but it was mostly old men. Kind of fat, not tall. He was real, real tired. He wanted to sit down on the rug, but his mother wouldn't like it.

Someone was looking at him from the other room. Someone in line, Paul Kincaid, who used to play with his dad when they were little boys. Grandma said she loved Paul and used to feel sort of sorry for him because he acted lonely all the time.

Paul winked at Jon with a sad face. It made Jon feel good, like somebody who liked his dad really liked him too. His mother seemed far away. Everybody seemed far away. He wanted to talk to Paul. Right now. He wanted to ask him about when Paul and his dad were little boys. What did they play? Did they play with the Matchbox cars? Was his dad fun?

Paul waited and waited and waited to see them. When his mother saw Paul, she hugged him for a long time. Paul was like an uncle. Not just a friend.

Paul sat on his heels in front of Jon and whispered so no one else could hear, 'I'm sorry about your dad, Jon. I'd like to get to know you better before you go back to California. I'll miss you. Would you like to spend some time with me, maybe tomorrow afternoon, the two of us?'

Jon nodded. Things were so mixed up. He was afraid about the man, and his grandpa wouldn't listen. And when his mother came back from the river, she wouldn't tell Jon what she saw. She could be dead, too, pretty soon. And he wasn't allowed to say anything to anybody. His mother was even mad at the police.

He remembered how his dad had given Paul a big kiss in New York. His dad had been laughing. Happy. Maybe Jon could tell Paul. Just Paul, nobody else, about the pictures.

24

Surreal, this parlor with Tim's body at the center like an altar. People had been drawn to the casket all evening, pausing, staring, weeping. Strangers to her. But not to him.

His skin held a radiance in the ambient glow of candles and under the filtered spotlights. An air of peace and even of resurrection surrounded him. The rest of the parlor was muted. The family milled about in shadows, among their own hushed voices. The mourners had departed. Deena had listened astutely to what each had said to her as they filed by. She had wanted to hear it all. Every word, every name.

186

When she and Jon had first arrived and were alone with Tim, Jon had cried in her arms. But as the visitors began to arrive, he had stood bravely beside her, searching the parade of faces. Was he looking for the same thing she was? Now, her mother beckoned to Jon and took him from the room. The others followed, and she understood. This was her chance to say good-bye to Tim. The next morning's service would be held with the coffin closed.

She limped through a few silent prayers, forgetting whole phrases, trailing off in thought. Leaning over him, she tried to feel the presence of his soul. A scent of perfume drifted strongly to her, one much more distilled than the atmosphere created by sprays of flowers. The aroma was actually coming from his body. What potion had they used on him? She visualized the backs of his legs, the bruises that must surely exist there, and winced.

This was not the time to pursue it. When she had amassed enough evidence, she could have him exhumed. Right now, she needed to appear cooperative in order to deceive Tim's killer and to send her family home, out of her path. She should not think of this burial as a defeat, but as a ploy.

She took Tim's wedding ring from her pocket. She would send it with him, as a sign of her faithfulness. His finger, under her grasp, was surprisingly soft and accepted the circle with the slightest push.

Still my husband. She stood with him for minutes, unwilling to relinquish him, remembering in detail his vitality and his kindness. She was only able to leave his side and walk away when she had decided what she needed to do for him next.

25

Mike would be in the recliner. Guaranteed. Paul shoved his house key into a pocket and carried his suitcase past the pine-paneled den. His father, sprawled in the chair with a magazine in front of his face, lowered it a fraction to give Paul a slight nod. Paul headed for his old bedroom, the hardwood floor growling under his feet. The cottage creaked incessantly – from age, from the wind, from mice in the walls. Some weekends the creaking was the only sound in the cottage. He and Mike seldom spoke. Paul noticed that when Mike did speak, his voice was hoarse from disuse. Fine. He'd had plenty of that voice. His father's silence had been an unexpected benefit produced by the death of Paul's mother. *Sarah*. He thought of her with a twinge.

He fumbled for the lamp. Just once couldn't his father leave it on for him? Was he saving a penny on the electric bill? It was more a stinginess of emotion than of money, Paul was sure. A dark room held no welcome.

He found the light and set his suitcase in the corner. This was not a boy's room, never had looked like one. It looked like Sarah. Her hand-crocheted bedspread. The decorative pillows. The lace curtains. The dressing table that had belonged to Sarah's mother. He had never been at home in this room, although the infusion of her personality into it had at times been consoling.

The birthday marks were still on the door jamb. She had measured his height every year of his life until he was twelve. Each penciled line had a date on it. Some years he had grown faster than others. He had wanted to grow up quickly. He rubbed his thumb across the red line at the top of all the marks: his father's height, unsurmountable in those days, although Paul was slightly taller than his father now.

How they had wrestled when he was a child, Paul trying in vain to twist away from Mike's painful grip. Even birthdays were a test of manhood. His father's punches, one for each year, permanently bruised the bone in Paul's upper arm. *Seven, eight, nine! And one to grow on!* Sick bastard. Tough guy. And she . . . Turning away. He had tried to talk to her about his father, but she discouraged it. He had seen them in bed some nights and early mornings, sleeping stomach to stomach, their limbs intertwined, not a wisp of space between them. How his father had adored her. Flowers and fruit, perfume, embossed boxes with giant bows. He could still see her face as she separated the pastel dresses and lingerie from pale pink tissue paper: unutterable delight, respect, a breathtaking undercurrent of sensuality between man and wife.

No, she did not want to listen. Paul didn't have a sentence for it back then, but her unspoken intent seemed clearer and clearer to him as he passed each mark: Sarah would love Paul only as long as Paul loved his father, or pretended to love him.

What choice was there? He worshipped his mother. She was all he had.

The pencil lines had crept up the wall and, between them, years of shame and labor under his father's fist. Paul's climb toward the red mark became an obsession, that height of five feet eleven inches his single goal. He stuffed himself with spinach, cottage cheese, all sorts of foods he disliked. He secretly bought extra vitamins out of his allowance. It was almost funny now, how he had nurtured hope, made plans. Fantasized about being big enough to kill the man.

26

In the damp parking area of the funeral home, Deena let Gene and Barbara go ahead of her and then stooped to talk to Jon quietly. 'I'd like you to go home in Grandma and Grandpa's car. I'll be along after a while.'

'Why?'

'I want to ride by myself. So I can think.'

'I'll let you think. I won't say anything.'

'*Please*. Do this for me,' she whispered.

'What is it?' Gene asked, backtracking.

She straightened up, Jon holding tightly to her hand. She couldn't make him do it. Not tonight.

'You need something, pal?' he said to Jon.

'Um. Yeah.' Jon let go of her. 'Can I come with you, Grandpa?'

'That okay with your mom?'

She touched Jon's hair and he bowed his head. 'Yes. I'm going to drive around a little. I'll be home shortly.'

'You got it,' Gene said.

27

It was well past dark when Frank Halligan heard the horses leave the back meadow and round the house into the front yard. This always heralded a visitor on foot.

190

The gate at the road was locked. No one could drive onto his property.

He stood still, listening for the animals to tell him whether it was a friendly presence or a threat. They were not complaining. A good sign. He could tell by the movements of the horses that the human was coming to the front door. A stranger, then. Since his wife had died, he had lived in less than half his house: the kitchen, dining room, and a downstairs bath. It saved expense and trouble. He had got rid of the dining room table and installed a bed. He came and went by the kitchen door only; the front door remained locked. Now the stranger was rapping on it. He walked toward the sound, turning on lights as he went, surprised to find, in the end, that it was a woman of about thirty, dressed in a black coat and high heels. A professional woman, he guessed. Glossy strawberry-blond hair. Smooth complexion. Brown, serious eyes.

'Dr. Halligan?' There was accusation in it.

'I am.'

'I'd like to ask you about an autopsy you did on a man who drowned Monday. His name is Tim Reuschel.'

Weakness took him. He had expected this for the past fourteen months, at least. And now it was here, on his doorstep: an insurance investigator, possibly the same one who had forced Jim Weding out of his job as Dunbar County pathologist. How long did those fools in the sheriff's department think they could keep up the charade? It was all going to fall straight on his own shoulders, straight on him, right now. He was going to lose everything.

'I apologize for intruding on you at home, but I wanted to speak with you privately.'

He was lucky. If she had cornered him at work, the

whole town would know about it in half an hour. This way, maybe he could explain himself, explain the situation, save his hide. This woman had the power to take his license. His reputation. His pension. God, she could even send him to prison. He needed to have his say with her before she approached anyone else. 'If I cooperate with you, will you protect my interests?'

'What do you mean?'

'Will you keep me from getting too badly hurt in this?'

She narrowed her eyes at him. 'Of course.'

28

The house had a musty smell. Deena followed Halligan through the living room and what seemed to be a makeshift bedroom into the kitchen. A dim bulb burned in a lamp on the wall. Two Irish setters jumped up from a corner to sniff her shoes and rub against her coat. She sat where he indicated, on a white enameled wooden bench at a matching table. He slid onto the opposite bench and adjusted his glasses to peer at her. She sensed his fear.

'What about Mr. Reuschel?' he said cautiously.

'He was struck in the legs from behind.'

'And you're here to find out why I didn't report the pattern injury. I'm not incompetent. I saw it. That particular wound was suspicious. I know that.'

Electrified, she opened the top button on her coat.

One of the dogs, in response to Halligan's agitation, came to him and nudged his knee. Halligan stroked the dog's head. 'I'm prepared to give your company information on this and other cases, but I'll have to have your full assurance of my protection. In writing. And I think I'd better get a lawyer before I tell you anything else, Ms.—'

'Mrs.,' she said.

'Mrs.—'

'Reuschel.'

29

The rhythmic motion stopped, as though someone had put a hand against a gently swinging hammock and brought it to a halt. But he was not in a hammock – he was lying too flat, the back of his head only slightly raised. Heat began to spread from the center of his chest to his neck, his chin, his lips. His heart knocked wildly against his breastbone as sleep held him down, down, and the dome of air above him turned slowly inside out, empty. He couldn't breathe. *God,* here it was again: He *couldn't breathe*.

He struggled to move. Warm saliva slid from the corner of his mouth, down his cheek. He could miraculously feel his wrist bone against a wall. He found a breath and choked on it, came up coughing, in pain. The wall was the cushion of the couch. He was on the couch. At home. In the dark.

Martin put an arm over his face, wiping his eyes and nose on his sleeve, coughing, coughing. Freezing. He stripped off his wet shirt and dried the fringes of his hair with it. Traffic noise filtering through the window panes told him it was still early. Before eleven o'clock.

Turning on the lights made him feel better. He found a can of ginger ale in the kitchen cupboard and opened it, hunting for ice without success. The bubbles loosened his throat anyway, eased some of the soreness. In the bedroom, he unfolded a T-shirt from the stack of laundry on his dresser, pulling it over his head as he positioned himself at the computer and booted it up. From the shelves over the monitor hung eight newspaper clippings in chronological order. The stories and photographs of eight dead women. *Jenny Cunningham*, Suzanne McVaugh, Allison Hout, Marie Sietz, Deborah Lundin, Rebecca Turregano, Beth Pyle, Carmela Azaña. He had spent hours contemplating their lives and their deaths. They waited silently above his desk, in the midst of the printed words. Some had waited for years.

They had all drowned while alone. They had all drowned within a hundred-mile radius of Manhattan. They were all between the ages of eighteen and thirty. All of the deaths were termed accidental. All but one of the women – Carmela Azaña – were engaged to be married.

If they were murdered, how were they chosen?

He had thought a time or two of using his NYPD connections to get an audience with a detective in Homicide. But he couldn't make himself do it. Civilians were perpetually at the paranoia game, piecing together ludicrous scraps of events and information into elaborate plots, bringing the whole mess by police stations, excited, begging to be listened to. Retired men. Middle-aged ladies whose husbands were overly busy with corporate life. Newly released mental patients. Martin had a reputation around the court-house for being vaguely oddball. He didn't need to add to that.

But he didn't have enough information. He wanted details about these women, touches that wouldn't be in any news account. He wanted to interview their families, their sweethearts, if he could find them. Some were already irretrievably lost. He'd bet on that. People in the wake of tragedy load up vans and move.

Jenny was the only victim to which he had sufficient access. He kept coming back around to her. He had arranged and rearranged the pattern of her twenty years, reviewed her friendships, her conversations, examined memory after memory. If she was the first of this string, why was she chosen?

She lived in Manhattan during the winter.

But they did not all live in Manhattan, or even in New York. Nevertheless, they had probably, at some time – perhaps often – been in Manhattan. Where? That's what he would ask if he could.

She lived at the lake in the summer. He had virtually ruled this out. Jenny was the only victim whose death had been reported in the *Cameron Star*. The paper would have done its homework. If any of the others had come to summer homes in the area, they would have been featured.

She was engaged. How would that border on the other murders? An engagement announcement in the newspaper, perhaps, complete with picture. Which newspaper? The women were from New Jersey, Connecticut, New York. Many different newspapers. Not a valid theory. Unless the killer haunted libraries. No. Too much trouble.

He had been through and through this, round and round.

Born in the same hospital during a single time span? Possible. But doubtful that someone in attendance would track them for so many years. Too far out.

And what about Tim? Wrong sex. Right age. Died

fourteen miles from where Jenny died. Had a connection to Manhattan. In fact, had just been there.

What if all of the victims had been in Manhattan directly prior to their deaths? What street, avenue? Did *what* in Manhattan?

He put his fingers on the keyboard and began to enter the data on Tim into the program he had designed to compare and contrast the victims. The computer might see links he had missed.

What good would it do? He didn't have enough vital information. He was going about this the way he went about everything – as a spectator. If he wanted to know, he'd have to *ask*. Ring doorbells. And ask.

30

Halligan had risen and left the room abruptly when he realized who she was, his boots scraping against the hardwood floors in the recesses of the house. She had listened for running water, for drawers sliding in a dresser, for the sound of a window being lifted or an outside door being opened. Had he gone into the bathroom? Was he looking for a gun? There were no sounds except the footsteps, roaming. *She had come this far*, she had said to herself. *She would stay*. The dogs had not followed him. They lay on their bellies dozing, observing her from under half-closed eye-lids. She had been raised with dogs and knew their language. These, which were secure enough to tolerate her presence in the absence of his, had to have been consistently well treated but not fussed over. Their demeanor bespoke the reason and compassion of their owner. She hoped she was right.

Suddenly, Halligan was in the dining room, hidden by the kitchen wall. Her gaze followed his footsteps. He emerged with his hands flung out and up, a gesture of surrender. 'You're in the catbird seat. You tell *me*.'

'Tell you . . .'

'What you want.'

'I want to know who murdered my husband.'

'Hey.' Halligan sat across from her, rubbing the palms of his hands on his pant legs. 'There's no certainty he was murdered. That pattern injury could have occurred any number of ways.'

'He was *murdered*.'

Halligan sat back, in a brooding silence, then leaned toward her. 'That may be. But don't count on getting competent help in Cameron County.'

'Including from you?'

'Listen, it was in the gray area. I simply passed over it.'

'A habit of yours, I gather. Who did you think I was at first?'

He sighed, a sigh heavy with weariness and regret. 'Let's talk bottom line. Tell me what you want.'

Thursday

1

Rain pelted the green canvas tent with such force that Deena could barely hear the minister who stood across the coffin from her, praying. Many more people had come to the grave site than she had expected, crowding beneath the shelter as the downpour intensified. The folding chairs intended for family had been taken away to make more room for the mourners. Still, some stood beyond the spilling curtain of rain under umbrellas.

The casket, with its giant spray of fragrant yellow roses, dominated the gathering. In the crush, Deena and Jon had moved so close to it that Jon could see little except its brass handles and polished wood. She continued to hold his hand, rubbing the back of it gently with her thumb. He responded now and then with a squeeze. Gene, shoulder to shoulder with Deena, supported her elbow in a tight grip. His other arm was around Barbara.

Through the drumming overhead, Deena heard Tim's name in the minister's sentences, but the rest of his words were obliterated. She opened her eyes slightly and focused on the cascading roses and ribbons that bobbed in the wind atop the casket. Would Barbara and Gene forgive her when she finally told them that Tim's body had not been in it at the church and burial services, that she had – in a sense – lied to them, lied to every person assembled here?

If the second autopsy proved nothing, she would not have to tell the Reuschels about it, would tell no one, not even Jon.

Where was Tim's body now? Halligan had promised that Bob Norville would remove it from the coffin overnight and secretly retain it at the mortuary. Halligan had promised that, while the funeral was in progress at the church, the body would be transported from the mortuary to Somerset Hospital for examination by the state police forensic sciences team. And he had promised that, when everyone had left the grave site, Tim's coffin would be retrieved from the open hole to await the return of the body. It would then be interred.

The minister concluded the prayer and raised his arms. 'And now, may the Lord bless you and keep you . . .'

What were Halligan's promises worth?

'. . . the Lord make his face to shine upon you and be gracious unto you . . . the Lord lift up his countenance upon you and give you peace . . .'

What other hope did she have?

'. . . both now and forevermore. Amen.'

2

He had not cried since he was a child. He had given it up deliberately, forcing his mind to go blank whenever he felt threatened. But he was close now.

Paul cleared his throat and tried to dispel the images of his mother that had drifted to him during the benediction. The crowd was in motion, some turning away from the casket, some navigating toward Deena. He had watched her all morning with a reverence that surpassed any longing he had ever experienced. In the shade of the tent, among the dark clothes of the mourners, her ivory skin and copper hair glistened. The beauty of her full lips and soft brown eyes moved him. She had been gracious at the visitation, at the funeral, aware, open. She had allowed strangers to embrace her and had wept with them. Now she, subdued but radiant against a background of roses, began to receive those who came to her. Should he speak? It was only proper that he introduce his father. Mike had already put his back to Paul and angled into line.

As he stood breathing the soap scent of Mike's sparse hair, he noted for the millionth time that he was an inch or so taller than his dad. He had passed Mike up slightly when he was sixteen or seventeen years old. But by that time, it didn't make any difference. He had not been measured on the bedroom door frame after the age of twelve. The last time was vivid in his memory, his mother surprisingly eye to eye with him, holding a pencil flat to his skull, marking the spot on the wood with a tiny horizontal line. His father had grown more fierce in his pursuit of Paul, more brutally challenging each year, and yet more tender and solicitous toward Sarah. As he grew, Paul had nurtured and expanded the idea of killing his father. The fantasy of it kept him going, held him spellbound for hours, soothed his injuries. He had worked out every detail, had begun to build his biceps in anticipation. It would be a bare-hands murder with no clues. A drowning, ruled accidental.

The ceremonial measuring of Paul on his birthday was increasingly fraught with emotion. His father, the day that Paul turned twelve, had stood at a distance with his arms folded, grinning at him, licking his lips as Sarah began the measuring. *You think you're such hot stuff, sonny boy. Let's see.* At a record five feet four, Paul was still seven inches below the red line, but – incredibly – the same height as his mother. She had laughed in delight when she discovered it and measured him again. The contrast between her flushed pride and his father's triumphant smirk cut savagely into his chest. It was then, with her smile nearly brushing his cheek, that he knew how best to conquer his father.

He was not yet big enough to kill Mike. But he was big enough to kill Sarah.

3

For a moment, it seemed there was not enough air under the tent. Light, diffused through the canvas, cast a greenish tinge over the multitude of faces all fixed in her direction. It was as though their intense sorrowing had used up every molecule of oxygen. In a flash of chill and heat, Deena put her head back and tried to draw breath from the sloping ceiling and the sky beyond. And then, someone grasped her arms with murmured condolences. A heavyset balding man. She responded and he passed by. An elderly woman in a veiled hat appeared in front of her, speaking words of comfort. Deena had met her the day before at the cottage. She tried to remember the woman's name. How had she known Tim? Deena had lost track of the ordinary flow surrounding the death and the funeral. The parade of people and customs had the flat repetition of a feverish dream, unreal in contrast to the vividness and urgency of her search for Tim's attacker.

A few spaces began to open around her as couples and

groups at the edges of the tent bolted into the easing rain. The slamming of car doors punctuated the hushed sentences of those who filed past her and Jon and Gene and Barbara. The woman staring at her now from beneath the hood of a cape gave her a small sealed envelope and said, 'I am truly sorry, Mrs. Reuschel.' Deena focused with shock on the blue eyes, the puffed fleshy cheeks. Before she could reply, Arlene had left the line and walked out onto the lawn.

Deena could not measure time except by the gradually clearing weather. During the endless minutes she stood next to the coffin, receiving mourners, the rain diminished and sun began to faintly dapple the headstones surrounding the tent. Paul Kincaid was nearly last in line, shepherding ahead of him a somber man who could only be his father. Their looks were so similar that she glanced from one to the other several times: the lean build and powerful posture, the aquiline noses and pointed chins, the sandy hair. The most perceptible difference between them was in their demeanor, Paul's vital and caring, Mike's withdrawn. Paul's presence suddenly infused her with energy, with will. She could feel her toes inside her shoes again. Paul Kincaid was one of the most valuable friends she had at this moment. And he would help her if she needed to ask.

4

The cemetery was deserted except for the solitary limousine and the boatlike rusted car rounding the curve toward it. Deena, walking down a grassy slope arm in arm with Gene, paused. The car pulled over and the features of Martin Trayne became visible behind the windshield. Barbara and Jon were already inside the limo, the chauffeur holding the door, waiting. 'I'll be right there,' Deena said to Gene, who released her.

Martin got out, leaning on the roof of the car, as she approached. 'Is it over?' he asked.

'Yes.' She moved closer and saw that he was dirty in smudges: his forehead, a sleeve of his coat, his fingers.

'The battery,' he muttered. 'It died. On the way.'

'Well, can you come to the house for a while? Have some lunch?'

'All right.' He ducked into the driver's seat. The shifting of gears produced a crunching whine.

She turned back toward the limousine, surprised to find that Gene and the chauffeur were not in sight. Bob Norville was holding the door for her. He must have been in the front seat all along, behind the tinted windows. As she neared him, she searched his expression for a sign that her wishes had been accomplished. His eyes told her nothing, but as he took her hand to help her into the limousine, he pressed Tim's wedding ring into it.

5

Paul drove the long way around the lake, to keep from passing the Reuschels' cottage, and turned onto the McNaughtons' property just south of it. With ten acres, the McNaughtons had the largest chunk of land in the neighborhood. Most pieces were five. Their paved driveway curved among hardwoods, which obscured the house from the road. It ended in a cul-de-sac twenty yards from the water.

He approached cautiously, but the cottage had the blank, shuttered silence of a summer place off-season. The McNaughtons were Canadian and never in residence here until June. He positioned the Maxima at the arc of the cul-de-sac, with its trunk toward the lake, and got out, resting his hands on his hips. Scanning the woodland, he felt satisfied with his choice of this site. He could not see or hear the dozens of visitors who must surely have come back to the Reuschels' cottage after the funeral. The McNaughtons' home was beautifully buffered on all sides by trees and on two sides by hills. Their lakefront was one of the few that naturally formed a harbor. Their dock had complete privacy.

He'd lure Jon quietly, disappear with him from the gathering, walk with him along the lake from Reuschels' cottage to McNaughtons' dock. He estimated that walk at four minutes, another three or four to drown Jon and get him into the bag. Paul would strip off his own wet clothing – whatever it may be – and put it in the bag, too, dressing quickly in dry clothes he'd stashed in the trunk. Ten minutes, tops, and it would be over. Paul would be gone, around the lake and out to the caves.

He had worried some about the red car. Red was showy, likely to be noticed. But he couldn't have driven the Bronco to the funeral. It was his rule not to use the truck where he would be recognized and associated with it. He'd been carelessly proud of that Bronco when he first bought it – sparkling new and for cash, had wheeled it around and deviled his dad with it a little. But within hours he'd sobered up about it. Its intended use was as a weapon.

He needed to hide it. He rented garage space in Midtown and stayed away from the truck except for the hunt.

And today? He listened for a few minutes, slowly pivoting in a full circle. It would be all right. Touching the car for luck, he set out walking through the woods. The weather was favorable, the clouds white, scudding, not ominous.

6

Deena – She did not recognize him but saw his truck. So far unable to get details. She is failing. Sleeping much of the time. Arlene.

Deena refolded the page, then unfolded it and read it again. A truck. She sat down on the commode lid, contemplating the dogwood blossoms on the bathroom wallpaper. If she had known this before, she could have studied the trucks in the church parking lot and at the cemetery. Were there any trucks here now? She would check. People had left vehicles all over the grass surrounding the cottage and along the street. She would go out and look on the pretext of getting some fresh air.

God, she wanted to stay in here forever. It was quiet in this sanctuary, cool. This cubicle offered the only privacy she was likely to get. Low conversation rumbled beyond the door like distant thunder. And after the guests had gone, there would still be family, so precious and yet so far from where she was now.

She needed to be patient. In the next twenty-four hours, they would all go home. She would regain her freedom, be mobile, able to investigate. She had already told Gene she wanted to stay at the cottage alone after their departure to 'sort out her thoughts.'

But she would still have Jon.

Could she send him back to California with her parents, just for two days? Would he agree to it? She could try.

She had no patience left. There was a creeping panic in her that made her hand shake. The paper trembled now as she tried to decide what to do with it. Finally, she tore it and the envelope into tiny pieces and slid them into the undersink wastebasket beneath a nest of trash.

7

Flakes of tuna and mayonnaise from his sandwich clung in Martin's mustache. He could feel them, wet and sticky, between bites. He wiped his mouth with a soggy paper napkin, keeping his eyes averted from the people milling around him. Small talk made him uneasy. He couldn't see a purpose to it. He'd express himself briefly to Deena and get out as soon as possible. He'd already spoken to Tim's parents. Saying something to Deena and Jon would fulfill his obligations. He wasn't sure where she was right now though. He hadn't seen her since he came in.

It was weird to be here without Tim. Martin hadn't been one to hang out with the Reuschels when Tim wasn't home like Paul had. Paul almost seemed to like it better when Tim was absent, playing the role of the son, helping Gene with the boat or whatever. Not Martin. He liked the Reuschels but had nothing much to say to them. Those kind, coaxing questions from Barbara only scrambled his brain. The great thing about Tim had been that he didn't need conversation from Martin.

Across the room, Deena slowly descended the staircase and hesitated, pale, frowning. Martin swallowed the last lump of his sandwich and hastily washed it down with Coke. He'd do it now and get it over with. She was moving rapidly away from him. He followed her into the kitchen, inching sideways past people clustered around the dining room table. As he caught up with her, he touched her shoulder. She looked at him blankly.

'I'll be leaving in a minute,' he said.

'Thank you for coming.' The sentence was devoid of inflection, as though it were the hundredth time she had used it that day. A pang shot through him. He had been like this – just like this – after Jenny died. In many ways, he still was.

'I wanted to say good-bye to Jon, too.'

Her mouth dropped open slightly as she glanced around for him, finally pointing back toward the living room where Jon sat alone on the floor beside the hutch.

'I'll write to you,' Martin said. 'Every Christmas.'

She nodded. 'I'd like that.'

He made his way toward Jon, who listlessly watched Martin's shoes as he advanced. Martin hunkered in front of him. 'I'm going now. It was nice to meet you. And . . . I'm really sorry about your dad.'

Jon stared at him as though he hadn't heard.

What else could he do? He wasn't good with kids. They didn't generally respond to him. Still . . . this little one resembled Tim so much. Martin knelt next to him. 'Jon?'

The child peered at him.

210

'Is there anything you want?'

'No.'

'Do you remember my name?'

'Martin.'

'I'll . . . be thinking of you. I hope that'll help.' He got up and took a last look at Jon who had not stirred and who was staring at Martin's shoes again. It was no use. It was all broken. Forever. Tim gone forever. The child was simply wise enough to know it.

Martin stumbled through the dining room, into the kitchen, heading for the sunlight beyond the screen door. Paul came through it just then, visibly startled to see Martin. 'I'm going,' Martin said flatly. He could sense that Paul was not in the mood to talk either.

'See you.' Paul held out his hand and Martin shook it.

8

More shoes in front of him. A man's. But this man did not lean over, just waited. Jon followed the pants and white shirt and red tie to the face. It was Paul Kincaid, with a happy smile. That smile was a surprise. Nobody else in the whole house was smiling. Paul wanted to have fun with him, make him feel better. Jon jumped up and Paul said, 'Let's play.'

'Play what?'

'What have you got?'

'Lots of stuff. In my room. You want to go up there?'

Paul smiled again. 'It's a nice day. Why don't you bring a game down and we'll sit on the screen porch.'

9

Deena stood in the road. There were no trucks parked along it. Not a single one. None in the yard either. A dazed exhaustion weighted her throat, her bones. Martin, in a blur, walked up over the rise and paused when he saw her. Lightheaded, she folded her arms across her stomach. If only she had a place to sit down. She needed to sit down. Right now.

Without speaking, Martin got into his car. She crossed in front of it as he tried the ignition and the engine gave a feeble wail in response. Opening the door on the passenger side, she crawled onto the seat next to him. 'I know it's crazy, but I'm suddenly sick. Give me a minute, will you?' She rested her forehead against the dashboard. A wave of nausea tingled along her ribs and gradually subsided. When she straightened up, Martin was staring out his window. He was such a strange man, so aloof, that it was hard to imagine why Tim had felt close to him.

'. . . crazy,' he murmured without looking at her.

'Pardon me?'

'It's not crazy.'

She knew that Martin had suffered terribly when Jenny died. He stopped speaking for nearly a month. He lost thirty pounds and had to be hospitalized. Tim's only description of Jenny's drowning and of Martin's ensuing agony had stayed with Deena, nearly word for word, through the years. Martin understood her pain. 'Did you ever . . .' It probably wasn't a good idea to talk with him about Jenny. He wasn't approachable like Paul.

'Ever—?'

'Feel guilty. I feel . . . guilty . . . about Tim. Like . . . I should have prevented this. I could have done better. Did you feel that about . . . Jenny?'

He didn't answer. She couldn't see his face. Finally, he gazed at her solemnly. She took it to mean that she was an intruder. His thoughts were his own

'Well, have a safe trip back to the city,' she said gently.

His eyes spilled tears. 'I still feel it. The guilt. I was late to meet her. Twenty minutes. I wasn't there. I . . . wasn't . . . there.'

Her own tears burned her cheeks. She couldn't think of a reply. She and Martin were quiet for several minutes.

'I don't want to accept it,' he whispered. 'I can't. I want to blame somebody, hold somebody accountable other than myself, other than Jenny. I start imagining that someone did this to her. I've wanted to believe it so badly that I do. I do believe it. But it can't be true. It's like an illness for me now. I can't let go of it. I keep going around and around, believing it. Wishing it.'

Jenny might have been murdered. Like Tim was. Stunned, Deena pressed her fingers to her lips.

'And *that's* crazy. That's what's crazy. *I* am.' He finished bitterly and tried the ignition, which made a few spiraling buzzes before it quit.

It wasn't safe to pursue this subject with Martin. She couldn't tell him what happened to Tim. Not yet. She couldn't even hint at it. She would jeopardize all her efforts.

'I guess I'll have to jump this battery again.' Martin's vulnerability had changed to irritation. She realized that he had been embarrassed by her nonresponse.

213

She searched for a comment that would put him at ease.

Deena's silence was his answer. If she suspected anything unusual about Tim's death, she would surely tell him so. Loneliness, stark and familiar, washed back to him. 'I've got cables in the trunk. Can I use your car for a jump?'

'Yes.' She did not move.

All the light had gone out of her since Sunday. She'd had a visible sheen when he met her at the Tavern, a springing energy. She'd been able, across the dishes and chatter, to infuse him with a foreign sense of well-being. There was none of that now, nothing left. A shell.

He needed to shut it off, this pity. Wasn't useful. He needed to get the hell out of her way, get her out of his way, forget that pathetic little boy, forget the whole damned incident. He couldn't do anything about what happened. He wasn't the law, for Christ's sake, didn't want to be the law. Didn't have a way to make anybody feel better either.

Didn't want to try.

10

'After the next hand, I'm going to have to take off,' Paul said.

'Whose deal is it?'

No. Jon pushed the cards together into a pile on the table. 'Three more hands.'

'Just one more. I think it's your deal.'

If Paul left, there wouldn't be any more fun. Paul liked to

play War. Liked it real well. It was fun sitting all alone with Paul on the screen porch. Paul acted like he loved it.

'Want me to shuffle for you?'

'I'll do it.' Jon lifted the top off the pile and made another pile. He'd shuffle slow and deal slow. 'Why do you have to go home?'

'I have a shop in New York where I make jewelry for people. Nobody helps me. If I'm not there, the shop's closed and people who come to see me are disappointed.'

'*I* want to see you.'

'I know.'

Jon mixed the cards by putting some from the first pile onto the other pile. He took some from the bottom of the second pile and stuck them on the first pile. He did it a lot of times.

'Go ahead and deal.'

'I'm almost ready.' He mixed them some more. When Paul left, everything would be sad again. He'd start thinking about his daddy all the time. He hadn't thought about him during the card game.

'Jon.'

'Okay.' He passed the cards out as slow as he could and they started to play. Paul was silly. He pretended to be mad when Jon won cards from him. He made noises when Jon's pile got bigger and bigger. *Ackkkk. Oowww! Yiiii*. Jon laughed every time. Then it was over. Jon had all the cards and Paul didn't have any.

'Gotta go,' Paul said, patting Jon's arm.

'One more hand.'

'Can't do it. Want to, but can't.'

'Why?'

'I told you.'

215

Jon made a face.

'Hey,' Paul said. 'I'll go around and say good-bye to everybody and then I'll come back and say good-bye to you. How about it?'

That would give Jon a chance to make him stay. 'Okay.' Jon kept watching Paul in case Paul might forget to come back. Paul went into the living room and talked to everyone and shook hands. Grandma Reuschel gave Paul a hug. Jon heard Paul ask for *Deena*. People started looking around, but she wasn't there. She must be up in the bedroom. She hid and cried sometimes. He saw her do it.

Paul came toward him. Jon could grab him and not let go. Then Paul would change his mind and not leave. Or he might get mad.

'Bye.' Paul held up his hands for a high five. Jon slapped them and held out his hands. Paul gave him a pretty good hit, but it didn't hurt. No wonder his dad liked playing with Paul when they were kids. Paul was good. 'See you, Jon.' Paul went out the porch door and walked by where Jon was sitting. Jon touched the screen and Paul gave his hand one more hit with a smile and walked away, around the side of the house. Jon looked at the cards on the table. He didn't want to think what he was thinking, about his dad going into the trees and never coming back, about his mother going into the ambulance.

'Jon.' It was Paul, using a quiet voice. He was standing by the corner of the house, waving in circles like he was saying *come here, come here*. Jon got up from his chair and went to the end of the porch to see what Paul wanted. Paul was excited. He said, 'A mommy duck and babies. Down there.' He pointed at a spot along the lake. Jon looked but couldn't see them. 'Hurry.'

The quiet voice again. A loud voice would frighten the ducks.

Jon wasn't supposed to go near the water without a grown-up. But Paul was a grown-up. Jon looked back at all the people in the house. Everybody was still talking. Nobody was looking back at him. Jon went down the steps. Paul was running along the lake, still waving at Jon in a friendly way. The ducks must be swimming fast. Jon started to run, too.

11

'Mission impossible,' Martin sighed, removing the jumper cables from her battery and from his.

'What's next?'

'Go to town. Buy another one. Put it in.'

'Borrow my car,' Deena said.

Martin nodded.

How long had she been out here? Her best guess was fifteen or twenty minutes. Too long. People had traveled across the country to be with her today. She needed to make herself available to them. 'The keys are in it.'

Martin slammed the hood of each car. She left him and took the steep driveway at a tripping pace, anxiety seeping back to her. If Jenny and Tim had both been murdered, they had been killed by the same person. The odds were that the death of two such close friends was no coincidence. She thought of Halligan and Bob Norville. Involving them in her suspicions may have placed her in more danger than she'd thought.

As she entered the kitchen, her mother came to her and

217

embraced her. Her magical power enfolded Deena. This woman had taken Deena rock climbing, wind surfing, ice fishing, had instilled curiosity and daring in her from childhood. Mariah Harper was lean and solid, painted in neutral tones: golden freckled skin, flawless white teeth, graying black hair. She wore no makeup and, in Deena's opinion, did not need any. Her eyes were brilliant with interest and acceptance.

'Deenie, how can I help you?' her mother murmured.

She inhaled Mariah's earthy scent, hoping to be strengthened. But weakness stayed with her. Would she ever be healed? 'Take Jon when you go tomorrow and keep him for a few days. I want to be by myself.'

'Will he let us do that?'

'I'll ask him.'

'All right.'

She released her mother in a rush of longing for Jon. 'Where is he?'

'Last time I saw him, he was out on the porch, playing cards with Paul. Maybe he's still there. Paul left a few minutes ago.'

'He did?'

'He said to tell you good-bye and that he'd be in touch shortly. We weren't sure where you were.'

'I was up on the road with Martin. His car wouldn't start. I didn't see Paul come past. Maybe he parked at his father's house and walked down through the woods.'

So many people were congregated in the living room that Deena could not see the porch clearly until she reached the French doors. The porch chairs were empty. The table held a scattered deck of cards. With a twinge, she went to the screen. The grassy yard and lake beyond were tranquil. A few birds hopped about in the greenery.

She walked back through the cottage, fielding comments and pausing to chat briefly, then excusing herself to move on. She shouldn't have left Jon for so long. She hadn't told him where she was going. Was he searching for her? Deena took the stairs two at a time and scanned the bedrooms, the bathroom. Could he be in a closet? She checked them and entered the bathroom to push the shower curtain aside. He was not there. Why did she think he would be? She went quickly downstairs to the master bedroom and bath. Someone was in the bathroom. She tapped on the door. 'Jon?'

'Be out in a minute.' A woman's voice.

Deena went back to the bedroom doorway. She could see the entire cottage from this spot. Her eyes searched the floor. Jon liked to sit in out-of-the-way places. He had been on the carpet next to the hutch earlier.

'What is it?' her father said, coming up beside her.

'I can't find Jon.'

12

The boy was lagging behind him, tiring, but the fact that he had run this far meant Paul had gained an extra minute or two he hadn't counted on. He'd slow up a touch but stay ahead of Jon in order to keep him moving as rapidly as possible. The scrub and hillocks of McNaughtons' harbor were in sight.

Paul monitored the landscape behind him. No one. And his sixth sense told him that no one was on the way. Nobody

219

had seen them go. They had been into the trees in an instant, obscured from view. He had pulled it off cleanly, simply. As usual.

Jon put on a burst of speed and ran alongside him. 'Where are they?'

'They're fast little critters. We haven't caught up yet. I know where they make their nest, though. Under a dock up here. Not much farther.'

Jon began to hang back again.

'They're worth seeing. Eight babies. Cute as they can be.'

'My mom might get worried about me.'

'It's not much farther.' They crossed a small rise and the dock shifted into view. Jon followed him into the basin and out onto the weathered boards. 'They like the shade underneath.'

'Will they come out?'

'You might have to get down on your stomach and lean over to see them.'

Jon knelt and then lay flat, with his head over the side. Paul stooped next to him. Prone, the child seemed tiny, delicate. This would take half the time of the other projects. He could hold Jon under with no effort at all.

A memory stung him: Mike with a foot on Paul's back, crushing the breath out of him, insisting on an apology for some transgression. Paul had been about this age, five or six. This is how he had appeared to Mike – this small, this fragile. He could still feel the increasing pressure on his spine, feel the air hissing from his throat. He hadn't been able to speak. He'd wanted to, but he couldn't. That was the first time the yellow fire had appeared, flashing and rolling at the edges of his vision. The Fire had made his dad stop. He owed it after that. He did whatever the Fire asked.

'I don't see them.' Jon started to push away from the dock and stand up.

Do it. He hesitated as Jon got to his knees. *Do it.*

Deena stood in the marshy grass next to the lake, paralyzed. *It couldn't happen again. Could it?* Her father had gone calmly up onto the road to hunt for Jon. There was no reason to worry, he'd said. Jon was probably with one of the guests somewhere. Or had wandered off by himself for a moment. Maybe he was upset and didn't want to face all the visitors. It was understandable, he'd said. Kids do those things.

But she knew Jon. He wouldn't.

The lake's surface was glassy, stirred only by faint wind ripples. She could see nothing floating for miles. Jon was a good swimmer. She had that assurance. He wouldn't drown accidentally unless he were injured or trapped somehow.

Mommy, I'm afraid of the man.

It could happen again.

Tim had died only a few minutes from where she'd been sitting. She could have intervened. She had failed him, made mistakes that were obvious in hindsight. She needed to do something decisive right away. But what?

Instinctively, she turned to her right and began to run.

There weren't any ducks. He didn't even see a nest under there. Just ugly spiderwebs with bugs stuck in them. Nothing good. And now he had splinters. Two or three. They cut his knees when he got up. His mom would have to dig them out with a needle and it would hurt. He didn't feel brave anymore. He wanted his dad. But his daddy was dead in the ground. They'd left him in a hill all by himself. He knew his dad must be lonely. But if he told his mother that, she would say no he's not because God is with him.

The way the sun shined in back of Paul made him seem like he didn't have a face. His head was just a brown circle. He put out his arms toward Jon, like he wanted to hold him. He bent over toward Jon to sort of catch him. Jon wanted Paul to catch him. He wanted to be held by Paul, to rest on his shoulder. Paul was sort of like a daddy. He played cards and was fun and nice.

He put his arms up for Paul. Paul stopped, like he changed his mind. He didn't pick Jon up. He didn't do anything. Then he grabbed Jon, around the stomach, pulling him up fast. The tight fingers felt like bites. He seemed to fly against Paul's hard chest. Paul put one arm under Jon's bottom and one arm around his back and held him in a strong hot hug that twisted Jon's neck. The hug was scary, the way Paul did it. It was too tight. And Jon's stomach was stinging, where the fingers used to be.

'That hurts,' he said to Paul, in the almost-crying voice Mommy called whining. She didn't like whining and told him every time he did it. Would Paul tell him he was whining? Paul's breathing was noisy. He didn't say anything. He let his arms go a little looser, but he kept on hugging Jon.

It was okay. Still too tight but okay. It wasn't the Bad Touch that his mother warned him about. It was just a hug. Jon hugged Paul, too, and put his face against Paul's shoulder. He knew Paul liked the hug. He put his cheek on Jon's hair and leaned slowly from one side to the other. He rubbed Jon's back. Jon pretended he was sleeping, like he used to sleep on his dad when his dad carried him.

In a minute, Paul started walking. Jon opened his eyes a teeny bit. They were going off the dock. Paul stepped down into the grass. The ride was bumpy after that. He peeked now and then. They were going along the lake, back to his grandpa's cottage. Pretty soon, he heard someone running up to them and Paul said, 'We were looking for the baby ducks.' Jon pretended to be asleep because he didn't want to get down. He wanted to be held and carried as long as he could. He peeked through his eyelashes to see who was walking beside him. It was his mother.

The three of them formed a unit: man, woman, child. With Jon warm against his chest and Deena at his elbow, Paul was a father, a husband. They moved slowly back toward the cottage in the hush of peace.

He had nearly forfeited his chance at this happiness. It awed him to think how close he had come to destroying the child. As he had seized Jon from the dock, the softness of the ribs and flesh under his grip had startled and shamed him. Jon was weightless, yielding. A boy. A baby. In the scarlet sea of his memory, he changed places with Jon. And could not hurt him.

They went into the house and he sat in the rocker with Jon in his lap, setting it in easy motion. Jon was not asleep, Paul was fairly certain, but he kept his eyes closed and lay slack in Paul's arms. Deena sat across the room watching, the light of gratitude on her face.

13

Martin poked at the items on his plate with a fork. The meal was the typical smorgasbord fare of the bereaved: casseroles and pies brought by neighbors. Au gratin potatoes. Meatloaf. Tuna-noodle bake. Rice pudding. He shouldn't be here, in the middle of this family gathering, but he never knew how to say no gracefully. After he'd installed the new battery, Gene had insisted he stay for dinner. Martin couldn't get a fix on how Barbara felt about it, but her exhaustion was evident. Martin and Paul were the only people left in the house who weren't immediate relatives. Embarrassed, Martin occupied a folding chair in a corner and tried not to drop food on his pants.

Paul was a different mind-set. Always had been. He sat on the couch, between Gene and Barbara, swigging iced tea and interjecting an occasional comment into what should have been a family-only discussion about whether Deena was to be left alone at the cottage for the weekend.

'I'll stay with you,' Deena's sister said to her. Linda was an older, more angular version of Deena, with hair a deeper red.

'I need to be by myself for a while.' Deena's tone implied that she had said this to Linda before.

'What's the problem? She's going to stay here,' Deena's father said. Martin couldn't find any resemblance between the gaunt, swarthy man and his daughters. Not in the shape of the head or the features, not in the coloring. But his amiable demeanor must have been the model for theirs.

'She's entitled to some privacy.' He gave the statement an air of finality and followed it with a wan smile at Deena. Martin guessed that this was as declarative as Mr. Harper ever got.

Jon sat next to his mother at one side of the raised hearth with the expression of the forlorn, his left arm and leg pressing against her right arm and leg. *Deena's asked him to leave, too*, Martin thought.

'I've got to go back to the city tonight, but I'll be here all weekend,' Paul said, 'staying with my father. I'll check on you a time or two.'

Deena nodded.

'And Jon's going to come with us, right?' Mrs. Harper, who was standing at the edge of the group, smiled at him. Jon did not react. It wasn't a question, then, but something that had already been decided. This didn't seem to be news to anybody but Paul, whose eyebrows lifted slightly.

Martin took a bite of pie: sugar, eggs, and pecan halves so richly blended that his tongue burned. His mouth flooded with saliva. The food to this point had been like ashes to him. 'Right, angel?' Mrs. Harper seemed to have less rapport with Jon than Barbara did, although she lived closer to him year-round. Deena's mother was magnetic, but Martin guessed she could be strong willed. Jon's nod was simply a bowing of his head. Deena took Jon's hand. The way she laid it on top of Jon's, completely covering his fingers, was a token of her authority. It must have been her idea for Jon to go, and he had acquiesced.

Paul was trying to get Jon's attention. He leaned forward until Jon noticed him. Jon left his mother and crossed to Paul, climbing onto his lap. Paul's embrace was possessive, almost crushing. Overdone.

225

When had they developed this relationship? Martin had missed something. Same old Paul. The man was showing off. This was an inappropriate time to demonstrate how much Jon liked him, while Mrs. Harper was trying to make contact with her grandson. She felt it, too. She watched them briefly, then turned sharply away. Blowing out the candles on the dining room table, she lingered with her back to the group. Finally, she brought one of the chairs over from the table and placed it outside the circle of relatives. When she sat in it, Martin noticed that she had placed it at an angle that blocked her view of Paul.

The pie was missing from Martin's plate. Had he already eaten it? He eyed the meatloaf and potatoes and laid his fork on top of them.

'I want to tell all of you how much it means to Jon and me that you're with us,' Deena said haltingly. 'Whatever we do now, we can't do it without you, without your help.' She was working hard to keep her voice even. When it thinned or cracked, she waited, then went on. Her candor was unusual, he thought. He wouldn't express himself to a group of people in such intimate terms if someone begged him to. 'Because all of us loved Tim, we're bound together forever in a special way. I want you to know that Jon and I appreciate each one of you.' He had listened for the hollow ring of falsehood. The sentences were perfectly constructed, but they hadn't been rehearsed. He was sure of it.

What was he *doing*? This wasn't a courtroom – this was *life*, real *life*. And he was dissecting the woman's speech as though it were testimony. What an insensitive crud he'd become, that he couldn't participate in any gathering without interpreting every nuance, every gesture. He leaned down and put his plate under his chair. He had to get out of here. He didn't deserve to be here.

Barbara had risen and crossed to Deena. She sat with her and they pressed their cheeks together, their eyes shining with tears.

He couldn't get up now, wouldn't. As awkward as it was for him, he had the humanity to remain still and silent. Deena was genuine. He could see it in the defeated curve of her back, in the rosy tinge of her forehead. She was stressed beyond imagining. And coping nobly.

He had started believing in her when they'd sat in the car and he had cried about Jenny. She hadn't answered but jammed her fingers to her lips, visibly withered by his confession.

Firelight on the dozen or so faces of this family evoked the artist in him. He couldn't help it. He had never seen a more arresting collection of expressions. Rapt, they concentrated on Barbara and Deena with an almost ethereal absorption. Communion. That was the word that came to mind.

Paul's expression, at the center of the group, differed. Martin was drawn to it: an unmistakable mixture of adoration and lust, the nostrils flaring, the lips slightly parted as Paul stared at Deena, transfixed.

The intensity of Paul's gaze riveted Martin. Desire. That's what it was. Did she know it?

Deena kissed Barbara and got to her feet, starting around the circle, kissing and speaking to each person. They responded to her with what appeared to be deep affection. Not one shrank, even slightly, from her. She was so utterly likeable.

It was perfect – too perfect, like a stage play, like

something concocted and enacted for the benefit of a jury.

The experience of a thousand days in court battered Martin with a thought: Had Paul and Deena been having an affair before Tim's death? She was obviously stricken by her widowhood, but not incapacitated. He would have expected her to lie in bed a lot and to be unable to eat. She was unconvincing.

God, he was one jaded creature, sick, even to entertain the notion of it. But he had witnessed betrayal too many times not to have his antenna up. He zeroed in on Deena as she paused in front of Paul and bent to kiss him. Paul was hampered by Jon lying in his lap, but he reached up and laid a hand against her hip. An overly familiar touch.

The placement of Paul's hand seemed to speed up Deena's motions. She gave him a light peck on the forehead and tapped him on the shoulder, stepping back, out of reach. An almost imperceptible air of formality possessed her for a second or two. Martin picked it up in the droop of the mouth, the straightening of the neck. It was a distaste, an inner bristling at the trespass of a stranger. He could see her deciding not to kiss Jon. To do so, she would have had to come within Paul's range again. She touched Jon's hair affectionately instead and went on to Gene, kissing his cheek with feeling and murmuring something that Martin did not catch. Paul's disappointment was evident.

Relief swept through Martin. She was innocent. He marveled at her toughness. What kind of upbringing did one have to have to be this composed and dignified under fire?

Tim would like it. Tim would definitely approve.

Deena left Gene and embraced Kemp. And then, she

was in front of Martin, hesitating. She didn't have to do this. He wasn't a close friend of hers, wasn't even a close friend of the Reuschels anymore. He hated to be on display, the others watching, Paul watching. She should give him a handshake. That would be enough.

He didn't move as she brought her face down to his and kissed him warmly on the temple.

14

It didn't seem right, everybody leaving so soon. There was intense grieving ahead. They all should have stayed for the weekend, at least. It was important to be together for as long as possible after a death for the healing. Barbara stood in the dark confusion of the driveway as cars were being readied for departure. She would not see Gail and Kemp in the morning. She would not see Linda and Christopher. Only Deena's parents would be back from their motel to pick up Jon and take him to the airport with them. It wasn't right. It was too fast. But it was Deena's wish.

'Good-bye.' Martin paused in front of her.

'Good-bye.' He was prickly, this sweet man. Had been a prickly boy. She knew better than to offer him more than a handshake. 'Thanks for coming.'

Gail rolled down the car window and beckoned. When Barbara went to her, Gail whispered, 'Are you sure this is okay?'

'It's okay.'

'Do you really want to go home tomorrow, Mom?'

'Dad does,' she whispered. 'The cottage is full of too many memories.'

229

'I don't want to leave.'

Barbara glanced about for Gene and Deena. They were well out of earshot, talking with people in other cars. 'Let's honor Deena's request. Dad and I will be back in a few weeks for the summer. We'll be with you then.'

'I'm glad we're only a few hours' drive from here. Mom, I'll really miss you.'

'I'll miss you, too.'

Deena appeared suddenly, to speak to Gail. Barbara walked toward the house and turned to wait and to wave. In minutes the driveway would be empty.

She was not a fool. She knew why Deena had requested to be alone at the cottage. Deena wanted the freedom to investigate Tim's death. After Gene had chastised her about the photographs, they disappeared and Deena had not spoken another word about them. Barbara had mentally gone over it a hundred times. Deena was no fool either. She had reasons for her suspicion – possibly more reasons than she'd said. Barbara would have been willing to listen. But neither she nor Deena would openly challenge Gene just now.

It seemed unlikely that Tim could have been murdered. The police had found no evidence of any sort. But what wife wouldn't ask questions? What mother wouldn't ask? Gene would, too, if he were thinking straight.

To do a thorough job of inquiry, Deena would need help, the help of someone who knew this area and its people. She couldn't begin to understand Cameron County the way someone like Barbara did. Yet there was no way Barbara could talk with Deena at length without Gene being present or at least overhearing. She wouldn't provoke him like that. He could have a heart attack, a nervous breakdown.

This was not the time to push him on any issue. He was as emotionally brittle as she had ever seen him.

Paul lingered in the shadows. Deena had been busy for minutes, moving from car to car to say a few last words to her relatives. He would be patient until they left and he could receive her full attention. She had devastated him tonight with that gentle, charming speech and her slow trip around the circle to touch each person physically. The anticipation had stolen his breath.

Deena was powerfully attracted to him. He had realized it when he first met her and she chose him for extended conversation at the brunch. Her body had been inviting, her comments flattering. She had gone as far as she dared with her husband sitting there. This afternoon, Paul had known for certain that the yearning had grown in her. When she had seen him carrying Jon back from the dock, her eyes had come alive with appreciation. She had fallen into step beside him as though they had always been together. Tonight, as she approached him in the circle, he had sensed her overwhelming longing and had pressed her hip as a sign that he understood. She had been discreet about it, pulling back, averting her eyes. She was a tempting, maddening blend of sensuality and shyness. And she possessed uncompromising ideas on what was proper.

He would give her time. He would not rush her. They both knew where they were going, but it would be unseemly to take it too fast. The accepted interval for mourning was one year. For now, their commitment to one another would remain their secret.

One by one, the cars backed up the driveway and into the street. Their headlights flashed and bounced. Deena waved until they were all out of sight. He was awed by her determination and insistence that she be alone for the weekend. It couldn't have been easy for her to effect this. She was even sending Jon away. But she had done it in order to make direct, unhampered contact with Paul – so they could find each other.

Deena started in his direction. Now, he would have his chance. The moon had risen but the driveway was dappled with the broadly cast shapes of trees. There was sufficient darkness to conceal their faces, their attraction to one another, even though Barbara and Gene and Jon still stood nearby.

'I'll see you,' he said as Deena approached.

'Yes, of course,' she replied as she brushed past and went up the steps into the kitchen. She had not said it unkindly, but the abruptness surprised him. He stared at the glowing rectangle that was the screen door. She did not reappear.

'You gonna walk home?' Gene patted his arm.

'Yes.' His car was still at McNaughtons' but he'd circle back for it. He felt for the penlight in his pocket.

'Want a lift?'

'No. Thanks anyway. Give me five,' Paul said to Jon. After they had smacked twice, Paul squeezed Jon's chin and Gene shepherded Jon into the house.

Deena had been smart not to stay outside with Paul. Her cleverness amazed him. It was much safer this way.

'You take good care of yourself,' Barbara told him.

'You, too.'

She contemplated him for a few seconds. In the milky light, he could see her searching his face. 'I'll walk up to the road with you,' she said.

* * *

This kid had been like one of her own. How many of her cookies had Paul Kincaid packed away in the first twenty years of his life? They were friends, he and she. He had been a puzzlingly needy child, leaping at the chance to stay overnight with the Reuschels whenever his parents permitted it. He had always appeared to be starving – for affection, for food, for fun. She had tried, and Gene had tried, but they couldn't fill him up. After his mother died, he was worse, eternally somber and eternally present. He had an uncanny knack of showing up at mealtimes and of knowing when they had bought something new, like the Ping-Pong table. They couldn't deny him. It would have crushed his soul. In truth, they liked him and couldn't resist trying to save him. He was a miracle, really, the way he turned out. Pretty okay. Better than okay. Better than most. A good kid, loyal.

They were approaching the road. She had less than a minute left in which to ask Paul for help. Should she? The idea of Deena at the cottage by herself, the idea of Deena pursuing a theory of murder, frightened her. Deena's decision was naive and unwise.

'I'll call you now and then, Mrs. R.' Paul was quickening his pace, widening his distance from her.

'Paul—'

He stopped.

'Will you watch over Deena this weekend? Just . . . keep an eye out?'

'Sure.'

'I'm . . . worried about her. Deena thinks –' *Don't tell him. You'll break her trust.*

'Thinks— ?'

'. . . that . . . someone . . . may have . . . killed Tim.'

233

It sounded ridiculous and was met with silence. 'I don't
. . . really think so. But . . . she does.'

He didn't respond. All she could see of his face as
he moved closer were the eyes, shocked, compassionate. 'Why?'

The photographs passed through her memory, the formidable blotch or silhouette at their center. She had
alienated Deena by looking at them without permission.
And Gene had made Deena angry by discounting them.
Deena had been gone for several hours twice after that
but had revealed nothing of where she had been. Barbara
and Gene were plainly shut out of Deena's thoughts and
efforts. They had let her down and they were paying for it.
Keep her secrets. 'I don't know. She won't tell anyone.'

He believed her. She could see it in his eyes. 'I'll
watch,' he said.

15

The train station at Maddox glistened in the darkness as
Paul approached. It was his favorite in the entire New
York system, and he had seen them all. Wooden, graced
with gingerbread and gables, it had weathered and faded
in this location for seventy-some years. The arch-necked
lamps with their gently slanted shades cast puddles of
misty light through the parking lot. Heartened, he left
the Nissan between two of the puddles and went into the
waiting room. A one-way ticket to Grand Central was still
thirty-two dollars. Luckily, he had the cash. He did not
need to ask the schedule. Trains were his specialty. The
young man behind the window barely spoke to him. Paul

kept his voice soft, his words to a minimum as he made his purchase, and went immediately to a wooden bench out of sight of the ticket window to wait.

Old train stations smelled as though their floors had never been washed, only swept with a broom daily for decades. Dust seemed to hang permanently in midair, powdery soil blown in from nearby farmland. It stuck in corners and mingled with the pungent odor of aging metal.

The ambiance of Maddox Station filled him with peace. He had dreamed of this freedom, the absolute minute-by-minute freedom to come and go, to ride or not to ride, as he chose. As a child he had sprawled, spellbound, across his bed, the train schedule in his hands, memorizing the names of the stations, the hour and minute of each stop. He had kept abreast of every schedule change in preparation for the moment of his escape from his father, the brilliant irreversible leap into the cosmos. It was laughable now, he supposed. He'd never dared to do it.

The rumble of the approaching train spurred Paul from the bench. He went out onto the platform, letting the train's thunder overtake him. The train slid into the station squealing and stood hissing at him. He boarded and took a seat by the window, overlooking the station and the parking lot. The Nissan was hidden in a fold of shadows, but he knew it would be all right where it was for twenty-four hours. His possessions were cloaked in a special way that protected them. He did not know exactly how that worked.

For an instant, he felt uncertain about his plan. Had he thought this out properly? He'd had to scramble to come up with something. Barbara had ambushed him in her typical unassuming style: *Deena thinks someone may have killed Tim*. Said with no more passion than a restaurant order. He had been momentarily struck mute. She didn't seem to notice. That was Barbara. She couldn't read him. He had sat in the car for twenty minutes before he could gather enough wit even to leave McNaughtons' driveway. Deena hadn't given him the slightest inkling of her doubts. Did that mean she suspected him? Or was she being generally cautious? *She won't tell anyone.*

If she was leading him on simply to trick him . . .

The train started with a lurch. The lurching was a flaw in American trains. In Europe, the trains glided slowly into motion. Maddox Station passed by the window and the sprinkling of lights beyond the station faded. His own reflection came up suddenly in the glass: startled eyes, rumpled hair.

Peace. He was still in charge. Deena would be transparent to him, now that he knew her fears. He had acted prudently, leaving the Nissan in Maddox. He might need the Bronco to take care of her this weekend. He'd have to bring it, be ready. That truck was a jungle cat, prowling through the brush, quick, quiet. He couldn't have done all he'd done without the truck. Call it superstition, but he needed the Bronco when he had the slightest doubt. The damned thing was strangely invisible. As far as he knew, it had never been reported in association with a crime. And that was flat-out unbelievable. He'd gone everywhere in it.

He would drive the truck to Maddox tomorrow, leave it in place of the Nissan at the station. The Bronco would be within range, then, in case he had to use it. The image of Deena struggling in his grasp injured him. He put his fist to his chest and held it there until the sadness eased.

She had so much promise as a source of joy, *his* source of joy. But he was cursed. The women he adored to the depths of his soul always gave him irrefutable evidence of their treason.

And Jon . . . hanging onto Paul's shoulder so sweetly, letting Paul cradle him. He would lose Jon, too.

A fragrance of flowers wafted through the train car. The dense, pure scent of hyacinth. He glanced around, shaken, confused. The other seats were empty.

16

Deena huddled with Jon under the covers, she still dressed, he in his pajamas. They sat cross-legged on the bed, facing each other inside a dome of sheets and blankets. In the glare of the flashlight, he looked ill to her, thin, pale, with black slashes beneath his eyes. The last time they'd held an 'igloo' meeting, Tim had been present. Jon had thought up the igloo idea as a way to shut out the world and have his parents' undivided attention for important matters. They had done it six or eight times, she guessed. Under his rules, Jon was the only person who could request a retreat to the igloo and the only one who could end the meeting.

The interior was beginning to get stuffy. Their time so far had been spent weeping for Tim, but they had run out of tears. A couple of times she had thought Jon was going to tell her something, but he did not. Deena raised a corner of the sheet to let in cold air from the darkened bedroom. She cupped a hand around Jon's bare foot and rubbed it.

'I miss my daddy,' he said.

'I do, too.'

'And—' He began to cry hoarsely.

Here it comes, she thought. *He's going to let it out.* 'Can you tell me?' she whispered.

'No.' He sagged forward, against her, and she put her arms around him.

'Is it a secret?'

'You'll think I'm not brave.'

'I think you're *very* brave. Amazingly brave. But you don't have to be for me to like you. Sometimes I don't feel brave either.'

He wiped his nose on his sleeve. 'I don't want to go away. With Grandma. I want to stay with you.'

'That's it?'

'Yes.'

She had lost. Her pursuit of Tim's murderer was over. With Jon at her side, she would have no mobility, no anonymity. She could not set him in harm's way, would not. No, if she kept Jon with her, she would have to give up the search. But how could she deny his plea? Nothing was more important to her than Jon. He had been damaged enough. 'You can stay.'

'Really?'

'Yes.'

He straightened up hopefully. 'Mommy, are you trying to catch the man? Is that why you want me to go away?'

He was so perceptive. And she was done hiding from him. 'Yes.'

'Why can't the police catch him?'

'They might be able to, but I want to help. I'm in

a hurry. I don't want him to escape. The more time goes by, the more chance there is that we won't catch him.'

Jon's eyes widened. 'He hurt Daddy.'

'Yes.'

'You're sure.'

'Someone did. I'm sure.'

'How do you *know*?'

A vision of Mimi made her hesitate. Mimi, helpless and frail, and Arlene. They were so vulnerable. She couldn't tell Jon about them. He might let it slip out.

'I just *know*. Don't ask me. Please.'

They were both perspiring. Jon turned off the light and drew back the covers. They lay back on the cool pillows. 'The meeting isn't over,' he said.

She laughed softly. 'Okay.'

He laughed, too, and coughed. 'Pretend we're still in the igloo.'

'Okay.'

'Do you know who hurt Daddy?'

'No.'

'Do you think *he* knew who it was?'

Did he? *Most victims know their attackers.* 'I . . . maybe.'

The way Paul Kincaid had touched her jumped into her mind. She could still feel his thumb and fingers on her right hip. He had pinched her flesh, a caress of sorts. A violation. Strange. It had made her angry, embarrassed. He had taken advantage of her at an emotionally precarious moment. The fact that he had done it publicly was even more abusive. He had realized that she would not rebuke him in that setting.

She had been over this. Several times. She couldn't release it, had hardly been able to say goodnight to Paul. Was she misinterpreting his intent? He might have made a mistake, had a lapse in judgment. He may have meant nothing by it. She needed to be careful with her accusations. He had been a friend of the Reuschels long before she had.

Jon nestled against her. 'Mommy . . . do you really think you can catch the man?'

That thing about Paul was nonsense. She needed to forget about it, forgive. He was not nefarious. Not in the least.

'*Do* you?'

'I can do anything I decide to do. Can't you?' She poked him playfully.

'I want you to catch him. I'll go home with Grandma.'

'Jon . . .'

'I will if you promise not to let the man hurt *you*.'

She was so tired that the back of her head seemed to be weighted. The feather pillow began to envelop her. She had told Gene and Barbara she'd be back to sit with them for a while. But she was drifting. She tightened her grip on Jon, an anchor as she floated.

'I'll go with Grandma if you promise me.'

She could barely hear him.

'Do you promise?'

She was standing in front of the empty coffin, in the rain, the yellow roses bobbing.

'Mommy?'

The words were slurred and heavy as she pushed them out.

'Okay, babe . . . yes.'

17

Myra aimed the remote control at the newscaster and pressed the red button with her thumb, knocking him backward. A sea of charcoal gray swallowed him. He deserved that and worse. The man had no sense, no sense at all, going on and on with such terrible news every night, every night, every night. Didn't have the sense he was born with. Less. A convict who caught fire in the electric chair, can you imagine, a baby eaten by a dog. Who needs to know? She got up stiffly and headed for the back hallway, running her hand along the wall for support. Daniel didn't want a TV in his room. He was smart, Daniel. Nothing but bad news on TV, you don't need that when you're sick, don't need it anytime, makes you sick, that's been proved.

He was still awake, twitching under the covers. Hardly ever slept anymore, couldn't sleep. How tired could he get lying in bed all the time? Wanted the ceiling light on day and night, like a sun, his own private sun. She never turned it off. They should have moved to Florida while there was still time, he could have had sun. Hindsight is always twenty-twenty. This was no place to die, the city, traffic in your ears, the room too small, the buildings blocking the sun. She couldn't move him now, didn't have the strength or money, he didn't want to be moved anyhow.

'How you doing, Daniel?' Same sentence all the time but she couldn't think of a new one, nothing much ever happened to her and she wouldn't tell him the sorry state of the world, not on a bet. He didn't want her to read from

241

books, didn't want to hear music, he was existing in total emptiness, his choice, not the illness but the emptiness, his choice after all, what could she do? He was sinking every day, what could she do?

'All right.' He spoke in gasps but he wasn't one to complain, Daniel, never was, fell from a beam once on the job, smashed his spine, never said a word, healed good as new. That was Daniel, good as new. Not this Daniel though, the younger one she had married in a blue velveteen dress.

Loud rapping startled her. The door. The front door. The rapping echoed inside her chest. She steadied herself and went through the hall, cautiously bringing the living room into view. A demanding knock, thumping, persistent. Rude. She could picture the door being suddenly lowered toward her like a bridge over a moat and hoodlums stomping in, punching her, throwing her down. No one but barbarians would knock this late.

She could call the police. The police, that lazy bunch, coming around in their own good time. She had tried once. It had taken them twenty-four minutes, nearly half an hour, she could have bled to death by then with her throat cut. She complained and they laughed, one said *buy a gun* and the other one said *be sure to drag him in after you shoot him or we'll have to charge you with homicide*.

The knocking stopped. It could have been someone banging for help, somebody could be on the floor out there, unconscious by now. She got the footstool and put it under the peephole. As she stepped up on it, she had an idea. Why didn't she think of it before? She could lay a nice handkerchief over the stool to protect the needlepoint cover from her shoes, a ladies' handkerchief, lacy, embroidered. She'd tack it on with white thread and take it off now and then to wash it.

Hair. That's all she could see through the peephole, the top of somebody's head. Hiding his face, maybe. A trick. Well, she wasn't stupid. She could wait. Skin, eyebrows, a nose. *Mr. Trayne.* Mr. Trayne again. Wanting to borrow something else, she supposed, coming around late, like she didn't know day from night, like she wasn't interested in sleeping. He was holding something up in front of his face, as if she could see it, which she couldn't, it was too close.

The keys. He was holding the keys. He'd brought back her car. Was this the funeral day? Was it last night he was here? The keys . . . Didn't make her come hunting for them this time, can you believe.

She pushed and rotated the latches and locks – a nuisance, a *nuisance*, some going some way, some the other, a test to get them right, manual dexterity, well she still had it, just took her a minute. His fuzzy face was smack in the door when she opened it. Glad she left the one chain on, like always. He resembled an animal wanting out of a cage. You never know.

'Did you fill it with gas?'

'Uh.'

Not uh-*huh*, just *uh*. He *forgot,* forgot *again.* 'Did you, Mr. Trayne?'

'Uh, no.'

She'd had zillions of boys like this in her third grade, she wished she had a nickel for every one, the boys, not so much the girls, the girls were eager to please, but the boys, *I forgot*, forgot their homework, forgot their books, forgot their lunch, forgot their milk money, forgot, forgot. She never could teach them to remember, she was too easy, the other teachers told her, *too easy*, and now they were all out there, her boys, letting people down in little ways, like this. 'You forgot.'

'Yes.' He had the decency to look contrite. Possibly ready to do penance. She thought of Daniel. He was still awake.

'Well . . . come on in . . . anyway.'

'Uh, not right now.'

'Why not?' He'd made a deal, a bargain, the car for a visit, now he was backing out, now that he had what he wanted, just like Daniel's boy Seth, forever sidestepping responsibility, even courtesy, if you can imagine, even common courtesy.

Mr. Trayne was reaching through the gap, trying to hand her the keys. He had hairy fingers. She backed up a touch and gave him a *look*. 'I'm done in, Mrs. Swenk. Thanks for the car. Truly. Thanks.' He dangled the keys in front of her, peering around the edge of the door. She gave the keys a *look*. She was not going to be easy on Mr. Trayne. If he had never learned anything, he could start now. 'You made a promise,' she said sternly.

'I know. I'll be back.'

'When?'

'Uh . . .'

'When, Mr. Trayne?'

'I don't know.'

'That's not good enough.'

The hairy fingers moved toward the peg board. Before she could say or do anything, he had hung them there, on the proper peg. The hand and face withdrew from the gap.

'I'm disappointed in you, Mr. Trayne.' She moved closer. He was gone.

She slammed the door shut and tussled with the chain, releasing it from its slot, and stuck her head out into the corridor. She could see him at the end of it, walking away at a steady pace. Anger rattled through her. 'Next time, *rent a car!*' she yelled. Mr. Trayne did not turn around.

Her chin began to burn, and her cheeks. She had *shouted*. In her own building. In the middle of the night.

Well, he deserved it, that man.

18

The doorman had packages for him, half a dozen – brown, with black-crayon UPS numbers handwritten on them. Most were padded bags, stapled or folded over and taped. One was a small box. Paul gathered them up and rode the elevator with them pressed against his chest. The varied shapes and textures comforted him, the softness, hardness, the clean perfection of the corners and edges, the computer printing of his full name on the labels, *Paul Michael Kincaid, Paul Michael Kincaid*. Their exteriors bore the trace scent of warehouses laden with newly manufactured goods: handknit sweaters, rain boots, twill trousers, top-quality canvas luggage, silk ties. He could not guess by smell what their interiors contained, because the products were invariably sealed in plastic.

Timers had turned his lamps on for him. He tapped the door shut with his heel, dumping the packages on the dining room table. They slid haphazardly to a halt, canted, upside down, right side up. Christmas bounty. An indulgence, this continual ordering from first-rate catalogs. A vice. But it satisfied his soul. He enjoyed slitting the tape on the boxes with a knife, ripping the zip strips from the bags to spill their contents. Invariably, some of the bits of paper that comprised the padding popped out like confetti. It had the feel of celebration, this ritual. It endorsed him, and he needed reassurance, tonight especially. Deena Reuschel was not sincere. The specter of her betrayal had chased him through the night, along the noisy tracks, in and out of tunnels, up the dreary hole into Grand Central, across Manhattan streets. He had run for blocks, arriving at his building breathless and lonely.

He fingered the dimmer switch until the chandelier bathed the table in brightness. Under the hinged lid of the only box, he discovered a cast-stone Egyptian blue cat from the Metropolitan Museum. The largest of the bags contained a cotton chamois shirt in heather gray from Eddie Bauer's. He undid the wrappings slowly, appreciating each purchase, checking style and size, laying the gifts he had bought for himself in a row: Pittard leather gloves, an analog-digital sport watch, Merino crew socks, a Japanese lacquer address book. Then, he placed the packing carefully in the kitchen wastebasket. A sprinkling of paper dust remained on the polished mahogany. He wiped it up gingerly with a damp flannel cloth and shook the cloth over the sink.

It surprised him to realize that he was still wearing his

overcoat. He slipped it off and hung it neatly away in the front closet, uneasy, trying to determine what to do next, trying not to think about Deena. The pile of merchandise on the table perplexed him. Its magic had evaporated. The rich fibers and surfaces had dulled. He didn't need most of this, and he was out of storage space. Lately, he had been repackaging some of his orders and sending them back.

He would put them aside until tomorrow, get on with the evening's workout. The weights would bring back his energy.

He stacked the items and carried them to his bedroom, pausing as he contemplated it. He knew beyond doubt that the drawers and closet were full. But it was not his habit to leave things lying around. Stray belongings disturbed his sense of balance and purpose.

He walked to the guest room. Apprehension shot through him. He did not like this room, did not like it at all. He seldom entered it, could not remember the last time he had done so. He laid the bundle he was carrying on the bed and went to the dresser. Forcing the over-full drawers open, one by one, he squinted at their contents: men's shirts, sweaters, accessories, underwear, stationery, objets d'art, obviously in their original wrappings, some bearing price tags. He did not recognize any of them. Not a single one. Had he ordered these? When?

It was more than bizarre, it was clearly unnatural that he could not recall. He was reaching some kind of watershed moment in his life, right now, right here, and could not figure out what it meant.

The closet door was tightly closed. He stared at it,

trying to imagine what he might have stashed inside. His only vision was of a sheer drop beyond the door, the concrete walls blown away, the stars beckoning him into oblivion.

19

An envelope hand-addressed by Jenny's mother appeared in Martin's mailbox each year, exactly one week before his birthday. He could always spot it through the slits because it was invariably pink or lavender. He didn't get much colored mail. Didn't get much mail, period. Utility bills and bank statements, that was about it. His parents and sister, when they did communicate, which was seldom, preferred the telephone. He didn't own a credit card, didn't subscribe to magazines, so he wasn't on junk lists. He looked upon the absence of letters and phone calls – especially personal ones – as restful. Attention from others brought with it a pressure to reciprocate or at least reply. No one at the office knew his birth date. He did not want to preside, flustered, over the ritual luncheon at a fancy French restaurant. He did not want co-workers depositing potted plants on his desk.

Lying on the couch, Martin fingered this year's offering from Patricia Cunningham: a wax-sealed lavender envelope. It had no distinctive scent – neither perfume nor smoke. Patty was a conscientious nonpolluter, environmentally friendly. The enclosed card would be printed on recycled paper and labeled on the back with the name of a wildlife or children's fund. The illustration would be sentimental in style. Correction, *effusive*. So would the message. Patty Cunningham refused to give up on him. She came around every few months, unannounced, and insisted he take a walk with her. She liked bench sitting in Central Park and lingering in a good piano bar. She liked Village antique shops.

He tore the flap and extracted the card. A teddy bear in a high-chair in front of a huge pink bow. The printed message read: With a Heart Full of Love. She had drawn several sets of puckered lips and jotted, *Happy Birthday, Martin. You're the best. Hugs and kisses, Patty.*

The objective eye viewing this card would wonder if she had a case on him. It was overboard. Juvenile. But she was the only one who seemed to understand where he had gone, the moonscape of his emotion, the only one who continued unabashedly to push affection on him. He had tried repeatedly to shake her off, but she hung on.

He didn't answer her cards or calls. As a policy. Someday she'd stop. It would be a relief. He had sympathy for Jenny's father who'd suffered under Patty's merciless optimism after Jenny's death and who'd finally withdrawn to a separate residence, complete with divorce. Patty was unrelentingly energetic, not as a reaction to her loss but because she believed that – no matter what happened to you – life was worth the trip.

Martin took aim at the wastebasket. The card fluttered toward it but smacked the wall, dropping to the floor like a stunned bird.

The building had grown quiet around him. The street sent up faint *whishes* now and then, fanning through the window glass. He blocked his thoughts and began to skate on the surface of sleep, determined not to go under, merely doze. Dripping water occasionally tapped the pan beneath the refrigerator. He could imagine the imperceptible flaking of dust from the curtains, from the layered wallpaper, from his books and clothing, even his skin. A tranquil snow. There was respite in neglect, in the untidy heaps of dishes, the matted carpet, the aging upholstery and blankets, the drying newsprint articles stuck with brittle tape to his shelves.

When he felt the pull of his lungs, he startled himself awake. The air was a solid, being forced down his throat. He sat up, his pulse quickening. He had been all right for a few minutes, he had been able to let go. What drew him back?

He did this to himself. Every time.

Disappointed and breathing heavily, he went to his desk. The women were waiting for him, their fresh gazes laced with hope. As long as he kept their pictures he would be bound. Obligated.

He lifted Jenny's clipping and stripped it from the shelf, then gently worked at the others. They came away easily into his hand. He stacked them on his blotter, an uneven stack, the paper squares and rectangles curved and rippling from seasons of humidity and furnace heat. Only Carmela's was still supple, and Tim's, as Martin added it to the pile as an afterthought.

He owed them nothing, needed to release them from his keeping, needed to be released by them into his own future. He carried the articles to the wastebasket and placed them in it. Retrieving Patty's card, he laid it on the stack.

20

Paul sat motionless in the guest room chair, staring, unblinking. It was important to try and comprehend what he had done, what had been done to him, what he had yet to do.

He had been flawed from birth, deserving of others' ridicule and deceit. All he desired had eluded him. He had been ignored, subtly taunted, shamed. Even his own mind displayed contempt for him, hid from and tricked him. He would never be chosen.

It was almost finished, the bitter yearning and the long illness of regret. Only one person could redeem him. He would go to her now, before it was light.

Friday

1

The room came at Deena suddenly, as if hurled in the path of her sleep. The impact made her groan. Strange shapes bulged and receded in the darkness. She lay still and tried to remember where she was.

Her hair and scalp, pillow and nightgown, were soaked, hot. She must have been having a dream, one of those feverish dreams. She would be all right in a minute. She would get up and change into her robe.

She reached for Tim, finding Jon.

Where was Tim?

There had been no nightmare. Reality was the nightmare.

The dampness beneath her cooled instantly to ice. Jon did not stir from his sleep as she got up and stripped the wet gown from her body in the shadows, pulling her robe around her and fastening the tie. Under the covers again, she turned the pillow over, tried to stop trembling. She had prided herself on not being one to flinch from circumstance. She had always done what was necessary, reflexively, fearlessly. She had rappeled off mountains, taken her sailboat through the slamming din of storms. She could do this, too, accept her widowhood. The sooner she made up her mind to do it, the sooner she would temper her suffering. She couldn't come awake like this many more times, shocked and terrified. She couldn't stand it. Wouldn't.

She would take charge – of herself, of Jon, of the certainty that Tim had been murdered. She would make the decision to outwit Tim's killer and, through deciding, bring it to pass.

Her feet began to grow warm and then her knees. She rolled onto her side. Her breathing eased. She lay in the cocoon of the blankets, alert, listening, trying to understand what else it was that drummed at her.

The night people were about, on benches, in doorways. Not one made a sound as Paul approached. They did not shift at his back either, but seemed to fall harmlessly away.

No one challenged his intended space; the murky sidewalks ahead of him were empty, block after block, the traffic sparse and silent beside him. As he entered the formidable neighborhoods surrounding the parking garage, all motion stopped. No car, no cat broke the stillness. The buildings were black, music and conversation so distant that they seemed to be traveling to him from another universe. He knew then that he had been summoned. For reasons beyond his comprehension, he had been granted grace again and would be led. He would find the most favourable site for whatever his purpose, and whatever he desired to accomplish would be given to him outright. He had only to follow his will.

He strode up the ramp and the steps, out onto the glacier of cement. The truck was as he had left it. It started on the first try.

The gate would open smoothly. The moonlit highway

would wind before him like an oiled track, and he would arrive without incident in a preappointed spot. All would go well for him. Once summoned, he was invincible.

At Maddox, he positioned the Bronco perfectly parallel and nose by nose with the Nissan and waited as the truck cooled, clicking. His were the only vehicles in the lot. The closed train station was a blank brown rectangle against a shell of luminous clouds. He rolled down his window, letting in the steady rhythm of crickets.

Was this right? Had he been directed to retrieve the car?

Minutes went by. A fine rain began, moistening Paul's collar and shoulder and sprinkling the windshield with pinpoint stars. At last, sanction touched him. He locked up the Bronco and unlocked the Nissan.

Because he did not dare to use his flashlight, Paul fell twice in the woods between McNaughtons' driveway and Reuschels' cottage. The spongy leaf blanket underfoot gave way to indentations in the earth, trapping one foot then the other and bringing him to his knees. Each time he went down, there was a corresponding thudding of creatures in the underbrush. Circles of dampness bled through the legs of his jeans. Feeling his way, he was mysteriously led back and forth between trees to a patch of high ground overlooking the stairs to Tim's room. There, the trail stopped abruptly in a nest of vines. The energy left him and he sat on his heels.

Beyond the wall of Tim's room, Deena and Jon swam toward each other in sleep, their shoes set out neatly on the floor at each side of the bed. He could see their features clearly, could see the layered surroundings: curtain and shade, blanket and sheet, the profusion of pastel flowers on fabric, cascading petals, pink and amber and blue. He lay between Deena and Jon, drinking the scent of their bodies, languishing in his own ventured pride. The vision kept him warm as the moon set.

Frost inched down through the trees. Blinded by darkness, Paul zipped his jacket and raised his collar, suddenly unsure what had brought him here at this hour. It was too early to approach Deena. Her people were still around her, would be until nearly noon. Why had he been sent? Always before when he had been propelled to a specific location, his prey had been drawn to it also. But, in this case, he had chosen no prey.

The strangeness was more than puzzling. It almost suggested that a victim had been selected without his knowledge. The thought awed him. He paced the hillside in small circles, continually halted by unseen boundaries. The exercise clarified his situation: He had been told to wait. He would wait.

Above him, birds gave the first isolated cries of morning. A thin crimson line began to travel along the horizon. Details of the cottage came into soft focus. He reassessed his position, deciding that he was adequately shielded from view in all directions by high bushes and dense timber. Someone would have to invade his territory to discover him. He pulled a candy bar from his pocket and ate it slowly. Heat spread through his stomach, filling his chest as though he had swallowed whiskey.

Deena watched the room turn gray, the furniture emerge like rocks in barren landscape. She had been awake most of the night, unable to sleep, unwilling to go downstairs and possibly encounter Gene or Barbara. She did not want to talk. Saving words somehow conserved her strength.

She left the room cautiously, in order not to wake Jon, and went into the bathroom. Rituals such as bathing and dressing seemed tiresome and endless now. She did them because she had to. She marveled at the bland passage of time in the realm of grief, day blending into night, night blending into day into night. Anticipation was absent, as well as eagerness and pleasure. When was the last time she had awakened in satisfaction and hope? Sunday. Sunday in Manhattan: the peach hues of the hotel room, the view of sunrise, the gentle teasing and the love, Tim beneath her, solid, immortal.

The tub was slick. With a hand against the wall, she stood in the shower for minutes, trying to loosen muscles and joints, trying to build a store of power, no matter how small. She would need extraordinary stamina in the next few days. Just letting go of Jon this morning would be a wrench and potentially damaging to him. Was she self-centered to do it? Was she deluded in believing she could single-handedly affect the outcome of this situation?

She thought with discomfort of a French clairvoyant whose evening lecture she had attended once. He had answered, in detail and without hesitation, questions from the audience about the past, present, and future, explaining that each of their lives was like a prerecorded tape to him. He had only to rack it back and forth to view the portion they wanted to examine. Further, he could do nothing to change what was on the tape. Each human life was cast in concrete, he said. He had tried his best to change outcomes and, failing repeatedly, had given up and accepted inevitability. The concept had so rankled her that she had left in the middle of his talk. Friends told her later that he had been amazingly accurate in his insight and his predictions about them. Their endorsements disturbed her, and she had actively erased him from her memory.

It disturbed her even now to think of him, his white hair and beard, the resigned severity of his expression, his barked, adamant pronouncements from the stage. *What was the point, then*, she would have asked him if she had been willing to hear the answer, *of attempting anything? Was human existence some sort of cosmic joke?*

No, she could never accept it, ever, the idea that fate was hurtling through the universe toward you like a meteor and you could do nothing to dodge it or avert it. No path was predetermined. You made your own way.

She washed quickly and cut off the water, expecting to be chilled as she retrieved a towel from the rack and rubbed her hair with it. But heat rose steadily from the floor register. Her in-laws must be awake. They had turned up the furnace.

There was comfort in it, that single act. She felt their presence as companions.

She put on her robe and scrubbed her teeth, taking a little time with makeup and the hair dryer. It had been days since she had tended herself in a caring way. The leisurely shaping of curls with the brush was a statement of deliberately renewed interest in her own well-being. No matter what had been done to her, something at her core wanted to thrive. She would try to be kind to herself.

2

Martin leaned toward the bathroom mirror with the razor poised. Shiny skin and innocent eyes accosted him. He'd done a pretty fair job of shaving off the beard and mustache. But without his mask, he felt naked, vulnerable. Everybody who wanted to could read his mind now. It was hanging right out on his face.

He checked the sideburns. Nice and even. But he needed to snip stray hairs from his nose and eyebrows to make a neat job of it. They'd all fall over themselves at the paper when he walked in. Faint. Laugh? Whatever. Well, fine. He was making changes. This was the first.

No, this was the second. Throwing away the clippings had been the first. He knew he was onto something when he woke up sane this morning. His sleep had been dreamless. The doggoned breathing thing hadn't jumped him.

Working at the nose hairs with the scissors made him sneeze. He sniffed as he combed his eyebrows and hacked at them, then contemplated the nest of hair in the sink. Giving the mirror his profile, he assessed his ponytail. Didn't go with the bald face. He'd have to cut it, too.

But not now. He was bordering on late. He'd have to go to work half-baked, as usual. Maybe he could get it cut in his lunch hour.

He rooted around in the kitchen for a paper bag and, finding one, policed the bathroom sink, wiping the hair up with toilet paper and dropping soggy hunks into the sack. He carried the bag to the wastebasket near his computer desk and stared down at Patty Cunningham's card.

She goes. He stuck it in the bag. Tim stared at him from the bottom of the well. Martin averted his eyes and scooped up the clippings, smashing them together into the sack and crushing the top of it to seal it.

Had to be done. They were making him crazy. He didn't want to be crazy anymore, didn't want to be responsible, *wasn't* responsible, for anyone but himself.

Wetness began to leak through the brown paper. He held the sack helplessly as it turned limp and damp. It was dripping by the time he burst from his apartment into the corridor and hurried toward the incinerator chute in the back stairwell. For a moment he was afraid he would not be able to let go of it. It stuck to his fingers and then to the drawer before it rolled out of sight.

3

Arlene smiled as she swished the cloth in the basin and rinsed Mimi's arms. Her mother-in-law was much better this morning. She had been hungry and had eaten well. 'You like having this change of scenery, don't you?' Arlene asked her with real happiness. 'It's lovely out there.' Mimi did not have to answer. To Arlene, Mimi's body seemed slightly more supple and strong; her attention was directed at the window. 'We'll move you back to your own room in a few months if you want to go. Or maybe we'll let you have Tony's room next so you can look out on the road for a while. I wish I'd thought of it before – giving you a new view. Why didn't I?' She laid the cloth in the basin and patted Mimi's arms dry with the towel.

How hard they had all worked last night to switch

Heather's furniture and clothes into Mimi's room and move Mimi in. It had seemed an impossible project at first, but it had only taken two hours with Nick and Tony and Heather all helping. Nick had protested privately to Arlene when she first suggested it. He thought Mimi didn't realize or care where she was. He was wrong. Arlene knew Nick's mother better than he did. Mimi cared. And the move had made a difference. Mimi no longer had to stare at the place where Mr. Reuschel had died. She was on the other side of the house now, facing deep woods. The squirrels and birds would keep good company with her.

Arlene changed Mimi into a fresh gown and stood beside the bed, massaging Mimi's scalp gently. Then she began to comb Mimi's hair, inch by inch, from the bottom up, slowly releasing knots and tangles. She should cut Mimi's hair, she supposed, but she was superstitious about it. A trim might sap Mimi's remaining vitality. It was Biblical, this concept, and Arlene half-believed it.

She and Mimi were bound together more tightly than ever since Mrs. Reuschel came to the house. Arlene still hadn't told the children or Nick about the incident. As devoted as he was to her, she couldn't predict his reaction. The last thing she wanted was police on their doorstep again and for word to get around that someone in the Trakas household had been witness to the crime. She and Mimi stayed by themselves too much for that to be a comfortable scenario. No, it was better hidden and left alone.

'There.' She laid the comb aside. Mimi seemed to be relaxed. This might be the time to ask her about the truck she had seen in the field. It would only take minutes.

Arlene had cut pictures of various trucks from magazines and had them ready. She would show Mimi crayons, one at a time, to get the color.

4

'Something's sticking out,' Barbara said. Deena let the lid of the suitcase pop up again and Barbara pushed the sleeve of a sweater away from one of the latches. 'Now try.' She and Deena leaned on the case, easing it closed. Barbara locked it and they moved it from the bed to the floor.

As she straightened up, Barbara assessed Deena's appearance. Deena's complexion had continued to grow pasty since Tim's death. Blue veins stood out prominently in her neck. Her elbows and shoulder blades were sharper than ever. Had Deena eaten yesterday? If she had, Barbara missed it. 'You take care of yourself,' she whispered.

'Of course.' The musical inflection so much a part of Deena's personality had disappeared. She spoke in flat tones.

'When will we see you again?' Deena would make sure Jon stayed in touch, Barbara was certain of that. But she was afraid Deena would drift away. She cared for Deena, as a daughter, as a friend. A change in their personal relationship would hurt. Had it already begun to change?

'I don't know.'

Deena had become more and more evasive with her since the incident with the photos. Barbara had handled that badly.

Gene and Jon came for the luggage, Gene taking the large case, Jon struggling to lift her weekender. She saw

264

Gene squelch the impulse to take the weekender away from Jon and carry it himself. Jon figured out a way to lift it and followed Gene out.

If she wanted a private word with Deena, this was the time. The kitchen screen door banged shut. Barbara stepped around the bed to make sure that Gene was not in the house. She could hear him talking to Jon, at a distance. Deena watched her in surprise.

Honesty was the only thing that could bring them back together. Barbara had to give up pretense. 'I believe you,' she said to Deena. 'About the photographs. About your suspicions. I'm sorry that I didn't take your side with Gene. I was afraid to upset him any further.'

An intensity filled Deena's expression. She nodded.

'I'm worried about you staying here, dealing with this. I want to help you. But I have to go with him.'

'It's all right.'

The metallic *crunch* of the car's trunk lid being slammed echoed in the house. There were only seconds left to reach a resolution. 'Tell me what I can do.'

'Just . . . *think* for me,' Deena said urgently. 'Be my brains. I'll call you.'

'Yes.' They were directly in touch now, as they used to be.

'And don't tell anybody what I'm doing.'

A thought of Paul pricked Barbara. She had told him. Because he was family. Like family.

It was dishonest not to admit to Deena what she had done. But she might alienate her again. Perhaps she could smooth the way for Deena to trust Paul. Then it could work out. 'I asked Paul to check with you this weekend. Maybe he would be a source of information somehow.

He has a lot of empathy. His mother drowned when he was a child.'

Deena's eyes narrowed. 'She *drowned?*'

'Yes. When he was twelve.'

'Don't you think that's unusual?'

'Why?'

'Three drowning deaths among neighbors? Where did she drown?'

Sarah Kincaid, thin and shy, came to mind, Sarah stooping to dig in the flower beds. 'On their property.'

'In the lake?'

'No. There's a pond.'

'Barbara?' Gene, calling.

'Coming!'

'Was it accidental?' Deena whispered.

'Yes.'

'With no witnesses?'

'Yes.' Could there be a connection among the three incidents? They had happened years apart and under differing circumstances. Should she have seen a link?

'Hey.' Gene was between them. 'We'll miss our plane, Barb.' He slipped an arm around Deena. 'Can't talk you out of this?'

Deena was looking at Barbara.

'It's not too late to come home with us – you and Jon. I'll spring for the plane tickets,' Gene said. Barbara ached for him, the groping desperation in his voice.

Deena shook her head.

There she was. Paul jerked to attention. Deena emerged from the carport walking beside Gene and Barbara's car, which was slowly backing up. She was sending them off as she'd promised. Cautious delight rose in him. He squinted at her form: lean, brilliant. Dew moved with her, behind her, a dazzling backdrop for the vivid sienna of her hair. As the car gathered speed, Jon ran next to it, waving. Paul drew back. As the car went out of sight, she called to Jon and, when he came to her, pulled him gently to her hip.

She would send Jon away this morning, too, wait alone for Paul's arrival. They could declare themselves then, in the veiled tentative ways of early lovers.

She was gone. Vanished. They must be in the house, but he could not see their silhouettes behind the silver panes of glass. His feet tingled from standing still for so long. He did a few knee bends, the leaves sighing beneath his boots.

He had always wanted Deena Reuschel. He knew that now. He had not consciously acknowledged it during the years of the Christmas letters and family portraits from Tim, but she had indelibly imprinted his brain: every pose, every dress, every sentence about her had stayed with him. This year he would replace Tim in the photographs and sign his own name.

Unless . . . Astonished, he stood listening to the farthest edge of his mind.

Unless she was the prey.

5

Martin's bare face tingled and itched. He'd forgotten how wind could slice it raw. He'd been running in the dry cold streets since he left the subway. Pointing to his ID tag, he galloped past the ground-floor guard and around the reception desk to the escalator. He had perfected the art of taking the steps rapidly, two at a time, then slowing as he reached the top in order not to attract attention to his arrival. As he glided up toward the city room, dozens of desks and people came into view. Mercifully, not one focused on him. The huge hoop earrings and massively snarled coiffure of Ella Chalmers were not visible inside her glass cubicle. He was safe, at least for the moment. Harvey Delittuso hunched over the phone, his skinny back bobbing as he chewed someone out. Beyond him, the mound of junk on Martin's desk seemed bigger than ever. He'd plunge in, get control of it today, throw stuff out. He was in the mood. Delittuso slammed the phone down and fell into his chair, sliding it toward his computer. With that motion, Martin caught sight of the mug, his coffee mug, a sheet of paper rolled and sticking out of it.

Another drowning.

'Never trust anyone in television,' Harvey snapped as Martin approached. 'I asked Jordan Baines for a simple – hey. You shaved your beard.'

Stricken, Martin walked around him and took the story from the cup. A wire account. Woman who drowned pier fishing alone.

'You know this one, too?' Harvey gaped at him.

Sandra Monroe Evans, 39. 'No.'

'Geez, I thought you did. Don't scare me like that.'

The breakfast bagel he had bought from a street vendor and wolfed on the fly had solidified in the past thirty seconds, a stone, just above his belt buckle. The words on the page did not fit together. He couldn't get them to make sense. He took off his coat and stuffed it under the desk.

Sandra Monroe Evans . . . Martin put a finger under the

line of type and moved it painstakingly along . . . *drowned*
. . . He read the account twice, finally absorbing what had
happened. She didn't fit the pattern. She was too old and
had been married fourteen years.

If there was a pattern.

'I'm not saving these anymore,' he told Harvey. 'You
don't need to pull them.'

'Whatever you say.' Harvey's manner had changed to
that of a hospital visitor.

'And don't humor me.' Martin slipped the story into the
round file and dug through desk debris for a sketch pad
that wasn't full. His charcoal pencils were blunt and stubby.
They'd have to do. He tore a few strips of sandpaper from
a sheet and stashed them in his pocket. He'd sharpen the
pencils in court. Drive Rachel Culver mad with his furtive
scratching.

'You going?' Harvey stood up.

'Gone.'

In the street again, he ran until his ribs ached, ran away
from memories of his sweet Jenny, ran as though they were
chasing him, over curbs, up steps, down steps, through
security, across buffed and glinting tiles. The bailiff saw him
coming and noiselessly opened the courtroom door. He
found Rachel and, huffing, sat beside her in the sweltering
crowded room, under the high-pitched buzz of a teenage
girl's testimony.

'Tardy,' Rachel whispered without looking at him, then
did a double take at his new persona and tugged his sleeve
in approval.

Martin gestured at the witness. Rachel wrote her name
on the edge of his pad: *Susan Yeager*. Daughter in a
custody case that had turned deadly, the mother shooting

the father. The mother had claimed the father sexually abused the child.

Martin zeroed in on Susan. He'd already heard the mother's testimony and judged her to be lying.

Susan punctuated her paragraphs with uneasy glances at her mother who sat with her back to Martin at a table peopled by her attorneys. After a few exchanges between Susan and the prosecutor Martin was sure Susan was being silently directed by her mother. Her statements sped up or halted without logical reason. And they were devoid of the kind of emotion that sprang from the recollection of abuse. He had seen the real thing: testimony by children so shattered that they needed recess after recess in order to get through the briefest details. This wasn't it. Not even close. She hadn't been rehearsed, though. She wasn't falling into the repetitious speech that resulted from rehearsal. A clever move. The mother was capable of orchestrating that. And more.

The posture wasn't right either. Not tight enough, not bowed and tremulous. Postures varied. He had to allow for that. Two people could tell similar true stories and be differently affected. But this . . .

He pulled a wad of sandpaper out of his breast pocket and began to rub the charcoal against it. Rachel's jaw muscle tensed in irritation.

Rachel never ventured to guess who was innocent and who was guilty. She'd dressed Martin down a few times for being so opinionated. *Not for me to decide*, she'd say. *I'm just here to record history*. But, if she didn't know the truth – really know, in her gut – she wasn't really looking and listening. You couldn't make a mistake if you really took it all in.

Juries made mistakes. He didn't. Things shook down into patterns for him. Physical poses, skin shadings, the shifting of eyes, verbal nuances. He knew too much. Some of the verdicts he'd seen rendered had seriously shaken his faith in the process. But he was still here, drawing Susan Yeager.

He was a hypocrite. *I'm just here to record history.* That's what he was doing with the drownings, the clippings, noting them for the record and sending them down the rabbit hole. He knew damn well there was an observable pattern in the confusing mix. And that there would be another victim.

6

Grandma and Grandpa Harper's rental car was big. If Jon wanted to, he could lie down on the backseat and stretch all the way out without bumping his head or feet. But he wasn't going to lie down on the way to the airport. Lying down in the car made him sick. He had to look out the window at the stuff going by or he'd have to stop and walk along the side of the road until he felt better. When he did that, he made everybody late.

This backseat wasn't good for sitting up. He rolled backward in it. It was too fuzzy. But he wouldn't say anything. This grandma and grandpa didn't like to hear bad things. His grandma Harper always said, 'You're not,' when he told her how he felt. Like when he thought he was going to throw up, she'd say. 'No, you're not.' She said it with kind of a smile, like she was trying to make him feel better, but it only made him feel worse. Sometimes she'd

271

say, 'Yes, you are.' But she'd only say that when he told her stuff like 'I'm not hungry.' She'd say, 'Yes, you are,' with that little smile.

His mother stuck her hand into the car, in back of Grandpa Harper's head and wiggled her fingers. Jon grabbed them and she squeezed. 'Put your window down, Jon,' she said. Grandpa Harper hit a button and the window beside Jon made a noise and went down about half. She let go of Jon's fingers and came up to his window. 'I love you,' she said. 'I'll see you in a couple of days. Can you put this down some more, Dad?'

Grandpa Harper hit the button again, but the window stayed in the same place. 'Only goes halfway.'

His mother pushed her lips out for a kiss. Jon felt mad at her. Sort of. He pretended he didn't know what she wanted. She made the kissing noise at him one time. 'You're my friend,' she said.

He felt scared. Would she come home to their house in California? Or would she die now? He wanted to say one more thing to her about the man. Tell her again to watch out. But she didn't want Grandma and Grandpa to know about any of it. A bunch of shivers came up in him. He could feel things moving around inside, fast.

'Bye.' His mother waved and he saw her sliding away from the car. The car was going. Backward. Up the driveway. And she was all alone, by herself. Without anyone.

'MOM!' It was loud. Grandma Harper's shoulder went up toward her ear. Grandpa stopped the car.

His mother came up and looked at him. 'What?'

Jon pushed out his lips at her. She turned her face sideways over the window glass and kissed him. 'You be good,' she said. She sounded like she had a cold.

'Dad, he doesn't have his seat belt on. Jon, put on your belt.'

'I don't want to.' This would keep her a few more minutes. She wouldn't let him go away without it.

'Jon . . .' She had tears and didn't say anything else, just stepped back and stepped back. Grandma and Grandpa saw that she had tears, too. Grandpa made the car go. Up, up. Jon kept watching his mother's pretty red hair as she got smaller. The car kept on climbing. He had to grab the seat to stay on it. *Bump*. The street. They were really leaving. His mother was just standing there. He knew she was looking at him.

They started to go forward, along the road. 'Put your belt on,' Grandma Harper said.

He got on his knees and looked out the back window. His mother was behind the trees. He couldn't see her at all. The car jumped and started to speed. 'I'm not going with you,' Jon said. Why did he say that? He had to go. He promised.

'Yes, you are,' Grandma Harper said.

'No, I'm *not!*'

'Jonny boy—' Grandpa started to talk, but Jon didn't want to hear it. 'I'm *not*, I'm *NOT!*' he shouted. 'Maybe we should—' Grandpa said to Grandma. Grandma talked over him. 'He'll be all right.'

'No! No! No! No! Noooooooo.' He sounded like his dog Candy when she heard a fire engine. 'Oooooooooooooo!' He had just meant to make noise, but he started crying, too, because he was thinking of his mother standing there with tears, all alone. Maybe the man was after her already. Maybe she would be gone if they went back. Even if they went back real fast. Maybe she was gone

273

right now. 'Nooooooooooooo! Oooooooooooo! Oooooo!' His crying was extra loud in the car, like when he hollered in the bathtub.

The car went *bang* to a stop. 'Mariah—' his grandpa said.

The man had hold of Jon's mother. The man was behind her, pulling her backward off her feet. 'I'm not going! Not *going!*'

'Jon!' Grandma Harper had turned all the way around. She was up out of her seat and trying to touch him.

'No! Nooooooooooooo! No!'

'Jon!'

He moved away so she couldn't get him.

'Go back,' his grandma said to Grandpa.

'I'll have to find a place to turn around,' Grandpa said.

'Do it.' Grandma was all the way over the front seat now. She grabbed Jon's arm. 'Jon, hush.'

But he couldn't. Screams were coming out of him without his help. His mother was dead. Dead, like his dad. He was so scared, so scared, so scared, so scared, so scared. Out the front window, the road turned into trees and turned into road again. The car made a big roar, then bounced and bounced. His tummy went up and down and up and down, but he held onto the seat. He watched for Grandpa Reuschel's driveway, the one with the castle for a mailbox. When he saw it, he looked for his mother, but she wasn't there anymore. 'Mommy! Mommy!' He tried to make his sounds go straight out the window. 'MOMMY!' The car went on its nose and down, down, straight at the house. Where *was* she? Why didn't she come?

He knew how to open the door. He knew it wasn't locked. He had to pull the handle in and *push*. The door came open and the driveway was moving under it. Fast, but getting slower. He could put his feet out and run. The door came toward him and hit one of his shoes across his toes. Then it let him go, but he was falling out at the ground. Grandma Harper yelled, 'Earl, stop!'

His shoulder went down. He turned his face so he wouldn't smash his nose. What he hit was soft and had arms. His mother was running by the car, holding him up. His feet were still inside. The car stopped. They stopped. She pulled him out and stood him up. The way she did it jerked his neck. His foot felt like something was biting it. 'What are you *doing?*' she said to him. Her face was crooked and white.

'I want to stay with you! I don't want to go! I don't want to! I won't!' She better not try to send him away. He'd make sure she didn't. He started to cry the loudest he'd ever cried. But not too loud because he wanted to hear what she was saying. It was: 'You don't have to go, Jon. You don't have to.'

7

Arlene unplugged the coffee pot and dumped the coffee grounds on top of the egg shells and melon rinds in the plastic bowl. One of the children had left toast on a plate. She picked it up along with the bowl and pushed the screen door open with her back. A postcard day, the sun bleaching the deck, blue sky popping between leaves and branches. She would try to ignore the butterflies in her stomach and think clearly. Mimi's reaction to the truck pictures had been devastating in its deliberate calm. It was the most lucid Mimi had been since her stroke, her attention total, the ringing of the bell definite and shattering. Mr. Reuschel's murderer had driven a jeep-like truck, heavy-duty, large, with big wheels. It was silver. Not gray, silver.

She set the toast on the deck railing for the birds and strolled to the compost heap to dump the garbage. *Waste not, want not.* They were almost proud of this decaying mound fenced by wire. It gave off a rich odor, not in the least objectionable, and provided fertile black soil for the garden. She poured the garbage on top of the heap and stared up at Mimi's window. The angle was too steep; Arlene couldn't see her.

Arlene's response to Mimi's serenely definite answers this morning had been rising emotion, a spilling wave that left her with a headache. The man in the truck was still out there somewhere. A threat. Arlene had followed the news closely. There was no mention of Tim Reuschel or any ongoing investigation. Where was Deena Reuschel? Had she left for California? Surely she would contact Arlene sometime to try and get the truck's description.

The idea of waiting for a call that might not come, the idea that Deena might abandon her efforts and go home, filled Arlene with anxiety. She had begun to have a change of heart about contacting the police. Suppose the killer came back to the scene and discovered their house like Deena did? Or had already discovered it? If Deena wasn't going to continue to pursue him, Arlene needed to know it and make a choice. Every minute that passed could bring him closer to them.

Tim Reuschel's obituary and accompanying article had given the location of the Reuschels' lake house. She'd

checked the phone number and found it had been disconnected. If she wanted to contact Deena, she'd have
to go there.

Arlene walked swiftly inside and laid the plastic bowl
in the sink. Could she leave Mimi? Her condition seemed
to have stabilized. Arlene had routinely left her for short
periods to run the kids to school or pick up a few groceries.
It would only take an hour or so to do a flying round-trip
to the lake.

It could be tricky there. Deena might be surrounded by
family. It was best to have a note ready, like last time.

Paul had begun to sweat. He took off his jacket and sat on it
in a cluster of saplings. Jon's presence changed everything.
Deena must be upset about it, but what could she do? The
car had simply reappeared, with Jon falling out the back
of it. She had to let Jon stay. He knew that. But he was
disappointed.

He had tried to leave the area after that, hunger and
sleepiness clawing at him. But the boundaries were still
in place. He was right where he needed to be for some
reason. He would wait.

8

Deena had spent an hour calming Jon down, rocking him,
humming, making sure that she moved slowly in a relaxed
and measured way. His shuddering breaths had finally subsided into deep, even ones. He seemed alert now, hungry.
He stood on a stool next to her at the stove stirring the
baked beans with a wooden spoon while she lifted the hot

dogs from the boiling water with a fork and placed them in the steaming buns. Birds chattered and sang beyond the window screens. A breeze puffed the curtains causing them to brush the sills. The illusion of routine had been good for her. She'd been forced to consider her situation at length and to narrow the possibilities. She kept coming back to Paul.

No one else that she had met here, and no one at home in California, troubled her mind the way Paul did. There might be many suspects beyond her immediate circle of acquaintances, but they were not presently accessible to her. She was limited in what she could see and do. So, it made sense to concentrate her efforts at the center of that circle and gradually work her way out as far as she could.

She'd have to be low-key about it. She had done enough to Jon, had told him enough. It was time to work on restoring his emotional health and his confidence. Gene had been right. For a moment, she meditated on Gene. He'd been uncharacteristically adamant about the photos. Had he glimpsed the truth but denied it in order to protect Jon's sense of security? In order to protect hers? Gene possessed an enviable wisdom, which she had admired over the years. He may have been planning to deal with the situation in a different way. Later on and from a different angle. She had no such subtlety.

She finished arranging the hot dogs, beans, potato chips, carrot sticks, and plastic glasses of apple juice on their plates. Turning off the stove, she handed Jon the napkins and forks. 'Bring these for me, okay? We'll eat on the porch, by the lake.'

He hopped down from the stool. She noticed as they

approached the French doors that the spring leaves beyond the screened porch had grown larger and more vividly green overnight, softening the landscape and enclosing the cottage. She thought again of the decades spent in the sanctity of this house by a family so kind and so devoted to one another that it seemed nothing but time could change them.

She and Jon were not safe here either. She mustn't forget that.

9

The air split in two with a single muffled *thwack* and fanned Paul's face. He tried to open his eyes. Through a haze, Deena and Jon climbed toward him. The tree trunk, jagged against his shoulder, took shape. He had been dozing. His left arm was numb.

Alarmed, he twitched, trying to rouse feeling in his legs, tracking the bobbing bodies as best he could. They were on the gravel, not on the grass, cutting at an oblique angle to him. He was not ready, needed to get ready. He shifted his weight, shaking loose his circulation. High sun told him it was midday. He had not been asleep long.

Their backs were to him as they hiked onto the road. He struggled up, a laming stiffness in his knees. They were heading east, toward his cottage. Their ambling gait suggested this was a recreational walk, not one with an urgent purpose. He could easily catch up. He contemplated the routes that would best conceal him. He could cross the road. Shrubs grew thickly there for half a mile.

He took a few tentative steps up the hill, caught by a

net of doubt. Beyond a tight radius there was resistance
to his passage. He perceived it as density in the atmosphere. Confused, he retreated. Deena and Jon were no
longer in sight.

A blue van coming from the other direction passed
slowly behind the bank of trees. It rumbled into the
driveway and all the way to the house. A heavy-set
woman emerged from the driver's side and went toward
the kitchen. He couldn't see her after that, but a soft
rapping reached him. It went on sporadically for a minute
or so. The breeze quit suddenly and sounds sharpened.
He heard the whine of the screen door's spring and then
a gentle latching. She must have put something between
the screen door and the main door. At that instant, he
knew beyond doubt that she was there for him. He had
been waiting all morning for her, for this woman.

Released into motion, he sprinted silently uphill, pushing
limbs out of his path and jumping logs. He was steady now,
his boots landing cleanly on natural shelves and propelling
him up the terraced slopes. His breath stroked evenly in
his chest, his stride loose, nimble.

He heard the van back up and turn around and then,
for a few heartbeats, he lost track of it. The ground leveled
out and he ran toward his car. He had left it unlocked,
the keys in it. He eased it into gear and brought it to
within twenty yards of the road. If she did not come
by in a few seconds, it would mean she had turned
right, toward Deena and Jon. He would not follow her
in that direction.

She would come by. He was in the right place.

He put his window down, the clay-flat odor of the lake
drifting to him, and watched the road.

10

Jon strolled ahead of Deena, dragging stalks of pussy willow and forsythia. Noonday sun reflected in the road's pavement was a shimmering backdrop for his honey blond hair, red jacket, and the curving yellow and gray switches. She put the camera to her eye and paused. This was nice from the back: the boy, the pose, the colors. Jon heard the shutter click and turned around. 'No, keep on,' she said. 'Just the way you were. It's great.' He grinned at her. *Here she goes again. More pictures of me.* That was nice too, that grin. She captured it and he walked away, with no self-conscious clumsiness. The gait of a five-year-old, easy, eager. She got down on one knee, taking a series, concentrating on his fluid motion, adjusting the frame with the distance.

Through the viewfinder, the log fence surrounding Mike Kincaid's cottage was crisp in the background. No sign of his car. She stood up and ambled behind Jon.

She wouldn't need long. Five minutes inside that fence. Maybe she'd be lucky. *Maybe.*

The Kincaid land was typical of this area: heavily treed, with natural ground cover. The single-story house, vaguely defined in a perimeter of brush, appeared to have a brown log exterior that matched the fence. The backyard and lake were not visible. Did the Kincaids have a garage? All of the cottages at the lake seemed to have been built with carports instead. She guessed theirs was on the side rather than in the back. She could probably see into it from halfway down the driveway. Then she could be sure Mike was not at home.

Jon was getting quite a bit ahead of her. Should she call him back? Was now the best time? She glanced at the far ends of the road and then at the cottage.

'Jon.'

He looked over his shoulder. 'Huh?'

'Come here, please.'

He backed up, skipping comically.

'You funny bug.' She smiled. 'Listen, I haven't seen Paul's yard and I'd like to. Let's take a peek. I hear it's pretty.'

Jon centered his body and stared at her. She could feel him scanning her with his kid radar.

'Okay?'

'Yuh.' He fell into step beside her. The way he watched his shoes as he walked told her that she hadn't fooled him. He knew this was some sort of a mission.

Guilt assailed her, but curiosity was stronger. She had to see the pond. Seeing always brought answers. It was as though her eyes and her brain formed a single organ. To see was to understand.

The driveway consisted of a coating of fine gravel over dirt, the borders defined by decorative rock. The gravel had not been replenished or raked recently, she decided; tires and a harsh winter had worked it well into the mud. She and Jon skirted some watery ruts. The cottage and grounds had an air of general, but not massive, neglect. Bushes had grown up over a couple of windows. The end of a rain gutter hung loose. Weeds tangled through the flower beds, yet hadn't choked their growth. Halfway to the house, she noted the location of the carport – on the side, as she had thought. It appeared to be empty. Sky filtered through a nest of vines cloaking it. She took a few steps to one side, squinting. Empty, yes, the cement floor of it dappled with standing water.

Paul grew up here. This was Paul's home.

Trees still dripped from the night's rain. Sunshine created an atmosphere of mist. Splotches of yellow, orange, purple, blue, red, white, pink in the backyard came into focus as showy plots of blooms. Tulips, tiger lilies, daffodils. Bulb plants, all. In astonishingly thick clusters. Hundreds. Beyond them, a sliver of lake glittered.

She heard the car before she saw it: the sound of wind and whirling wheels on the far stretches of the road. Zooming into sight, it geared down with a whine. An old car, black, slightly rusting. It pivoted at a right angle and flew toward them down the driveway, showering stones behind it. The thunder shook her. *Mike Kincaid. Had to be.* He pulled up next to them with a wary glance.

'Mrs. Reuschel. Hello.' Polite, but not cordial. An invitation for explanation.

She had rehearsed a sentence or two, but they seemed lame under his scrutiny. *Wanted to see where Tim had played as a child. Wanted to say hi to you. Wanted to see the flowers.* She touched Jon's head for reassurance and courage but could not think of adequate words. She was clearly trespassing and unwelcome.

'Can we see your yard?' Jon said, wrinkling his nose.

Mike zeroed in on Jon. 'My yard?'

'Yeah.' Jon gave a toothy smile.

The lines in Mike's cheeks softened. 'Why?'

'For fun?'

'Help yourself.' He pulled the car on around, into the carport.

Jon sobered as soon as Mike went out of sight and gave her a conspiratorial glance.

She pinched the lobe of his ear.

11

Martin covered the phone's mouthpiece with his hand. 'Ed, do you speak Spanish?'

'Nawsah. Kin barely speak English.'

'Smart shit,' he hissed.

'Who's this?' Flanders tipped his chin up in a gesture of mock impatience. 'I thought you were callin' your office.'

'Just give me a minute.'

'Usin' my phone, boy. Better be official business.'

'It is.' Martin put the receiver to his ear. 'Señora, I – am – looking – for – the – family – of – Carmela – Azaña.'

'No comprendo. *Carmela?*' He guessed this woman to be past seventy, perhaps having trouble hearing as well as understanding.

'Si!' His high school Spanish was virtually extinct ten years after graduation. 'Carmela – Azaña. *Familia.*' Was that right? 'Por favor.' He was shouting. Flanders made the time-out sign at him. Martin ignored him.

'Carmela csta muerta,' the woman said feebly.

Muerta. *Dead.* He had the right number. She knew about Carmela. He could use the address from the newspaper article. Someone close to Carmela still lived there. 'Muchas gracias, señora.' What was *good-bye?* 'Buenos.'

That was 'good.' He couldn't think of the other word. It didn't matter. She had hung up on him.

12

The Kincaid cottage sucked at Deena's back as she and Jon weaved along cracked stepping stones toward the lake. Mike had gone inside but was watching them. She didn't need to look to know that.

'This is creepy,' Jon said.

The path ended quickly, lost in a storm of blooms: tulips, hyacinth, narcissi, lilies, their bulbs obviously planted in sections years ago, now growing wild, untended. Giant cobwebs, spun between overhanging branches and the tumble of blossoms, sparkled faintly. Their sticky silk clung to her skin, her hair, as she crushed flowers underfoot and kept walking.

'How much farther are we going?' Jon was up to his hips in petals and leaves. Vines tore at his pant legs.

'Want me to carry you?'

'No.'

Where was the pond? The land sloped very gradually toward the lake. About halfway between the cottage and the water, the dense plantings thinned out slightly, meeting high grass. From a low spot, she would be able to survey the grounds. 'Stay here. You'll be able to see me the whole time.'

He went back to the last stepping stone and stomped his sneakers on it. 'Feels like bugs up my jeans.'

Her legs were itchy, too. Gnats, maybe. She rubbed her ankles through her slacks and socks. 'I'll be right back.'

She chose her steps carefully. Roiling swarms of tiny flying insects seemed to bar the way as she moved among dripping trees. The weed-choked flower beds tapered off at a stand of tall coarse grass that whipped at her as she passed through it. At the edge of the lake, she scanned the acreage surrounding the cottage. Jon, small against the broad sweep of nature, waved.

If there had been a pond here, it was gone now, filled in or covered over. She could not find a patch of water anywhere. Her experienced eye divided the scene into sections, framing each, hunting. And then she saw it.

13

The red car had been in Arlene's rearview mirror for miles, perhaps since she had left the lake. It lagged far enough behind and had such darkly tinted windows that she could not see the driver. The idea of an anonymous pursuer gave her the jitters. With each bend in the highway, she lost sight of the car, but it always emerged again, keeping a steady distance.

She was nearly home. Whoever it was could trap her there, in the lane leading up to the house. Once in, she couldn't get out if the red car blocked the way. Should she drive past her turn, go on into Somerset, and ask for help? What about Mimi?

She'd have to make a decision momentarily. Was it nonsense to think that she was being followed? Why would anyone follow her? Did it have something to do with Mr. Reuschel's murder?

From habit, she slowed down as she approached her

cutoff. The red car slowed, too. She would end it now, right now. She would rather know than not know. Nick's shotgun was in the corner of the garage. She would drive rapidly toward the house, hit the remote to open the garage door, get inside, and get ready.

The red car was on her tail now, riding her bumper as she prepared to turn. She wheeled into the lane and tromped the accelerator. Her fingers were already on the garage remote control, but she was too far away to trigger it. In the rearview mirror, the red car flashed past the lane, headed downhill, on the highway. The garage door was opening in front of her. She pulled the van inside and sat staring at the mirror in amazement and shock. Nothing was reflected in it but the busy skitter of birds against tranquil greenery. No red car. She needed to stop imagining things and calm down.

The van had gone into an unmarked, nearly invisible dirt road. Its location told him all he needed to know: *There had been a witness to Tim's murder.* A dizzying sense of disbelief possessed him, and for a moment, he could not think.

He had known she was there, had felt her presence when he was getting into the truck. It was true. True. He had to accept it, work from here.

Paul signaled a left turn and rode the brake, searching for a place to leave the car. It would have to be a sheltered spot so that she could not see it from the mountain. She might have noticed him following her and be watching for the car.

Rocky embankments closely lined the shoulders. The highway narrowed to two lanes as he reached the bottom of the hill. He didn't want to go too far out of range, in case he had to get away quickly. There might be suitable niches uphill, above the driveway, but it was a bad idea to go back into her line of sight. Nervousness flooded him and then ebbed. A place would be provided. He would be taken care of, as always.

Tim's wife had left her little boy and gone all the way to the lake. Now she was circling back, toward the pond. Mike could keep her in sight by moving from one window to another. The grounds were a jungle. Mike had not been able to bring himself to work in the yard since Sarah died. He had let it take its course, the flowers multiplying and the weeds flourishing. He did not even look toward the lake or the pond most days. He had managed to block that entire section of the earth from his mind. Paul got out there occasionally and did some mowing when Mike wasn't around.

He mowed around the flowers. They had been so much a part of Sarah that he knew Paul couldn't touch them. While she was alive, they had filled the house with their fragrance. She had smelled like roses, hyacinth, lilac. *Sarah*.

Mike hadn't brought a flower inside since her death. Sometimes he imagined the bulbs proliferating under the soil, saw them in their silent darkness nudging the dank earth aside, sending out layered buds to expand and break away. Each year brought more and more blooms, as though she were still among them, nurturing their glory.

Deena Reuschel had almost reached the pond. Had someone told her that Sarah died there? Mike had found her floating, her beautiful face bruised and empty, her arms stretched out to embrace a cloudless sky. He had thought that no future grief could exceed that one.

Deena seemed transfixed by the setting. What did she see? Only remnants of the way it had been when Sarah tended it. She had kept the pond as a showpiece, ringed by New England rock and a low white wire fence. At any time of year, color had flecked the surface of the water: reflections of spring irises, summer ageratum, fall marigolds, and winter holly. It was overgrown now, the fence gone to rust, the rocks displaced by seasons of frost.

He should have maintained the pond as a tribute to Sarah. He had reproached himself about it many times. But remembering Sarah was not possible without remembering her inexplicable death and the strangely uneven reaction of their son. In the beginning, it felt to Mike that Paul was pretending his sorrow. He had been twelve at the time and full of false bravado, a quirky, defiant front he had displayed from early childhood, a front that Mike had tried repeatedly to knock out of him. Paul's mourning, though it might have been profound, seemed to coexist with a measure of satisfaction. In quiet moments, he would catch Paul watching him with a barely concealed air of triumph.

Yes, Mike had loved Sarah best. And Paul knew it.

It was only when Mike's devastating day-to-day grief began to subside and Paul's began to escalate that Mike entertained a new thought, one so horrendous he could not put words to it for months: that the child may have been willing to sacrifice his mother in order to wound his father – and that he had, at last, realized it could not be undone.

*   *   *

The slope was steep but so heavily wooded that the under-brush had rotted. Paul's progress was unhampered as he climbed toward the sun. Climbing down would be another item. There'd be no way to take this hill slowly. He'd have to use the trees as stoppers for a rapid descent. At that angle and speed, the mulch would be slippery.

He looked back, glimpsing bits of the road far below. He had almost reached the crest and he was still breathing effortlessly. His weight training kept him in superb shape. Whatever was at the top of this hill, he would handle to his advantage. He would not make any more mistakes.

The terrain gradually leveled and a two-story house emerged from the horizon. Paul, disoriented for a moment, considered its setting: high, heavily treed, and so close to the river that the sound of tumbling water rose behind it. He crouched and summoned a mental map. He was south of the river and west of the field where he had parked on Monday, coming at the house from the side. The other side must overlook the width of the river. That meant the house had been built facing upstream, possibly opposite the field and the ridge. If so, it was new in spite of the camouflage coloring, which gave it an aged appearance. New in the past year or so. That's how he had missed it.

Skirting the house to confirm its exact position in regard to the murder site would waste his time. He knew he was right. But he'd do it anyway just to be sure. Then he'd figure out how to get inside.

The pond was smaller than Deena had expected, perfectly round and bordered by small rocks. A profusion of weeds and flowers nearly obscured them, but she could see that they were all approximately the same size. She guessed they had been set in evenly and precisely, long ago, although weather had dislodged many of them. The water bore the charcoal hue of great depth. Deena wondered if it were connected to the lake by an underground spring.

It was difficult to imagine how Sarah Kincaid could have made a fatal mistake here. The rocks were at the very edge of the pond – a barrier of sorts, a caution zone. Around the rocks was a band of flowers, and around them, a knee-high wire fence, bowed and broken in spots. Sarah had to have been inside the fence when she fell. She may have lost her footing in the flower bed and slipped, striking her head on a rock.

Or had she been working the muddy earth with a trowel when the unexpected presence of a second person made her look up?

Or . . . had she been – like Tim – absorbed in her thoughts when she was attacked from behind and knocked into the water?

Deena stepped over the fence, glancing superstitiously over her shoulder and then at the pond. Was it possible to know what had happened to Sarah Kincaid? She stood for minutes in the midst of full-bloom irises shivering on thick stalks. It was the only flower Sarah had planted here. They must have been her favourites. Deena could count half a dozen distinct varieties, at least, in differing combinations of purple, white, blue, and gold. Many grew at an angle due to the pressure of the weeds, but they grew heartily still.

In the end, Sarah did not speak to her. She could not sense Sarah's presence any more than she had been able to sense Tim's. Wherever they had gone, it was a place apart. Disappointed, she crossed the fence again. A cloud rolled pale shadows over the pond, touching the irises, row by row, making their fragile, flowing petals somehow more vivid. The wedge of sunlight that remained on the irises grew smaller and smaller until it disappeared and the circle closed.

Deena stared down at her hand, at the wedding ring she wore. A circle of irises. Taking it from her finger, she ran her hand over the engraved blossoms. Irises in a circle. Paul had patterned it after this pond.

14

The kitchen comforted Arlene, the children's splashy art-work adorning the refrigerator, letters from good friends stuffed into the cubby holes of her built-in maple desk, neatly folded lengths of uncut fabric stacked next to her sewing machine in the corner. She had been baking for over an hour: tollhouse cookies with nuts, banana loaf with raisins. Mimi was still napping. Blue jays scrapped with each other on the deck railing in the spot where she had left the toast that morning.

The oven aromas and the pine-scented air rushing at her through the window screen above the sink affirmed for Arlene that her world was fully intact, secure, even inviolable. She carried the banana skins to the compost heap and returned to the kitchen in a leisurely walk, the sun stealing through the knit of her sweater, heating her blouse and the skin beneath. A great day to be outside. A beautiful day. She would stroll down to the end of the lane and meet the school bus. It was almost time.

Should she lock the kitchen door? She'd only be gone a few minutes. She never locked it. Why should she today?

She'd have to lock the window, too. A nuisance. Stepping into the kitchen, she responded to the red light on the stove. She had left the oven on. She clicked the knob, listened for a moment to the chattering jays, then closed and locked the door and the window. Terrible to live this way, uneasy, defensive. It went against her grain.

She stepped into the garage, thinking again of the red car and the panic it had caused her. She'd been silly. Pressing the buttons on the automatic system, she raised the door and peered down the lane. Should she take the remote control with her or leave the garage open? She'd be able to see it the whole time. She might scare the children with that locking-up business. They'd want to know why. She didn't want them to be frightened in their own home. No, she wouldn't do that to them. She'd just be vigilant.

Paul edged along the back wall of the house. He would only need two seconds to get into that garage. The woman was glancing at it repeatedly as she moved toward the road, clearly spooked by something. He didn't like the setup, but he had to try. It was impossible to tell whether the second story had a view of the river and field. He had to be sure before he targeted her. It worried him that she might not be alone, although he hadn't seen anyone else in the hour and a half he'd been watching. She'd had a solitary air, but the house was too large and too isolated for her to be living in it by herself. And she'd parked on one side of the garage, as though leaving room for another vehicle.

She took another glance and then faced the road. He sprang from the wall into the garage and slid quickly behind the van. The floor next to it had a fresh oil stain in the middle. She was probably married and the husband had the other car at work. Where was she going? She was nearly to the end of the dirt road, still watching behind her. He clung to the shadows as he let himself into the house.

A nice house, in good order, smelling of baked goods. The furniture had some age on it but was not antique. He went immediately to the front windows. Treetops swayed in the distance, overlaid with a huge stretch of sky. The river could not be seen from here. He needed to go upstairs.

The staircase gave him pause. It led to a landing; he couldn't see what was beyond the bend. Someone could be waiting for him. He crept from tread to tread with his neck stretched, his head tilted back. No one was in the hallway. He noted as he reached it that the attic access was in the ceiling. That meant there was no third floor to speak of. He would find what he was looking for on the second.

He turned right into the front bedroom. This was the one. Pink bedspread and a dressing table, old dolls, girl clothes. Outside the bay window, pale green leaves formed a screen. Days ago the leaves would have been smaller, the view of the river clearer. Through gaps between clusters of leaves he could see the water, the ridge, the field. But who had witnessed what he did? The girl, home from school for illness? Or the mother, lingering in the girl's room? Both? Neither?

Had they filed a police report? If so, he hadn't gotten a whiff of it. His best guess was that the woman was the only witness and that she had chosen to protect her family by staying off the official record.

But she had contacted Deena. *How?* She could have found the Reuschels through newspaper accounts of Tim's drowning. Was this why Deena believed that Tim had been murdered? Because the woman had told her so?

The other window looked out on the dirt road. The woman was standing at the end of it, gazing at the house. He made sure to stay to one side, his body concealed by the drapery, as he focused on her. She had ruined everything by becoming involved, and he could do nothing about it. He did not know what actions she had already taken against him, how many people she had told. It was out of his control.

He could be discovered. Discovered and punished, his life taken from him. Deena would never be his.

The woman pivoted toward the road. A school bus was winding its way toward her, a long way off. If she were in the house with him now, he would exact a price from her for the damage she had inflicted on him.

He moved away from the window and prowled the second floor. One of the bedrooms clearly belonged to a boy and one seemed to be the master bedroom. Neither had a view of the murder site. At the farthest point in the back hall, he paused, glimpsing what seemed to be a sick room. Medicines lined the dresser. A bedpan rested on a wooden chair. A walker stood near the foot of the bed. The shape of a small body lay under the covers. He inched closer, bringing more of the bed into his vision. He could not see a face yet, but it seemed to him that the person must be sleeping because the body did not stir at all. Cautiously, he leaned into the doorway. The head belonged to an old woman, white haired and shriveled. Her eyes were closed. At the instant he looked at her, they flickered open and fixed on him in alarm.

A mistake, letting her see him.

He had a split second to make the call. It was foolhardy to leave her in a position to identify him. He started toward her, his anxiety and anger intensifying so suddenly that the world went silent. He was aware of nothing but those black eyes, which seemed, inexplicably, to recognize him.

Her mouth fell open. The back of her throat and her tongue began to convulse. Her chest heaved and a piercing, inhuman screech cut through him. *Aaarrraah*. The fear in her eyes had been replaced by fury. *Eawraaaww. Awwaaaaa*. She knew what he had done, who he was, she said. *Yarrraaaaw. Waaaraaa*. The fierce, warped language hammered at him. Poised over her, he felt the vibration of her voice strike the core of his brain, closing off his thoughts, his reasoning. Her arm jerked up, down, up, down, smashing a bell against her side, sending clatter at him and against the walls, the ceiling.

A steady, shrill bell began to answer hers from another place, bringing him to attention. He was in danger here. Harming this old woman would serve no purpose other than revenge. She obviously could not speak. She must have had a stroke. She could not describe him to anyone, was no threat. And she could not have recognized him – she was in the wrong room. Could not have seen him, could not have seen what he did. Her window faced the wrong way. She slumped to one side, still jangling the bell, her eyes accusing him, her garbled words ripping at him. He took the stairs at a run, realizing that the other bell was the sound of the telephone.

The shouts of children were already echoing in the garage. He could not go out that way. There were only seconds left. He unlocked the kitchen door. The warm afternoon enfolded him as he emerged into it, easing the door shut behind him.

15

She had the right number. Mimi's bell was clanging in the background. 'Arlene?'

'Yes?'

'It's Deena. Is this a bad time?'

'I've just come into the house with the children and Mimi's asking for me.'

'Okay. But please – could you tell me – did she say anything else about the truck?'

'Yes. I put it in a note. You didn't get it?'

'No.'

'It's in a sealed envelope with your name on it. I stuck it between your screen door and the main door in your carport. About one o'clock.'

After she had left the house to walk with Jon. When they had come from Mike's, to get the car, they hadn't gone into the cottage.

'She said it was an off-road vehicle, four-wheel drive. Like a Land Rover, you know?'

'Yes.'

'Silver. She said it was shiny silver. Not gray. Listen, I have to go. I'm sorry.'

Loneliness gripped Deena as she listened to the vacant line. With the description of the truck, she possessed another significant piece of information. If only she had someone to talk to about it, an adult she trusted. She left the pay phone and peered through the window of the

Cameron Toy Shop. Jon was in a corner of it, watching a large electric train scoot along a track overhead. There were holes cut in the walls and the train would disappear through one of them, only to emerge from another. She could call Barbara, while he was still occupied, ask her for details about Paul. She and Gene were probably home by now.

No, she wouldn't do that. Barbara and Gene were in too much pain. Paul had been a friend from birth. They might find her inquiry offensive, ill-timed.

What should she do? She had called Bob Norville. Tim had been interred, the autopsy complete. But no conclusions would be drawn right away. They would move slowly, be accurate. There was no telling when she would have the results and when – or even if – they would launch an investigation.

She would not go back to California until they did, if she had to supply all of the evidence herself. The clues were here, not at home. She had checked with her answering service and with Tim's office. There were no messages other than condolences and business inquiries. Going home would be fruitless. Worse than fruitless. She would lose momentum. She would stay here. Stay and observe Paul. Instinct had led her to him. Instinct would tell her the truth about him.

Were the garlands of irises on the wedding rings he had made for her and for Tim commemorative of Sarah Kincaid's death? Had he been so impacted by it that it had tainted his entire life?

Was there a connection between her drowning and Jenny's? And Tim's? Had they all been murdered? By *Paul*? *Why*?

If he had killed them, he was cunning. He had laid out nearly infallible plans that had gone undetected for years. Was it naive to think she could deceive such a man, defeat him?

She thought suddenly of Martin and his lingering anguish over Jenny. *I start imagining that someone did this to her. I want to believe it so badly that I do. I do believe it. But it can't be true.*

She checked her watch. Four o'clock. Martin would be at work. She couldn't call him there. He was such a private person, he would hate it. She'd try him tomorrow, at home, and hope he wouldn't shut her off when she started asking about Paul.

Was going back to the cottage the right thing to do? Paul was bound to show up. She mustn't underestimate him. She tapped on the toy shop window and motioned for Jon to come out. He pointed at the train. She nodded.

Paul would not get the best of her. Whatever Paul's innate resources, she had more. Whatever his feelings, hers were stronger. If he had killed Tim, she would snare him, bring him down.

Jon left the store, barreling into her, hugging her.

'Let's buy a couple of ice cream cones before we get the groceries,' she said, hugging him back.

'Did you see the train?'

'Yes! Wasn't it wonderful?'

She would buy a couple of flashlights, too – one for the cottage and one for the glove compartment of the car – and fill the tank with gas in case she felt she had to take Jon away from the cottage in the middle of the night.

16

The address was a brownstone in a decent neighborhood. That surprised him and shouldn't. He knew better. He'd learned in court that prejudice was one of the most useless things you could haul around. It kept you from seeing.

No one answered the door. He had come all this way for nothing. What happened to Carmela was not his business anyway. Her family would resent his intrusion. Why would they agree to speak with him even if they had been home?

He should have cut off the ponytail. He still looked like a drifter. People often crossed the street when they saw Martin walking toward them. He must be carrying around a deranged expression, too. They averted their eyes as they hurried past. What was it? He could never catch himself at it in the mirror.

He sat on the Azañas' front steps, his hands in the pockets of his trench coat, the stone slab cold through his clothes. Cooking odors wafted to him, making him hungry. Onions, beef, garlic. He *was* a drifter, constantly pressing his nose on the glass, unable to make meaningful contact with the human race.

Dusk filtered over the houses and the hush of the dinner hour set in. Sidewalks emptied. Inside the Azañas' house, laughter rattled softly. He stood up and peered at the windows. A light was on in one of the back rooms, downstairs. He knocked again, unable to find a doorbell. No one came.

* * *

Jon had been singing softly since they left town, kindergarten songs about rowdy bears and mama ladybugs and skinny pigs. At the end of each, he would give himself applause and make a mock bow. As they rounded the last bend before the cottage, he stopped abruptly in the middle of a line and followed Deena's gaze to the red car in their driveway. 'Paul's here!' he said.

So early. Hadn't he gone to work today? She hadn't expected him to arrive until well after dinner.

What if he'd found Arlene's note? She guided the car down the hill, past his, the outline of his shoulders and head behind the darkly tinted windows filling her with foreboding. Why was he just sitting there?

Before she had turned off the engine, Jon was out of the car and running. She watched in the mirror as Paul stepped into his path and lifted him, grinning. Jon patted Paul's cheeks as they talked. She couldn't hear what they were saying, but there was affection in the way Paul held him. Guilt touched her. What if Paul were innocent? He was walking toward her now, carrying Jon. She grabbed her purse, but before she could push the door he was there, opening it for her, standing so close to it that she had to brush against him. *Look him in the eyes.* 'Hello, Paul.'

The eyes seemed guileless. 'How are you, Deena?'

'All right, I guess.'

'I thought you and Jon might be lonely, so I quit at three and came on up.'

She nodded. Paul set Jon on his feet and hefted the bag of groceries from the backseat for her. She noticed, as if for the first time, the powerful build of his upper body. He had the thick chest and biceps of someone who worked out with weights.

'We saw your yard today,' Jon said. 'You have millions of flowers. Too many!'

Paul hesitated for a split second, then smiled. 'You're right. There are too many.'

'Why don't you give some away?'

He put a hand on Jon's head. 'If you want some, I'll give them to you. Plant them in Grandma's yard. Want to?'

'Will you do it with me?'

'You bet.'

Ordinary banter. The banter of an ordinary man, a trusted neighbor. Paul did not drive a silver truck. He was not sinister. He was not the one she was seeking. Embarrassed by her thoughts, she fished in her purse for the house key and went up the stairs.

'Is Paul having spaghetti with us?' Jon asked.

She unlatched the screen door and swung it cautiously toward her, scanning the doorsill for the note.

'Is he?'

Reaching inside the kitchen, she turned on the porch light.

'Mom?'

There was no note.

'Mommy?'

'Will you, Paul?' she said evenly as he took the groceries to the counter.

'Love to,' he said without turning around.

The backyard was minuscule and occupied by a chunky beagle on a chain. Martin assessed him in the twilight. The tail and ears were up and moving. This one wouldn't bite – wouldn't even bark – he'd make book on it. Martin let his shoes be sniffed and licked, then stroked the dog's silky ears. Dogs liked him for some reason. He'd never had a problem with a dog.

People were another story. And this group might be an especially tough audience. There were more than half a dozen folks milling about in the clatter of the kitchen, none of them speaking English.

He squatted next to the dog, with a whisper. 'Hungry?' The dog gave a yip and put its front paws on his chest. 'Okay. Lessee.' Martin patted his pockets, coming up with a package of saltines left over from lunch. He unwrapped them and fed them to the beagle. The dog understood English. A good sign that someone else in the house did.

A floodlight came on, pinning him in its glare. 'Quien es?' A middle-aged man, calling to Martin from the doorway.

'Mi nombre es Martin Trayne.' Brilliant. He was getting the hang of this. A little more practice and he'd have it.

The man consulted with several other men in the kitchen. Martin couldn't understand any of it, but the tone conveyed wariness.

'Por favor, señor, may I talk to you?' Martin shouted. *That wasn't right.* May I . . . How would he say it?

'About what?' A younger man now, hands on hips. A break-through. He could go ahead in English.

'Carmela Azaña.'

Silence. An undercurrent of murmurs that included female voices. Silence again.

'I rang the front bell, but no one answered,' Martin said as he approached the house, holding his hands up so they could see he was carrying no weapon. The young man opened the screen door to him and propped it with his foot, a gesture that Martin took as an invitation to enter. The other men stepped back.

Martin was center stage. Every person in the kitchen observed him carefully as he joined them. He had interrupted the preparations for a meal. Bowls of steaming food were on the countertops. Beyond the dining room archway was a long table set with white linen.

The women seemed especially affected by Martin's presence. He guessed that one of them must be Carmela's mother, the one with the raw, injured gaze. The other women were paying homage to her, even shielding her, by the position of their bodies. She was clearly the center of the gathering.

'Am I in the right place? Are you Carmela's family?'

The young man nodded.

Martin's story suddenly seemed lame. He was not a detective or a reporter. He was a curiosity-seeker, of sorts. A stranger wishing intimate information he had no right to. And he was stoking their sorrow.

Jenny, whimsical and shy, pivoted in front of him, a vision so distinct that it stole his voice. He put a hand to his throat.

Their faces softened. No one moved.

'I was engaged to be married,' he said haltingly, 'to a woman . . . who drowned before our wedding day. Her name was Jenny Cunningham.'

The young man began to speak softly in Spanish, his sentences echoing Martin's. Martin realized he was translating.

'In the past few years, I have come to wonder whether Jenny may have been murdered. She drowned while swimming alone, at a lake, seven years ago. Since then, I have seen newspaper articles about several women of her age who drowned while alone. I wondered about them, too. Whether they could have been murdered. Possibly by the same person. I am here to ask you about Carmela. I hope my asking does not make you angry. I need to find peace. I need to ask.'

He paused. Nothing he had said registered in them as surprise. They studied him intensely.

'The first thing I want to know is whether she was engaged to be married. All of the women who died were betrothed. Except . . . I am not sure about Carmela.'

This was not immediately translated. The young man looked at Martin with suspicion. The translation, when it came, was delivered with a tinge to it. Martin, not recognizing any of the words, was startled by the obvious change in tenor. People eyed each other nervously. The translator seemed to be awaiting their permission to reply. Martin's guess was that Carmela had, indeed, been engaged but – for some reason – it was a taboo subject. Had the fiancé rejected Carmela? Had she been a suicide?

'Please,' Martin said to the man. 'Yes? Or no?'

Some sort of signal passed among the group. 'Yes.'

'Is it possible for me to talk with her intended husband? Is he here?'

In the wake of the translation, Martin felt himself being appraised. They were judging him, trying to decide whether to trust him. What was their secret? If only he dared to stare at each person, as he did in court, he could pick this scene to its bones, understand the essence of it. After an uneasy moment, he allowed himself to scan them lightly, picking up resemblances, quickly assigning roles: the mother, the father, and their two adult daughters. A teenaged son, who was the translator. An aunt, perhaps – the sister of the mother. He was not sure about the other three men, who stood together. They did not appear to be related to the rest. Two might possibly be boyfriends or husbands of the daughters. The third . . . Very different in style from the rest of the gathering. Mid-twenties, dressed in black clothing and bearing the somber formality of a person twice his age. Martin did a rapid retake of him. Misery at the eyes, in the pinch of the mouth. *The fiancé? Carmela's fiancé?* Conservative garb, nondescript. Mourning clothes? No flash except for a gold pinkie ring. And a ring identical to it on the next finger. Wedding bands? His and hers? The rings they had not been able to wear because Carmela had died before the wedding day?

Martin zeroed in on them, on their faintly sparkling patterns, with shock. They were exactly like the ones Paul had made for Martin and Jenny. And for Tim and Deena.

Then the man stepped forward.

17

The Fire was back. It had gradually seeped into the fringes of his vision during the evening. He knew why it had come. Jon sat near him on the floor in Tim's old room, Deena in a corner.

'We need boats. Are there any boats?' he said to Jon.

Jon crawled over to the dresser and sifted through the toys in the bottom drawer. 'Yes!' He dropped two onto the carpet. A tugboat and a ferry.

Paul picked them up and placed them on the hand mirror they were using for an ocean. They had aged like the other toys, their paint faded, chipped since the days when Paul and Tim played with them. 'What else?'

Jon surveyed the miniature country they had built, the airfield and planes on the bed and the network of roads and cars that covered the carpet, running between houses and churches and gas stations. He sighed.

'You getting tired?'

'No.'

Deena spoke for the first time in an hour. 'A few more minutes, Jon, then we'll have to clean it up.'

'I'm not tired.'

'It's almost time for bed.' She got up slowly and went into the hallway. A few seconds later, the bathroom door clicked shut.

Jon flung himself on Paul's back. 'Will you be here tomorrow?'

Paul leaned forward pulling him gently into a somersault. 'If you want me to. If your mom wants me to. She seems sort of nervous tonight, don't you think?'

'Yes.'

'Your grandma Reuschel told me why.'

Jon lay on his back considering Paul curiously. 'Why?'

'You know.'

This registered. Deena must have told the child something.

'Right?'

Jon gave a slight nod.

'But your mom didn't tell me herself. So I won't say anything to her. The thing I wonder is whether she's sure. Do you think she's sure about it?'

Jon stared at him uneasily, without answering.

She had evidence. 'It'll be okay.' He patted Jon's leg.

'Let's clean this all up.' He dragged the plastic basket out of the closet and began scooping toys into it.

18

'I get it, Mart, but you damn well know we can't do that. Can't go through anyone's stuff on a wild hair. Got to have a search warrant. You want a warrant? I'll go after it for you. But it's Friday night. We're into the weekend. It'll take time.'

It was bitter on the street, soot blasting at him as traffic whizzed by. Martin held up his hand, hoping for a cab. This conversation was going nowhere. He shouldn't have bothered to call Flanders. 'You gonna help me or not, Ed?'

'I'll help you.'

'Now. I mean NOW.'

'I'll help you search, but not without a warrant. You gotta do this right or it won't stick. That's the bottom line. It has to stick.'

'I'm outta here.' The white light on the top of a taxi was crossing toward him.

'Hold it. Don't screw this up. Mart? Mart? Hold it. Hold it a minute.'

Martin dropped the receiver. It was still swinging at the end of the cord when his cab pulled away.

Jon was asleep on his shoulder, but Paul did not want to quit rocking him. When he quit, he would have to begin the other journey. The Fire was waiting, supremely patient, wise. Waiting to receive Deena.

He had fouled things up for himself. He had spurned the

gifts he'd been granted. This was the natural consequence: His truck had been seen at the river. His impulsive disobedience had rendered it visible to a witness for the first time. The woman had described it perfectly in her note to Deena, the note that now rested in his pocket. Could she also describe *him?*

He would not let himself be caught, imprisoned. He could not tolerate an existence at the whim of a captor – dominated, taunted. How many other witnesses were there? How much did Deena know? The situation had grown too complex for him to solve alone. Only the Fire could erase it all, release him.

Deena, wrapped in a blanket on the couch, was watching with gentle eyes as he rocked her child, the honeysuckle scent of her hair a temptation, the sweet ripe curves of her flesh a lure. He must not be swayed. He must go back and start over. Sacrifice her. Make things right.

'Mrs. Swenk. Mrs. Swenk!' Martin, in a full sweat, stopped pounding the door with his fist and rested his forehead against the jamb in frustration. 'Mrs. Swenk!' She had to be in there. She never went anywhere. 'Mrs. Swenk!'

Clunk. She had dropped that thing against the other side of the door – he always imagined it was a stool she stood on to see out the peephole. *Thump, thump.* Climbing up. Thank God.

He backed away, so she could get a good view of him. Did she recognize him without his beard? 'Mrs. Swenk, it's Martin Trayne. Please. Open up.' He addressed the round glass spot with respect. 'Open the door. Please!' *Beg.* 'Mrs. Swenk, please! *Please!*'

He was a specimen under her microscope. He straightened his tie and tried to look appealing.

Squeeee. She was getting down, moving the stool. He counted to nine. The locks began to shift. He smoothed his coat, his hair. *Whump*. She was peering at him from beyond the chain. Disapproval.

'Mr. Trayne, it's after ten o'clock. What do you want?'

'Your car. I need to borrow it.'

'Rent a car.'

'I don't have time. It's an emergency.'

'No, Mr. Trayne. *No*.' She tried to shove the door at him, but he had a foot against it.

The keys were on the board, right next to her. Within his reach. He shot a hand into the opening and snatched them from the peg.

19

If she could fool Paul for a few more minutes, just a few more minutes, it would be over. He would be gone and she would have a chance to get out, run, take Jon with her. She stood by the bed as Paul lowered Jon into it. Jon was deeply asleep, limp. It would be difficult to get him up quickly. Perhaps she could carry him. It would be risky to move the car. Paul might hear it start. Sound ricocheted off the lake on clear nights. And he would be no farther away than his father's cottage.

She hadn't anticipated the whole thing escalating this fast. When she realized Paul had taken the note, she was trapped. Throughout dinner and the evening, he had studied her with caution and with what she interpreted as desire. She could sense the capricious, cunning nature of him now and she had worked to keep his emotions even. He could turn on her whip-quick.

She slowly descended the staircase behind him. Surely he would go. It was nearly eleven o'clock. Halfway across the kitchen, he stopped. She wished she could see his face. She didn't like it when she couldn't see his face.

She walked around him. His expression was one of bemusement and determination. He held out his arms to her. *She had set all this in motion with the brunch, the Sunday brunch, her invitation and her attention to Paul. She had led him on in some way. And he had murdered Tim to have her.*

She moved toward him. He put his hands on her upper arms. Then his body was against hers and he caressed her back. Weakened by fear, she laid her cheek against his shoulder. He wanted her affection. As long as she was willing to give it to him, he would not hurt her or Jon. She must let him do what he wanted to do.

His lips came down to hers. His was a lover's kiss, full of promise and lust. Acid tears burned her eyelids. *You son of a bitch.* He crossed his arms behind her back, pressing her to his chest, his abdomen. As he eased away from her, she glimpsed Jon behind him in the dining room. *She was lost, falling, falling. Falling. Lost.* She blinked to stem the tears. Jon had disappeared. Had she really seen him there?

Paul kissed her on the forehead. 'Good night.'

'Good night.' She kissed her fingertips and laid them against his cheek, then stood in the doorway, waving at him as he drove away.

Jon was on the stairs, sitting near the top, his face wet

with tears. She climbed up and sat next to him. They leaned against each other. She was tired, so tired. 'Jon, I need to tell you something. About Paul.'

'Did you want him to do that to you?'

'No. But . . .' How much should she say? 'It was important to keep him happy.'

'Why?'

'Because – Paul is mixed up. In his feelings. He feels bad inside. And I think that sometimes that makes him want to hurt people. He might . . . be the one who hurt Dad.'

'I would hit him if he did!'

She put her arm around him. 'I would, too.'

'Will he hurt *us*?'

'No. Because we're going home to California. As soon as the sun comes up. We'll let the police take care of him.'

'Why don't we go now?'

'Because he might be watching. I don't want to try it at night. In the morning we'll pretend we're going to the store. We won't even take our suitcases.'

'What if he tries to come in here when we're sleeping?'

'He won't. There's no reason for him to do that. I kept him happy. That's what he wanted.'

'He asked me if you were sure.'

'Sure about what?'

'Something Grandma Reuschel told him.'

'What was it?'

'I don't know. Maybe about Daddy?'

'What did you say?'

'Nothing.'

'Good.' He was barely holding his head up. 'Come on back to bed and let's snuggle.' She took him by the hand.

'You stay with me, Mommy.'

'I will.'
'All night.'
'I will.'
'I don't like Paul anymore, Mommy.'

Paul parked in the weeds at the swimming area. The wooden raft, washed with palest moonlight, was the only gray patch in a black sea. He concentrated on it, trying to control his anger. Deena had been patronizing him. She knew what he had done. If she hadn't known, she wouldn't have let him kiss her. She was too proper for that.

He would have been willing to save her, to defy the Fire for her. But she was faithless, false like the rest.

20

Barbara Reuschel lowered herself into the dark pool from the side. The solar heat panels had kept it at a constant eighty-four degrees while they were gone. She was always grateful for the luxury of their Florida pool, but tonight more than ever. Swimming before bed relaxed her. Perhaps she would finally be able to sleep a little. She slid through the water and floated on her back, Tim a tremor in her chest. Beyond the tented screening, hundreds of stars floated in blackness. Where was he now, her boy?

And Deena and Jon . . . What would become of them without the anchor of his love?

Jon . . . and Deena . . .

All day, in the airports and on the planes, Barbara had tried to think of what knowledge she might possess that would be useful to her daughter-in-law. If Barbara believed – as she had told Deena – that Tim might have been murdered, then she must also believe the concept that the three drowning deaths might be related. She had to get past her own denial and think.

Barbara had not been at the cottage when Sarah drowned. It had happened in the springtime. April? She and Gene were at their winter home in Manhattan with Tim. He was twelve then, Gail twenty, married and gone. Patty Cunningham had called with the tragic news. Barbara hadn't been close to Sarah – Sarah was only close to Mike. So Barbara found herself sorrowing more for Paul than for Sarah. He had adored his mother and, predictably, her death crushed him. It altered his personality severely and permanently.

And Jenny? Barbara had been there, at the lake, with the whole family when she died. July. It was July. Details of that morning were hazy except for the events after Jenny was found. Those were terrifyingly vivid: Tim and Martin stunned and sobbing uncontrollably, nearly suicidal. It had taken all of her emotional resource, and Gene's, to support them.

And about Paul? She didn't remember his sharing fully in the great hard stretch of anger and guilt that swallowed the other two boys for weeks. He seemed affected, certainly. But in a much different way.

Paul's father and Martin's parents stayed in the background throughout the siege. She remembered thinking that the situation must have staggered Mike Kincaid because it was a throwback to the most devastating event of his life. Martin's parents were, well, composed. They were forever composed. That was their way.

Barbara slipped slowly through the water of the pool, back and forth, end to end. The exercise worked on her muscles, limbering her back and loosening her joints. Star formations were ascending slowly, diagonally, over her. Spectacular. A show. The same show she had watched with appreciation from girlhood. The vast, unchanging scope of the universe held enduring hope for her.

She left the pool and put her arms into the sleeves of a terry-cloth robe, tying the belt around her waist. She hated to go into the confines of the house. If she were a child, she would drag her mattress out here, lie peacefully under the everchanging, changeless sky, sleep.

What could she tell Deena about Jenny? Barbara had promised to help. Was she too broken-spirited to receive inspiration right now? Somewhere inside her rested a clue, a scrap of first-hand detail that would be constructive. But which memory was it?

Martin had been late to meet Jenny at the swimming area. Not unusual. From the time he was a toddler, he had existed in an abstract space, a dreamer. He was the boy who could be absorbed for hours by a piece of blank paper and a few colored pencils, the boy who had trouble mastering the concept that you could not leave someplace and arrive someplace else at the same instant. He was always running behind the clock.

But that morning . . . He was more than five minutes late – the time it would take to drive from his house to the swimming area. He was twenty minutes late. Because . . .

Why? Barbara lingered at the edge of the pool, trying

to recall exactly what had happened. He had overslept slightly. And . . . Paul had borrowed Martin's car the night before – that was it. Instead of returning it to Martin's driveway, he had parked it in his own. That meant Martin had to hike down to Paul's to get it.

If only Paul had put the car where he was supposed to put it, Martin might have been able to save Jenny. But Paul had been out drinking beer that night, the boys said, had lost track of himself. He was a college kid then, doing college-kid things. It should have been a harmless mistake.

As far as she knew, Martin hadn't blamed Paul for what happened. He'd blamed himself.

Was still blaming himself.

21

Martin had been in Gino's once before, with Patty Cunningham. She didn't like it, and they had left after a single drink. He didn't like it either. It had a quicksand atmosphere. No air, just smoke. Threshold-of-pain amplifiers for second-rate rock. A crowd that a fire marshal would disperse if he weren't on the payroll. A twelve-dollar cover charge.

It could take an hour to find someone in Gino's, everyone up and dancing, a forest of twitches and undulating arms. Martin, urgently pushing his way through the crowd, examined the howling faces, looking for Derek Vealey's. Derek was at the geographic center of the action – his natural habitat – hopping and sweating, clapping, shaking his rump for laughs.

22

The cooling spot next to her in the bed woke Claire Flanders. The lawns and orchards of a dream slithered away and the creak and tap of her husband dressing came softly to her. She rolled over, locating him in the mellow shaft of light from the closet. He was in front of the full-length mirror, buttoning the jacket of his uniform. 'Ed?'

'Shhh. Go back to sleep.'

'Where are you going? It's Saturday.'

'No, it's still night.'

'Why are you up?'

'I've got something to take care of.'

They'd had long years of wee-hours dressing and leave-taking. She'd hated it. The city was cruel at night. She had lived as though camping out in her own life, waiting for a fellow officer to appear at her door with an ashen face. She'd been almost relieved when it had finally happened and she'd been taken to an airless hospital room to hold her husband's hand and cry over him. They'd nearly killed him, the nameless ones, leaving him on a Brooklyn dock. After that, he was safe, assigned to courthouse duty. 'Take care of what? What is it?'

He placed his cap on his head and tugged at his jacket. 'Go back to sleep.' He lifted the blanket from his side of the bed and folded it over her side. 'Cozy up now.' He leaned down to kiss her, his trademark spearmint chewing gum spreading sweet breath at her lips.

Saturday

1

'I owe you one.'

'Owe me one? You owe me your firstborn child,' Derek said as he let Martin into Paul's studio. 'I wish you'd tell me what's going on.'

'Just . . . trust me.'

'If I didn't, I wouldn't be here.'

'Give me the flashlight.'

'I'll hold it for you.'

'I'm not going to steal anything, I just want to look.'

'So look.'

Martin crossed the room and stepped behind the counter, Derek at his heels. 'Let me see the desk.' Derek ran the beam over it. *Tidy*. The drawers were locked. 'Those shelves.' *Art supplies. Books*. 'Show me the back wall.' *A safe. And half a dozen large wooden compartments, all with locks*. Martin tried to open each of them, without success.

'What are you after?'

'His customer records.'

'They're in here.' Derek rapped on one of the compartment doors.

'Shit.'

Derek bowed his head slightly and backed up. 'Let's go.'

'You have a master key.'

A jerk of the chin in Martin's direction.

'Right?'

'How would you know that?'

'Lucky guess.'

'Listen, I can't—'

'You're the manager. You can do anything you want.'

'But—'

'Do it! This is important, man – I'm not joking around.'

Derek picked through the keys on his chain, selecting the smallest. 'And your secondborn, too,' he muttered. He released the lock and pointed at a long brocade-covered box on a shelf. Martin lifted the box to the counter, fingering the rich fabric with a feeling of premonition. Its hinged lid raised smoothly. The file was alphabetized, dividers separating the twenty-six letters. The cards were neat, not dog-eared. They smelled new. It was typical of Paul to be so precise. These cards would be in perfect order, either typed or hand-done in Paul's meticulous printing. 'Give me more light.'

'Damn, you're bossy.' Derek moved closer.

Martin studied the first card. India ink. Paul's writing. *Aardema, Justine, 1235 Lochmoor Circle* . . . He skipped to the detailed sketch of the piece Paul had made for her. A silver necklace with a rectangular onyx stone.

Abingdon. Horace and Constance, 346 Park Avenue South. Apartment . . . A brooch. Diamond clusters.

He went to the T section, searching for his name. It wasn't there. Neither Tim nor Deena were listed under R. What about Jenny . . .

'How long you gonna be? I could get boiled in oil for this.'

*Cuisette, Walter. Cullen, David. Cummings, Gena.
Cunningham, Jennifer. 84512 Timberline Drive* . . . Her
ring. Carefully drawn with the iris pattern. No mention of Martin and his matching ring. The card was
dated and marked with the word *Gift* in the lower
right corner.

Why wasn't Deena in the file?

What about Carmela? *Azaña, Carmela, 4431 Rem* . . .
The same ring. Iris pattern. No mention of Carlos Leal.
Not under L either.

'Mart—'

'Hang on, Derek.'

Beth Pyle, the victim before Carmela. Was she here?
His heart gave a single jolting thump. *Pyle, Beth Anne,
946 West 13th Street* . . . A wedding ring. Drawn with the
iris pattern. A fine cold sprinkling of perspiration tingled
Martin's upper lip.

'What is it?' Derek was reading over his shoulder.

'Just . . . wait . . .' Rebecca Turregano. The one before
Beth. The joints of his fingers seemed enormous. He
had trouble pulling the card. *Turregano, Rebecca, 258
Lexington* . . . Iris wedding ring.

Paul had killed Jenny. She was the first.

He should have seen it. Paul adored Jenny. No one
could miss how upset he'd been when she and Martin
became engaged.

Had Paul been jealous of the rest?

They would all be here. Suzanne McVaugh, Alison
Hout, Marie Sietz, Deborah Lundin. Murdered because
they had come to his studio for a piece of jewelry. *What a
setup. My God.* The pool of potential victims ideal: random
and infinite.

Had Paul marked every bride-to-be the same way? Martin scooped out one entire section and examined each card. No. Some of the wedding bands had a leaf design. Ivy. He did not recognize the names. Had Paul selected some brides and not others?

It was no use. He could not fathom the man's mind. There was too much here, tangled and baffling.

'That's enough,' Derek hissed. 'Let's roll.'

'One more minute.'

He tucked the cards back between the dividers. Why had Paul made the iris ring for Deena six years ago but allowed her to live?

She had to be in this file. Somewhere. He went through the R's again. Harper. Her maiden name was Harper.

Harper, Deena, 31776 Coronado Parkway . . . The iris pattern. He turned the card over. *Reuschel, Timothy, 77 Idlewood* . . . A sketch of Tim's matching ring. The grooms were on the back of the cards, then. That's how it worked.

Had Paul killed Tim *instead* of Deena? Why? Was he the only male victim? How many people in the file were future targets?

It would take all night to figure it out.

Martin tapped the cards into alignment and put the box back on the shelf, exactly where he'd found it. His breathing was getting tight, shallow. 'Does Paul come in on Saturday?'

'Supposed to. But that might not mean anything. He was scheduled to be here today and he wasn't.'

'He wasn't?' *Deena*. Paul had tracked her with such obvious interest. Had he gone to the lake early?

She was in a dangerous position. Paul found her attractive, and she evidently didn't care for him. If he had killed Tim in order to put the moves on her, he was in for an unhappy surprise. She didn't look like she'd back down from a confrontation. And she sure as hell didn't know who she was dealing with.

Or . . . had Paul always intended to kill her, too?

2

Night sounds kept Deena alert. The cottage seemed to lean with the wind, tilting almost imperceptibly, righting itself, tilting in another direction, righting itself, sighing. The wind sent low rushes of old leaves against the walls and whistled softly in the eaves. When it withdrew, the house settled, board upon board, with an audible ticking.

Jon, warm against her under the covers, slept the sleep of exhaustion, occasionally lapsing into snoring. When he did, she shifted him into another position so that he would stop. She had to be able to listen. Listen for Paul.

3

Derek let fly with a string of muttered curses. Martin had practically kidnapped him from Gino's, dragged him here so that he could muck around in Paul Kincaid's stuff for who knows what reason, then bolted without saying one syllable, not one bleeping syllable. He couldn't wait two minutes for Derek to lock up. Not two bleeping minutes.

Thanks a lot. This was a skunk neighborhood. He could get mugged just trying to get out the back door and reset the alarm. And Martin had taken off with the car. He'd have to hail a cab. No one in his right mind would walk from here.

Thanks a lot.

He tinkered with the alarm system, punching the buttons into place. The alley was dark as the inside of a cow. His flashlight rays faded to yellow. Great. He was about to lose the batteries. Wonderful. He'd get his throat cut by a homeless person and they wouldn't even find his body until Monday.

He hurried toward the faint glow of the street, keeping clear of dumpsters and barrels, watching his back in quick starts. Like an apparition from a nightmare, a figure appeared in front of him, backlit, faceless. A man in a brimmed cap. It was going to happen now. This is what he got for being a good guy. He wouldn't be able to get back through the alarm system fast enough to save his life. Maybe he could just hit a few buttons, set it off. He cut the light and back-pedaled slowly.

'Police officer!'

Brightness burned his eyes. He was caught in the beacon of a lantern.

'Sergeant Ed Flanders, NYPD. I'd like to talk with you.'

4

Flanders flagged a patrol car and bent down to see who was in it. Kevin Doland. Len Patterson driving. *Friends.* Lucky. He could use some luck. He had been too late to snag Martin at the art guild and the manager could tell Ed little except Kincaid's home address, phone number, and a description of his car.

Doland shook Ed's hand. 'What's up?'

He caught Doland's air of surprise. No one had seen Ed out on the street for a couple years. The surprise was mixed with pleasure. They were still a fraternity, a close one.

'Got a line on somebody. Suspicion of homicide. No warrant yet but I need to locate him fast. Paul Michael Kincaid. Lives around the corner.'

'Not home?'

'Don't think so. He didn't answer the buzzer or phone. His car's not in the parking deck. Red Nissan Maxima. Late model. I don't want him to know we're looking for him.'

'You think he's out there doing someone else?'

'I've got a bad feeling about it. Three a.m. and he's out of pocket. Run him through DMV, get a plate. I want to know where he is. Here's his address. I'll watch his place. Meet you back here in twenty minutes.'

Doland took the note from him. 'What's this other address? Martin Trayne.'

'Informant. Can you get somebody to go around there for me? Knock on his door. Find out if he's home. I get nothing but an answering machine when I call.'

'Sure.'

The cruiser pulled away, taking the warmth of the engine and exhaust with it. A chill radiated at Flanders' core. Ever since the beating, he'd had a permanent case of the jitters. Had not been able to get comfortable in any circumstance, to settle down inside his skin. Even at home. Probably never would. It had been over two years and his mind still told him he was a perpetual target in or out of uniform. Especially in uniform. Especially on the street.

Tonight, pins were jabbing his stomach without letup. He had no partner, no car but his own, no real authority for this vigil. But he couldn't abandon Martin. He'd tried. Got into pajamas and slept briefly. Got up with his intestines cramping.

5

Martin punched the accelerator. What was happening? The battery again? Nothing was happening, that's what was happening. The car was rolling to a stop. He wrenched the wheel and steered it onto the shoulder of the road. Of all the God-forsaken places to . . . He squinted at the fuel gauge. *Empty*. He had done it to himself. Flat damned done it to himself.

Where was he? Near nowhere, that's where. Near goddamned nowhere on hell's highway. That's where. Nobody was going to stop for him, give him help. He looked like a goddamned slasher.

He released the hood and got out of the car. Had to put the hood up. Maybe someone would report him. He lifted it and then went to stare into the trunk in the dim glare of a small bulb. Mrs. Swenk hadn't added anything new. A tire, jack and jumper cables, that's all there was. She hadn't even driven the car since he had. Of course. *He* was the one who hadn't put gas in it. He slammed the trunk and looked around. At this time of night, a car would happen along this road once an hour. He couldn't even see the glimmer of houses. And he was still miles from Cameron.

His only hope was that someone would give him a lift to a telephone. Fat chance.

He rooted in the glove box for the first aid kit, pinching it open and finding a small pair of scissors. He'd get this ponytail off right now. He grasped it near the rubber band and sawed at it until his fingers hurt. The scissors were just about useless – the kiddie kind with no points. He could only cut a few strands of hair at a time. Eventually, he felt the ponytail separate from his head. He held it up and looked at it, the pelt of a dead animal.

It was a joke, chopping it off like that. *He* was a joke. His life: a joke. No one was going to pick him up from here, take him anywhere. He was going to be late. Late again. Too late for Deena.

6

Paul dressed quietly and made the bed. His father wouldn't miss him. He was used to Paul's coming and going at odd hours. It was Mike's policy never to question him. An ironic shift from the days when Mike kept tabs on Paul minute by minute, sadistically restricting his activity.

He gathered his belongings and rolled them in yesterday's shirt. Mike was not in his room. He'd be in the recliner chair. Did he ever sleep in his own bed, the bed he had shared with Sarah? Probably not. Paul hadn't seen him lie in it since she drowned.

So long ago. He had almost perfect recall of life before she died. Her death drew a line in his mind. On this side of it, details were vague. He had few crystal portraits from the intervening years. But he could remember – precisely – his

329

father's face after he discovered her in the pond. Whatever Paul had wished to see was there and more: horror and disbelief, emptiness and agony. It was as though a giant had thrown his father against a wall with incredible force. He had been utterly broken.

Paul put the roll of clothes under his arm and checked the living room. Mike was in the recliner, slumbering. He no longer evoked emotion of any kind in Paul. That single, shattering event had settled the score. Paul hadn't expected it. He had expected to hate his father forever.

At the back of the cottage, Paul emerged into the exquisite, dewy night. This was the best hour: the stars at their brightest, the wind growing calm in preparation for morning. He started the Maxima without problem and backed it up slowly, headlights off.

Mike listened to the fading sound of Paul's car. Where did he go at night? The mysterious arrivals and departures of his son had contributed to an evolving fear: that Paul might be engaged in something illegal, even nefarious. It was not something Mike liked to dwell on. He had no control over Paul. Had never had control, though he had tried. He had brought Paul up the way he himself had been brought up, under two basic tenets: Don't coddle children – they grow up to be cowards. Don't praise children – they become vain and lazy. Whatever Mike had done to guide and correct Paul, he had done for Paul's own good. But somehow it hadn't worked. God only knew why.

Paul had thought Mike cruel, he knew that, but he had hoped someday Paul would understand that his tactics were in the boy's best interest. Mike had never been cruel, simply exacting. It was important to toughen children before the world got hold of them. The world could break a person who wasn't tough.

Mike sat up in the recliner, thinking of the dog. He couldn't remember its name, only that it favored Paul, slept on Paul's bed. The elementary school year that Paul had goofed around and messed up his grades, Mike had given the dog away as punishment. It worked. Paul's grades were perfect after that. It was only a dog and not to be compared to one's future. But somehow Paul never forgave Mike.

7

'Two vehicles registered. New York plates,' Patterson said.

'Red Nissan Maxima and . . . ?'

'A silver Bronco.'

Flanders, standing at the side of the patrol car, took off his cap and rubbed his scalp with his fingertips, his favorite trick for reviving himself. The early morning hours were the worst. He was in a gully. 'One residence listed?'

'Yes.'

'Wonder where he keeps the truck.'

'Garage?' Patterson handed him a plastic thermos cup of coffee out the window.

'Needle in a haystack.'

'Start with the city garages. When they open.'

It didn't matter where he kept it. The only thing that mattered was where it was now. Where Kincaid was now. Flanders scorched his throat with the coffee. His sinuses started to melt. He didn't have a particle of evidence against Paul Michael Kincaid – only the word of Martin Leland Trayne, such as he was, and he was a bird.

Martin in a panic. Right there you had a strange item. Half the time he wasn't even sure Martin was conscious, he was so low-key. This was the one and only occasion he'd heard Martin cranked up. High.

Mart knew police work and he knew courts. He had to have something amazingly concrete and urgent or he wouldn't have called Ed at home. He could prove beyond doubt that theory about Kincaid and the rings and the brides or he wouldn't put his foot in it, not Martin. Martin was mangy and off-center, but he was not nuts. In the past half-dozen years, Ed had grown to trust him without question. Mart had the razor touch. Could smell people the way cops could. Ed didn't even have to ask him to know what he thought. Just had to pick up the evening paper and look at Martin's sketches. It was all there, just the way Ed would draw guilt or innocence in faces if he could draw.

'Martin Trayne home?'

'No sign of him.'

This was twitchy. Surveillance could tip off Kincaid. He could slip through. Disappear.

Where the hell was Martin? Trapped with Kincaid somewhere, looking down the barrel of a gun?

'Check hospital emergency and admissions for Trayne and Kincaid. Notify if either comes in. And let's get an APB on both of Kincaid's vehicles. Locate only. Do not alert.'

'You got more than a hunch?' Doland stared at him pointedly.

An APB was ass-chewing territory. You didn't request

it without a good reason. He didn't have one. Except the hole in his gut. That was worth something. His jitters had begun to subside slightly as the old instincts came to the surface.

He mentally leafed through his contacts in the state police. Several of them owed him favors. Long-standing. He'd call in one of his markers. Nightside . . . nightside . . . *Sheldon McGuire*. 'Shelly McGuire still in dispatch?'

'Yuh.'

'Let me talk to him.'

8

The Bronco, alone in the center of Maddox Station parking lot, rose like a monument from the flat shiny pavement. The sight of it reassured Paul instantly. He had worked out as many details as he could. The rest would be taken care of for him. He needed to give himself over to faith. Symmetry would be restored in the universe. Balance. As soon as Deena was gone.

He did not trust enough. That was his defect. He wanted to be able to understand the twists of life, events he had not planned or foreseen. Sometimes he believed that whatever directed him was toying with him. He did not trust it at all. Sometimes.

He transferred the sleeping bag from the car to the truck. Having the bag in his hands made him sad. But there was nothing he could do. He could not alter tomorrow. Or yesterday.

He left the Maxima behind, the Bronco growling under his touch. The roads were wide and desolate, swept clear for his use. *Sarah*. He had not ever understood the sharp, sliding twist that came after her death. She had been punished for her lack of love, for the benign passivity that had allowed his father to torment him year after year. She had abandoned Paul. And, for this, she had paid.

And he had been satisfied. Until her will was opened. Her lawyer, lumped in a chair reading to Paul and to Mike in a monotone, revealed her last wishes: that all of her worldly goods be placed immediately in the name of her only child and held by the bank for him until he was twenty-one. This included the considerable inheritance she had received from her parents, which was providing enough interest that neither she nor Mike had to work.

With the will was a single letter, addressed to Paul, in which she spoke to him in words of adoration, calling him her 'dear and precious son.' Mike was not mentioned. Not in the will, not in the letter. Not once.

She had seen what Mike was. Seen what Paul was. And, in her secret heart, had chosen.

9

'Nick . . .' Arlene was shaking him. It seemed like he'd only been asleep five minutes. Couldn't be morning. The bed dipped at the edge where she was sitting on it. He slid toward her.

'Nick . . .' He saw her through water and then clearly. She was dressed, a sweater, slacks. 'It's Mimi.'

He raised onto his elbow. 'She worse?'

'I know what's wrong with her! She told me, just now.'

'Okay.' He reached for the sweatshirt he kept on the headboard. 'We need to take her in?'

'While I was at the bus stop today, a man . . . got into the house. He came into her room.'

Impossible.

'She thought he was going to kill her.'

'*What?*' He had the sweatshirt on now, but she was hanging on him, hard, nearly crying.

'I know why it happened, Nick.'

'*Why!*'

'I . . . have to tell you something.'

10

This one was stopping. Martin squinted at it nervously as it angled onto the shoulder of the road and pulled up behind his car. A small truck, hazy behind high beams.

A good way to disappear, stand on the highway with a stalled car at 4 a.m. An easy mark. Martin shivered, shrinking into the collar of his overcoat and shoving his hands deeper into his pockets. Did he have a choice?

The guy swinging his legs out was wearing a baseball cap. Long hair fanned from beneath it. Mustache, beard. Barrel build. He approached Martin casually. 'Kint git it goin'?'

'Out of gas.'

'Oum.' He went back to the truck.

Martin's eyes had adjusted to the headlights. It was a pickup truck. He recognized the shape of a shotgun on a rack in the back window. The man was on the flatbed behind it, bending over. Then, he was down and walking rapidly toward Martin with a gas can.

11

Through her veil, the scene sparkled: the tall stained-glass windows and ponderous pipe organ; her bridesmaids, scrubbed and smiling; Tim, red cheeked in a white tuxedo. Deena held his gaze as she walked down the aisle, her father's arm firm beneath her hand.

An explosion shoved her against the headboard of the bed. Instantly conscious, she searched the room. Jon was beside her, wrapped in the covers, snoring. What had she heard? Four twenty-three by the clock. Tim. The dream had been so real.

Thup, thup. Downstairs. Not in, but out. Glass. The French doors. The lake side of the house.

Thup.

She untangled the blankets and reached for her robe. No – she was dressed. She had gone to bed fully dressed. Except for shoes. She fumbled for them. *Thup.* The porch door banging in the breeze? She listened. There was no wind. She tied the shoes quickly and crept into the hall. She had been right not to leave a lamp on. She did not want to be seen from outside.

She sat on the top step. Silence seemed to smother her. She was pulling in air, but it was not getting across somehow. She began to breathe through her mouth. Why hadn't she taken Jon away from here last night? She would have had the car under her, a tool. This way she had no advantage at all.

Thup. In the kitchen. Window? Window glass. Outside. He was still outside.

336

If only she could see. Darkness always confused her, shut off part of her brain. She lowered herself, stair by stair, to the bottom and stood leaning against the banister.

There were no more sounds. She waited minutes, picking out the glint of windows in the blackness. What was it she had heard? A raccoon? A cat? If it had been Paul, he would have broken the glass by now, let himself in. She would have felt the soft, blowing draft from the jagged chink, sensed his heat as she came down the stairs.

12

Barbara Reuschel lay in bed, eyes open. The weather was choppy. The date palm at the front of the house had been tapping on the roof for hours. She wouldn't have been able to sleep well anyway, but the sporadic knocking annoyed her. She'd ask Gene to trim the fronds today. She had dozed several times, spiraling through feverish mental chatter, sentences and phrases spoken to her in many voices. Each tap on the roof poked her brain into alertness, a reminder – of something she had left undone. But what? She could not rest. Would she ever be able to rest? She had failed. Their son was lost.

Who would have wanted to kill him? He had been a good-natured and flexible man, straightforward with them, nothing hidden. Surely they or Deena would have known if he had been troubled. He must have been taken unaware.

The only time he seemed to be holding back in telling his feelings to her and to Gene was the year Jenny became engaged to Martin. Barbara had always thought Tim loved her. She was lovable. Dear and sweet. Barbara had always thought Paul loved her, too. There was tension surrounding that engagement. Then she died.

Barbara shifted onto her stomach. A drowsiness seeped through her. Who would have murdered Jenny Cunningham? Deena had to be wrong.

Sarah and Jenny. And Tim.

If Jenny had been murdered, a stranger must have done it. The only people who knew she was going to be at the swimming area were Tim and Martin and Paul. Tim, in his usual morning exercise routine, had jogged down to meet Jenny and Martin, arriving just after Martin pulled her from the water.

Martin . . . No. Martin was squeamish. Would go fishing with Tim just to keep him company. Wouldn't catch fish. Wouldn't kill anything. A little boy who would unscrew the tops of jars and release the lightning bugs and spiders other boys had captured. No. Not him. Not Martin.

Paul. A cunning streak. She hated to say it. Sneaky at times. Jealous. But capable of murder?

Maybe. God forgive her for the thought.

If he did . . . if he did kill Jenny, how did he know he could get away with it? Martin was supposed to have been with her at the swimming area from the outset.

Paul had Martin's car. Could Paul have kept the car from Martin on purpose, so that Martin would be more than a few minutes late?

Yes. He could have done that. He manipulated things to his advantage. She had seen it dozens of times. But why would he? Was he angry that Jenny chose Martin?

About Sarah . . . No. Paul was only twelve then, too young.

Tim. Did Paul murder Tim?

Why would he?

If he did. If he did murder Tim . . . Barbara had told him that Deena suspected murder. He would surmise she had reasons, proof. He might go after her. And Jon.

She got up, panic jumbling her thoughts. Deena did not know what Paul might be. And Paul was there. Right there at the lake.

It would take too long to explain it to Gene, convince him. She needed to make the decision and she needed to do it now.

She could call the police to go by and get Deena and Jon, take them into protective custody. That could take an hour. More. Cameron had one police car and two deputies. Better to call someone at the lake to get them. But at this time of year, it was mainly deserted.

The fronds tapped the roof again sharply. She put her hands to her head. It could be happening. She mustn't wait.

The closest person – the *only* person – who could help was Mike Kincaid. And Paul was with him.

A wail. Another wail. Loud. Mike crashed forward, lowering the footrest on the recliner. The phone. Careful. He'd been asleep. He didn't want to go leaping up, bashing himself. Another ring. He'd left the television picture on. By the light of the blank screen, he lumbered to the desk. Had to be bad news. Or a wrong number. It was the middle of the night.

'Yo.'

'Mike?'

'Yes.'

'It's Barbara Reuschel.'

'Bar—'

'Mike, don't say anything. Just hear me out. I need you to help me. Please, help me. I need you to go and pick Deena up, pick Jon up, without telling anyone, even Paul. And I need you to do it now. Take them to the firehouse in Cameron and tell them to stay there, to stay inside. I'll send someone for them.'

In all the years he had lived next to Barbara Reuschel, she had never asked him for a favor. She had been polite, cordial, and had sidestepped him constantly. She'd had minimal dealings with Sarah, too. But had lavished attention on Paul. Why, suddenly, was she sidestepping Paul?

Because it was *about* Paul.

'Will you? Mike, it's important.'

'Yes.' He laid the receiver gently into its cradle.

13

Deena made herself tea in the flickering light of a gas burner and sat drinking it at the kitchen table in the dark. A chill curled around her legs and receded as the hot liquid began to warm her. Beyond the window, trees, outlined against a sky full of fading stars, grew faint in a gathering fog. She ached from tension, from listening, watching. The silence was total. Had Paul been here and gone? Or was he perched on the hillside, waiting? How soon did she dare to dress Jon and take him to the car?

Was she right about Paul? Or was someone else stalking them? Had she become unstable and begun to imagine it all?

A buzzing whine in the distance made her stand up. Where was it? Did she truly hear something or were her ears ringing? It became more distinct. She placed it on the lake road, coming toward her. The hillside branches and tree trunks cast moving shadows. *It was turning. Into the driveway.* She gripped the tabletop, which was cold as a slab. A truck rumbled through the fog, shining dimly. Silver. The silver truck.

It stopped in her sight, mist swirling through its headlight beams. The driver got out slowly and stood in them, facing the house. It was Paul.

She had the eerie feeling he could see her in spite of the darkness. He was looking right at her. She backed up a few inches at a time, away from the window, finding the edge of the kitchen linoleum with her feet, the carpet of the dining room and then the staircase banister, slippery under her hands. *Easy. Go up easy. Save it.* She would need all her strength.

She would carry Jon out the door in Gail's room. It was on the side of the cottage opposite the driveway. If she heard Paul in the house before she could do that, she would take Jon out the door in Tim's room and up the hillside. The nearest occupied house was . . . Mike's. Was Mike home? Would he help them, or were he and Paul partners in this?

She ran through the hallway into Tim's room, flinging the bed covers aside, groping for Jon.

He was not there.

'Jon!' The scream seemed to echo from a thousand surfaces. 'Jon!' *He would answer. If he could.*

Paul had him.

Somehow.

341

The grinding of gears and squeal of tires cut through her bones. The truck was in motion. He was turning it around. Leaving.

The man had him. That man, the one who made his daddy die. Was he trying to make Jon die? The blanket was too tight around his face. He was hot, sick. Getting carsick from how bumpy it was. Where was his *mother?* He woke up when the man pushed a blanket on his face so hard he couldn't yell or even breathe and wrapped him up in the blanket, tight. Then, he wrapped something else around him. It had zippers and the man closed them. Was it Paul? Was the man Paul? He took him out the door next to the bed, down the steps and up the hill and put him lying down on the flat floor in a truck. It sounded like a truck. Did his mother know the man had him? Did the man have her, too? Had he already made her die?

Mike stared through the open window of his car. Paul's Bronco was slamming back and forth in Reuschels' driveway, turning around. He hadn't seen the Bronco in years, not since Paul first bought it. In the backwash of the headlights, Deena Reuschel appeared, screaming. '*Jonnn! Jonn!*' She ran from the carport, chasing the Bronco as it gathered speed. What had Paul done? Taken the child? Mike pulled the car across the end of the driveway, set the emergency brake, and jumped out. Paul would stop. He would make him stop.

The Bronco veered onto the grass, aiming for the clearing behind the car. Mike moved into the path of it, holding up his hand. He had to end it, right here, right now. He knew what Paul was, had known it since Sarah died. He had messed it all up with Paul. Had been too hard on him. Then looked the other way. Out of guilt.

If he could start over . . . bring the baby in the blue blanket home . . .

The Bronco climbed rapidly toward him. He had wanted the baby, his son, had such hope for him, still wanted him. 'Paul! Stop! Stop!' The words blew back to him in the roar of the engine.

His father. Shouting orders. The mouth, the teeth, the raised hand. Always in his way, teasing him, sparring, jabbing. No place to go, to go from him. Mike in the way, between the car and the trees. Between him and freedom, hand up, ready with a slap. *What's the matter, Paul, huh? What's the matter? You a sissy? Take me on.*

Get out of the way. His father stood centered in his vision, unyielding. *Get out, damn you.* Paul stomped the accelerator. *Out.* Mike did not move, even at the last minute. His expression never changed. He was still shouting at Paul as the front bumper grabbed him with a jolt, shoved him under quickly. It was so unreal that Paul did not feel surprise. There was no other jolt, just steady bouncing, as the Bronco continued to climb over stones and uneven turf, up onto pavement, into the solid curve of the road.

She was doing everything mechanically, fast, as fast as she could. *Ignition. Not too much gas. Brake off. Lights on. Reverse. Back, back, around, forward, around, more gas.* She couldn't afford a mistake, couldn't afford to stall, couldn't afford to think, really think. Paul had hit Mike. She had seen Mike running toward the truck in the flare of its headlights. Her view had been blocked as the vehicle bore down on him but she heard the thud, saw Mike's broken body emerge from beneath the truck, tumbling. He might need help, but she could not stop for him. If she did, she would lose Jon.

Mike was in the path of her car now, bloody, his head twisted to one side and lying at a sharp angle to his body. Dead. Dead beyond doubt. In a single horrifying instant, she wheeled around him and went on.

Deena was in Paul's mirror so suddenly that he swerved. The shoulders of the road reached for him. He applied his full concentration to keeping the Bronco in the center of the road. She was on his tail, constant, close, trying to pass, her lights flashing in blinding streaks.

It wasn't supposed to be like this. She was supposed to be in the distance, barely in sight all the way to the caves. Lured. She was supposed to be taken unaware, disposed of down the sheer rock staircase. He would let the boy go then, the boy who had seen nothing, heard nothing. He would simply lay the sleeping bag on the ground in a spot where Jon was likely to be discovered.

But it was flying apart, into pieces, as though the center had let go, as though he were no longer being directed. His father had appeared in front of him like an apparition. Why? What had sent him? Paul had struck him, the flesh giving, collapsing under the weight of the truck. Not a ghost. Mike himself. Flesh. And she . . .

Tapping the truck with the front of her car. Speeding into curves, forcing him over, first one way, then the other. He could not see her face in the mirror, only a blaze behind him, like something inhuman or subhuman gaining on him. How could it possibly be Deena?

In the weaving and jarring he waited for control to be returned to him, believing it would: the gift, settling as always over the scene, positioning him to advantage in the malleable universe. He had done what he had been asked to do. He would be protected.

She came to the outside then, nudging the truck so that he had to slow it. They were in the great sweep at the far end of the lake, where the road narrowed to a single lane. Suddenly, he was on the gravel, on the dirt and grass in the wide dry basin that bordered the swimming area, headlights shining on the water as trees snapped past. He braked frantically. The Bronco smashed into a stump and quit, slamming him against the windshield, bruising him with fury. She doubled back, careening at him, angling her car behind the truck so that he would not be able to move it.

He realized then that he was being tested. The Fire would not intervene. He would have to prove himself worthy.

The truck must have crashed. Jon had felt a terrible punch in the back and now there was no motor sound. The blanket was looser. If he could get it off, maybe he could get out. He tried to wiggle his arms and it made his chest hurt worse, so he pushed with his knees and feet.

That was doing it. He wasn't all tied up anymore. But there was that other heavy thing over him. He felt it with his fingers. It had a zipper around the edge. Just like he thought. It might be a sleeping bag, like the one he got for

Christmas. If it was, he knew how to get out. He just had to find where the zipper started.

She mustn't wait. If Jon were still alive, Paul might be doing something to him inside the truck. She had blocked his escape with the car. She needed to leave it where it was and confront him.

Paul backed out of the truck, a large sack over his shoulder. What was it? *Was it Jon?* Paul did not look in her direction. He walked slowly toward the lake. The unhurried gait terrified her.

She would not be able to catch him on foot. She released the brake and let the car drift forward, keeping Paul centered in the glow of the headlights. They shined across the black water, outlining the wooden raft. He began to walk faster. She sped up, and he began to run, heading for a short dock that jutted into the lake. She brought the car up behind him with a single thrust of her foot on the accelerator and yanked the emergency brake. She stumbled out and onto the dock, as he reached the end of it, drawing the sack from his shoulder, swinging it to one side, using both arms. *He was going to throw it*. His body strained forward. She thought she heard a short, muffled cry. The sack was falling behind Paul as he turned toward her. The water took it with barely a sound.

14

The sight of Mike Kincaid's car parked across the top of the Reuschels' driveway hit Martin like a fist. The car appeared to be empty, the door on the driver's side open, exhaust smoke rising past the glowing red taillights, the headlights illuminating the trees. Martin stopped and got out. Beyond the quiet idling of the engines, a vast stillness spoke to him: *He was too late*.

He passed behind the car, noting tire ruts that led onto the road in the direction of the McNaughtons'. A figure lay heaped on the ground halfway down the hill. Behind it, the cottage was dark.

Numb, Martin became uncertain of his footing and inched down the incline. As he drew closer, he became aware of two things at once. The person on the ground was dead. And Martin was walking in his blood.

She mustn't dive. It could be shallow here. Paul had his arm out to hook her. Deena spun to one side, feeling his fingertips brush her ribs as she dodged him and jumped. The icy water broke over her legs, seizing her shoulders, wrenching her head. It was deeper than she expected. She searched with her hands and feet, her lungs searing her. The crystal globe was limitless. She could not touch bottom, could touch nothing. Then, something touched her, wrapping around her neck.

Jon couldn't find the zipper part anymore. He was upside down, kicking, trying to get out of the bag. The man had thrown him in water and now it was coming in the bag, slow, cold. He was going down, down, easy. He was on his stomach, heavy stuff pushing on his back, then it was the other way around, he was lying on his back under a mountain. Each time he tried to find the zipper with his fingers, he moved or the bag moved. 'Mommy!' he had yelled, but it sounded tiny. She didn't know where he was. If she did, she would let him out. The water was in his clothes, in his hair, up his nose. Freezing. Pretty soon the bag would be full of water. He couldn't see anything but black and he was all mixed up in the blanket.

Maybe his dad would let him out. His dad was already dead and could go anywhere, like a ghost. Jon tried to call him but couldn't. He didn't have any more voice. Outside the bag, his father was walking through the water, straight from heaven, looking for him.

As he trapped Deena's neck in the crook of his arm, she drew against him, startled, then arched her back. Paul tightened his embrace with a thrill of pleasure. It was always like this, the silken flinching, the most intimate moment. He imagined that lovemaking at its height must be similar, the woman convulsing slowly as if under water, stretching toward the man and then twisting away into her own ecstasy as he held her in place. They had all done it. All of his brides.

Deena was strong. He had predicted it, her determination and power. She did not try to bite him as some of them did. She was muscle and strategy, locking her legs around one of his knees, reaching up and back with her arms to pull his head sideways toward the same knee, trying to put him beneath the surface so that he, too, would need air.

He let her tip him, let her get a breath, and could tell she was encouraged by it. He liked to make them think they could win. They would try longer then instead of giving up.

This struggle had the feel of all the rest. A peaceful

confidence infused him. By his act of sacrifice, he was being redeemed, accepted. It would be well for him from now on.

The water began to burn his skin. He must not allow it to warm him. Hypothermia was lethal. He needed to go on and finish rapidly, more rapidly than he'd like. He shoved her under again, holding her against him with her back to his chest, his arm around her neck. After a few seconds, she stopped fighting and let go. Her limbs spread out. Her head lolled. But he could feel a pulse in the well of her collarbone. Some of them did this, pretended to be unconscious. He kept a steady grip and waited.

The zipper thing was under his thumb. Jon tried hard to get hold of it as the bag bumped something and stopped. Water was all over his face, banging in his ears. He couldn't breathe but he had the zipper thing. There were two. You could pull each one a different way to open up fast.

They were stuck. He tried to get a finger in between them. One of them moved. He pushed. His finger felt like it was on a knife, but he was making a hole and water was coming through it. He had to bend his hand bad to keep his finger on the zipper thing, then the water started helping him push it back and the hole got bigger. He could stick his head in it and get halfway out.

He pulled the bag off his legs like pants. It was warmer out of the bag and he felt sleepy. Too tired to swim. The water started to take him up to the top without his help, just like they told him in swim class, but he was not going fast enough. He would have to breathe before he got there.

Deena's heart thrashed against her breastbone. She knew Paul could feel it beneath his elbow. He would wait until it stopped. She wasn't fooling him. That's why he didn't let go.

Weakness had set in. She could no longer buck to try and exhaust him. She was his.

It didn't matter. Those she loved were gone. She could give herself over to the current now, slide away into the stars. She hoped for unconsciousness so that she would not feel the stark, stabbing rush of water in her chest.

A parade in the distance narrowed her attention. She could not see it yet but could hear the confusion of voices and the tinny horns. Drums, faint and steady.

A blow knocked her out of Paul's arms, up into the wind. The water churned and air flew into her throat. In the shadows made by the headlights, Paul was grappling with another man. Someone she had never seen before. Paul was besting him quickly with smashing punches to the head as they wrestled toward the raft. 'Deena . . . get Jon out!' the other man called to her in a moan.

She looked around. Jon was floating near the edge of the lake. How was it possible? He was treading water silently, his mouth open in shock. 'Jon!' she shouted.

He didn't answer.

'Jon! Are you all right?'

'Yes.'

'Go on then! Get out of the water! Run away!'

Jon leaned into a crawl. She watched him slowly reach the bank. Paul had gripped the other man's hair and was beating his forehead against the side of the raft. *Paul would kill him*. She had to do something. She propelled herself toward them, seeing in the dazed face of her rescuer strangely familiar features. *Martin*. It was. Without his beard and mustache and with short hair. When she had almost reached him, Martin's head sagged forward and he slipped under. Paul held on, seemingly dragged down by Martin's weight, and surfaced alone.

It couldn't be so that Martin was gone. He was pretending. He would emerge from the water behind Paul, attack him.

But it was so. On the smooth, silent surface of the lake, there were just the two of them, Paul moving deliberately and steadily closer to her. She began to swim away from him, awkwardly. The temperature of the lake had caused a great heaviness in her. He would be on her in seconds.

She heard him change direction, gliding, then swimming in powerful strokes. She paused to look. Jon was in his path, bobbing up the embankment. Paul overtook him easily, lifting him, staggering, with Jon on his hip. They were on the mud, on the dirt, in the grass at the side of the truck. Then, *in* the truck, its lights dimming, its ignition whining as Paul tried to start it.

The ceiling tapped Martin's head. Tapped it again. And again. He put his hands up to stop it. The ceiling was made of boards. He opened his eyes, seeing pale golden straws evenly spaced over him in the darkness. He was in water. Cold *cold* water. Up against something metal. With difficulty, he held the ceiling away from him with one hand and explored the metal with the other. It was a metal drum. He was under the raft.

Memory leaped at him. He and Paul. Deena. Jon. Seeing them out on the lake, Paul taking Deena down. Martin had left his car with the headlights trained on Paul and dived in. It was no match. *Where were they now?*

Fear and pain made him gasp as he felt his way to the edge of the raft and submerged himself to duck under it. The scene came up in a blur, a single car's headlights shining at him. His own car. Paul's truck and Deena's car weren't there. He was alone.

Dizziness. He hung on the side of the raft, desperate, waiting for it to pass. It grew worse. He wouldn't be able to hold on. He slid along the raft, hand over hand, searching for the ladder and got it under a foot. If he could just pull himself up. He did it with his feet, pushing, pushing. He was blacking out. He fell onto the deck, a loud crackling in his ears, and rolled onto his back. The sky rotated over him, the pale stars winking out, the crescent moon fading as it plummeted into the trees.

15

Two sharp reports at his left side catapulted Flanders into consciousness. He tried frantically, in split seconds, to locate the source. Doland and Patterson had pulled up next to him. He could tell by the position of Doland's fist that he'd just knocked on Ed's car. He shook himself awake. He'd been dozing with his head on the steering wheel. Doland motioned for him to put his window down.

'Nothing at the hospitals, but they found the Nissan.'

'Where?'

'Maddox Station.'

Flanders waved off the bag of donuts Doland shoved at him. 'Check the other stations for the Bronco.'

'Done.'

'What do you think?'

'About Kincaid?' Doland talked around a wad of donut.

'Yeh.'

'Drove up from the city, parked the Nissan, went somewhere on the train.'

'Picked up the Bronco at one of the other stations?'

'Maybe.'

The murk of dawn hung like low fog over the street. *The truth is never what you think. Flanders' Law. It is always infallibly the opposite.* 'He's in the area.'

'Of Maddox Station?' Patterson now.

'Within thirty miles.'

'Get a chopper?' Doland had started on another donut.

'Can't see spit 'til eight o'clock,' Patterson said.

The end of the line. Only God could ask for a helicopter and get it. No one was going to put a chopper up for him, no matter how many markers he called in. Whatever happened next would have to happen on the ground.

16

Deena managed to keep the truck in sight as main roads merged into smaller ones and then into winding lanes with no markings. Paul was speeding into deep country, remote areas with no buildings at all, no other cars. For miles, she had used her flashers, leaned on the horn, hoping for help from a passing police car or concerned motorist. But traffic was sparse and no one followed her. Paul kept an incredible pace. He obviously knew the terrain well. She didn't dare floor the accelerator to try and catch up. There were massive bumps and hook turns, steep drops with no guard rails. Her only ambition was not to lose him. She pictured Jon constantly, how terrified he must be, how much he had already endured, and hopelessness overwhelmed her. She was assaulted by images of Martin calling out to her across the lake, suffering, slumping away from her to die alone. Water still flowed from her hair, her clothes, soaking into the seat, puddling underfoot. To her amazement, her sneakers had remained tied in place over her socks. They were heavy and viciously cold, but she would need them. The presence of mind that sustained her at the lake had dissipated, leaving in its place an unwieldy dullness. Her brain was shutting down, unable to react correctly. The car slammed from side to side as she attempted to control it. The blast of the heater was not reaching her at all. When Paul finally stopped, what then? She was without resource. For the first time, she understood. There was such a thing as chance. She had not invited catastrophe. It had fallen randomly to her as it had to so many others. And, in spite of her will, the outcome was random as well. The seed of compassion: to know that the worst can befall anyone, unbidden and undeserved. Her eyes smarted. She blinked against a hot torrent of tears. When she had cleared her vision, she could no longer see the truck.

17

'Why don't you pack it in, Flanders, get some sleep? We'll tell them to call you when they find the Bronco.'

The Manhattan sidewalks were still largely empty, but the streets were coming alive with garbage trucks and cabs. In a matter of minutes, Ed's car would be blocking traffic. It was time to move. Give up. For now.

'Stay *with* me a minute.' He had blown this somehow. Martin was still missing. Kincaid had not come home. Were they together? What was going down? Was it over?

Cabs cruised silently around the double-parked patrol car. Doland and Flanders stared at each other through their open windows. What more could Ed do? He had followed all his own rules, especially the primary one: *Ask, ask, ask.* He had even hit Shelly up for the chopper. It simply couldn't be engineered from where Ed sat – or from where Shelly sat. Ed didn't have sufficient cause.

The whole thing was cockeyed. Ed couldn't see it clearly at this point. He wasn't street material anymore. They had beat it out of him. He had lost. For the second time in a row. 'Okay, I'm gone.'

Doland nodded. The patrol car pulled away. Ed shifted into gear and left the curb. Ahead, the light changed to green, but the patrol car didn't move. Ed instinctively crept up behind it to cover it. Doland got out and walked back to him.

'They're timing speeders up there.'

'What?'

'Cameron County. Near Maddox Station. They've got

a clear morning and a Cessna already in the air, timing speeders. They're going to pull it off for a few minutes to look for the Bronco. Shelly sends his regards.'

18

She wasn't behind him. Paul took his foot off the gas pedal. If he touched the brake and Deena were still watching, she would know he had slowed down for her. The brake lights would tell her so. He had been careful to do it properly this time, staying well ahead of her but within her scope. Jon began to squirm again and Paul tightened his arm around Jon's chest until he lay quiet in his lap. Morning was spreading dusty pockets of glare through the landscape. He squinted at the rearview mirror. She hadn't made the last turn. But she was sharp. She would back up when she couldn't find them.

As if on cue, the side of her car appeared. She was in reverse. A pause, then the car jerked forward, headlights gleaming as she wheeled it onto the narrow dirt road. He led her over a mile down the snaking incline, going faster and faster, leaving her farther and farther behind until her car blended into the landscape. He took the final rapid swing into the parking area of the caves with satisfaction. She would locate the truck at exactly the right moment. When he was ready.

The vicinity had been sealed for him. There was not a soul here, no movement of any kind. Not even a bird in flight. It would remain sealed until he had finished. He would come out into a pristine world, one arranged for him. If he kept his covenant.

Jon was limp under his arm as Paul carried him toward the cave and flicked on his battery lantern. It would take less than three minutes to dispose of the boy. Then he would come back for Deena.

What was this place? There had been no road signs, but she was approaching a paved level lot. Paul's truck sat to one side of it. From her angle, Deena could tell it was empty. She covered the remaining distance quickly and parked next to the truck with a lurch, scanning the trees, the brush, the boulders, her blood pounding in her ears. A lone trail led downhill to a low, wide vertical opening in rock. At the center of the black archway, a single flash drew her attention. Had she truly seen something? She was staring at darkness. There was no other movement.

A cave. She would not be able to follow Paul there and he knew it.

She had bought a flashlight. Yesterday. Her fingers wouldn't work. She clawed at the glove box, finally forcing it open and snatching the flashlight from it. How deep was the cave? Would Paul be hiding just inside? Or were there labyrinthine formations through which she would have to chase him? She had been caving with her mother twice and had learned she did not like it. Caves were unpredictable, strewn with natural traps, macabre surprises. It was folly to explore one without a map, without proper equipment.

The overhang shielded a huge tunnel. As soon as she stooped under the rock and stood inside, she felt a drastic difference in temperature. Her wet clothes seemed to stiffen with frost. She could freeze to death in minutes. Had Paul really brought Jon in here? She listened, hearing the rhythmic hush of footfalls. Why wasn't Jon making any noise? Was he already dead?

The tunnel was made of soft pulverized black rock that glittered in spots. Coal? She tried to measure the length of it with the beam of light, but it seemed endless. She trained the light on her feet and on what was immediately in front of them as she moved cautiously forward. Paul would not hide here, in this section. There was no place to conceal him. She walked faster as her eyes became accustomed to the darkness. Her clothing stung with every step and her skin itched wildly. At intervals, she paused and could still hear him lumbering ahead of her – unevenly now. He must be carrying Jon and getting tired. Hers was the only light. The tunnel was becoming stony, solid, as she descended into the earth where the temperature grew colder still. She began to trip from clumsiness.

His light was suddenly visible, diffused in the splintered terminus of the cavern. She could not identify shapes. She became afraid of falling, afraid of the protrusions and clefts in the walls. Was she simply disoriented, or was her flashlight dimmer than before? The tunnel widened into a vast, level sheet of ice. A room. Enormous. She absorbed it all in an instant: Paul standing at the other side of it, clutching Jon by the hand, the immense cathedral ceiling, the mist, the countless entrances to other rooms and natural shrines. In the glow, the rock walls spread out and up like spun lace, graceful apertures leading to other apertures, and on to still others. A majestic maze.

'Give me my son!' Her words caromed back to her, magnified, fractured into a dozen pitches.

'Come and get him.'

Jon began to cry softly as she crept onto the ice. Was

there water under it? How deep? Paul would not have come this way if he had been threatened by it. She pushed ahead. As she did, he backed up, taking Jon with him. Jon was crying slightly louder now, through chattering teeth. It was an eerie cry, without spirit, a measured keening. She became aware of the ceiling as something alive, pulsing, and knew it was covered with clustering bats. Their fine rain sparkled around her. A snow.

For each step she took, Paul guided Jon back a single step. Then he lifted Jon and their silhouettes seemed to be sinking, disappearing into the earth. Her light flared as she shined it on them.

'Paul, let him go.'

'Come and get him.'

She could no longer feel her feet or the calves of her legs. Jon had to be close to collapse. His body weight was a third of hers. She could lose him any second to exposure. Paul continued to move backward and down as she came toward him. She reached the rim of the ice, realizing that she was standing at the top of a natural staircase. It was astonishing, a phenomenon. Seven or eight steps carved into the rock. They varied some in depth and width, but were incredibly uniform. Water must have flowed though the caves at one time, rushing along this pass to rooms below, creating tiers.

Where was Paul going? The staircase appeared to end at a wall. At the bottom he stopped, facing her, waiting for her. Jon, slack in Paul's arms, whimpered.

She took each step cautiously. They were slimy in patches. Halfway down, she was close enough to read Paul's eyes: eagerness and confidence. 'Give him to me.'

He did not answer.

She had the precognition of doom. He had tricked her in a way other than the obvious. There was something else, something she wasn't seeing, wasn't expecting. Something he was waiting for her to discover. She sensed it before she saw it: the sheer drop directly behind him, between the last stair and the wall. When she touched it with her light, he smiled.

A chasm, four feet wide, Paul's bleeding bare feet within inches of the edge. It would be easy to hurl Jon into it and seize her when she was close enough. They would never be found. She had no doubt about the depth of the pit. She was in the presence of a master planner.

She was in the presence of insanity. Paul could not win. His truck would be linked with Mike's death and, possibly, with Martin's. It was *over*. Did he understand that? How much should she say to him?

The smile lingered, and she saw that it didn't matter. His only task was to punish her for transgressions he had invented. What had gone wrong in this man's life to damage his soul so completely? If she knew, she might know what to say.

Deena's courage entranced him. She did not falter. She descended the steps with uncanny poise, pausing on each to watch his eyes. As she drew closer, she held out her hands, silently begging him to surrender the boy.

The Fire spread its wings behind her so that she could not retreat. She was unaware of the magnificent unfolding.

'You don't want to hurt him, Paul. Give him to me.'

She was within reach. He stared past her at the splendor.

What did Paul see? He was looking beyond her and up,

his face reflecting awe and homage. She resisted the urge to glance behind her, because in Jon's face, she could read the truth. Jon was focused blankly on her. He did not even blink. There was nothing above her on the stairs.

Did Paul believe he was in the presence of something supernatural? Disturbed people often thought they were being directed by a force only they could see or hear. It was a wild guess – her only one. She had to use it. She dared not hesitate. Paul could kill them at any instant. She had to try.

She turned slowly, slowly, in order not to startle him, and feigned controlled amazement at catching sight of his vision. When she eased back to him and glimpsed the wonder in his eyes, she knew that she was right.

'You don't want to hurt Jon,' she whispered. 'You never wanted to hurt anybody, did you?'

The boy stirred against his chest, and Paul *saw*. It was a game, a vicious game. The Fire had despised him from the outset, had meant to separate him from everyone who cared for him. He had been seduced into destroying them, one by one.

Sarah by the pond, the irises in full bloom. She had been kneeling, with her back to him, unaware of his presence. He crept up silently, snatching her from the ground, an arm around her waist, the palm of his hand tight across her eyes. She must not see him, must not guess who had come for her. The thought that she might know was intolerable. He would not be able to go through with it then. It would break his heart.

He pulled her into the pond, the purple and yellow hues of the irises closing over them. The temperature of the water shocked him, made him angry, bold. He tightened his grip. She struggled in his arms, reaching back, clutching at his shoulders, pushing at his face. The pushing slackened quickly to a touch. She felt his cheeks, his forehead, rubbing, probing. A quiver traveled through her. She slumped forward, her hands stroking his arms in a gesture that was familiar to him. She had soothed him to sleep that way many nights as he grew.

It wasn't too late, was it? She was alive, conscious. Sobbing, he tried to lift her to the surface, but she would not help him. She was like a stone. He grappled with her slippery weight, unable to hang on, losing her, diving futilely after her in the inky water.

She had known. Had believed the child she loved hated her. And had chosen death.

Deena stood in front of him and then beside him on the ledge, gently patting his shoulder. He leaned toward her and pressed Jon into her arms.

'Come *with* us,' she said quietly. 'It will be all right.'

The Fire, hungry, demanding, was waiting for them. It would not let Paul pass. He knew, at last, the crux of its voracious desire. And knew, at last, how to satisfy it.

She was so numb that she could not hold onto Jon. She felt him slipping from her as she tried to regain her balance. He put his feet down in panic and teetered on the edge. The abyss sucked at them.

'Hold my hand.' Her voice was a stranger's. She could barely feel Jon's fingers on hers. She gripped him under the arm instead. The first step seemed insurmountable. If Paul did not go with them, they would have their backs to him. *Dangerous*. But Paul wouldn't have let her approach him if she hadn't been close to right about the vision. He wanted to be saved from it, whatever it was. 'Come with us,' she said to him again. Paul did not respond. His gaze was fixed on the staircase.

Jon sagged against her. She did not go while he could still walk, they would perish here. She could not carry him. And there were only moments left before the ice would defeat them.

With all of her strength, she guided Jon onto the first step. They must mount the stairs in a deliberate cadence or they would never reach the top. Paul had not moved. She was attuned to his shallow breathing, listening for the slightest deviation.

The second step.

Paul was in motion. Deena tried to turn quickly, but her reflexes were maddeningly slow. He straightened up from setting his lantern on the ground, its glittering shaft aimed at the ceiling. He was not looking at her, but past her. They were still in Paul's range. He could drag them backward with a single sweep. She mustn't think about it. She must go on. She focused on the third step and helped Jon onto it. Paused.

Behind her, the world gave way in a crackle. The energy Paul released was stunning. She had the sensation of impact, of being drawn toward him. She realized at the same moment that he had not touched her. Jon was still steady under her grasp. She crouched, staring dumbly at the spot where Paul had been standing.

There was nothing but the lantern on the ledge.

He had fallen. Or jumped. Suddenly dizzy, she crushed Jon to her and held him. Paul did not cry out, but a faint thunder stayed with her for many seconds, growing more and more distant.

In the tunnel, Jon stopped breathing and uncurled slowly in her arms. She had carried him up the rest of the stairs and through the cathedral talking to him, shaking him to keep him awake. He was nearly weightless now, his hair crusted with ice. The flashlight, frozen in her hand, sent a dim white circle bobbing along the wall. She could not see what was in front of her, could see only the white hole that must be the entrance through which she had run years and years ago. She could not remember how to run. Could not remember how to drive. Could not remember the road upon road she had taken to get to this place. There was no use to hurry.

The white hole was low. She had forgotten that. She laid Jon down gently and pulled him through. The entire earth came at her as a black and white photograph, no color at all. Not even gray. Leafy trees, a curving trail, a car, a truck. Behind the truck, a police car.

She tried to shout but could hear only the wind in her throat. Jon was too heavy to lift. They were on her then, the uniforms, men, laying him out flat, listening at his breastbone. One crossed his big hands over Jon's heart and the other bent to kiss his mouth.

Epilogue

1

Martin clutched his bandaged head as he ran along the concourse. His brain was loose in his skull, banging painfully against the top of it. He should have started earlier. But who could have predicted the snarl of traffic on the FDR? And then he'd discovered he had to use the money machine at the airport to pay the cabby. Someday he'd get it together. *In his dreams*.

Gate 46. Lord, how far was it? 41, 42, 43, 44, 45, . . . 46. The waiting area was nearly deserted. He glimpsed the tail of the plane out the window. Parked, still parked. 'Listen, can I . . .' The uniformed woman at the jetway door squinted at him. 'I need to get on there.'

'Ticket?'

'I don't have one. I just want to . . .' He couldn't find the right words since his concussion. The doctor said it would take weeks. '. . . visit. I want to visit someone. Please.'

She started to shake her head. 'Well—'

'All I need is a minute.' *His fault*. If he had gotten here sooner . . . The weakness inched up on him again, bringing with it a full-blown sweat. Why couldn't he ever get it right? Just once.

She looked him over sympathetically, her gaze lingering on the bandages, then picked up the receiver on the intercom behind her. 'I have a gentleman coming aboard for a moment to speak with a passenger.' To him he said, 'We're about ten minutes from departure.'

He sprinted down the ramp. It seemed to be rocking under him, but he knew that it wasn't so. He felt like he was on a boat a lot of the time now. The two flight attendants near the cockpit were talking with each other. He eased past them into first class. The plane was full. He had the attention of almost every person as he started through the coach cabin. His face grew hot with embarrassment as he searched among them for Deena.

She was about halfway back, in an aisle seat, with her eyes closed. Pale. She was hardly there at all. He would never again look at her or think of her without feeling sorry for her.

As if she could sense his presence, she opened her eyes. Affection lit her face. He hunkered next to her, hiding from the curious expressions around them. They clasped hands and said nothing. Teary, she put a finger to his bandages. Her tears brought his own, but he swallowed them.

Jon, strapped into the center seat, unfastened his safety belt and reached for him. Martin gave him a playful poke and got one in return. 'Where you goin', partner?'

'Home,' Jon said. It was friendly, but there was no smile with it.

'Okay. I'll . . . write to you.' He wasn't good at this stuff, had never been good at it, never would be. The elderly man next to Jon was taking it all in with evident concern. 'Well . . . keep in touch,' Martin said to Deena.

Her answer was hushed. He had to strain to hear it over the warming jet engines. 'I can't. For a while.'

He nodded, straightening up into frank stares from the passengers around them. The flight attendants were already closing the overhead bins for takeoff. He patted his pockets, finding nothing to give Jon. Gave him a thumbs-up instead.

As the jet gathered speed on the runway, noisily vibrating the cabin and pressing Deena back in her chair, she had the sensation of being slowly crushed. The entire mosaic of her life began to fall on her in pieces, a few at first, and then more. And more. Scenes, emotions, scraps of information, remnants of prayers, tender memories, coming at her in rapid succession. She was being pummeled by them, injured, taken down. Hopes, regrets, flowers, photographs, river currents, smiles from Tim. Amid the jostling and the thunderous noise, the huge hangars and the distant city hurtling by the airplane windows, whole conversations and fragments of songs and the sunlit corners of rooms tumbled at her. Secrets. Questions. *So many pieces:* the frantic flurry surrounding Jon in Emergency and in Intensive Care . . . the shock and joy of learning that Martin had survived . . . the hospital visit from Arlene, who had cried in Deena's arms. The state police autopsy report, verifying Deena's claim that Tim had been struck . . . the opening of Paul's files and the finding of the bridal records . . . the wall safe, the identical sets of rings . . . the affidavit from Mimi. Mike's quiet funeral . . . the newspaper articles and photographs of Paul. The policeman she went to see – the one who had hung on all night in pursuit of the silver truck.

Mysteries. Pretenses. Hungers. She. And Jon. Alone now.

The wheels left the ground and they were away.

* * *

The taxi driver set their suitcases in the foyer and went out into the brilliant California afternoon, closing the front door behind him. Deena and Jon stood listening to the silence of the house. It did not seem to belong to her, this tranquil vista, the pale blue carpet and cherrywood furniture, the gilt-edged antique mirror, brass candlesticks, the glass curio cabinet bearing her collection of porcelain angels. This was a museum re-creation of a place where she had once lived. She had wanted no company for this moment, no relatives or neighbors, just Jon, close beside her. She had told her parents not to pick them up at the airport and had explained to Jon that she needed for him to be quiet when they came in.

They moved through the rooms without speaking. Her parents had respected her wishes in not touching or adding a thing. There were no welcoming notes, no bouquets, just their own belongings the way they had left them the morning they flew to New York. The photography magazine on the coffee table, open to the page Deena had been reading while she ate her toast. Toys strewn on the couch. Tim's mud-encrusted yard shoes at the kitchen door. The grocery list, some of the items written in Tim's hand. In the powder room, she found Tim's toothbrush next to the sink. He had used it after breakfast and forgotten to pack it.

Gene had been right about the mourning. She had missed the timing of it. Now that she had space to grieve, she would not be able to. Not in the way the others had. Her grief would be a permanent, fine glaze over the minutes and hours of her life, over her heart, over the facets of this house. Nothing would ever again be ordinary. She knew.

2

The garbage truck woke Martin, its familiar rumble rattling window panes. He lay still as the bright ceiling spread out over him. He was in his bed. In his pajamas. The night had passed without his knowledge. Air was strong in his lungs.

The eleventh day in a row. He was beginning to believe the nightmares were gone for good and that the breathing problem had gone with them. Wouldn't make book on it. But he hadn't slept in his clothes since before the hospital. He sat up gingerly. His brain dipped only slightly as he did.

Comfort. And relaxation. Comfort and relaxation. Foreign feelings. A marvel. He could get used to this. Chalmers would try to crank him up a little on Monday when he got back, but hey. He might be ready.

Might not. The concussion had taken the edge off his senses. He couldn't see through situations like he did before. It had made him normal, he supposed, getting walloped like that. Normal people saw things through a screen.

His gaze went to the gathering of dish gardens on his dresser. Hospital gift plants. He hadn't been too keen on receiving them. They were like babies someone had left on his doorstep to take care of. He wasn't up for it. Maybe he'd take a couple to Daniel when he went by to see him this morning.

He sorted through them visually. A few brown leaves, the rest green but dimpling from thirst. Not too bad. He went into the bathroom and filled a paper cup with water, poured it into the twiggy nests and spongy soil. The dish garden colors reminded him of the man next to Jon on the plane, his clothes, green, two shades. Green sweater, green slacks, but not a match. Jarring. Well, most men were color-blind in the greens and blues.

No woman would have let her husband out of the house wearing those greens together. That gentleman had dressed himself. But wasn't used to dressing himself. Life-long bachelors learn what goes together and what doesn't. And he was elderly. Married?

More water. Martin stood over the sink with his hand on the faucet. The man had looked at him – at Deena and Jon – with concern. Empathy. A countenance of kindness. Sad, accepting eyes. This was a man who had known love. And was himself in some kind of emotional pain.

Martin filled the cup slowly. A wife used to dress that man. And he was traveling by himself, a long distance. New York to San Francisco. You didn't go that far without staying a while. A retired man wouldn't make that kind of a trip without his wife. If she were well enough to travel.

That sort of man wouldn't leave his wife at home if she were ill.

A widower. New at it.

He turned off the faucet, confronting his image in the mirror with surprise. He could still do it, pick it to the bone, couldn't he? My God. He was back.

3

Pastel sunset. She, flying. In the crystalline air over the tree-lined narrow street, autumn leaves seem suspended like stars. The wind has puffed her jacket. The bicycle tires sing under her. She looks back. Jon, who has been pedaling like fury, is coasting now in the splashy swirl of leaves kicked up by her bike. Behind him gallops a happy dog.

They take the driveway fast and drop their bikes on the lawn, instantly running. They are a jam and jumble coming through the door. Candy is worked up. She doesn't want to quit. She continues to race through the house in clumsy golden retriever style, plowing into Jon every time she comes around the circle.

He throws himself on the family-room floor, laughing. Candy jumps on his back, licking his neck, sniffing, letting out little yips. Deena is down, too, exhausted, rolling on the carpet. She hides her face from Candy who finds and nuzzles it with her cold nose. 'Quit!' Deena laughs. 'Quit, you rascal!' Jon leaps on Deena too, hugging her, digging under her hair with his fingers, wiggling them on her scalp. She kisses him and gets to her feet with difficulty, stumbling over Candy.

Pulling off her jacket, she tosses it on the couch. She is whipped. Almost too tired to make the pizza. She has spent the hours since dawn at Jon's soccer game, at the library, at the garden shop picking out a birthday present for her father, in the backyard raking leaves. She washes her hands at the kitchen sink and starts to dry them, stopped by a thought. It is about Tim. His memory has been with her in the shopping and the raking, in the bike riding, at the game. Like always. But she hasn't felt wounded by it. For the first time. This was an ordinary day. No tinge to it.

The first ordinary day.

A selection of bestsellers
from Headline

GONE	Kit Craig	£4.99 □
QUILLER SOLITAIRE	Adam Hall	£4.99 □
NOTHING BUT THE TRUTH	Robert Hillstrom	£4.99 □
FALSE PROPHET	Faye Kellerman	£4.99 □
THE DOOR TO DECEMBER	Dean Koontz	£5.99 □
BRING ME CHILDREN	David Martin	£4.99 □
COMPELLING EVIDENCE	Steve Martini	£5.99 □
SLEEPING DOGS	Thomas Perry	£4.99 □
CHILDREN OF THE NIGHT	Dan Simmons	£4.99 □
CAPITAL CRIMES	Richard Smitten	£4.99 □
JUDGEMENT CALL	Suzy Wetlaufer	£5.99 □

All Headline books are available at your local bookshop or newsagent, or can be ordered direct from the publisher. Just tick the titles you want and fill in the form below. Prices and availability subject to change without notice.

Headline Book Publishing PLC, Cash Sales Department, Bookpoint, 39 Milton Park, Abingdon, OXON, OX14 4TD, UK. If you have a credit card you may order by telephone — 0235 831700.

Please enclose a cheque or postal order made payable to Bookpoint Ltd to the value of the cover price and allow the following for postage and packing:
UK & BFPO: £1.00 for the first book, 50p for the second book and 30p for each additional book ordered up to a maximum charge of £3.00.
OVERSEAS & EIRE: £2.00 for the first book, £1.00 for the second book and 50p for each additional book.

Name ....

Address ....

....

....

If you would prefer to pay by credit card, please complete:
Please debit my Visa/Access/Diner's Card/American Express (delete as applicable) card no:

Signature ....Expiry Date ....